Mary's Child

By Celia A. Leaman

To Sue
Best Wishes
Celia Leaman

Twilight Times Books
Kingsport, Tennessee

Mary's Child

This is a work of fiction. All concepts, characters and events portrayed in this book are used fictitiously and any resemblance to real people or events is purely coincidental.

A previous edition of "Mary's Child" published by Earthling Press, Dubuque Iowa 2002

Paladin Timeless Books, an imprint of
Twilight Times Books
P O Box 3340
Kingsport, TN 37664
www.twilighttimesbooks.com/

First paperback printing, June 2005

Library of Congress Cataloging-in-Publication Data

Leaman, Celia A.
Mary's child / by Celia A. Leaman.
p. cm.
ISBN 1-933353-11-2 (pbk. : alk. paper)
1. Orphans--Fiction. 2. Poor women--Fiction. 3. Workhouses--Fiction.
4. Suicide victims--Fiction. 5. Unmarried mothers--Fiction. 6.
Maternal deprivation--Fiction. 7. Illegitimate children--Fiction. 8.
England--Fiction. I. Title.
PR9199.4.L43M37 2005
813'.6--dc22

2005006923

Cover art by Judith Huey

Printed simultaneously in Canada and the United States of America

For Mary Jay who inspired me

With gratitude to Chris
for his encouragement and support.

Acknowledgments

Thanks to my family, friends and many acquaintances for their interest and encouragement.

To the staff of the Kitimat library in Northern British Columbia, who obtained the many reference books I requested.

Last but not least, thanks to the Hand that guided my own, and for the gift of imagination.

Celia Leaman
British Columbia 1998

Foreword

Jay's Grave

There is a lonely grave by the road not far from Hound Tor on Dartmoor that is never without flowers. It is marked on the Ordnance Survey map as Jay's Grave.

Around 1860, men working on the road unearthed what they thought were, at first, the remains of a pony. These were later discovered to be the bones of a young woman, and the local squire ordered them to be reburied in their present position. One of the road-mender's wives recalled being told by her mother that it was the grave of a young girl known as Mary Jay. When the law forbade the burial of suicides in consecrated ground, they were buried outside parish boundaries, often at a fork or crossroads. It was believed this would confuse their spirits and render them unable to return and haunt the living. Sometimes a stake would be driven through their hearts.

Research has revealed the girl was most likely an orphan, apprenticed out from the Wolborough workhouse in Newton Abbot.

This novel is based around these fragile facts. All characters are fictitious, except for Mary Jay. Some place and farm names do exist, and in this story they are embellished by the author's imagination.

Part I

1809

Mary Jay

I will not wish thee riches, nor the glow of greatness,
but that wherever thou go some weary heart shall gladden at thy smile,
or shadowed life know sunshine for a while.

And so thy path shall be a track of light,
like angels' footsteps passing through the night.

Words on a church wall in Upwaltham, England

Chapter 1

Although the sun shone through the windows, it did little to relieve the sadness in the Wolborough workhouse. In a chestnut tree outside, sparrows chirruped and hopped from branch to branch, their freedom a stark contrast to the forlorn souls within who never celebrated any joy in living, but merely existed from one day to the next.

At the end of a long corridor, a young girl knelt, wearily scrubbing the flagstone floor. She paused for a moment to stretch and ease her aching back. Unfortunately, it was just as Kat Black, one of the workhouse assistants, came around the corner.

"Slacking, Jay?" Kat said. "Well, you can leave it. Brimley wants you in his office." She took a step forward and clipped Mary's ear. "You should have finished by now if you weren't slower than everyone else. Well? What you waiting for then? I said go, didn't I?"

Mary got up quickly, wondering if she should first empty the bucket. Another look at Kat's face relieved her of that decision and she scuttled along to the flight of stairs that led to the top floor, where the master of the workhouse, William Brimley, had his office. She couldn't think why he would want to see her, unless it was with respect to the couple that had arrived some time ago. However, she shook the foolish hope away, knowing she was the most unlikely candidate to be chosen.

She knocked and entered Mr. Brimley's office. He asked her to stand in front of his desk so that the couple beside him could have a look at her.

"This is Mary Jay, of whom we have been speaking," he said to them. "Mary Jay, this is Mr. and Mrs. Bennett from the parish of North Bovey on Dartmoor. They have need of an apprentice to work on their farm."

Mary's eyes darted towards Mr. Bennett. Of course, she knew she must not stare; but at a glance she could see he was a chubby, jolly-looking man with a face as rosy as a red apple. When he caught her quick, shy look, he smiled and nodded encouragingly at her.

Harriet Bennett, however, didn't look impressed at all, and pursed her lips. "Haven't you got anything else?" she asked.

"Owing to the men going off to war laborers are in short supply everywhere," Mr. Brimley pointed out. "I'm afraid there is no one else who would be suitable for the work you describe."

"Humph, if that be the case why hasn't she gone out before?" Harriet grumbled. "She must be fifteen if she be a day. What be wrong with her?"

"Mary is coming into her sixteenth year," Mr. Brimley said patiently. "There is nothing wrong with her except she is unable to speak, and others have not been comfortable with it, you understand. That is the only reason she is still here."

As Mary listened to this all too familiar conversation, her spirits fell. When people knew this, they generally assumed she was also deaf, and thus too daft to take instruction.

In the silence that followed, while Mr. Bennett looked thoughtful and Mrs. Bennett's expression seemed to suggest there was a nasty smell in the room, Mary waited for the inevitable rejection.

Hope flared again when Mr. Bennett said, "Poor maid. From birth, was it?"

Mr. Brimley shuffled in his seat. "No, Mr. Bennett, it was shock so I am led to believe. She has no problem with her other senses."

Harriet sniffed. "That's what I be afraid of. I don't know that she'll be at *all* suitable." She lowered her voice to Ronald. "What about *Matthew*, Ronald?"

"Aw, you don't have to worry about him, he's sweet on that maid Clara at the Manor."

Harriet frowned. "Oh? And how long has that been going on?"

"Now, don't get in a huff. I only mentioned it so you would give the maid a fair chance," Ronald said, sending a somewhat embarrassed look towards Mr. Brimley.

"We aren't here to give anybody a *chance*," Harriet said. "We are here to find someone to suit our needs, and if the maid be simple—"

"Mary is far from simple," Mr. Brimley pointed out, a little testily. "To the contrary, I would say she is very bright. She has been a good, willing worker and learns quickly."

"Well, that's the main thing—"

"I'll thank you not to interfere, Ronald," Harriet interrupted sharply. "It isn't you who'll have the trouble of her."

Ronald's color rose a notch. "Trouble, you say? It's help we have come for, to save your legs. If you're that put off we'll go home and say no more about it."

Harriet stayed him with her hand. "Now wait just a minute. It's just that we've hardly been given any choice, and she is *not* what I came for."

Mr. Brimley gave a deep sigh. "It is better not to come to the workhouse with any preconceived ideas, Mrs. Bennett, especially with the war on. As I have tried to explain—"

"Everyone blames Napoleon for everything and anything," Harriet snapped. "*I* don't count *him* as an excuse for anything at all."

"It will be all right, my dear," Ronald said in a conciliatory voice. "I'm sure Mary will work out very well."

Mr. Brimley shuffled the papers on his desk and stood up. "Well, if it's settled then I do have rather a lot to do and I'm sure you'll want to be getting along. We'll just get these papers signed."

Ronald rose to his feet. "Yes, indeed, sir. I do believe the matter is concluded well enough, and I thank you for your trouble."

Mr. Brimley turned to Mary. "Fetch your things, child. You don't want to keep these good people waiting."

Mary could hardly believe what she had just heard. It was as if someone else curtsied and left the room, not her. No, not her, because she was so dumbfounded she had to lean against the wall for a moment. They'd *accepted* her! Well, Mr. Brimley had persuaded….

With a sudden burst of energy, and feeling something akin to happiness, Mary skipped along the hallway. She was sure that Mrs. Bennett would change her opinion of her once she saw how hard she worked. It was only Kat who said she was slow.

Kat was waiting for her at the bottom of the stairs, and smiled her ghastly smile. "Turned you down then, did they? In here a bit *longer,* are you?" She lowered her voice to a growl. "I knew they wouldn't take you. No one will ever take you out of here. You're stuck here for life. And so you should be, the child of that—" She suddenly saw Tilly coming down the corridor, and lowered her hand.

Tilly smiled kindly at Mary. "Start putting your things together, dear. I'll come and help you in a moment." As Mary hurried away she turned to Kat. "For your information, they *did* accept the girl. Now, thanks be to God, she'll be free of you."

Mary heard the sisters fighting their private battle. She had no idea why Kat was so mean to her. Tilly, who was as different from her sister as cream was to coal, told her it was jealousy, but Mary doubted this because she couldn't understand why anyone would envy such a miserable existence as her own.

ꕥ

"My, this is a day to remember, isn't it?" Tilly said, minutes later as she helped Mary fold her belongings into a neat bundle. "I bet you're as pleased as punch."

Mary was. Of course she was, she told herself, and she nodded and smiled. But as she watched Tilly tie her bundle securely together she suddenly realized she might never see her again, and she burst into tears.

"Oh, Mary," Tilly whispered, embracing her. "I don't want to say goodbye either; I shall miss you more than you'll ever know. But this is what I've always hoped and prayed for." She wiped the girl's eyes. "There'll be someone else to take care of you now, the Lord always allows for angels on the way. Show them what you're made of, work hard and be a good girl. The years go by like nobody's business and one day, when you've worked out your indenture, you'll be free to come and see me. Why, by then you might even be married and have children of your own."

If Mary could have spoken she would have told Tilly she loved her and would miss her, too. And yes, one day she would seek her out. However, she doubted she would ever marry. It may well be the fate of most young women, but she wanted no part of it. She would be quite content to stay working on a farm, where she could breathe the sweet air of freedom, blessed freedom, until the day she died.

They heard footsteps coming down the corridor and Tilly's expression changed. "I'm going to tell you something else now and don't you ever forget it," she whispered quickly. "Your mother was a lady who died because of the wickedness of others. It was those with their hearts of granite that brought you in here, not her doings, and don't you ever let anyone tell you otherwise."

Mr. Brimley stood in the doorway. "Is she ready, Tilly?"

"As ready as she ever will be, Mr. Brimley." To Mary, Tilly whispered, "Be brave, my dear. When you walk out of this place you can put it all behind you. You'll never have to come back in here again."

Mr. Brimley was a man who always seemed to be in a hurry. He was also a man of few words, but he had a tender spot for the young girl who, in his opinion, should never have entered the doors of his establishment. Before he handed her over to the Bennetts, he bent for a moment to speak to her. "Do your best child. You don't want to return here, do you? If you aren't a good girl, that's what will happen. And if you should lose your virtue you will also face eternal damnation, so don't invite mischief."

He shook hands with Mr. Bennett, but Harriet declined the back of hers and looked directly at Mary. "Any hint of trouble and I'm telling you, she'll be right back on your doorstep."

Ronald winked at Mary as if to say, don't take any notice of her, then he tucked her arm into his and led her down the front steps towards the waiting cart.

Mary paused as she heard the loud, resonant *clump* of the doors closing behind her, and she turned as if to ensure she was actually shut outside the cursed building. She felt quite stunned. For years, she had wanted to get out of that detestable place. Now that part of her life, which had begun so suddenly, had ended just as abruptly. Ended. It was over.

"Go on," grumbled Harriet, giving her a shove. "You sure you aren't daft?"

Mary did as she was told and climbed up into the cart. As they drove away, she promised herself that Mr. Brimley need never worry. She had no intention of losing her virtue, or ever setting foot inside those walls again.

When Mary had gone, Tilly sat down on Mary's bed and allowed her tears to flow unchecked. Although she was relieved a home had been found for the girl, she wished desperately it had been to somewhere else. She sighed deeply. Her dear girl was free at last. But after all these years, to think she was going back *there*.

She looked up as Kat came to the doorway.

"So, she's going back to the place of her making then," Kat said.

"I'm well aware of where she's going," snapped Tilly.

"Now there'll be *proper* retribution. The Lord always—"

Tilly leapt off the bed. How she kept her hands off her sister's neck she never knew. "You can quote the Bible all you want to me Kat, but I'll always be left wondering just who *your* god is."

Chapter 2

It was market day and more people than usual thronged the streets. Ronald patiently threaded the cart in and out of the chaos, avoiding those who made no attempt to get out of his way, so involved were they in their own business. A man leading a cow, who could hardly walk because her udder was so full, stumbled out in front of them and Ronald pulled up sharply and got down to grumble to him about it.

"He's always been one for the underdog," Harriet said, turning down the corners of her lips. "Sarah says he's far too soft."

Mary wondered who Sarah might be, and felt a tinge of anxiety. She thought anyone who said unkind things about Ronald couldn't be very nice.

There were no more incidents to delay them, and they trundled away from the hustle and bustle of the market town and headed towards Bovey Tracey. There, they turned westward and began their trek down through Reddaford Water, on towards the moors.

There had been a shower of rain earlier that day and everything smelled as if it was newly made. A fine, fading mist hung in and about the treetops, drawn there from the ground by the sun. Primroses peeked from the hedgerows, and Mary closed her eyes and took a deep breath of the sweet, pure air that to her smelled like paradise.

Going up over Trendlebere Down they saw several rabbits, and Harriet cursed a fox that ran across the road in front of them and dove between some boulders. Swallows swooped around the cart from time to time and Mary smiled and held out her hands to them. Only a bird, she thought, who must not be able to bear captivity, would really be able to understand how she felt.

When Ronald wasn't struggling to keep the cartwheels out of the deep ruts and potholes left by the ravages of winter he chatted about Blackthorn Farm. "The missus does a bit of dressmaking," he said. "That's why she needs your help. We have an old dog, a few sheep and pigs, and some cows, chickens and ducks." He chuckled. "Us be a bit like Noah's Ark really. Know who Noah is, do you?"

Mary nodded her head enthusiastically. Of course she knew who everyone was in the Bible, for she had learned in Sunday school even though they thought her too simple to take anything in.

At the top of Trendlebere Down, Ronald pulled the cart off the road to give the horse a rest. "Just look at that view, Mary dear," he said. "Look how far we've come. That's Bovey down there, and further still, Newton Abbot. And there, as far as you can see is the seaside. I don't expect you've ever been, have you? No, well, we'll have to take you there one day."

Harriet clucked her tongue. "Ronald," she warned reprovingly.

Mary barely heard her new mistress speak; she was staring in awe at the view. She felt as if she was on top of the world, and it was almost impossible to think she had been down there only hours ago with little hope of escape.

After a while they set off again, wending their way through Manaton and past the church to Langstone Cross, where they turned towards the parish of North Bovey.

"Not long now, my dears," Ronald said cheerfully. "We'll soon be home."

Mary's smile faded. The word 'home' made her feel strange and her stomach churned uncomfortably. During the transition of the journey, she hadn't thought too much about the destination. Now she began to worry. Oh, not about the work, she was used to that; getting up at four in summer, five in winter and working until nightfall when she sank exhausted onto her pallet. Rather, she feared Matthew, the boy the Bennetts had mentioned. What if he bullied her, or even worse, tried to do things to her like some of the boys in the workhouse? She was very frightened of boys.

And then there was the Sarah whom Mrs. Bennett had spoken of. Mary wondered if she was their daughter, and if they would have to share a room. What if Sarah didn't like her and was hurtful and unkind, like others who had made fun of her and called her horrid names because she couldn't speak?

Ronald sensed the change in her and reached out to pat her hand. "Don't you worry, my dear," he said kindly. "Everything will be all right, you'll see."

When they reached Blackthorn, Mary got down off the cart to open the gate. She saw the pleasure on Ronald's face, but her effort to please made very little impression on Harriet, who grumbled about all the tasks there were now to do. Even when Ronald said, "You've got the maid to help you now," she didn't respond enthusiastically.

Mary followed the cart down the yard and looked with pleasure towards the farmhouse. The front of it was smothered in greenery and she imagined the joy of waking in the summer to the scent of flowers that might later bloom. Wave upon wave of strange and interesting scents wafted towards her on the warm evening air. At her feet, daisies poked their faces from between the cobblestones, and she bent to touch their delicate faces.

"Whatever be she doing now?" Harriet grumbled, clucking her tongue. "Picking weeds? Mary Jay? You come here this instant!"

"Now don't forget the maid's been shut up in that awful place," Ronald said, but sighed when he saw his wife wasn't going to give that any thought at all. He turned from her scowl to the tall, red-haired youth who appeared out of the barn. "Hello, Matthew," he said, relieved to see a smiling face. "Everything all right then?" He beckoned Mary closer. "Look who we've brought home with us. This is Mary Jay. And Mary, this is Matthew Steer. He came from a workhouse some years ago. We don't have any chillern of our own."

"He be as daft as you be dumb," Harriet threw over her shoulder as she went in. "But like you, he was all we could get."

Ronald frowned and turned away to the back of the cart.

Matthew's face darkened. When Harriet was out of hearing he whispered, "Take no notice, Mary. She's got one of those tongues that gets sharper with use."

Mary had heard Tilly use that expression, and she smiled shyly. Matthew met her smile with candid blue eyes, and she sensed that Mrs. Bennett was very wrong in her estimation: Matthew looked far from being stupid. He also seemed as kind as her new master and she felt sure she would be able to trust him.

Feeling less anxious, she helped to carry the packages into the farmhouse. The ceilings were low and beamed and the windows had deep sills set into the cob walls. There was a large table in the center of the kitchen with several chairs placed around it, and a rocking chair beside the huge fireplace. What a contrast, Mary thought, to the austerity of the workhouse.

ꕥ

"Now didn't you find Mary helpful?" Ronald asked Harriet after they had finished putting everything away.

As would be her way in the future, Harriet spoke as if Mary was either not in the room, or was deaf. "She's willing enough, I will say that, but they be bound to try and make an impression when they first come—look at what we took her from. Time will tell if she can keep it up." She looked at Mary. "Come on then, I might as well show you upstairs."

Ronald looked apologetic on Harriet's behalf, yet nodded encouragingly for Mary to take her bundle and follow his wife. They went through the stair door to the first floor and along the landing to another steep and narrow set of stairs. Harriet wheezed her way to the top and paused to get her breath before opening a door into a small room.

"As befits your station, you will sleep here," she said. "I expect you to keep yourself and the room clean and tidy. You must sweep and dust, and change your bed linen regularly, as well as doing your other duties. When you've put your things away you can come downstairs for some supper."

Because of their steep and difficult negotiation, Mary hoped her mistress wouldn't venture into the attic too often. For that is where she was, in a room so tiny some would have considered it an insult. But she didn't care about that. Compared to what she had been used to, she felt like a princess in a castle.

She ran to the window to look out and saw that her room, situated above the front porch, had a fine view over the farm. It was the time of evening when the animals were settling themselves in for the night, before the nocturnal creatures began their own foraging and sounds. Mary thought of the ducks and ducklings that Ronald said lived by the pond in the orchard. He had also told her they had an old pony as well as the young horse, and that if she behaved herself she might be able to ride him. He'd chuckled and added, that was if the pony behaved himself, too. Mary could hardly wait for morning when she could go and explore.

She looked back into the room and her eyes filled with tears. Although her mistress might believe she was of the lowest order, to her, this room with its small cot, chest of drawers and one rickety chair, was more than she could have ever hoped for. A bubble of joy welled up inside her and she expressed a prayer of gratitude before getting down to business and unrolling her bundle of clothes.

Mary took out her Bible. Although she couldn't read, she liked looking at the pictures and knew by heart all the stories that went with them. She opened the cover and ran her finger over the inscription inside. *To my darling child, Mary. From your loving mother, Celine.* Mary knew it said this because Tilly, who could read, had told her. Beneath, Tilly had written, *Love from Tilly Black, Wolborough 1809* and put several crosses, which she said stood for kisses.

Mary had lost her mother at a very early age and could only recall her as being a gentle, rather fragile person. She had often puzzled why she was alone in the world, because for some reason she'd always felt there was a family somewhere. She thought this because, although the memory was elusive and made little sense, she could vaguely remember being taken to a house, where an imperious old lady had peered at her through an eyeglass and said, 'so this is the child.' A man had shouted at her mother and she'd become distressed, caught hold of her hand and pulled her from the room. Mary could remember running down a driveway with the air so thick with drizzle that her mother's face looked as if it was streaming with tears. It wasn't long after that her mother died and she was taken to the workhouse.

It was shock, they said, that took her voice away. And indeed, what greater shock than being torn from her dead mother's side and incarcerated in such a place? To begin with, it was thought she wouldn't thrive. Nor might she if Tilly Black hadn't come along, because it was only Tilly's kindness and encouragement that had sparked in her the will to live. "No matter what circumstances you find yourself in, you must always try your best," was Tilly's motto, and gradually she instilled into Mary the hope that her life wouldn't stay the same: that one day she would leave the workhouse.

Mary often wondered what might have happened to her if Tilly hadn't been there to protect her, although until that very moment she never once considered *why* Tilly had looked after her so well. And wasn't it strange that she'd echoed the same words once spoken by her mother? Words that she had never forgotten, because of the tone of Celine's voice when she had cursed those with the hearts of granite.

"Mary Jay, where are you?"

Harriet's imperious voice rose from below and Mary quickly put on one of her aprons and ran downstairs. An aroma of stew met her and her stomach growled hungrily. Ronald was sitting at the table and patted the chair beside him for her to sit down. Matthew, who sat opposite, nodded kindly at her. Mary was so overcome with gratitude for her change of fortune she ran over to Harriet and shyly embraced her.

"Lord alive," Harriet said, shrugging her off. "For goodness sake sit down do."

"Aw, the poor maid's only grateful I dare say," Ronald said.

Harriet grunted and began dishing up the supper: a stew of dumplings, bacon, onions and greens. On the table was a loaf of fresh bread, cheese and dough cake. After grace was said they began to eat, and Matthew smiled as he watched Mary tucking in. "I've never forgotten the first proper meal I had after I left the workhouse," he said. "Likely you never will either, Mary."

Ronald smiled. "Well, that's all over for the both of you now."

"Humph," Harriet said. "You're here to work, not to be fed like pigs for market. And there's to be no nonsense either, do you understand?" She looked meaningfully from one to the other. "*And* no time wasted gabbing." She almost choked on her mouthful of stew as she suddenly burst out laughing. "But what am I thinking? She'll hardly stop anyone working with chatter, will she? There's that about it I suppose." And she bent her head to eat, oblivious of the embarrassment on Ronald's face, or the protective and anxious look Matthew gave Mary when he saw tears start to her eyes.

Chapter 3

1810

A year later, Ronald Bennett was still as nonplused by his wife's attitude towards Mary as he had been in the beginning. He had also gathered a multitude of battle scars on the girl's behalf, and was feeling very weary about it all.

He wasn't tired of Mary, not by any means. She, who tried so hard to please, who worked solidly and cheerfully at anything she was set to do, was the light of his life. He liked to imagine she was his own little girl, and had endless patience teaching her this and showing her how to do that. She responded to his kindness like a flower opening its petals to the sun, and he was proud of how quickly she learned: as Mr. Brimley had said, she was indeed a bright little thing, and when Harriet wasn't around, he lent new meaning to the words by calling her his angel.

With Mary in his life, he looked forward to each day with renewed vigor. Even the winter wasn't so dreary because in the evenings he would tell her stories in front of the fire. More often than not Matthew would be there and in a kindly way tease his master into telling them about the 'olden days.'

"You may laugh," Ronald would say, looking at them sadly, "but you'll be old before you know it." He would feel a pain in his heart when he thought of Mary growing up and leaving him, as inevitably she must one day.

Harriet rarely joined in their camaraderie as if it wasn't the proper thing to do, but hovered in the background, and if she could find any excuse to break them up she would.

"If she smiled," Matthew said once to Mary, "she'd crack her face." Although Ronald overheard and gave him a reproachful look, he didn't chide him. Matthew was like a son to him, and he would have been the happiest man alive had Harriet's attitude only been different.

Not that Ronald blamed her entirely. Her detestable sister, Sarah, didn't help. It was she who put the foul seed into Harriet's mind about the dairy, saying Mary could be a witch and thus turn the milk sour. "What bleddy nonsense!" he said when he found out. He, who so rarely swore. "The woman's mazed, and you're no better if you believe her."

Nevertheless, even though Harriet subsequently allowed Mary to work in the dairy, Ronald noticed a rowan twig suddenly appear on the lintel of the door, professedly to ward off the evil eye.

Mary was aware of the tension between her master and mistress and wished for all the world it wasn't so. She realized Sarah was an instigator, who, for some reason, had taken an instant and violent dislike to her. She had once heard her say that Harriet was nursing a viper in her bosom. Although Mary was stung, it would have hurt more if she had ever heard Sarah say a kind word about anyone. However, she came to dread her visits because the outcome was always the same: Harriet would generally find fault with her afterwards and make an excuse to send her to bed early without supper.

Matthew tried his best to reassure her, but Mary's constant companion was insecurity; her frequent worry was that the day would come when Ronald would tire of soldiering for her, and Harriet would have her way and return her to the workhouse. And always, always, Mary was determined that would never happen.

࿇

After a good dry spell of weather, for the first time that year the roads were passable enough to allow the Bennetts to go to Newton Abbot.

The day before, Harriet gave Mary a list of chores she must do in her absence, one of which was to deliver a dress to Betsy Berry, the innkeeper's wife. "And mind she pays you before you hand it over," she instructed.

Sarah, who had arrived with a list of errands for her sister to perform in the market town, added, "Yes, they Berrys be as tight as a duck's ass."

Mary fled from their vicious laughter. She didn't think the Berrys were mean at all. They were very kind and generous, to her at any rate, and like Matthew and the master, treated her like a normal person, not some freak they had the misfortune to meet.

The next day, a few hours after the Bennetts' cart trundled off down the lane, Mary finished her chores and set off in the opposite direction to the village. The hedge tops were a mass of fragrant, snowy blossom that would later turn into sloe berries, from which Ronald would make wine. The hedges themselves were full of bluebells, Mary's favorite flower.

Betsy was delighted to see Mary and gave her a big sloppy kiss for the flowers that the girl thrust into her hands. She was also pleased to see the dress and said she'd waited ages for it to be altered; Mrs. Bennett must be very busy indeed. However, when she saw the bill her eyebrows shot up. "I'm sure I don't know why at these prices," she added. Then she noticed Mary's forlorn look. "But don't you worry, dear. I'll go and see Tom for the money. Want something to eat, I bet?" And she bundled Mary along to the kitchen where she was given cold duck, pickled onions and the crust off a new loaf of bread. Mary ate every morsel on her plate and was given more, plus a large piece of apple pie and clotted cream.

"That poor maid's always starving," Betsy told Tom. "That bleddy woman should be reported."

"And who is there around here that'd listen?" Tom said. "No one cares, my dear."

"Well, it isn't right. I'd like to see that old skinflint spend a week in a workhouse. That'd bring her down off her high horse. You should see what she's charged me for that dress. It's downright robbery and I've a good mind to send her what I think it's worth, not what she's asking."

Betsy returned to the kitchen and handed Mary the money wrapped in a piece of paper. "You can give her this, Mary. Between you and me, I shan't be asking her again, she's too expensive and there's a woman in Moretonhampstead they say is just as good."

It wasn't the first time Mary had heard this from one of Harriet's customers and it distressed her; when her mistress considered she wasn't making enough money, her tongue was sharper, and—always out of Ronald's hearing—her threats to return her to the workhouse uttered more frequently.

"Don't worry." Betsy gave Mary's arm a squeeze. "It isn't your fault, is it? Now run along home, dear, before the old tartar gets her hackles up."

Mary set off down the passage. She cupped her nose and mouth as she passed the bar. She hated the cold, bitter smell of beer and was afraid of the men's raucous laughter. She hurried on across the yard and almost collided with a man riding in around the corner on a chestnut horse. The horse was spirited and fidgeted a little, and his rider patted his shoulder, speaking to him soothingly.

"Lovely horse, Mr. le March, sir," Tom said admiringly, coming up behind Mary and putting an arm protectively around her shoulder.

Justin le March smiled. "Hector is young yet and has a long way to go, but I think we'll get there. He seems particularly intelligent and I thought I'd train him for young Master Thomas." He chuckled. "I believe they'll both be ready for each other at the same time."

"That boy's lucky to have you," said Tom, speaking of the squire's infant son. "But we haven't seen you for a while, sir?"

"No, not since Squire Gordon's funeral I believe. I've been overseas."

Tom chuckled. "Aye, sir. Thought you looked a bit healthier than if you'd just spent the winter around these parts."

Justin's saddle creaked as he shifted. "Particularly bad, was it?"

Tom glanced towards the bar. "In some ways, yes. It's the very devil to get paid by some folk."

Justin's expression darkened. "I'll have a word with him, Tom. Good day to you then." He glanced at Mary and nodded, and moved Hector forward.

"He's no fool," Tom said quietly to Mary. "It's a pity he wasn't the new squire instead of his brother-in-law, useless piece of work that he is." He shook his head sadly. "Dark days ahead, my dear. Dark days ahead."

Mary was aware that few people liked the new squire, who had taken over the manor when his father died. She often heard Harriet and Sarah gossiping about him. They reckoned Hartley Gordon would more than likely come to a bad end, and Harriet said she hoped she would live long enough to see it.

Sarah had cackled about no woman being safe with him around, and how there would be mouths to feed that he would have the pleasure of making, but not the trouble of raising. Sometimes Mary's cheeks burned with what they said in front of her. They appeared to forget that although she couldn't speak, her ears worked perfectly well.

"You hurry along home now," Tom said, interrupting her thoughts.

Mary gave him a quick hug and crossed the yard. At the corner, when she saw he was still looking after her, she waved. How kind most people were to her, she thought. If only her mistress could be the same.

She glanced longingly towards the village pump in the middle of the green. Sometimes she liked to sit on the stone trough, watching the hustle and bustle of life going on around her. But that day she had too many chores to do; she had dallied enough as it was and must get off home.

Nevertheless, before she ran down the hill, she paused to listen, as once she had heard a cuckoo from that very spot. She had been fascinated to hear the call bounced back and forth across the valley by an echo, but that day there were hardly any sounds at all, apart from the occasional barking of a dog somewhere in the village.

She climbed the stile at the bottom of the hill into a meadow full of buttercups and leapt over the stream that chortled its way through beds of marsh marigolds and wild cress to the river. She skipped through the lush grass to climb the stile out into the lane. Further down the road were two bridges, and she paused briefly to peer over the granite wall to see if she could spy any trout. Ronald said the plumpest ones lived under the bridge, where the water was quite deep.

He had told her that last night, after creeping upstairs to bring her a crust of bread and a chunk of cheese. He'd also said she could ride the pony to the village if she wished. However, that morning, after going to the orchard, he said he was sorry, but the old pony had put his foot down a rabbit hole and was lame.

Not that Mary minded walking except it increased her appetite, which was voracious enough as it was. Harriet's helpings were rarely enough to satisfy her. Matthew sympathized, and at the supper table tried to help by passing things to her without Harriet noticing. Although she was grateful, Mary discouraged him, not only because he might get into trouble, but also because Harriet wasn't over generous with his portions either and she considered he needed every morsel for himself.

Sometimes he would share scraps of food that his beloved Clara managed to get from the manor kitchen. Clara was the Lady Leonora's maid, and also helped to look after young Thomas. Apparently the lady was often not well, and Matthew said since the old squire's death, things had become very lax.

Matthew was by no means a gossip, but Mary thought he found some of the things Clara told him to be quite shocking, and he repeated them to her to share the burden, knowing they could go no further. One thing he told her was that the squire had only married his wife for her money, and if it wasn't for her brother having some control over the estate there would be nothing left by now. He also said

Mary should be watchful of the squire. He was a philanderer and no woman was safe when he was around.

She was ruminating these things and still on the bridge when she heard horses approaching. To avoid either being run down or startling the creatures, she kept into the side, pressing herself against the cold, rough stone.

The riders were jocular, and from their expressions, Mary gathered they had just come from the Blackbird and were probably in their cups. Her heart picked up a beat when they slowed and turned their heads to look at her. One man on a black horse, reined in. The horse sidled frighteningly close to her, champing at the bit and pawing the ground, eager to get on.

The man cussed him and pulled cruelly on the bit. Then he turned his attention to Mary, and lifted her chin with the tip of his riding crop. "What a pretty maid," he drawled. "And where have you been all my life?"

It wasn't quite a memory, yet something about his voice struck a chord. One of the others said, "An unbroken filly too, I'd wager."

Terrified, Mary averted her eyes as raucous laughter broke out. She glanced over the bridge and swore if any one of them touched her she would leap over the side. Better to drown in the whirlpool than fall into those arms.

She suddenly heard another horse approaching and with some relief saw it was Justin le March on his chestnut. The crop, now touching the tip of her breast, was withdrawn, the horse kicked on, but not before the man gave her a rakish wink.

Mary's world wavered beneath her. Justin inquired if she was all right before he rode on, but she barely heard him, and it was several minutes before she could even move.

Matthew was in the yard when she came up from the orchard, her breast heaving and her face red with exertion and fear. She had run all the way home across the fields to avoid the lane, tearing her legs on the brambles and sticks in the hedgerows over which she'd climbed.

Matthew threw down his fork and ran towards her. "What's happened, Mary? What's up?"

They had found a way to communicate, and she indicated for him not to worry; she was merely upset because she'd stayed overlong in the village and feared she wouldn't have time to finish her chores before the mistress came home. Followed by Matthew's dubious expression, she ran indoors. Even if she could have told him her fears, he, who said he loved her next to Clara, couldn't have done anything to help her. To the likes of those men on the bridge, Matthew was just a simple farm laborer, worthless and expendable.

ജ്ഞ

When the Bennetts arrived home from market, they both had long faces. Harriet banged things about and told Mary to put them away and look sharp about it. Then she took her own purchases into what she called her sewing room and slammed the door behind her, only to storm out again shortly afterwards to ask Mary if she had delivered the dress. In her consternation Mary had forgotten all about it and now felt in her pocket for the money. Harriet clucked her tongue as she unwrapped the piece of paper.

"And what's the meaning of this?" she demanded.

Ronald looked up. "What's up?"

"The damn cheek of it." Harriet showed him the note. "Giving me 'what she thinks my work is worth.' Who the hell be she when she's at home? Mary'll have to go over again tomorrow. It's her fault for not collecting the full amount."

"Don't be daft, Harriet, how can it be her fault? How could she say?"

"I knew we shouldn't have taken in that dimwitted slut," Harriet retorted.

Ronald's face suffused with anger. He looked quickly at Mary. "Go and shut the chickens in, there's a good maid. You haven't done anything wrong."

"That's right," Harriet said, in a tight, bitter voice. "Take her side."

Normally Ronald backed down to keep the peace, but this time he turned on his wife. "I'm getting damned sick and tired of this, Harriet. You've been acting queer ever since Sarah was here yesterday. Blaming Mary for some trumped up reason and sending her to bed with no supper last night. Poor maid, I dare say she's known starvings enough."

"No one goes to the workhouse without good reason," Harriet cried. "She didn't weed that path properly and she has to learn. Letting anything live that's got a face on it—"

"It's just her way. She's kind, that's all. Unlike some others I could mention," he added bitterly.

"Oh, yes? And who might that be?" Harriet's eyes flashed challengingly.

"You know who I mean. Nobody can please you, or your bleddy sister. And every time she comes here and stirs things up you find some excuse to take it out on the maid."

"It's you who's making excuses," Harriet cried.

"What the hell are you talking about?"

"You don't need me to tell you."

He met her eyes. "Tell me what? Come on, out with it. I know you've got a bee in your bonnet about something."

Harriet lifted her chin. "I'm beginning to think Sarah was right. You got that maid for yourself."

"What filth is this?" he growled.

Immediately she was on the defensive. "Why else would you make such a fuss of her then? It's Mary this and Mary that. Anyone'd think I didn't exist."

"I care about Mary, it's true, but I only treat her like any decent soul should be treated. Is that what you're jealous about? Someone who's never had a home or someone to love her? This time won't last forever, Harriet. Soon she'll be fully grown and will find a young man—"

"She is fully grown," Harriet said stonily.

"She's the same age as our own maid would have been," Ronald continued, the painful memory too much for him to heed her interruption. "Imagine if we'd perished and our maid had been forced to live in such a place for all those years. Wouldn't you be glad when she found some kindly people to take her in? Wouldn't you want them to treat her right? I just don't understand you."

"Oh, don't you? She be ripe for the picking, that's what Sarah says. And she says you'd have to be blind not to see it."

Ronald looked at his wife as if he had never seen her before. "Then I am blind. I haven't seen it because I haven't been looking. It's just in your bleddy filthy minds!" He walked out and slammed the door, saying he intended to spend the night in the barn with Matthew.

ꟹ

Harriet was in a furious temper the next morning. In a voice that indicated she had made up her mind and there would be no argument about it, she told Mary that she would have to return to the Blackbird and collect the rest of the money, and hadn't better show her face until she had.

Mary couldn't look to Ronald to save her as he had already left with Matthew to go to Moretonhampstead. After she completed her morning chores, she took the note Harriet gave her and set off. There was no lightness in her step this time.

She wished the old pony hadn't been lame, as she could have ridden him there and back in no time, even though she doubted the mistress would have been agreeable: Ronald might like to see her and pony getting along, but Harriet didn't approve. Sorrowfully, Mary thought her mistress seemed to be disapproving of her more every day.

When she reached the inn, Betsy hugged her to her ample bosom. "What, back again? Want more duck, I bet? But what's that face for? What's wrong, my dear?"

Mary drew the note out of her pocket and reluctantly handed it over.

Betsy frowned as she looked at it. "Well, I go to say," she murmured, but nonetheless disappeared into the bar to find her husband. "I shall have to pay her," she told him. "You should see the look on that little maid's face. It wouldn't surprise me if she didn't get the blame. Oh, Tom, whatever have I done?"

"Don't you fret, my dear, Mary won't hold it against you," he said. "Give her a piece of your apple pie, that'll cheer her up."

But when Betsy tried to entice her into the kitchen, Mary glanced towards the bar and declined. "She seemed in a dreadful hurry to go," Betsy told Tom later. "I hope I haven't upset her so she won't come again."

"You know our Mary wouldn't do that," Tom said, consolingly. "She's probably been told not to linger and you know she's a good, obedient maid."

All the same, Betsy worried all day, and for some reason felt she should have run after Mary and escorted her home to Blackthorn.

ꟹ

Mary didn't go by way of the meadow this time but hurried down by the church, alternately running or walking very fast while she caught her breath. She hoped she hadn't upset Betsy by not staying. In truth there was nothing more she would have liked than a piece of apple pie because she was very hungry, but she was too afraid to linger, she was sure she'd seen him watching her as she'd crossed the yard. She ran over the bridges without giving the trout a thought; she just wanted to reach the safety of the farm.

Sometimes a person senses their fate before it is upon them, and so it was with Mary. She knew what was to befall her. She had seen the determination in his eyes when he'd practically pinned her against the bridge. She'd known he would watch and wait for her: she was the rabbit to his fox. And now, when she heard the horse coming behind her, she had no burrow to run to. No escape.

With her heart pounding in her throat and her breath coming in great gulps, she ran as fast as she could, stumbled over a gate and hid behind the hedge.

It seemed an eon but it was barely a few minutes before she heard the horse stop. The man dismounted. And then she heard him urinating by the gate. She could see him, but he hadn't yet seen her, and she kept as still as stone, hoping he wouldn't. However, that was too much to hope for, and when he spied her, he grinned and climbed the gate.

"Well, well, what do we have here, an invitation?"

Mary shook her head. He was still partially disrobed, and she saw that part of him that would hurt her rising in anticipation. She shook her head again and backed away.

"Don't be afraid," he said. He took a step nearer and took hold of her chin. His breath was rancid, an insult to her senses, and she averted her face. This irked him. He grabbed her roughly, and began to feel beneath her dress. Mary fought him as best she could, but he tumbled her to the ground and pinned her beneath him.

Pain racked her as he ripped into her body. "Tight little wench," she heard him say through the roaring in her head. Then, mercifully, she fell unconscious.

ꕥ

Shocked and shaken, Mary made her way home. Every now and again she stopped to vomit, even though she only brought up bile. Still, her body felt the need to eject his filth from her. Her hair was disheveled, her dress grass-stained, and it made her sick to think of it even, but there were flecks of blood and his cursed slime on the insides of her legs and on her underskirts.

She came up from the orchard, grateful that no one appeared to be about, and hurried into the dairy where there was a pan, soap and water. She was whimpering, and shaking so badly, she could hardly think straight, but knew she must wash his foulness off her. She lifted her skirts about her waist and sloshed water over herself, then began to scrub her body.

All of a sudden, Matthew was in the doorway. She would never forget the look on his face, his head bent under the lintel. A moment frozen in time, it seemed he stood there for ages. Their eyes met. His questioning: hers wide and fearful, begging him not to ask her what she was doing.

In reality, it was seconds only. While she dropped her skirts momentarily, he mumbled an apology, albeit a puzzled one for coming upon her like so, turned and went out. Mary resumed scrubbing herself until her flesh was red and sore.

ꕥ

At supper, Mary couldn't eat a morsel of food. Neither could she meet Matthew's eyes that looked at her so inquisitively, for she knew he would realize something terrible had happened to her. She signed she wasn't feeling well and was excused from her evening chores and allowed to go upstairs to her room.

She closed the door and undressed, but instead of getting into bed, she stood looking out of the window.

Tears rolled down her cheeks as she watched the world grow darker and the stars come out. Now and again, clouds crossed the moon blotting the light out of the heavens. That was how she felt her happiness had been blotted out that day. Now she would never be able to walk those lanes again and feel safe. Never pause on the bridges or dally in the meadow. She would even be afraid to go and visit Betsy at the inn. That beast, that devil, had robbed her of far more than her virtue.

Through her tears, she saw a star twinkle. Tilly reckoned after people died they went to other stars, one of which was called Heaven. Tilly had told her lots of things that were quite the opposite of what the preacher in the workhouse said. He contended they were all sinners and had committed a crime merely by being born. Condemned to hell he said, all of them.

Mary felt at that moment she was already in hell, and that what was to come after death could only be an improvement. Because, really, in God's vast creation, what worse could have happened to her? Although even that she could, and would, survive. What it might lead to, however, she might not.

"You all right, my dear Mary?"

She heard Ronald's voice outside the door and quickly got into bed. Just in time, for the door opened and he stood there.

He scratched his ear and looked at her anxiously, but didn't cross the threshold. "It isn't like you not to want your supper," he said, sounding concerned. "I just wanted to make sure you were all right." He hovered for a moment longer. "Well, good night then, my angel. Sleep tight."

As Ronald closed the door, Mary turned her head into her pillow and wept. How she loved that dear man who cared for her so deeply. She couldn't bear it if she let him down. Yet she knew it may only take one time. In the workhouse she had watched women's bodies swell and witnessed their unwanted babies born into an unwelcoming, uncaring world. And she had heard a woman take her last breath when she'd done something to avoid such an outcome and it had gone wrong.

She tossed and turned in inconsolable grief, afraid that a similar fate might await her.

ജ്ജ

After what seemed hours, she eventually fell into a fitful sleep.

In the early hours of the morning, she dreamed of the dark rider. She was on his horse and he was pressing into her, and she was squirming and crying out for help, trying to get away from him. Then she did, and she was running and running, and getting nowhere.

She awoke, drenched with sweat and carrying the memory of her screams into the cold room. Now she remembered her voice. Strangely enough, the last time she had heard it was when she had found her mother's lifeless body. She had been screaming then, too.

Chapter 4

Across the other side of the parish, Peter Peardon smoldered in his own hell as he made his way home along the rutted, muddy lane from the Blackbird Inn.

He rode under a starlit sky and brilliant moon, and when he got to the crossroads, could see the gibbet dangling a corpse, its chains clanking as it swung on rusty hinges. As he stared grimly at the shriven, rotting thing, which the crows had in places picked clean to the bone, Hartley Gordon came to mind. Gordon was like a crow, Peter thought, a dark pestilence who fed off the tender parts of others.

A cloud momentarily covered the moon and shadowed the corpse. Shuddering, Peter rode on.

He passionately regretted going to the inn that evening, especially into that back room where it wasn't unheard of to see a man ruined, the tide turned in his life forever. Peter knew the innkeeper's wife, Betsy Berry, didn't hold with what went on in there, but times were hard and her husband's social conscience didn't extend as far as stopping his customers having a good time as long as they paid their bills. Not even a virtuous wife was enough to save a man from his own ruin, Peter thought, grimly. He of all people could attest to that. His own pious Felicity would be mortified if she knew about his habit. But whereas some men got a tingle when they looked at a pretty woman or a fine horse, gambling did it for him and he hadn't the willpower to resist.

Fortunately, he was often lucky at cards and had been winning that evening too, until that devil Gordon walked in and doused his luck with brandy. Peter didn't normally drink while he gambled; he liked to keep a clear head. However, this had irked the squire who insinuated he might be cowardly. So, he accepted a drink and after the first one, his glass was never empty.

He should have known better than to dull his wits like that. It had caused him to hang in when normally he would have quit and gone home. But it wasn't only the brandy that stalled him. In that dimly lit, smoke-filled room with all eyes upon him, he wasn't going to give Gordon the satisfaction of his backing down. He could barely tolerate the squire's lazy arrogance and would have done anything to beat him. But he lost to the bastard and along with it was made to look a fool when, near the end of the last game, someone said, "You can hardly afford to lose, Peardon, having a daughter with such extravagant tastes."

That snide remark stung, because it wasn't without a grain of truth. Still, he might have laughed it off if that damned Gordon hadn't put his spoke in. Ponderous and sly he looked across the table and said in that detestable drawl of his, "Is that so?"

What business is it of yours? Peter thought, bristling even further. Then one or two others decided to further the evening's entertainment by enlightening the squire of a few occasions when Peter had indulged his only daughter.

The squire listened. Then as he put his last, and winning card down on the table he gave Peter a sly wink. "Your Leah sounds quite the gad-about. I should get her a husband and be quick about it if I were you."

While Peter scribbled his signature on the promissory note the squire shoved towards him, somebody sniggered, "He's been trying to marry her off ever since Robbie Barnes disappeared, but she's like a bleddy contrary mare. She won't have none of them, isn't that right, Peardon?"

"She even turned the vicar down, didn't she?" someone else said, snorting with laughter. "Perhaps she was worried he'd find out she hadn't been *pious* enough."

Raucous laughter followed, and Peter threw back his chair and told them in no uncertain terms that his affairs were none of their business. Amid roars of laughter and more coarse jokes he made for the door, the squire shouting after him, "Don't forget the husband, Peardon."

"Damn that brandy, and damn Gordon to hell!" Peter uttered now in sudden fury, causing his horse to snort and quicken his pace. Being made a fool of didn't sit well with him at all: those jibes seared like a branding iron in his mind.

As each mile passed Peter concentrated on what he could do to remedy the situation, and by the time he turned into Furze lane, he already had a plan.

ꕥ

Peter would have been even more disconcerted if he had known his daughter's own thoughts that evening. Leah paced her room, up and down, in and out of the shaft of moonlight that streamed through the window, alternately wiping her eyes and wringing her handkerchief around her fingers. She was also brooding over what the squire had said to her that day and felt renewed pain when she recalled his words.

Until now, she had conveniently ignored the gossip, and put aside the possible danger she was courting by having an affair with him: but it had been so long since anyone had aroused that sweet, delicious sensation of desire in her that she was simply unable to resist him. Even thinking of him now, despite her anguish, made her body weak with longing.

She sank onto her bed in misery and despair. If only Robbie hadn't disappeared none of this would have happened. But her former lover had gone to Plymouth, been press-ganged into the navy and never seen again. After she had recovered from the shock, she had vowed she would never give herself to anyone else. Yet look at her. What had she become? Even today, after the squire treated her so inconsiderately, her body had betrayed her at his touch. Afterwards, as she did now, she wept tears of self-pity for her weakness.

ꕥ

In the morning, both Leah and her father bore the brunt of Felicity's temper when they could barely eat what was placed before them. Peter hardly spoke a word until he went to go outside. "John Pugh coming this afternoon?" he asked, pausing in the doorway.

"Yes," Felicity said. "Tuesdays are when he usually calls. Why do you ask, Peter?"

"I want to see him," Peter said shortly, but offered no explanation. He felt the matter had to be handled very carefully. Only when things were arranged would his wife and daughter know his intention, else there would be so much fuss and inquiry of the whys and wherefores he'd be lucky to get Leah within a mile of the church, let alone to the altar. *Foxy* was the name of the game: *stealth and speed.*

While Felicity watched her husband from the kitchen window, Leah slipped outside. Grateful to have her mother's inquisitive eyes on someone else for a change, she went behind the dairy and retched. Further down the yard she saw her father doing the same into the dung pile, and she wondered what he might have been up to the night before to make him so sick and bad-tempered.

But Leah had enough to worry about without the addition of his problems. She hurried on with her work, intending to finish up as quickly as possible so she could take her pony out again.

ꕥ

Later that afternoon, Felicity opened the window to allow the scent of the forsythia to come in and freshen the best room, then returned into the kitchen to check on the pudding she had boiling. In another pot, she stirred the sauce to pour over it.

When a knock came at the door, she hurried to answer it. "Come in, John," she said warmly to the fresh-faced young vicar who stood there. After they exchanged a few pleasantries about the weather, she ushered him down the hall. "Peter would like to see you today," she said. "Wait in the best room if you will and I'll fetch him." And she left him before he could question her about it.

When Peter came in, Felicity poured the sauce over the pudding and, with a tray of tea, followed him down the hallway.

"Ah," said John Pugh as she set it down before him, "there's no one to touch you for your puddings, Mrs. Peardon. How you do spoil a man."

Felicity always felt regretful and guilty in this young man's presence, as if she alone was responsible for Leah having refused his attentions after Robbie Barnes had disappeared. Barnes was no loss as far as she and Peter were concerned, and John would never know how much she regretted her daughter's decision, or how she would have welcomed him into the family.

Peter ate in silence while he listened to their small talk. Eventually, as it seemed they would go on forever, he interrupted. "I have a devil of a lot to do, if you'll pardon the expression, John. But first I'd like a word with you if you don't mind." He turned to his wife. "You may leave us now, Felicity."

Felicity took umbrage in being so dismissed, but left them with all the dignity she could muster. Only the fear of discovery propelled her into the kitchen and prevented her from listening at the door.

Peter put down his plate. "I'll come straight to the point, John. It's about Leah."

John Pugh's heart picked up a beat. Esther, his wife, had once said that in her opinion Leah Peardon was a hungry woman if ever she saw one, and it wouldn't bode well for her. John hadn't been able to meet her eyes, for she'd just confirmed what first attracted him to Leah.

"Oh?" he said. "She's not in any trouble, I hope?"

"'Course not. No, it's nothing like that." Peter gave an embarrassed cough as he remembered how keen John had been on her. However, he felt no guilt. In his opinion John was no match for his willful daughter and he was far better off with the prim and prissy woman he'd married. "I didn't pursue it before... That is, when you and she... because I didn't feel it was right. To push her, I mean. But certain things have made me reconsider. Now I think it's more than time—"

"Are you *ill*, Mr. Peardon?"

"No, of course I'm not ill," Peter snapped. "You know how it is. A man doesn't get any younger. Has to think of the future. And well, it's about time Leah was wed. She isn't getting any younger either."

John looked around him at the somewhat luxurious furnishings and compared them to his own meager lodgings. "And who might the fortunate man be?" he said, unable to repress a twinge of envy.

"That's why I wanted to see you," Peter said. "That's where you come in. It's quite simple and straightforward really."

ᘓᘐ

For the remainder of that day John mulled Peter's request over in his mind. Having been born and raised in the parish he knew that as far as his parishioners were concerned very little was simple and straightforward. Peter's request for him to quickly find someone to wed his daughter smacked of an ulterior motive, and while John had said he would help if he could, he was reluctant to go so far as to actually choose a husband. Under the circumstances, he thought it a bit of a cheek for Peter to ask.

Still, he had always liked Peter Peardon, and when he thought of the man's urgency he decided there must be fair reason for it. So he came to the conclusion that it was his Christian duty to put his personal feelings aside, and prayed he would be guided to do the correct thing.

Later that same week, while John met with the churchwardens and discussed business, Esther visited with their wives and reflected on parish news.

Their conversation ranged from how Betsy Berry had taken offense at Harriet Bennett's outrageous dressmaking fee, to Harriet's unbearable sister, Sarah. This in turn, led to Colan, Sarah's younger son, who had found favor with the squire's wife. He had apparently saved her day by lending her his horse so she could carry on the hunt, as her own had gone lame.

He wasn't as handsome of course, one of the wives said, but he was strong and had served her all day, so she had been led to believe.

"You talking about the horse, or he?" someone else asked.

This was followed by cackles of laughter, and further speculation about the state of the squire's marriage. And speaking of that devil, yet another said, he'd been seen riding alongside Leah Peardon down Broadmeads way. Now what did they think of that?

Esther always bristled when she heard Leah's name mentioned. The girl, with her voluptuous body and sloe eyes, was a thistle in Esther's otherwise weed-free garden of life. Her mother-in-law had once told her that, although John had lusted after the Peardon girl, she was pleased he had come to his senses. Esther had never been sure whether this was a compliment or not, but in any event it was hard to live with being John's second choice.

Now her ears pricked up and she leaned forward into the company. "Oh dear," she said, in an impeccably innocent voice, "do you think we should worry about Leah Peardon's virtue?" And was rewarded by cackles of laughter.

ഇ

Later, when John asked Esther how her evening had gone, she told him she had learned something that might distress him. She feared she might be correct in her estimation of Leah Peardon, and felt she must, on this occasion, repeat what she had heard. She added that perhaps it was John's duty on the one hand to resolve Colan's bachelorhood, to lessen the chance of any more scandal in the Underwood family, and on the other, to banish Leah's vulnerability. And what better way than perhaps bringing them together? What did he think?

"Praise be," John said. "The Lord surely works in mysterious ways."

Chapter 5

Sarah Underwood sat by the fire in the kitchen at Lower Farm, endeavoring to mend a tear in her eldest son's shirt. She squinted in the failing light and uttered a profanity as she jabbed herself with the needle. Joshua, her husband, who was feigning sleep, winced as he heard her suck the blood from her finger and wished she would take such chores to her sister Harriet.

"I wonder what the vicar wanted today?" Sarah glanced at Joshua and clucked her tongue with pique when he didn't respond. She knew it was hopeless to ask Colan, their younger son. He went around with his head in the clouds thinking of goodness knows what. Now he was engrossed in one of his books. What good learning to read and write would do him she didn't know. If it had been her favorite son straining his eyes she would have chided him, but Hern had never bothered himself with learning; he didn't believe in it. He sat opposite his brother chewing his dirty fingernails and staring through the window. As his mother opened her mouth to speak again he scraped back his chair, and without a word, went outside.

Colan looked up, closed his book and followed him.

"I'm surprised you could leave that book of yours," Hern said, as Colan caught up with him, but there was no sarcasm in his voice; Colan was the one person in the world Hern thought was all right.

"You weren't the only one who needed some fresh air," Colan said, nodding his head towards the farmhouse.

"Is that why you read, so you have an excuse to ignore her?"

"No. Well, partly I suppose. But I'm hoping my efforts will come in handy one day."

"When will you ever need to know anything, stuck in this bleddy place?"

They walked up the lane towards the field that led onto the moor and sat on the top rail of the gate.

"I'd leave. Up and go like Margery did, if I had what she had," Hern said of his twin sister. "There's an easy way to get ahead if ever there was one."

"That isn't fair, Hern," Colan said reprovingly. "She's just had some lucky breaks, that's all. And by all accounts she's worked very hard for them."

"Huh! It's men that do all the work, I reckon. Women just lie there with their legs open."

Colan knew Hern was jealous of Margery who had one day up and left the farm without a word to anyone but himself. He didn't blame her; their mother had worked her like a slave, and their father never had any time for her. Joshua hadn't even cared when she'd gone, and said more than once, 'good riddance to bad rubbish.'

But Colan didn't think Margery was rubbish. For a start, she could read and write, and he had known she would find a way to get on. He wasn't at all surprised when she secured a position with a family in Exeter. Then later she had written to say she was living with the le Marches in Whitmouth. He didn't want to know how she'd come by such luck. He supposed he didn't want to know really; he was only glad she hadn't ended up in the gutter as Sarah had predicted. It was no use saying all this to Hern, however, as he and Margery had never gotten along. He merely said, "You're incorrigible, Hern."

Hern wasn't sure what Colan meant, but thought it must be a compliment of sorts as his brother was never mean to him. He chuckled again, and then sighed. "I don't know what I'm smiling about. What chance is there really of ever getting away from here? As for bringing a maid here...."

Colan duplicated his brother's grimace. He believed their mother must be one of the hardest people to get along with in the County of Devon: although men might give her the time of day, most women avoided her as if she had something catching. "It would be hard," he agreed.

"Hard? Bleddy impossible you mean."

"Is that why you've never had anyone?"

Hern looked sidelong at him. "Who said I'd never had anyone? Though mine doesn't come riding by." He chuckled. "Nancy only rides at the inn."

Colan smiled at his brother's crude humor.

Hern's smile faded. "You want to be careful," he warned. He knew what his brother was up to, and although he secretly admired him for his gall, he also worried Colan was looking above himself and could get into a lot of trouble.

"I am being," Colan said quietly. Then, to change the subject added, "Nice and peaceful out here."

"Bleddy well is." Hern spat to the ground, relieved to be off the other matter, because in truth he was embarrassed by his brother's involvement with the squire's wife. "I don't know how Father puts up with her."

Colan sighed. "Men have murdered for less, I'm sure."

"Beats me how they got together in the first place. Never have been able to imagine them doing that. But we're here to prove it, so I suppose they must have."

Colan's room was next to his parents'. Over the years he had heard a lot and could have told Hern a few things. But now was not the time, he decided: before he went away perhaps. "What did the vicar want, by the way?"

"I dunno," said Hern, who was curious himself. "He said he wanted to see Father alone, so I left them to it."

"Mother can't stand not knowing, can she?"

Hern chuckled. "Be over to her bleddy sister's tomorrow, gossiping and trying to figure it out. Making poor Ronald's life a misery. And that maid of theirs, I dare say."

Colan knew that his mother's viciousness, although aimed at Mary, was really to hurt Ronald because he'd spurned her in favor of her sister. He knew this because he'd once heard his father shout to Sarah that Ronald had been lucky to see her coming, unlike himself who hadn't.

"Sounds a bit of all right to me," Hern said of Mary. "And if she's come from a workhouse, well you know what they say, those maids are used to it and they like it, too."

"You can't say that, Hern. It doesn't do to make assumptions about people before you know them."

But Hern had lost interest. He was watching the sky, and he suddenly gave a cry and jumped down off the gate. "Bleddy hell, did you see that?"

"No. What?" Colan followed his brother's eyes.

"It was a bleddy great light, tearing across the sky."

"Oh, that'll be a shooting star, but you've seen them before."

"Not one like this. It was a bleddy great thing. The biggest I ever saw."

"You'd better wish on it then," Colan said, amused. "Come on, it's *bleddy* cold out here." They laughed companionably as they walked down the lane towards the farmhouse. But while Colan hurried inside and over to the fire to warm himself, Hern hung around outside for a little while longer, searching the sky.

ഌഌ

A few days later, after Peter received word from John Pugh, he rode over to Lower Farm and knocked gingerly at the door. Sarah eyed him suspiciously when he asked to see Joshua, and would have closed the door in his face if Peter hadn't persisted. She only very reluctantly pointed to where her husband was.

Joshua was out in the potato field, checking the plants. After digging beneath one or two, he saw that the tubers were swelling nicely and there would be a fair crop. He straightened up and nodded with satisfaction: potatoes were the one crop this land could grow. His pleasure deepened when he saw someone coming across the furrows towards him, knowing it was likely to be Peter Peardon.

"Early crop by the looks of it," Peter said, shaking Joshua's outstretched hand, and he went on to talk about potatoes, not quite knowing how to broach the subject he had come about.

Eventually, as Joshua did his best to put him at ease, Peter said, "This is a bit of a delicate matter. I expect you're wondering why the hurry?"

Joshua scratched his head. He had only been thinking of his own pleasure, and thought little—and cared even less—about Peardon's motives. Even if there was more to it than the reason the vicar gave, it mattered not a cuss to him. It would even add some spice to his revenge if Sarah's son suffered the same fate as himself.

"Not at all," he said. "Sometimes young people need a bit of a push."

Peter was pleasantly encouraged by Joshua's attitude and went on to say how he wasn't getting any younger and what a relief it would be to have someone to take over the reins. He ignored a niggle of doubt as he said this, however, because he noticed Lower wasn't kept like Furze. But beggars couldn't be choosers he supposed. It was true what John Pugh said, there were so few men available owing to the war.

Although John had suggested Colan would be a good match for Leah, as the conversation continued it became apparent that Joshua was proposing Hern should marry her. Peter was perplexed. It seemed unthinkable that a man would choose his eldest son to leave a farm that should be his by rights. But he said nothing; worrying that if he made a fuss he might lose even this opportunity. Hern, Colan, it mattered not a whit to him. All he cared about was seeing his daughter married as soon as possible to stop the sneers and the jibes, and embarrassing gossip.

ꕥ

After Peter left, Sarah hurried across the yard to the field. Although she had racked her brain, she couldn't think what the two men might have been talking about.

"I thought you'd be along," Joshua said, without looking up.

"What do the likes of Peardon want with us?" she demanded.

"You'll find out tomorrow. We're going over to Furze."

"And why might that be?"

Joshua didn't answer, but whistled under his breath while he continued to hoe between the rows of potatoes. Despite Sarah's whining and wheedling, he wouldn't say another word, and eventually she got fed up with his silence and went in.

Joshua looked after her and smiled with the exhilaration and liberty that comes with the acquisition of power. He'd been waiting for something like this for years.

ꕥ

As Joshua drove down the lane to Furze the following day it occurred to him what a gift he was handing to Sarah's son, but then the satisfaction of his revenge quickly overcame any regret. Besides, he told himself, when all was said and done, it was only right that his true son should inherit the farm that had been in his family for generations.

Sarah, however, was not at all impressed. She was still furious at Joshua's secrecy and very sure she wasn't going to like the outcome of this meeting, the reason for which she still didn't know. When they were met by the glorious show of spring flowers in the beds beneath the farmhouse windows, she sniffed and turned her head away. She considered flower gardening to be frivolous and a waste of time, and she suspected Felicity Peardon would reflect the same attributes.

Peter met them in the yard and showed them through the front door into the best room, where Felicity was waiting with light refreshments. She was as puzzled as Sarah about this meeting, and greeted them coolly.

Despite the obvious ill ease of those around him, Joshua was quite relaxed and praised Felicity for her superb pudding, the remainder of which was then eaten in silence, punctuated by awkward and stilted conversation and Sarah pointedly refusing a second helping. Felicity sipped a cup of strong tea. She was more than a little discomfited by Sarah, and hoped she wouldn't have to tolerate her company again.

To add to her chagrin, she was also feeling stung by Peter, who blamed her in front of the Underwoods for being too lax with their daughter. He completely ignored the fact that she had grumbled more than once in recent weeks that she was thoroughly fed up with Leah's behavior. Taking Duffy out every day, coming home looking miserable, snapping at her every word. Not eating. Why, if she hadn't known better, she would have thought the girl was in love.

She put down her cup as she heard the back door open. She intended to go and give Leah a piece of her mind, but Peter beat her to it and was out of the door before she could even get up from her chair.

"Where do you think you've been?" Peter demanded, as Leah removed her riding boots. If he noticed she was upset, he said nothing of it but took hold of her arm and shook her slightly. "Come along. I will not have them kept waiting any longer."

Pale and shaken, and not only because of his welcome, Leah followed her father down the hallway. As yet unable to believe that her affair with the squire was over, and telling herself that his present indifference was because he must need more time to deliberate about the situation, she had ridden out to meet him at their usual rendezvous. When he hadn't shown, aware that her company was required at the farmhouse, she had turned for home in bitter disappointment.

Her hopes had risen, however, when on the way home he'd passed her in the lane. But there had been no more acknowledgment in his eyes than what he might give a casual acquaintance at a county fair. No one would have known he had stolen her heart and given her a child. While Leah had scrambled desperately for words to say that might touch him, he had ridden away.

Peter frowned at his daughter's lack of enthusiasm as he introduced her to the Underwoods, and was thankful he hadn't divulged his plan to either her or his wife, whose anxious looks he kept avoiding.

When they were all seated his eyes finally met Felicity's, and he began.

"Yesterday, Mr. Underwood and myself came to an agreement," he said, his chin jutting forward stubbornly. "There is to be a wedding between the two families. Leah, you are betrothed to Hern. The bans will be called immediately, and the wedding will take place at the end of the month."

He looked at Joshua as if to say, 'there, it is done,' and Joshua nodded with a satisfied grunt. Both men ignored the stifled cries that came from Felicity and Leah, and the sharp intake of breath from Sarah.

Hern was stunned. He glanced at his mother. She obviously hadn't known anything about it because she looked livid. Well, he knew it certainly wouldn't fit in with her plans. She never stopped telling him how, once Joshua was out of the way—and she made no bones about how she relished the day—she would make sure Lower Farm would become his.

Then he remembered the shooting star. Bleddy hell, he thought, he *had* made a wish, feeling stupid as he'd done so, but all the same, he'd asked for something to come along to take him away, and it had. Marriage to Leah Peardon would mean no more nights stuck at Lower listening to his mother's prattle, or his parents' bickering. He would be in his own home stuck into Leah Peardon. He'd *be* someone.

While the others had been sipping tea and making banal conversation, Hern had been looking around him appreciatively. Compared to Lower, the furnishings in this house were like they belonged to gentry. Of course, he knew the Peardons were of good stock and thought a lot of themselves because of it. They were also very highly spoken of in the parish. That's why he'd been at a loss to know what the likes of his family were doing there, but one didn't ask questions of a father who rarely spoke except to chide or give orders.

Sarah was the first to break the uncomfortable silence. "Well, *I* was not informed about this," she said. "As Hern is our eldest son, I assumed he would be taking care of *our* farm in the future."

Barely loud enough for anyone else to hear, Joshua leaned towards her and said, "Your son, *my* farm."

Sarah's face suffused with color and she turned on him.

"Be quiet," he warned, in a low, hard voice. "It is arranged now, and the marriage will take place." He cleared his throat and turned to Hern, "What say you then, boy? Sound all right to you, does it?"

Hern colored and thought it must be shock that made him want to giggle. It was the first time his father had ever asked his opinion about anything, and it was puzzling to see him so keen on his behalf.

He sobered suddenly, wondering what might be the reason, and why Colan hadn't been chosen. But then, he thought, why dwell on it? He glanced at Leah again. His impression of her so far was very favorable, and he thought she would be nice and comfortable, too. He could see himself in the evenings to come, sitting beside his own hearth while she made supper. Afterwards she would make sure his needs were met. There would be no need for Nancy now.

Not only that, but when her parents passed on he'd have Furze. You'd grow a damn sight more than potatoes here, he thought. This farm wasn't some piddling acreage you could barely scrape a living off, but a real farm. He caught his mother's eyes. She was looking at him as if he'd betrayed her, and he looked away. How could he tell her that no one would want to stay at Lower in that atmosphere if they had a choice? As for him having Lower, it had always been her ambition, not his. If she really loved him the best, as she swore she did, wouldn't she be pleased for him to have a better future anyway?

Being unable to say anything of that, however, he croaked, "Well, I reckon so, Father. Yes, it sounds all right to me."

Leah glanced at the emotions flickering across Hern's face, and she grimaced and decided something must have possessed her father. She knew he sometimes acted rashly; her mother was full of stories about his eccentricities, and not all of them were funny. But *this*? She felt as if everything had suddenly become very unreal and she wanted to run from the room. But as Peter beckoned her forward to take Hern's hand, she obeyed. Although she wanted to tell him she had no intention of marrying the son of these doltish farmers, what choice had she but to play along until her lover came up with an alternative solution?

"Hern and Leah, you are betrothed, and that is my word," Peter said, holding his hand over theirs, clasped together.

Joshua beamed. His thoughts went back to years ago when his mother had warned him about Sarah and begged him not to marry her. He hadn't listened of course, what son ever did? But when she lay on her deathbed he'd wept and admitted he wished he had.

Sarah had been a striking woman in those days and he had wondered what she saw in him. He never realized just how devious she was until after her twins were born, two months early. But when he confronted her with it she had laughed in his face. Called him a fool. How he ever managed to touch her after that he never knew, and once Colan was born and thriving, he hadn't. Now, finally, after years of bitter frustration, he was having his revenge on that scheming bitch. His mother would be smiling in her grave this day, proud of him, he thought. Now it was his turn to laugh, and he did.

Peter caught his mood and chuckled, too. He had actually brought it off. *Now* see who would be sneering at him behind his back.

Behind them Felicity sat as still as Haytor Rock, staring at her daughter who looked about to faint; at her husband who was laughing like a jack-ass and offering Joshua a drink; and at the silent, furious mother of the bridegroom-to-be.

She shivered. This was not at all how she had envisioned her daughter's betrothal. This was medieval, the conjuring of men. And she didn't get a good feeling about it at all.

Chapter 6

The following Sunday, Leah was beside herself when she learned the squire had gone to London and no one knew when he would be back. She sat in church listening to her banns being called, and afterwards suffered severe scrutiny from those in the congregation who were curious to know how this had come about so suddenly when they hadn't even heard she was courting.

It wasn't until the end of the week, and quite by chance, that she discovered the squire had returned. It happened when she went into the village shop and walked into a heated conversation between the shopkeeper and a servant from the manor.

The squire had come home unexpectedly the previous evening, the servant said. It had thrown them into a tizzy as it always did. But that wasn't all. Without even consulting the Lady Leonora, he then ordered supper and a bottle of wine with two glasses to be taken to her room. They all knew downstairs what that would mean, and drew lots to see who would be the unfortunate to take up the tray. It was himself, he said, and he was thrown down the stairs afterwards for his trouble. Not only that, he was dismissed for the broken dishes, the food on the stairs, and for spilling a good bottle of wine. Now, was that his fault? Could he help it if the lady wouldn't sup or have anything to do with her husband so that it was driving him mad?

Leah had learned what she needed to know, and when someone else came into the shop she slipped out without being served. Although she knew how much she risked in the way of gossip, she was running out of time and felt she had no choice but to go to the manor.

She recognized the servant who opened the door. He was called Maddox. Once, he had worked a season for her father and she'd told him to get on with his work and stop gawking at her. She could see he still bore a grudge over it, but she told him she had come to see the squire on behalf of her father, and he let her in. She was shown to the library and told to wait.

When the squire walked in he didn't smile. "I believe you have come here on behalf of your father," he said abruptly. "You have something for me?"

Leah frowned, not knowing what he meant, but her own desperation overcame her curiosity. "Forgive me," she said, blushing. "It was a ruse. I really needed to see you and I feared he would not allow me in."

"More lies?" he said, with a touch of sarcasm.

"I do not tell lies," she said defensively. "I only used the excuse because I urgently needed to see you."

"I thought I had made the situation quite clear. I neither want to see you, or hear any more about the matter."

Leah put her hand to her breast to catch the pain she felt in her heart. "But we *have* to talk about it. Even if you no longer care for me, there is still the child."

His dark eyes bored into hers. "By all accounts you are rather a gad-about, Leah Peardon," he said, as softly as a cat might tread. "I hear you have turned down at least one good man's hand in marriage. I also understand you have a taste for luxury. Might I suggest that perhaps none of your other suitors would be able to keep you in the manner you desire, and that is why you are targeting me, believing me to be a man of considerable means?"

Angry tears sprang to Leah's eyes. "Why sir, that is quite the most outrageous accusation! How could you say such a thing? Have I not made clear my feelings for you? The child I carry is *yours*, and if I recall correctly, you assured me if that ever happened you would take care of the situation."

"But I have," he drawled. "I was the one who suggested to your father that you should be married. And according to the banns, that I believe were read on Sunday, that has been arranged, has it not?"

"You did *what*?" she whispered.

He shrugged. "I promised to take care, and I did. Now, if you would leave now."

"No, please, you cannot dismiss me like this. For me to marry Hern Underwood is no solution at all. I cannot! Oh, won't you cast a thought to what we had between us? You cannot say you were displeased with me. And I...." She swallowed. "Well, I thought if I should fall for a child you would make arrangements."

"What *arrangements*?" He cocked an eyebrow.

Leah had envisaged he might provide a cottage for her. In her mind's eye she had seen him visiting her. He would admire their child then she would take his hand and lead him to her bedroom. There, in the summer afternoons, while bees droned in the flowers outside the window, they'd lie in each other's arms....

She blinked away bitter tears. That wasn't going to happen now. It had been a dream. A foolish, foolish dream. And one that she daren't verbalize, because in doing so she would only confirm his opinion of her; that she was mercenary. Now, she didn't know what to say.

He picked up on her hesitation. "This is the best and tidiest solution. And really, we cannot meet again, Mistress Underwood. I understand your wedding is to be held forthwith and I would not dally with a newly married woman."

As well as being embarrassed for having stooped so low as to beg him, together with her disappointment and disbelief at his cold, calculating mind, Leah was now infuriated. "I doubt that fact has ever stopped you before from your wenching," she cried. "I have heard the rumors of why your lady wife does not allow you into her bed." She gasped as he grabbed her arm before she could even blink. His eyes were like dead coals, his grip like steel. "Please," she whimpered, "I didn't mean it. I'm just so distraught. Let me go, please, you are hurting me."

"You don't know what pain is, *yet*," he growled, pinching her arm spitefully.

She managed to shake herself free and ran to the door. "You are being completely unreasonable," she cried. "I cannot believe you would do this. I come from a respectable family and I will not be—"

"Your father is a sot, and you are nothing but a strumpet," the squire said icily. "Now, get out of my sight before I have you thrown out."

ꕤ

Upstairs, Lady Leonora happened to be crossing the landing when she heard the commotion downstairs. She edged back into the shadows as she saw a woman hurrying towards the front door.

"Who was that earlier, Hartley?" she asked him later. "Something on the estate I should deal with?" He looked at her blankly, and she added, "The woman who came. I saw her leave."

"Oh, that," he said vaguely. "It's nothing you need worry about."

"But something must have happened that she should come here?"

"It was inconsequential. Leave it alone, Leonora."

"Inconsequential," she said bitterly. "You keep me in the dark about everything. In this room—"

"When you come to your senses things will be different," he said tersely. "I won't have gossip being spread about you. It was foolish of you to venture near Lower Farm again; you know what these peasants are like." He caught her face in his hand. "If I thought there was any truth in it...."

She snapped her chin out of his grasp. "Don't be ridiculous. What would I be wanting with Colan Underwood?"

"Something you don't have with me," he said, his dark eyes boring into her.

"And whose fault would that be?"

"Witch," he growled. "You only have yourself to blame for the way I am."

"Oh, I'm to blame," she agreed bitterly. "But not for the way you are, rather for the fool I've been."

"I'm a man, for God's sake. What do you expect?"

"A man?" She laughed. "More like an animal you mean. Why, you're positively indecent with your affairs. Oh, get out. Get out and leave me alone."

Thomas stirred from his bed and whimpered. Hartley looked from his wife to their child, then flung himself out of the door and called for Clara.

Shortly afterwards there was a knock at the door and the maid came in. "The squire asked me to take care of Master Thomas, madam," she said.

"It's all right, Clara," Leonora said. "I can manage, thank you."

"Are you sure, madam? The squire said—"

"I don't *care* what he said," Leonora said. "Please. Leave me."

The door closed and Leonora reached for Thomas. "Darling," she whispered. "It's all right, my dove." And she took the restless child with her to sit by the window, where she rocked him to and fro and sang in her low, sweet voice until he closed his eyes and drifted back to sleep.

She knew in one way it would be easier to give into her husband's demands. He was using every ploy to coerce her and had even gone so far that day as to suggest she couldn't mother her own child. She knew the only reason he didn't beat her into submission was because of the money her family provided. One mark on her and Justin would make sure he'd receive no more of it. All the same, she was making a dreadful enemy of him by stubbornly refusing him her bed. But her fear was that one day he would bring home more than the welts and bites he received on his sojourns to London. It wasn't only that she risked disease; his infidelities had completely killed her love for him and she couldn't bear the thought of him ever touching her again.

Leonora thought again of the woman who had visited that afternoon. Hartley might say it was inconsequential, but she'd heard the anguish in her voice. Curses on him, she thought. Even though his London escapades occasionally, and embarrassingly, reached her ears through their acquaintances, he had promised he wouldn't bring disgrace to their doorstep. But pity the poor woman, whoever she was and whatever truck she had with him; she would soon find out what he was really like, and how worthless his promises.

She gave a shuddering sigh. God willing she wouldn't have to put up with this for much longer; surely she would hear from her cousin soon. And surely Hartley would let her go? He had what he wanted now, an heir and her money, although thank goodness, he couldn't get his hands on all of it. How prudent her father had been to appoint Justin to manage the remainder at his discretion, even though it hadn't helped their marriage. But if it hadn't been that to irk him it would have been something else. Hartley wasn't a man who could keep a woman happy beyond the bedroom.

"My precious," she murmured, as she bent her head into Thomas's fine, blond hair and kissed him tenderly. The only good thing that had come out of the union was the child. But then she began to sob quietly, knowing what she might have to give up in order to gain her freedom.

Chapter 7

Leah was so distraught after leaving the manor, she couldn't trust herself to return to the village to do the shopping. Nor did she feel she could return home immediately to her mother's scrutiny. So, as many times before when feeling out of sorts, she called to see her friend, Flo Endacott, who lived at Forde Farm, just a field away from Furze. Flo was a midwife, and whether it was due to her experiences in that capacity, or whether she was naturally wise, Leah didn't know, but she had a knack of being able to make her feel better in any given circumstance.

When Leah arrived, Flo was in the kitchen having a cup of tea with her husband, Acheson. He excused himself, saying he had things to attend to outside and had better get on with them.

"I dare say you'd like a cup of tea?" Flo offered. She noticed Leah had been crying, and wondered what could have happened. She had been acting strange of late, and Flo suspected she might have a lover. Perhaps, she thought, they had quarreled.

"Here you are," she said, handing Leah a cup of tea into which she slipped a drop of brandy. "You look as if you need a strong one."

Leah lifted the cup and although she grimaced at the taste, sipped the tea gratefully. She couldn't yet trust herself to speak. Over the years they had known each other, she had confided many things to Flo, but never anything like this. She didn't know how to begin, or if she should even tell her such shocking news.

"I know something's up." Flo placed her hand on Leah's arm. "And a problem shared is a problem halved, you know."

"I don't know if I can tell you this one," Leah said faintly.

"Aw, it can't be *that* bad, surely—"

"Oh, Flo, it *is*... it *is*." Leah buried her head in her hands and began to weep.

"In my job I get to know all sorts. I could fill a library with it all. But I'll tell you this, I've never repeated a word to a soul, if that's what you're worried about."

"It isn't that." Leah gripped Flo's hand. "I had no idea things would turn out like this. I didn't think, and now I'm so ashamed."

"If it's that secret lover you've had a quarrel with," Flo began, with a knowing smile. Then she saw the look of horror on Leah's face. "What is it?" she whispered. "Leah, what can be so bad that you are afraid to tell me?"

Hesitantly, and tripping over her words, Leah revealed her affair with the squire. As she did, Flo began to feel very uneasy. Was Leah mad? she wondered. Oh, she knew the Peardons spoiled their daughter, and *that* didn't help Leah's whimsical or impetuous nature, but to get mixed up with a Gordon? Acheson said that to call them reptiles would be an insult to a snake. Now Leah was to have his child?

"If only I could rid myself of this... *need* for him," Leah was saying after two cups of tea and brandy. "Even today, after he said those things, I'm still finding it hard to believe that he really, probably, doesn't care."

Of course he doesn't care. Flo wanted to cry. Why couldn't Leah see that? He cared for no one and nothing but his own satisfaction. But she could tell her friend was still in love with him, and probably would be for some time to come. And without the man himself she'd live off the memories and the fantasy, so it was no good condemning him. She didn't wish to damage their friendship, and Leah was surely going to need her during the months ahead.

"There's many a woman suffers delusions about the men they takes up with," Flo said, diplomatically. "But some men are like bad fleas. Once you've been bitten, their poison goes around and around in your body, and you keep feeling the itch. The only thing that'll help is time." A thought suddenly occurred to her. "This isn't why your father arranged the marriage is it? Oh, Leah, whatever did he say? He hates the Gordons."

"No, that wasn't the reason. In truth, I don't know what put that particular bee in his bonnet. I do believe there is something going on between him and the squire, but I don't know what it is. As for this, he and Mother have no idea, and don't you ever tell them, Flo. Father would kill me if he knew."

"But what about Hern? What do you think he's going to say when the baby comes early?"

Leah's cup rattled in her saucer. She hadn't given that, or indeed the marriage any serious thought. She had been so sure the squire would eventually come to his senses and help her. She'd even planned what she would say to Hern; that her father had made a dreadful mistake when planning her marriage. He hadn't realized she was in love with another, and so now she wouldn't be able to marry him.

But now that wasn't going to happen. Now she was being swept away in a fast-flowing river of events with no rescue in sight.

"Oh, Flo, how am I going to bear it?" she cried, bursting into fresh tears.

Flo found it impossible to find anything to say that would console her friend. "You will," was all she could say. *You will have to now,* she thought.

ꕤ

When Leah arrived home late without the shopping, Felicity didn't mention it, nor did she comment on her daughter's miserable countenance. Instead she said excitedly, "I've something to show you. Do you know I'd forgotten all about it? And I was wondering what on earth we would do in so short a time. I only hope Mrs. Bennett can oblige us."

Grateful not to be plied with questions, Leah obediently followed her mother upstairs to see what was so important, and was shown the bolt of material that had been intended for her wedding gown when she was betrothed to Robbie. Once before they were all set to take it to Mrs. Bennett, but then Robbie's father had come over with the news about his son, and the material was put away and since been forgotten.

It was history repeating itself, Leah thought, except there would be no cancellation of her wedding this time. With a jolt, she realized it was only weeks before she would be joined forever to a man, not to Robbie, but a stranger. She wanted to cry to her mother, "I can't. I just can't do this!"

But of course, she had to. She was trapped.

ꟸ

The next day, Peter drove over to Blackthorn and waited while Felicity and Leah took the material inside to Harriet Bennett. Although Harriet was a little put out by the haste required to make the gown, she agreed to do it. It wouldn't be cheap, she said, and they would have to come over for each fitting, as she wasn't doing any of the running around herself. She took Leah's measurements and told her she must come back at the end of the week, as she would have the gown cut out by then and tacked together.

Leah showed little interest and when they went outside, Felicity admonished her daughter for her poor attitude.

Spurred on by a handsome fee, and with Mary's help, Harriet made remarkable progress. In less than three weeks, only days before the wedding, Leah and her mother traveled to Blackthorn to collect the finished item. But when Felicity got down from the cart, Leah refused to budge. The tension of the past few weeks had just been too much for her. Her mother, who couldn't possibly understand, accused of her having moods that were up and down like the weather and said that if she wanted to have a successful marriage, she'd better improve her attitude. Leah retorted angrily that she didn't want a marriage at all. And she almost added that if not for necessity, she would have utterly refused to carry through with it. She burst into tears of rage for having fallen in love with someone who had abandoned her, and shed more tears of frustration for still wanting him in spite of it.

For a while she couldn't control herself. She didn't care that she had an audience of Matthew and Mary, but hoped, even knowing it was childish, that somehow her lover would hear gossip of her misery, would intervene and pluck her out of her unbearable situation. Hern had come over the previous Sunday, and although she tried, she found it impossible to imagine being his wife. How she would pay for those few moments of pleasure with the squire, she thought bitterly: a lifetime of misery living with an uncouth clod.

Eventually she pulled herself together and got down from the cart.

Matthew acknowledged her as she passed, and afterwards commented to Mary, "I get the impression Mistress Underwood isn't too pleased about something."

Similar thoughts had been passing through Mary's mind. She sensed Leah was dreadfully unhappy, and wondered why. Up until then she had envied the woman who would wear the most beautiful gown she had ever seen.

Inside the farmhouse, Leah caught her breath when Harriet proudly showed them the finished garment. The material was a cream French brocade, and it fell in shimmering folds to the floor. It was indeed beautiful, she thought miserably, and would be completely and utterly wasted on her.

"You know, that bolt was contraband from a wrecked ship in my father's time," Felicity said, clasping her hands to her breast.

Harriet had been wondering where they had managed to get hold of such frightfully expensive material. "Well, no one need know anything about that."

"Oh, I'm rather proud of it," Felicity added. "It doesn't matter now anyway, it was so long ago. But I think the history of it makes it more interesting, don't you?"

She didn't say so, but Harriet thought that wearing stolen goods would more than likely be a bad omen and not bode well for the married couple. So far, she hadn't been at all impressed by Leah's tardiness and wondered how her sister would tolerate such a daughter-in-law; she hardly thought the two would get along. Sarah had already cursed Peter Peardon and aimed venomous remarks at Leah for taking her son away.

However, she had to admit her nephew's wedding was a blessing. Business had dropped off a bit lately and the making of this gown would more than see her on for a while. With this in mind, she put her prejudices aside, and proudly turned Leah this way and that to show off her handiwork.

"Oh, you *have* done us proud, Mrs. Bennett," Felicity cried. "You have provided us with an heirloom."

"It's nice to start these things off," said Harriet. She gathered up the remainder of the bolt and held it out. Her eyes raked Leah's figure as she added, "There's ample left for a nice christening gown, too."

ꕥ

Harriet could have never finished the wedding gown on time if it hadn't been for Mary's help, although it had been a mixed blessing for Mary. Working late into the early hours of each morning meant she was too tired to think by the time she went to bed, and at least had a few hours of dreamless and untroubled sleep. The sadness was that for once she and Harriet worked together companionably and in accordance. "You sew a tidy seam," Harriet had even said, and Mary felt overwhelmed, not only by the rare compliment, but knowing that just when things might have improved between them, they were soon to be blown apart.

When her menses hadn't arrived it didn't take much reckoning to realize her worst nightmare had materialized: the seed the devil had sown in her had taken root. Before any time passed at all, she began to feel nauseated and found it hard to hide it from Matthew who asked more than once if anything was wrong. Consequently, although it hurt them both, Mary tried to avoid him as much as possible.

She was in such a quandary. She knew she couldn't bear to be returned to the workhouse, which would be her fate when her mistress discovered her condition.

But not to go back there meant she had to make a choice. Either she ran away and let fate take care of her, or she took care of the situation.

Once, in the workhouse, there had been a woman who described how she rid herself of unwanted pregnancies. When Tilly heard about it she had become quite irate and emphasized to Mary how doing such a thing could result in having an idiot or crippled child, or how a woman could die an agonizing death. It was both dark and ugly, she said, and Mary must forget she ever heard such a thing. She must remember that every creature that came to earth had a purpose.

At the time, Mary was sure Tilly had only said that to comfort her, to somehow justify her meager existence. However, after years of watching that kindly woman help souls survive the rigors of the workhouse, she was now haunted by the next words Tilly had spoken. "What if my mother had decided to get rid of me?"

Now Mary thought, what indeed? For although her child had been conceived in such a way, what if it should be another Tilly waiting to be born? Was it right she should deprive the world of such a person?

Every waking hour of the day, these thoughts were on Mary's mind. On the one hand, she was thinking of Tilly's words, and on the other, she knew that if she could be rid of the worry it would be a blessed relief. Although Tilly had made her promise she would forget what the woman had said, Mary never had. Now that memory hovered in her mind, tempting and tormenting her.

Chapter 8

Leah's faint hope of intervention by the squire didn't manifest itself and inevitably, the day of her wedding arrived. Flo went over to Furze in the morning to help out. Upstairs out of Felicity's hearing, she held Leah while she wept.

Flo was anxious her friend should stop crying before Felicity got suspicious and demanded to know what was going on; she had already hinted enough times that she thought Leah might be keeping something from her. "Think about that child of yours," Flo whispered. "You don't want it born without a father now, do you? And Hern Underwood is better than no father at all."

Leah gave Flo an ungrateful look, but all the same, wiped her eyes and had a smile on her face by the time she went downstairs.

ℵ⊃Cℑ

As Leah walked up the aisle of the church, there was a sudden hush as heads turned to look at Harriet Bennett's latest and most marvelous creation yet. There were murmurs of, 'no wonder she charges so much,' and even Betsy Berry, sitting at the end of one of the pews, was tempted to regret her hasty decision in changing dressmakers.

When the service was over, Hern and Leah went outside into the brilliant sunshine where they were showered with rice and flower petals. Unused to being the center of attention, Hern was rather overwhelmed with everything, especially the beauty of his bride. He was anxious to get across the green to the reception where he could have a drink and bolster his confidence a bit. Followed by the cheering guests and onlookers, he took Leah's hand and hurried her down the path and through the lych-gate.

As they crossed the road, they noticed the squire sitting astride his horse, talking to Leah's father. Hern scowled, thinking of the previous evening when he and Colan had gone to the inn to celebrate his last night of freedom. He had been having a whale of a time, jug after jug all bought for him too, when everything suddenly went quiet. It was as though a shadow fell over them, and then he turned to look into the blackest eyes he'd ever seen.

"I assume you are the bridegroom," the squire said, and there was a cheer as he ordered a round of drinks. Frivolity and conversation resumed then, although Hern felt sober all of a sudden. How had it gone? Someone said something like Hern had got himself a pretty little filly, and the squire laughed and replied, mares were much more fun once they were broken in.

It had niggled Hern then and it niggled him now, although he couldn't quite grasp why. It was just the disrespectful way in which it had been said, he supposed. He didn't think it was a very proper thing for a man of the squire's standing to say. He turned away and pulled on Leah's arm because she didn't seem to know where she was going all of a sudden.

Leah followed him blindly, tears blurring her vision. Although the habit of the old squire had been to attend local weddings and funerals, it was noted that the new squire and his lady didn't appear to have the same intention. Leah could hardly say so, but she was relieved he hadn't been in the church: and she'd hoped she could get through the day without him crowding her thoughts. Now, seeing him with her father not only brought back all her memories and desire, but also made her wonder once again what might be going on between them.

People were in the hall already, chatting and laughing, and they set up a great cheer of congratulations when Leah and Hern arrived. Hern was enticed away from Leah by the young men who wanted to carry on where they'd left off the previous evening.

As Hern left her side, Colan took his place. "I suppose this is why there has to be a best man," he said, hiding his annoyance with his brother who he considered could have stayed with his bride a while longer; Leah looked overwhelmed and very pale. "Would you care to sit down?" he said, leading her to a chair. "Most people are helping themselves and will come to see you of their own accord."

"Thank you," Leah said gratefully. "I've never been married before you see, so I'm not quite sure what to do."

Colan smiled at her attempt at humor and wondered why she appeared so sad: from what Hern had said, she'd accepted the arrangement without question. "I'll get you a selection of food," he said. "Better start your celebrations on a full stomach."

As Colan went away, Flo sidled over to Leah and handed her a glass of wine. "My, what a crowd. And half of them weren't invited I don't suppose." She looked worriedly at her and whispered. "Drink up. One or two glasses won't hurt the baby and will do you a lot of good." She suddenly turned around. "Oh, my goodness. Well, look who's here."

Leah gulped down a half glass of wine before turning to see a well-dressed female version of Hern coming towards them.

"Why, Margery, my dear friend," said Flo, hugging her tightly. "But look at you. I didn't expect to see you here."

"I made sure she knew about the wedding," Colan said, coming up behind them with a plate of food he handed to Leah. "No one else would have, and Leah's parents wouldn't have known where to send an invitation. Leah, may I introduce my sister, Hern's twin, Margery. She lives in Whitmouth now, and is at loggerheads with most of the family except me."

Margery took Leah's hand. "They don't approve of me at all, I'm afraid. But how lovely to meet you, Leah. When Colan wrote and told me Hern was getting married, you could have knocked me down with a feather." She scolded her brother. "You are naughty, Colan. You might have written to warn me, I had no idea he was even courting."

"Well, he wasn't for long," Colan chuckled.

"It really *was* very sudden," Leah said, with a hiccup. "You could have knocked me down with a feather, too." And she broke into wild laughter that threatened to turn into tears.

"Come on," Flo said quietly, pulling her to her feet. "I take back what I said about the wine. Perhaps you'd better have a strong cup of tea instead. We can't have you breaking down in here else we'll never hear the last of it, do you hear me?"

ꕥ

By the end of the day, Leah felt as if the smile on her face was pasted there and had nothing to do with how she felt. A day that should have been one of the happiest of her life hadn't been at all. What was worse, now she faced the days and nights ahead with a man she didn't know, or even want to know.

She remembered how the squire had looked so handsome sitting on his horse, and how he had, for one brief moment, looked at her. Was there a chance he still desired her? she wondered. Had he thought she looked as beautiful as others said? That is, except for her mother-in-law who'd hardly said a word to her. Leah felt inadequately equipped to deal with such a woman. Sadly, she didn't see any ground on which she would grow close to either Sarah or Joshua: he had spoken to her briefly, but their conversation had been stilted and difficult.

She and Hern rode home from the church without speaking to each other. They really had nothing to talk about. Not a thing in common. Only Felicity and Peter made conversation, and occasionally Felicity would give Leah a meaningful look and nod towards Hern. But Leah had no intention of pleasing either of her parents any further. She had been forced into the marriage, and that was as far as she was prepared to go.

Felicity and Peter retired early to their room, leaving Hern and Leah downstairs. Before he went, Peter suggested that Hern might like a drop of whiskey, and hinted Leah might fetch it for him. Leah was about to retort that Hern could fetch his own drink; she considered he'd drunk quite enough already. But then she changed her mind and poured him a large measure, hoping that with any luck it might put him into a stupor.

However, Hern had no intention of allowing the night to end without consummating his marriage. As soon as they were in bed, he grabbed her. Leah kept her eyes closed and her head averted from his foul, stale breath as he fumbled, grunted and snuffled like a pig at its trough until he found what he was looking for. Then he thrust himself into her and pumped away until, finally, he gave a grunt of satisfaction and collapsed on her. All the while she tried to think of anything but what he was doing to her, and once it was over, pushed him away and turned over.

Hot tears welled from her eyes. He'd hurt her, and he didn't care. He probably didn't know. *Oh, God,* she cried inwardly, *to think. Years and years of this to come.* How would she ever bear it? Oh, Hartley. *Hartley.*

Hern was puzzled. He thought virgins were meant to have pain and cry out. "That wasn't how I thought it would be," he said.

"Shh," Leah whispered. "You'll wake my parents."

Disgruntled, Hern turned over. Until now he hadn't given Leah's past too much thought as he had been too wrapped up in getting the wedding over with and securing Furze farm for his future. Now he was ensconced, so to speak, he was in a position to take a closer look at things.

"You done it before then?" he said, his voice leaping out of the darkness.

Leah started. She had thought him asleep. "What does it matter?" she whispered. "I'm yours now, that's all that counts isn't it?"

Hern's thoughts were in turmoil. What sort of answer was that? he wondered. She had looked a real treat that day, and although he hadn't told her so, he'd been real proud to stand beside her in the church. It was more than he could ever have hoped for; a woman like that and a farm like Furze. The thought: *almost too good to be true* flickered like a distant light in his mind, but he put it out immediately.

He supposed if he wasn't the first then it was the price he would have to pay. After all, as she said, she was his now, and wasn't that all that mattered? And, he reasoned, she wasn't *his* first.

But still, he went to sleep with resentment festering in his mind.

Chapter 9

People said they had never seen anything like the torrential rain that fell in the late summer of that year. Gray skies obliterated the sun, and the river flooded its banks, taking trees and livestock along with it on its tumultuous passage to the sea. When the rain did hold off for a few days and the flooding subsided, it left in its wake rutted, almost impassable roads and huge muddy puddles. The air felt oppressive and the skies were heavy and dull.

These climatic conditions did nothing to alleviate Peter's depression. He had hoped, once the wedding was over, that things at home would return to normal and become comfortable again. It hadn't been easy holding out against Felicity's silent reproach beforehand, or keeping patience with Leah's sullen moods since. However, any relief he might have felt now he had got things settled and would no longer be subject to ridicule, was overridden by the feeling he'd been duped. Hern was proving to be much less of an asset than he had hoped, and it began to dawn on him that he'd done Joshua Underwood a favor to the detriment of himself.

One night, when disappointment and frustration overtook him, he told Felicity he was going out. She knew better than to argue with him, but followed him to the door with her hand to her throat and a sense of foreboding in her heart.

Peter hadn't been near a gaming table since that night, all those months ago. When the squire had spoken to him on the day of Leah's wedding and asked him when they might settle things up, he'd asked for time. He had, he said, a wedding to pay for. But the truth was the last gambling episode had left a bad taste in his mouth that had barely worn off.

At the Blackbird, he nodded to the regulars and one or two who weren't. Ronald Bennett was one. Peter recognized him from the wedding, where Felicity had introduced him as the husband of the dressmaker. After a quick drink and a chat about the appalling weather, Peter left the bar and made his way down the passageway to the back room.

There were five men sitting at the table, and four looked around as he walked in. It wasn't long before their game was over. One of the men scooped up his winnings, three others got up to stretch their legs and have a drink. Peter was left alone with Hartley Gordon.

Peter cheered up considerably as the night wore on. Not only did he satisfy and retrieve the note he had signed at their last game but he took all Gordon's previous winnings of the evening, too.

The squire, furious at losing and too drunk to be prudent, took off his ring and threw it onto the table.

Peter couldn't believe his luck when he won again. He slipped the ring into his coat pocket and, despite the squire's coercive attempts to keep him there, announced he was quitting while he was ahead.

ꕥ

The reason Ronald Bennett was at the inn that evening was because there had been a terrible row at Blackthorn. After Harriet discovered Mary was stealing food, she had sent the girl to her room and told Ronald she wouldn't tolerate a thief in the house. Mary would have to be returned to the workhouse.

Ronald went upstairs and questioned Mary, who to his disappointment, didn't deny Harriet's accusations. The argument occurred after Ronald accused Harriet of being too stingy with the meals, saying it was no wonder the maid stole, she probably did it to keep herself alive. Harriet threw a plate at him, something she had never done before. As Ronald watched it crash to the floor, he also did something for the first time: he stomped out of the farmhouse and said he was going to the inn and didn't know when he would be home.

After he left, Harriet flew upstairs in a fury and burst into Mary's room. "This is all your fault!" she shouted. "It'll be a good job when you've gone, and you will. I'm having no more of this, I can tell you. You've been taken care of more than adequately and this is how you repay us, you wicked maid. You'll be returned to that workhouse as soon as the roads are passable."

Mary listened dully. In any case she had decided to run away. She had only been waiting for the right moment and for the inclement weather to improve. After Harriet's outburst she knew she couldn't wait any longer, and now planned her escape.

It was past midnight when she heard Ronald's horse in the yard. A while later, she heard him come upstairs. When he reached the bedroom it sounded as if a ton of verbal bricks dropped on him, and while he and Harriet were arguing, she climbed out of bed and tiptoed to the window. She wrapped her Bible in a cloth and tucked it into her clothing, then squeezed through the small space and carefully let herself down onto the porch roof. She scraped herself badly as she slid to the ground, but the softness of the flowerbed broke her fall. Much to her relief, the dog ran over and licked her face, so his barking alerted no one.

Mary felt very sad as she set off up the lane. Once or twice, she looked back towards the barn where Matthew slept and wished she could have confided in him. She knew he would be very upset in the morning when they found her gone. He had been so good to her, always kind and considerate, and she felt distressed to think that she might never see him again.

The sky was troubled-looking and mottled with clouds. Now and again, the wind gusted and sent a chill right through her. Mary had never been out at night beyond the farm, and when the moon came out from behind the clouds and threw weird shadows about the place, she felt frightened.

When she reached the gate, she hesitated, not quite sure in which direction she should go. She knew she must avoid the well-traveled tracks that crossed the moor to the south and yet she was unfamiliar with any other way. Once though, Ronald had taken her with him to an outlying farm and said the road they were on led to the center of Dartmoor. Mary remembered this now, as he had also commented on how few people went there. She wondered if she would be able to find that way again. The problem was, she hadn't given a thought as to where she would end up eventually, or how she would survive meanwhile; in her mind was only the need to hide so that she wouldn't be returned to the workhouse.

She made her decision, and knowing she must skirt around the village, she hurried on towards the bridges. When she got there, she was relieved to find the flooding had subsided enough for her to cross. But suddenly a movement from the other side alerted her. Although it was dark, and impossible to hear because of the water thundering beside her, she could tell something was going on. Instinct told her that she should hide, and she quickly ran back the way she had come and hid in the bushes.

She waited what seemed ages until finally, bevering with the cold, she decided she would have to trust to luck and go on. But as she crept out she felt the vibration of a horse's hooves coming towards her and she hid again. The rider didn't notice her, but the horse sensed her there and shied. His rider cursed, and Mary closed her eyes in absolute terror when she heard whose voice it was. Only when she was sure he had gone up over the hill did she crawl out of her hiding place and run as fast as she could across the bridges.

She began to pick her way along beside the river. However, she had barely gone any distance at all when she suddenly heard the nicker of a horse. Her heart leapt, and for seconds she was too paralyzed to move; terrified that someone would appear out of the darkness and grab her. But she had no need to fear. The man who might have asked her where she was going was lying in the long grass at his horse's feet. When Mary turned him over she saw he was beyond asking anyone anything again. She recognized this man; he had come to Blackthorn once with Leah Peardon, and had spoken to her kindly.

Fingers of dread closed over her heart. She looked in the direction the rider had gone. Tilly had told her about such souls who seemed to be guarded by the Devil himself. Mary backed away, suddenly fearful that by some uncanny, evil knowledge, he might sense she had come upon the scene and return to find her.

She hurried away from the lifeless body and raced as fast as she could alongside the river, climbed over a gate and ran uphill into a copse. There, she stumbled and fell to the ground, breathless and sobbing in the dirt.

ꙮ

The next morning, after Mary was discovered to be missing, Ronald hurried into the village to ask if anyone had seen her. But apart from Betsy and Tom, who expressed deep concern, all anyone else could talk about was the discovery of Peter

Peardon's body down by the River Bovey. Ronald was so shocked he could hardly believe what he heard, especially when it was said that Peter might have fallen into the river on purpose. A likely story, Ronald thought, although he kept that opinion to himself.

He returned to the farm more downhearted and troubled than ever, and he was silent and thoughtful while he and Matthew took the horses out to look for Mary. Although they searched the lanes and the immediately surrounding moorland, she was nowhere to be found.

ꙮ

Mary might not have survived being on the moors if the weather hadn't stayed fine. Even so, although the days might be warm, there was much dampness in the ground after all the rain, and she froze at night because of her inadequate clothing. Owing to the poor summer, a lot of the bushes hadn't fruited properly. The berries she did find, and gobble down greedily, did nothing to appease her gnawing hunger but often made her stomach ache. However, she kept her spirits up by telling herself that no matter how hungry or frightened she was, she was still better off there than being returned to the workhouse.

It was several days before she dared venture near a farm, and when she did she was driven away by the farmer who shouted at her and said she wasn't welcome. As she bolted away like a frightened rabbit, a laborer called after her in a vulgar fashion. Trembling and crying, she returned to hide on the moors.

Several days later, she awoke one morning to find she could hardly uncurl herself from her sleeping position. Her head felt light and fuzzy as if it were stuffed full of wool, and she dragged her leaden body along, not knowing and barely caring in which direction she went.

It was late afternoon when she heard a horse coming behind her in the distance. She hurried in by a crossroads and scrambled through brambles to hide behind a beech tree. But the pain of those scratches was nothing compared to the fear and misery in her heart when she recognized the rider.

After he passed, Mary wept with exhaustion, all hope now swallowed up by the knowledge that she had more or less wandered around in a circle and ended up back in *his* territory. Too weary to run any longer she stumbled on down the lane, and when she came to Forde Farm, stole into the barn next to the road and collapsed.

ꙮ

Flo and Acheson were in the kitchen, and he was teasing her.

"When's supper ready then?" he said, grabbing hold of her and rubbing his whiskers into her neck.

"Sooner or later," Flo said.

"I'd rather it be later," he said suggestively.

"Get away with you." Flo giggled like a young girl. "It's all you men think about. That and what's for supper."

"Ah yes. Supper." Acheson laughed, and when Flo tried to flick him with the towel, ran outside before she could get him.

Flo smiled to herself to think that Acheson still treated her like a young bride. Then her smile faded. There was only one thing that marred their complete happiness, although she tried not to think of it too often, believing that dwelling on the matter only made it worse. If they were meant to have children they would one day, she just had to be patient.

Her thoughts were suddenly interrupted by a commotion outside and she looked out of the back door. The dog was barking madly and the hens were kicking up a racket. She quickly wiped her hands and ran outside to have a look in case it was a fox. Although they generally hunted at night, except during hard weather, she wondered if one might have chanced it earlier in the day.

She went into the barn to have a look around. One or two hens were still fussing around, but there was no fox that she could see. However, lying face down in the hay was a girl. Flo bent down and turned her over, then ran outside to call Acheson. He came immediately and carried Mary upstairs.

ꕥ

Flo was sitting by the window, and when she saw Mary open her eyes she smiled with relief. "Well now, you're still with us," she said. "There's no need to be frightened, my dear. You're quite safe, and when you're feeling better you can tell us who you are. Meanwhile I'll fetch you something to eat."

Flo returned a while later with a bowl of steaming broth. She put it by the bedside and propped Mary up on the pillows, frowning to feel the girl's thin frame: she was as fragile as a little bird.

She pulled a chair over by the bed, tucked a bib beneath Mary's chin and began to feed her. "That's it. Slowly does it. Been a while since you've had much to eat by the looks of you, poor maid, so you mustn't have too much to begin with."

While Mary sipped the broth, she never took her eyes off Flo. Wild and frightened, they followed her every move. She felt so weak, so strange. Even taking the nourishment ebbed her strength, and after a while, she fell back onto the pillows and shook her head to indicate she was unable to take any more.

Flo was puzzled to know why the girl hadn't yet spoken. When she had removed Mary's filthy clothing she'd seen the slight swell of her belly, and was certain sure she was pregnant. Now she wondered if the poor girl was frightened they would turn her away because of it.

In an attempt to put her mind at rest she said, "You mustn't worry, my dear. You really are quite safe here. I'll take care of you and make you well again. That's both of you, I mean."

Mary's eyes widened at the knowledge that Flo *knew*. She buried her head in her hands and began to sob. But she still made no sound.

Suddenly, Flo realized the girl *couldn't* speak.

ꕥ

That night Flo couldn't sleep for thinking about the girl in the next room. She suspected she had come from the workhouse originally, because of the inscription inside her Bible. Also, she recalled Betsy Berry mentioning something about a workhouse girl. Flo decided she would pay Betsy a visit the following morning, and find out what she knew.

How contrary life was, she thought. There was that little lost maid expecting a baby. Then there was Leah, who had gone into a relationship without thinking about the consequences, and who, if her father hadn't for some strange reason taken it into his head to marry her off, would have had an illegitimate child. Then there they were with a home of their own and the means to care for a family that never came. It didn't make any sense to her.

Acheson stirred. "Can't you sleep, my dear?" he murmured.

"No," Flo replied softly. "But I'm all right. You go back to sleep."

He turned over and put his arm around her. "Now, how can I sleep if my Flo's got something on her mind? Can't you tell me about it?"

Flo was reluctant to say what was on her mind. Although it was hard for her, she believed it could be worse for him. Somehow, a woman learned to cope with being barren, but a man's esteem took a real beating if he was unable to father a child.

"Well, it's just that I don't understand why some things happen," she said eventually, because Acheson always required an answer.

"Like that poor girl in there you mean. You're wondering why she's in the family way, and you aren't. That's it, isn't it?"

She buried her face in him. "Acheson, you know I didn't mean—"

"I know you'd never say, my dear, but I'm well aware of what might be on your mind. Don't think it doesn't bother me, too. But it may be something we have to live with, and if it *is* my fault, I would ask you to forgive me."

Flo drew him close. "There's nothing to forgive. You know how much I would love a child, but I'll tell you this. I'd rather have you and no child, than a child without you. My mother always said you start as two and end up as two, and children come and go. We're just missing out on the middle bit that's all."

"You say that, but I know there's an ache in your heart, and I'd do anything to take it away. You know, I've been giving some thought to that girl, too. Wherever she has come from, I think it's unlikely she will be able to return; otherwise she wouldn't have run away in the first place. So I was thinking she could stay here if you like. You'd have your hands full, but then there'd be the baby. I know it wouldn't be ours, but—"

Flo put her finger to his lips. "You *have* done a lot of thinking," she whispered. "Oh, Acheson, I so hoped you would say that. But… are you sure?"

"I'm as sure of that as I am of what you will say if I do this," he said, letting his hand stray to beneath her nightdress.

Chapter 10

When Flo went to the Blackbird the next morning, Betsy Berry told her she reckoned the girl Flo spoke of was Mary Jay, who was apprenticed to the Bennetts. Betsy was quite happy to chat about Mary and said she had always been such a friendly little soul, but then had suddenly changed and become like a stranger to them. "I don't understand it," she said sadly. "I can't think what I did."

"I don't think it was anything you did, but circumstances that might have changed her," Flo said. "So you can put your mind at rest, Betsy."

"Well, that's a relief to know," Betsy said. "Poor maid, I always felt so sorry for her. Can't have been easy for the poor little beggar, living with that old sourpuss can it? Anyway, you make sure you send her our love."

Flo nodded and said she would. However, although she liked Betsy, she didn't feel it prudent to tell her what had happened to Mary. She believed the fewer people who knew of the girl's shame, the better.

Flo next went to Blackthorn. The Bennetts were out, but Matthew, whom Flo had met on various occasions, assured her the girl she spoke of was indeed Mary Jay. He added that he thought she had probably run away because his mistress was planning to return her to the Wolborough workhouse.

"Why on earth was she going to do a thing like that?" Flo asked, wondering if the Bennetts knew of her condition.

Matthew shrugged. "The missus was always threatening her with it. And then the master said she'd been stealing food." He couldn't tolerate even the thought of Mary being labeled as a thief. "If she had, well, I told him, there must be a reason for it. Not that the master disagreed with me, mind you. He was really fond of her. He called her his angel."

"Aw, did he now," Flo said.

Matthew colored a little. "Oh, there wasn't anything funny going on. Mr. Bennett loved her like she was his own. He said they would have had a daughter just her age if she'd lived."

Flo nodded. Most people knew of the Bennetts' tragedy of losing their infant daughter. "Funny the mistress didn't take to her then."

Matthew recalled the time Ronald had stormed out of the house and spent the night in the barn with him. He had been shocked when his master told him why.

"The mistress was jealous of her I think," he said diplomatically.

"Yes, well, jealousy can cause no end of trouble," Flo said. "Perhaps you would tell Mr. Bennett that Mary is with us, and I need to speak to him as soon as possible."

ꕤ

Ronald went to Forde the next day, but his delight at finding Mary alive and well was snuffed out when Flo told him about her condition. While looking thoroughly embarrassed, he made it quite clear it was not of his doing.

"I can hardly believe it's true," he said. Then, after a moment or two added, "But she has been very somber lately, poor little thing. Oh, to think, my Mary." And he put his head in his hands and wept.

"I'd like to get my hands on the man who did it," Flo said, flushing angrily. "A young girl like that, who couldn't even call for help." She sighed with frustration. "It's hardly likely we'll ever find him though." She paused, and then added, "You will keep this quiet, Mr. Bennett?"

"No worry on that score, my dear. I agree with you entirely… although I must say, I shall have to tell my wife. When Mary ran away, Harriet's first concern was what people would say about us. Because the girl couldn't speak, she thought no one was likely to believe Mary was a thief, but would think we had ill-treated her in some way. I don't give a darn what people think, but I did hope that if Harriet was *that* concerned about others' opinions, she might change her mind and allow Mary to come home." He shook his head. "Well, there's no hope of that now, is there?"

It was as Acheson suspected, Flo thought; and she had no doubt Ronald was only revealing a little of his domestic strife. "Well, the little maid's welcome to stay here," she said, as comfortingly as she could. "They both are."

"My dear Mrs. Endacott, that's wonderful news," Ronald said, wiping his eyes. "It's a miracle she's ended up with such a kind person. I can't thank you enough."

"And will you tell Matthew?"

"You think I should?"

"Well, yes, I do. He seems very fond of the maid."

"He is," Ronald agreed. "He'll be devastated about this, I can tell you that."

"I hope it won't get about too much. But perhaps it won't, with your wife feeling like she does," Flo said, biting her lip. "After all, no one will see much of Mary."

"Let us hope it will be a case of out of sight, out of mind."

"Let's hope so," Flo said, with a resigned sigh. "And rest assured, Mr. Bennett, we will do our best for the little one when it comes. Now, would you like more tea? And perhaps a scone or two?"

Ronald accepted Flo's offer, and his expression gradually lightened as he momentarily forgot the bad news, and shared with her the happy times he and Mary had spent together in the past.

However, as he left Flo's pleasant company and rode home, a cloak of depression descended on him. Flo might say he was welcome to visit Mary at any time, but he knew he would never be able to go to Forde, for what Harriet would say. Now, without the little maid in his life, he saw the years ahead stretching like a long, lonely road to nowhere.

When he got home and Harriet asked him where he had been and why he looked so downhearted, Ronald plucked up courage and told her. Better he suffer Harriet's wrath sooner than later, he decided. If Sarah found out, she would be only too pleased to tell her the news and wonder how she couldn't have known.

Harriet took it as a personal affront that such a thing could have happened under her own roof, and blamed Matthew. "I told you there'd be trouble right from the start," she said, "but you wouldn't have it. Oh no. *You* knew better. 'He has that maid at the manor,' you said. Well, I'm not standing for it, Ronald. What will people say? There's nothing for it, he'll have to go."

"Don't be daft." Ronald was aghast at her suggestion that he should lose Matthew as well. "It wouldn't be him. And why should he suffer for something he didn't do?"

Harriet's eyes blazed. "I don't care *who* suffers. Better rumors are spread about him than you. I'm not having Sarah say *I told you so*."

ꕥ

Sarah had something other than her sister's affairs on her mind, however. In the village she was pulled up sharp by one of the servants from the manor who hinted that there might be things going on in her own family she didn't know about. Unfortunately this coincided with Sarah's own suspicions, and when she got home and found Colan just about to leave, she snapped at him, "And where do you think you are off to?"

"The blacksmith," Colan said.

"What again? You only went last week."

"Aw, leave him alone, woman," grumbled Joshua, coming out of the shed.

Sarah's eyes narrowed as she glared from one to the other. "You old fool," she growled. "You wouldn't see something if it jumped up and bit you." Giving them a withering look, she stomped off into the house.

"What the hell's up with her now?" Joshua grumbled.

"I've no idea," Colan said, but he had his suspicions. He knew where his mother had just come from, and worried she might have been gossiping with someone from the manor.

The Lady Leonora, who had managed to slip away from her husband's watchful eye, was waiting for him in their secret place and excitedly showed him a letter she had just received from her cousin in Derbyshire. "At last!" she said, her face aglow with excitement. "He offers you employment and says we are welcome. We must tarry no longer, my beloved."

Colan held her close. How he loved this woman, who swore she loved him too and told him he was her savior. He liked to think he could believe her, of course, but there was always the chance she might be just using him as a stepping-stone to escape from her husband. Still, even if that were the case, it was too late now. His heart was hopelessly committed and he felt helpless to do anything about it. He was willing to take the chance and get her safely away from that beast. The future would take care of itself no doubt, and he would be richer by far for the experience if that was all it turned out to be, and not the lasting love he hoped for.

"Yes, Leonora," he said firmly. "Yes, we will make plans now. I fear some gossip may be getting about, and it is definitely time to make our move."

ᘓᘐ

On his way home, Colan decided to call in on Hern and tell him his plans. However, when he reached Furze he found things in turmoil. Leah had been collecting elderberries and fallen out of the hedge. Felicity explained there was some question as to the health of the child, and as Flo Endacott was out on another call, the doctor was upstairs with Leah and Hern right now.

Hern looked out of the window when he heard a horse in the yard. He cheered up a bit when he saw it was his brother, but he didn't go down to greet him because he didn't want to miss anything the doctor might say. Since Peter had passed away, he felt his mother-in-law was next to useless and if he lost Leah's help he didn't know how he would keep up with the work on his own.

"Her ankle will be all right in a few days," Dr. Morrison said, "but she must rest it. As for the baby," he smiled condescendingly at Leah, "women who are so far advanced in their pregnancies do *not* go clambering around in the hedgerows, Mrs. Underwood. You really must be more diligent."

Hern blinked. He was about to ask the doctor if he was sure, but when he looked at Leah and saw her expression he knew what a silly question that would be. He hardly knew how to contain himself until the doctor left. He stood there with all manner of thoughts going through his head. He'd known it was too good to be true. His bleddy father! Him *and* Peardon, the plotting, scheming bastards. Making such a fool out of him.

His resentment at not being the first to have Leah had always been smoldering just beneath the surface, and now it bubbled up in a hot torrent of rage. He went to the bed and grabbed the front of Leah's nightgown.

"What the hell's all this then?" he said, shaking her. "Don't lie to me. Don't bleddy lie to me. You and your family must have been laughing all the way to the altar." He poked her stomach cruelly. "You already had that in there, didn't you, eh? No wonder your father was so keen to get you married off."

"It wasn't like that," Leah cried. "My parents didn't know."

"But *you* did, didn't you? You married me under false pretenses. Who was it then? Come on, who was it? Who's the bleddy father?"

Leah intended never to tell him. She *could* never tell him. "It was no one from around here. It was someone passing through. From the military."

Hern let her go and stared at her. "You bleddy silly cow," he said slowly. "You might have got a sight more than a bastard out of that, and given it to me!"

Leah blushed at his insinuation. She had to admit that fear had crossed her mind. Knowing how promiscuous the squire was, she'd probably had a lucky escape. As for the child, however, her anger rose like bile.

"My... the baby won't be illegitimate," she said tightly. "You may be a bit disgruntled about this, but you got Furze in the bargain. I don't see what you have to complain about."

"Yes, I might have Furze to come," Hern growled, "but I'll never be a father to that bastard of yours, you can be sure of that!" And he left her, slamming the door behind him.

There was no one in the kitchen. Felicity had retreated to the best room where she spent a lot of her time, lying down. Normally Hern grumbled about it, but for once, he was pleased she wasn't there to see his face.

"What's up?" Colan said as Hern came outside.

Hern shook his head. He couldn't say anything for a moment. He had the ridiculous inclination to cry and he couldn't do that.

"That bleddy baby," he said at last. "It isn't mine."

"Oh." Colan paused. "How did you find that out?"

"The doctor said. She's too far gone. I might have known. I might have bleddy known."

"What has Leah to say about it?"

"Told me lies I expect. How can I ever believe anything she says now?"

Colan didn't see her as a liar, but one never knew. Still, he remembered how sad Leah had seemed on her wedding day and felt like giving her the benefit of the doubt. "There could be several explanations, Hern. Perhaps someone took advantage of her." Hern looked at him dubiously. "I mean, it happens all the time. And if she was a bit wild riding about the countryside on her own, like you said, that's when it could have happened."

"She said it was someone from the military and her parents didn't know anything about it," Hern said sulkily. "Though that's bleddy hard to believe isn't it? I mean, why else would Peardon have wanted to rush things?"

"By all accounts her father was apt to be a bit hasty about things," Colan said. "Or perhaps someone made a promise to her and then didn't carry it through. She was probably too afraid and ashamed to say anything to her parents. And then with the coincidence of her father arranging the marriage, well, it stands to reason she wouldn't turn it down, doesn't it?"

Hern thought about it for a moment or two. "Mother'll make a bleddy meal out of this one," he said miserably.

"She needn't know," Colan said, nevertheless feeling relieved he wouldn't be around to hear about it. "You know firstborns, they can come at any time. But anyway, she can't say anything."

Hern looked at him. "What do you mean?"

"Well, you and Margery were early too, remember? You must have given that some thought."

"Well, 'course I *know* about it, I'm not stupid." Hern frowned as he saw his brother's face. "What about it?"

Colan had never been sure whether he should tell his brother, but at least it would give him something to throw back at their mother if she got on her high horse about Leah.

"It wasn't Father, Hern. You and Margery aren't his." And then, to pile surprise upon astonishment, he told Hern some of the things he had overheard over the years.

As Hern listened, things that hadn't made sense before now began to fall into place. After a while he said, "So that's why he didn't want me to have Lower."

Colan heard the hurt in his brother's voice. "Well, what one man would forget, another can't. You know Father. Anyway, it wouldn't have done any good if he had proposed me for Leah, would it? But I will tell you this, had my interest not been elsewhere, I'd have been more than pleased to have married her. She's a damn fine woman and she'll make you a good wife. Father may not have intended it that way but he's done you a real favor. You're better away from Lower at any day of the week."

Hern was mollified, but only slightly. He felt that something had been stolen from him, and even if he had ten children with Leah, there was no way he could ever forget his first hadn't come out of him. His mind was so beset with resentment that when Colan told him his own plans he barely heard him.

ᘓᘐ

When she returned home, Acheson told Flo what had happened at Furze that afternoon, and although she was tired, she took up the lantern and ran across the field to see Leah. Hern was sitting in the kitchen and barely acknowledged her. Felicity, however, said she could go upstairs.

Between tears, Leah explained what had happened. "He knows, Flo," she cried. "He *knows*."

Flo was filled with sorrow for her friend; the circumstances were most unfortunate. From what she had learned about husbands and wives so far, although given time a man might forget his wife's indiscretion, especially if he happened to feel vindicated by straying once or twice himself, he may never forgive a child of such a union. Because of Hern's background and having no example of forgiveness himself, Flo thought things didn't look very bright for Leah's child.

Chapter 11

The weather cleared up through September and, although the air was chilly, the days were sunny. The flowers put on another show as if to make up for lost time and the birds sang as if it was the middle of summer, not the end of it.

The rest Leah was forced to take helped her, and she showed no further signs of miscarrying. During that time, she had to put up with Hern's jibes and Felicity's recriminating looks, although whether her mother was sour due to being forced out of her lethargy and into some work, or to the doctor's revelation, she wasn't sure: Felicity hadn't yet spoken to her directly about it.

One morning, she was outside hanging the washing on the line, when she saw a rider coming down the lane. Many used the right-of-way and as the sun was in her eyes, she didn't see who it was at first. But as he came nearer she recognized his horse, and she clutched at herself for fear the baby would slide right out of her there and then. It was the first time she had seen him since the wedding.

"Is your mother at home?" Hartley Gordon asked, dismounting and tethering his horse to the hitching ring.

"Yes, she's inside." Leah wondered what business he might have with Felicity, but she said nothing except for him to follow her. Before her eyes could adjust to the change in light she stumbled as she went into the kitchen, but he said no words for her to take care, nor lent a hand to steady her. Leah led him down the hallway, her heart filled with grief.

Felicity looked up as they walked in. "Why, Squire Gordon." She roused herself and patted her hair self-consciously. "What brings you here?"

"I wish to speak to you." His dark eyes settled on Leah. "Alone."

Leah's lips tightened, but she left them and went back outside.

It was hardly any time at all before the squire came out. As he was mounting up, his horse lifted his head and whinnied, and Leah turned to see Hern coming down the lane on Duffy, who nickered in response. Leah's eyes filled with tears: although humans might choose to have short memories, she thought, animals made no such pretenses.

"What was he doing here?" Hern said, dismounting from the mare.

"I don't know." Leah turned away so he wouldn't see her tear-streaked face. "He came to see Mother."

Hern scowled, but he didn't pursue it and went off down the yard. Leah immediately ran indoors. Felicity was still in the best room, sitting on the settee. She looked pale and stricken.

Leah closed the door. "What did the squire want, Mother?"

Felicity looked at her with eyes of stone. "First you, then your father. Have either of you ever told me the truth? Lies, deceptions. It's shameful, Leah, simply *shameful.* Indeed, I hardly know how to speak of it."

Leah's heart picked up a beat. She quickly closed the window, just in case Hern walked by and overheard their conversation.

"He said he'd waited out of respect," Felicity continued. "Respect? When have any of the Gordons known the meaning of *that* word?" She gave a shuddering sigh. "My father hated them, and when your father took over Furze he took that on too, as if it was part of being here. Now we have to suffer the consequences of his hatred, for that is what must have pushed him to go so far. I don't know how he could have *done* such a thing."

Leah was both bewildered yet relieved; obviously, it was her father who had done something unpardonable, not herself. "But Mother, what is it you are talking about?"

Felicity looked her straight in the eye. "We have lost our home. Your father was a gambler. Imagine, in my family for all these years, and now gone. *Lost* over a game of cards."

Leah sank into a chair. She remembered the squire and her father conferring outside the church on her wedding day: what Hartley had said to her at the manor. *I believe you have something for me?* Now it all fell into place: so *gambling* was their connection.

"You mean… he gambled *Furze*? But why would he do such a thing? It doesn't make sense."

"He *lost,* Leah. He *lost* our home!" Felicity's eyes filled with tears. "I shall never be able to hold my head up around here again. Oh, what will *happen* to us?"

"We must not panic," Leah said quickly, trying to get her thoughts together. "And you are not to say anything, do you hear? Not to Hern. Not to anyone. Promise me."

"But, my dear girl, how can you stop him finding out? *Everyone* will get to know. You can't keep something like this a secret."

"No, I know that, but just give me a little time, will you? And meanwhile, bite your tongue."

It wasn't hard for Felicity to relent. In truth, she felt too numbed to do much else. "I wish it had been me who had drowned that night," she muttered miserably. "I would give anything not to be here."

ꕥ

"What's wrong with your mother?" Hern asked later that evening. "There's something up and it's ever since that bleddy squire was here. I've a good mind to go and ask him what he said to her, seeing as neither of you will tell me."

"I don't think that's a very good idea," Leah said. She wished he wouldn't say things like that. It made her heart race, and the child didn't like it because it wouldn't stop kicking and she was getting sore from it. However, she was sure Hern was only bluffing. He threatened to do a lot of things he never followed through on, and she was beginning to find his procrastination very frustrating to live with.

"I'm going over to see Flo," she said. "Perhaps she can suggest something."

"Like what?" He scowled at her.

"Well, I've been thinking. Perhaps Mother could go away somewhere, to help her get over the shock. She hasn't been the same since Father died."

"I don't care where she bleddy goes as long as I don't have to stare at that bleddy miserable face of hers," Hern said, scowling.

Leah threw a shawl around her shoulders and hurried down the yard. Hern's relationship with Felicity was getting worse. He resented her authority and Felicity detested what she called his pig ignorance. What with having to deal with their constant bickering and now having the worry of losing their home, plus being married to a man who didn't inspire one ounce of love in her, she felt as if she'd stepped over a threshold into the kingdom of hell.

"Oh, Lord," said Flo, when she saw Leah's face. "Whatever's happened now?"

Tearfully, Leah told her. "I just can't believe it, you know how Father felt about the farm. It was his life."

"Yes, it was." Flo was puzzled herself to know why Peter would have gambled with his livelihood; it didn't sound like him at all.

"Now we'll become the squire's tenants. We'll be at his whim." Leah didn't think it boded well for them either, knowing just how much she was out of favor at the moment. "But Flo, I just can't get over it. I simply can't believe my father would have been so stupid."

"That means you must think the squire is lying. But why would he do something like that?"

"I don't know about *lying* exactly." Leah sighed. "In truth, I don't know what to think."

"Nor must your poor mother. As if losing your father wasn't enough."

"That's another reason I came over to see you. Mother's in a dreadful state, and I have been thinking perhaps it would be an idea if she could go away somewhere. She and Hern are always at each other's throats. It's driving me to distraction. Now, with this, I must get her away before she lets slip anything to Hern. At our wedding, Margery kindly made the offer to help out at any time. I've been wondering if her benevolence might not extend to having Mother to stay there for a while, to give me time to sort this out. It seems the le Marches are very kind, hospitable people."

"From what Margery says it does indeed seem that they are," Flo agreed. "Would you like me to write to her and ask?"

"Would you? You know her better than I do. But please, don't mention a word about the farm matter. You mustn't say a word to anyone, not even Acheson."

"What, tell him, and fuel his grudge against the Gordons?" Flo smiled grimly. "You've no worries on that score, my dear. But, Leah, you say you will sort this out? How do you believe you can do that?"

Leah pressed her lips together determinedly. "I'm going to the manor to talk to the squire. Mother might take him at his word, but I want to see proof of this. He *has* to show me proof of such a claim."

"Now you be careful," Flo warned. "If you upset him he'll never let you forget it, and you'll only make things worse."

"What *can* be worse?" Leah said, miserably.

ꕥ

When market day arrived, Leah persuaded Hern to take Felicity instead of herself, pleading she felt too unwell to ride all that way. Ignoring their protests she bundled them off together, then later on, saddled Duffy and with considerable difficulty and discomfort, mounted up and set off to the manor.

There had been a frost the night before and where the sun hadn't yet lent its rays the ground was still white in places. Along by the river bottom a fine mist rose from the water and hung among the trees. Once, such a pretty sight would have entertained her, but today Leah was oblivious of anything except her intent. As she rode past the manor gates, she was trembling so much that when a dog barked it startled her rather than the pony, and she almost became unseated.

She dismounted and tethered Duffy, then took a deep breath to steady her nerves before going to the front door.

"I'd like to speak with the squire," she said boldly, to Maddox.

"He's busy," Maddox said, looking her up and down, his eyes hovering around her midriff.

"It is a matter of extreme urgency," Leah insisted. "I will not leave without seeing him."

With a sour look on his face, he relented and led her down the hall. As Leah followed him into the library she could hear angry voices upstairs. One of them was the squire's. That didn't bode well for her, she thought uncomfortably, but she simply must speak to him.

Leah waited what seemed an age, and all the while she paced the room, too nervous to sit down. At last, the squire came, and closed the door behind him.

"May I ask why are you here again?" he said testily, sitting down at his desk.

"It is regarding Furze," Leah began. "Mother told me why you came to see her, but you see, I feel it is impossible that my father would have ever done such a thing. He thought too much of the farm to ever risk losing it at a gaming table. That land has been in our family for generations on my mother's side. One could even say perhaps that he didn't have any *right* to—"

"He had every right, it's the law, dammit. You know very well that when a woman marries, her property becomes her husband's. Unless it is entailed," he added bitterly.

"But I am *sure* he would never have done such a thing."

The squire sighed impatiently, and he opened a drawer, took out a piece of paper and flung it carelessly towards her. Leah picked it up. It was crumpled and stained, and was hardly legible, but there was no doubt it was her father's signature upon it.

Her heart fell. "But even so," she began, "under the circumstances—"

"There *are* no circumstances."

"Hartley…." She saw his eyes harden at the use of his first name. "Squire Gordon," she corrected herself, though it irked her to do so. "I beg you, have some thought to our situation. Why, if you do this you will be taking your own child's inheritance from him—"

"My child's inheritance is quite safe," he interrupted, fixing her with his dark eyes. "Part of which will now be Furze. If, as you continue to insist, I did perchance put some breeding into your belly, that is my only contribution to *your* child's future."

Suddenly, Leah's despair turned to anger. She flung the note at him as if it might contaminate her. "Your unspeakable insults and indifference are intolerable," she cried. "Oh, I have heard how love can turn to hate, and now I know it to be true. Because, believe me at this very moment I hate you, Hartley Gordon. And I curse you to your dying day. I hope I never have to look into your detestable face again."

"Nor will you after you are evicted," he shouted back.

Leah gasped and ran to the door, wrenching it open so suddenly, she collided with a man who was standing outside. They looked at each other for the briefest moment, and then Leah fled.

She was too upset to be able to mount her pony, and she gathered Duffy's reins in her shaking hands and led her down the driveway as quickly as she could.

When she was out of sight of the house, she fell against the mare's neck, weeping with frustration and regret. What a pawn of her emotions she was. Now, through losing her temper, she'd ruined their only chance of a reprieve. She'd made things even worse. *Eviction?* She should have approached him in an entirely different manner; not let his arrogance get to her. She cursed her stupidity. Whatever had possessed her to say those things to him?

She was startled suddenly, as she heard someone coming up the driveway. She looked around to see Ronald Bennett and Matthew Steer, and she quickly wiped her eyes.

"Why, Mrs. Underwood," Ronald said, reining in. "What a surprise to see you here." He looked from her to the mare. "Are you all right, my dear?"

When Leah didn't reply he dismounted and handed his reins to Matthew. "Why," he put his hand on her arm, "you're proper shaken."

"I can't mount up," she said lamely, unable to think of any other reason to explain her demeanor. Blushing, she added, "It's… it's my condition."

Ronald had heard Sarah gossiping to Harriet about her daughter-in-law's pregnancy. "Well, in my opinion, you ought not to be on horseback on these roads, my dear. It's proper slippery."

"I thank you for your concern, Mr. Bennett, but perhaps you could help me? I will be quite safe once I am mounted. Duffy is a very sure-footed mare."

"Well, all right, if you're sure." Ronald looked dubious, but he helped her into the saddle. "Before you go, might I ask how your dear mother is?"

Leah's lips trembled as she thought of the shame they would all face when the news of their loss got about. *When they had to leave Furze.* "It has all been a dreadful shock for her. For all of us," she said, her voice shaking.

"Indeed it has, my dear. A dreadful shock." Ronald felt sorry for the young woman who had lost her father so tragically, and who might have to bear the malicious gossip he'd heard Sarah tell Harriet; that Peter had lost at cards, got drunk and drowned himself out of shame. Of course, it was no good arguing with those two about it, they thought they knew everything, but to Leah he said, "I must say, my dear, when I saw your dear father that evening I thought he had all his faculties about him."

Leah blinked rapidly, and wiped the tears from her eyes. "You saw him that evening, Mr. Bennett?"

"Well, yes. I don't usually frequent the inn, but I was there that night and we had a kindly word or two. Then, as I was about to go home he came outside. He looked proper chuffed, he did. He was whistling, and he patted his pocket and smiled at me. Well, God rest his soul, I wouldn't want to say anything out of place like, but I thought to myself at the time, *he's* been having a flutter and he's won by the looks of it." He leaned closer to her. "You know what I think? I think he was set upon by a thief—that's what really happened to the poor man."

Leah jerked her head towards the manor. Then she shook her head, dispelling an idea that was too horrible even to contemplate.

Chapter 12

It was Justin le March who had collided with Leah. He happened to be visiting his sister and nephew that day and had seen Leah arrive. Already curious, he was further intrigued when Maddox sidled to the library door once the squire had joined her in the library. Fearing what was said inside might be broadcast around afterwards like a spring seeding, he shooed the nosy servant away and took his place.

When Leah suddenly burst through the door, he was immediately embarrassed in case she thought he was eavesdropping. It was true; he had unwittingly overheard her conversation with the squire, and now was torn between confronting his brother-in-law, or going after her to talk to her about the matter.

He chose the latter, but in his moment's hesitation, by the time he went outside, she had disappeared from view.

The mist that had lifted earlier was now coming down again off the moor and already obliterated the sun. It shrouded the trees, and Justin walked out into a silent world. As he cut across the lawn to intercept Leah, he heard every word that Ronald said to her on the other side of the hedge.

By the time Ronald and Matthew arrived in the courtyard Justin made sure he was there to meet them. When Ronald explained that he had come to see about a position for Matthew, Justin said he would have a word with the squire on his behalf. "It might be better to put it before him another day," he said. "But before you go, I would care to have a word with you alone, Mr. Bennett, if you would oblige me."

Matthew took no offense at being dismissed. He told Ronald he would go home via Forde, touched his forelock to Justin, and rode away.

When he was out of sight, Ronald turned to Justin. "Nice young man Matthew is. You won't go far wrong with him if you take him on."

"I must say I'm curious to know, if he is to be so well recommended, why you are letting him go?" Justin said.

"It isn't my idea," Ronald replied darkly. "But the missus blames him for something and won't have him at Blackthorn."

"May I ask what it is? His future employment may depend upon it."

"It's a very delicate matter indeed, but the boy has done nothing wrong."

"Is it so delicate you cannot speak of it?"

"Pains me, sir. Pains me terrible. We had a workhouse maid, a nice little soul she was, but she couldn't speak. Not that it was a concern, you understand, but I'm afraid someone took advantage of her and the missus blamed Matthew. Oh, it wasn't him, I can assure you of that. He's one of the best is Matthew, very loyal."

"Loyalty is a fine trait that should be highly valued. Your loss will be our gain no doubt," Justin said. "But what a shocking thing to have happened to the girl. Do you have any idea who might have been responsible?"

"I don't, sir. But I think very little of a man who would do such a thing."

"I agree. And I would like to think he could be brought to justice."

"I doubt we'll ever know who he was. But in any case, there's very little justice in these parts that I can see." Ronald glanced sidelong at him. "I hope I'm not speaking out of place, sir?"

Justin assured him he was not. "It is in my own interests, and the interests of my sister and nephew, that I come here. I like to be kept abreast of what is going on."

"Well," Ronald said, warming to him, "the rents were raised not long after the old squire died." He lowered his voice. "None of us have got nort for it and I don't suppose we ever will. If you don't mind me saying so, all the squire'll do is pee it down the drain in the Blackbird."

Justin could sense Ronald's uneasiness at saying such a thing. "Don't be concerned, Mr. Bennett, your observations will be kept confidential. I take it you see the squire in there quite often?"

"I don't frequent the place myself," Ronald said. "Indeed, the last time I was there was the night poor old Peardon died. Dreadful night it was, what with one thing and another." He looked around him uneasily. "Sometimes it makes you wonder if something doesn't get abroad."

"What do you mean, exactly?"

Ronald's voice became low and onerous. "Evil is what I mean, because that was the night my Mary ran away and the night Peter Peardon died." He shook his head. "If only I'd accompanied him home. But I didn't see any need. I saw him myself walk across to his horse as straight as a die, his pockets chinking with coin. I thought to myself, he's been gambling, and by the looks of it he's won. He must have been playing with the squire, because he was the only one left in the inn besides me. I wouldn't have been there myself if I hadn't had a tiff with the missus."

"I'm sorry about the tiff. Er... did the squire ride with him, do you know?"

"Not with him, no." Ronald hesitated. Then he met Justin's eyes and added, "But I do believe he might have ridden in the same direction."

Justin put his hand on Ronald's arm. "I thank you for your confidence. Be assured that no harm will come to you because of it, but that I shall do my utmost to see that justice is done."

"I'm glad to hear that, sir," Ronald said. "I feel better now I have been able to unburden myself over the matter. It's been on my mind a great deal."

ꕥ

For the remainder of the afternoon Justin rode around the estate, endeavoring to get his thoughts together. If he had felt perturbed over what he heard spoken in the library, his unease had doubled since overhearing what was said in the driveway and his subsequent conversation with Ronald Bennett.

He might have been able to dismiss the matter, put it down to village gossip and coincidence if it had been an isolated incident. However, years ago when his sister announced she wished to marry Hartley, he had been tipped off that the Gordon family left much to be desired. Because he loved his sister, and didn't want to sacrifice her happiness on account of what might be hearsay, he'd said nothing to her. However, he had spoken in confidence about the matter to his father, and that was why appropriate arrangements were made with her fortune. He thanked God for that, and his father's prudence.

He returned to the manor some time later and stabled his horse. When he went indoors, he found his sister upstairs in her room. It tore at his heart to see her looking so pale and unhappy. "Have you not yet resolved your differences?" he asked. "I thought I would find you downstairs by now."

She shook her head. "I rode out a few days ago when I shouldn't have and Hartley discovered it. I'm being kept an eye on."

"Is that what this is about, going for a ride? Good heavens, Leonora, but that is ridiculous. Allow me to have a word with him."

"No, please don't. It would only make matters worse. This is between us."

Justin knew how stubborn his sister could be, so he didn't press her. "By the way I met a Matthew Steer today who is looking for work. I am assured he is a good worker and very loyal. However, I didn't think it was a good day for him to call, so I have said word will be sent later."

"If he is such a good employee, why is he leaving his present position?"

"There is an irresolvable misunderstanding between him and his mistress." Justin decided it would be indelicate to relate what had happened to the Bennetts' girl. "Nothing more than that. And nothing that would affect his work elsewhere."

"Very well. Not that it will affect me for much longer." She arose from her chair. "Actually, I need to talk to you, but not here. Let us go out into the garden. I am sure there will be no objections if you are with me."

"It's rather chilly outside."

"It wasn't too chilly for the woman who came here earlier," she snapped, and then closed her eyes in contrition. "Forgive me, Justin. It is very wrong of me to take it out on you. Who was she, do you know?"

"A woman from one of the farms," he said, avoiding her eyes.

"I'm sure she has been here before. I asked Hartley at the time but he wouldn't tell me." She noticed his expression. "Oh, Justin, *you* know why she came, don't you." She looked away, her eyes filling with tears.

"Leonora... you know how some men—"

"Oh, I'm aware of what goes on, though I find it no excuse," she cried bitterly. "Well, come along. God knows I need some fresh air."

They went outside and walked down through the garden into the paddock, where the brook ran into the fishponds. "Our voices will not carry here for the sound of the water," Leonora said. "The manor walls, I have discovered, have ears."

"Yes, and they more than likely are carried around on a very large, dour-looking head," Justin said, thinking of Maddox. "So what is it you wished to talk about?"

She hesitated for a moment. Then she blurted out, "There is no easy way to tell you this except bluntly. I am going to leave him."

Justin was taken aback. For one moment, because he had been thinking of Maddox, he didn't quite catch what she meant. Then suddenly he realized she was talking about her husband. "Leave *Hartley*? What *are* you talking about, Leonora?"

"I'm going north to our cousin in Derbyshire."

"But this is outrageous." With receiving so many shocks in one day, he was beginning to think Ronald was right; perhaps something did get about. "But you've never said anything about this before. Not even hinted."

"No, I haven't. But I can assure you it isn't a sudden decision. It's just that before, I didn't have the means, and now I have. I won't be traveling alone."

"What do you mean, you won't be traveling alone? Who is going with you?"

"A good man who cares for me and will look after me," she said quickly. She saw the look of dismay cross his face. "Oh, Justin, please, you must not try and stop me. And for God's sake, don't tell Hartley."

"Of course I won't tell him anything." But even though Justin abhorred her husband and everything he stood for, he wasn't sure he liked hearing his sister's remedy for her unhappy marriage. He knew how impulsive she could be and hoped she wasn't taking another step she would later regret. He was concerned about Thomas too, and said so.

"Although I may try and take him, I am sure Hartley will never allow it," Leonora said. "I know he intends to send him away to school as soon as he is old enough, and that time will fast approach. He doesn't believe in what he calls my mollycoddling, which is really an excuse to part us. Because he can't have his own way with me he seeks to punish me in whatever way he can, and that means using our son. So I tell myself, I will barely miss any years. I tell myself that because I have to. And I have to keep faith that one day he will grow up and understand." Her voice caught. "And hopefully forgive me."

"But are you sure this is the only answer?" Justin asked. "Why don't you come home to Whitmouth with me?"

"No. Hartley would only come after me. But he'll never find me where I'm going." Her voice broke with a sob. "Don't deny me the chance of happiness. I feel so broken inside I do not know if I can be mended, but I want to try before I die for lack of being loved. Hartley has no compunctions about hurting anything or anyone. I had no idea what I was getting into. I have been such a fool."

"No one is ever a fool for loving, though it is wise to discern who is worthy of our love," Justin said gently. "For your sake, Leonora, I hope you have learned that."

"You needn't worry, the person who is accompanying me will never hurt me. I beg of you, please don't judge me. I am relying on you to make Thomas understand that if I can't take him with me, it isn't because I don't love him. Indeed, I am *depending* on you to help me until he's older, when I can talk to him myself."

Justin took her hand and held it tightly. "Now try and calm yourself, my dear. You know you can rely on me. If only I had spoken up years ago I could have saved you this misery. I knew things, but you seemed so sure of what you wanted."

"Oh, I was. So very sure of myself." She gave a bitter laugh. "Don't blame yourself—I would have hated you for telling me. Such is life's way that I had to find out for myself. But please, promise me you'll do your best to take care of Thomas. You're his godfather and Hartley won't refuse you access because of the money. However, you know what he's like, he'll try and turn my son against me."

Justin nodded. "I'll do my best. Yes, of course you can count on me. But I have to say I don't totally abide by what you are doing. And for God's sake, you must be careful, my dear. Very, very careful."

ꝏ

Justin was shocked by all accounts and would rather have not eaten with Hartley that evening. When he hardly ate or drank anything, Hartley commented upon it.

"I'm afraid I have no appetite, Brother-in-law. There are one or two things that have stuck in my gullet today," Justin said.

"Oh? And what might those be?" Hartley drawled, helping himself to more wine.

"To stop Maddox eavesdropping I stood outside the library door. I'm sure you would prefer my ears to his."

"Good Lord, yes," said Hartley, eyeing him warily. "Who'd want a load of codswallop spread about the parish." He waved the decanter. "Want more?" Justin declined and Hartley regarded him sullenly. "Look, old fellow, I don't come to your place interfering in your affairs now, do I? I'd forget all about it if I were you. Of course, you *heard.* But you needn't take any *notice.* The woman's demented. A liar out to satisfy her own ends."

"Not all your tenants can be lunatics, *or* liars," Justin said. "I rode around the estate today. I neither liked what I saw, or heard." He knew many of his fellow landowners treated those they considered beneath them very poorly, and as he had ridden around the estate, it had become obvious to him that his brother-in-law was one of them. He couldn't find any evidence that the le March money being poured into manor coffers was being used to help the tenants. He also remembered how Hartley had once scoffed at him for warning there would be trouble in the future if things didn't change. He'd been called a doomsayer, with his bleak and depressive outlook, yet the condition of the estate only supported his prediction, not weakened it.

"Bloody complainers, the lot of 'em," Hartley muttered. "Got nothing else better to do. No concern of mine."

"It is indeed your concern," Justin retorted. "And if I were you I would be very much concerned, especially over what is being said about Peter Peardon."

Hartley lowered his glass to the table. "Still gossiping about the stupid sot drowning himself, are they?"

"To the contrary." Justin watched his brother-in-law's face closely. "By all accounts Peardon had every reason to live. Coming out of the Blackbird whistling a tune, his pockets chinking with coin. I wouldn't say that sounded like a man about to do away with himself, would you?" He paused. "I'd say more likely he was set upon by a thief."

"Peardon was a conceited ass, and had it coming to him," Hartley blustered.

"Drownings seem to be quite common in this neck of the wood, wouldn't you say, Hartley? Didn't you once have a gardener who suffered the same fate? He was another nuisance conveniently disposed of, was he?"

"My family's affairs are none of your damned business!" Hartley shouted, banging the table and making the candelabra shake and the candles to flicker.

"They are when you're married to my sister and I'm continually supporting you. But that's something that can be changed."

Hartley stared at him. "You bastard," he said slowly. "What is it you want?"

"Before I leave for Whitmouth tomorrow you are going to meet me in Moretonhampstead where we will visit Coldswill's law office. In there you will swear an affidavit that Peardon owes you nothing, which will put Furze back in the hands of the Underwoods. The only reason I'm not pursuing the matter further is because of Thomas. God help the boy, having you as a father is going to be bad enough without adding any more scandal to the name."

"Damn you to hell!" Hartley shouted. "What's that Underwood bitch got over you? You want to tumble her, too?"

Justin found it very hard to resist knocking his brother-in-law to the floor. "You *will* sign," he said tightly. "Or else, when I return to Whitmouth, despite my concern for my sister and nephew, I shall make sure all moneys stop flowing into your coffers."

Hartley didn't reply, but sat twirling the wine in his glass, staring at it sulkily.

Justin got up and walked to the door. "Very well. You leave me no option."

Hartley tossed back his wine. "I'll sign," he growled. "But only for her lifetime."

Justin put his hand on the door handle. "Not good enough. We've had these skirmishes before, but this time I mean what I say. *Both* lifetimes. Leah Underwood and her child's, or you can suffer the consequences."

"Damn you," Hartley shouted. "Very well then. Both lifetimes."

"Moretonhampstead at ten," Justin said. "Or I swear I'll forego my benevolence and see you hang, Gordon, make no mistake about it. Damn it, man, what were you thinking of?"

"It wouldn't be this way if your sister didn't have a lump of ice for a heart," Hartley snarled. "It is she who is to blame for this."

Justin's eyes glinted. "It is indeed a coward who blames others for his misdeeds," he said, opening the door. As he went out and it closed, he heard a glass shatter against it.

Despite the cool evening he took his cloak and went outside, for he badly needed some fresh air. He walked past the gardens, to where he had been with Leonora that afternoon. From there he looked back towards the long, low building of the manor. It looked dark and foreboding, silhouetted against the night sky. He could understand why his sister would have no qualms about leaving the place.

Eventually he became chilled and walked back to his room. He made very sure his door was secured before he retired for the night.

Upon waking, a dream of a little girl, laughing and picking flowers in the lanes, resided in his memory. Strangely enough that image had a soothing effect, and accompanied him all the way to Moretonhampstead, where an irritable and brooding Hartley awaited him in Coldswill's office.

Coldswill was rather perplexed by Justin's request, but he was a good man and did what was asked of him. The affidavit was drawn up and signed by the squire in front of two witnesses.

Justin regretted he couldn't have done more to help Leah, and seen justice properly done. However, although he had little doubt that his brother-in-law was guilty, he knew how hard it would be to prove. Very few of his peers were interested in justice for the working class or the poor, and there were those who would have wondered at his sanity, going, as it were, against his own kind. At least, he thought, Leah and her child would be secure for a number of years. Hopefully, when Thomas was of age they could resolve the matter altogether.

Meanwhile, when he returned to Whitmouth he would write to Leah and put her mind at rest. He felt it was the least he could do considering she was carrying the squire's child. He shook his head, wondering what future complications, if any, might arise out of that fact.

Chapter 13

Matthew's dismissal from Blackthorn hit him very hard because it was the only home he had known for years. Neither was he too thrilled about going to the manor, although in some ways he thought it might be no worse than working for his vicious mistress.

After leaving Ronald and Justin, he rode directly to Forde where he found Flo in the yard. When he told her where he had been, and why, she looked worried.

"Aw, Matthew, I'm very sorry to hear that," she said. "But isn't there anywhere else you could go? I don't know about you working at that manor."

"Don't worry, Mrs. Endacott, I can take care of myself," Matthew said. "I've come to tell Mary, because I might not be able to see her as often from now on, and I want her to understand why. Is she around?"

"She's down the yard with Acheson." Flo knew what Matthew's next question would be and sighed. "No change, I'm afraid. Whenever a horse comes down the lane she runs and hides. Why, she dropped a whole pan of eggs the other day when one of them stopped."

She knew Matthew wouldn't like what she was going to say next, but she and Acheson had discussed it and decided it was probably the best thing to do. "Acheson thinks if she can be persuaded, she'd be better to go away somewhere. I have a cousin down Plymouth way and she could go there for a while. When she comes home again, we could pass her off as a war widow. God knows there are enough of them about, and people will think little of it. Hopefully they won't put two and two together, and it'll be easier for her to raise the child."

"I'd miss her terribly," Matthew said, "but it might be a good idea. People can be so cruel. Still, it's that bastard who did it to her that they should go after. Mary would have never invited the advances from any man, and only a fiend would have taken advantage of a poor, helpless maid. It just isn't fair."

"I don't think there is much that is fair about life," said Flo, sighing. "You'll gather that as you go along, my dear. But try not to upset yourself—there's little we can do about Mary's predicament now except to help her." She squinted towards the yard. "There she is now, bless her."

Mary's face lit up when she saw Matthew, and she waved as she came up the yard. She took Matthew's outstretched hand and pressed it against her cheek to show she was pleased to see him. Then, laughing, she tugged on his arm to go with her.

Flo watched them, with a smile on her face. Normally, the poor girl hid from all who came to the farm except Matthew and Leah. Even then, Flo knew how hard it had been at first for Mary to face him, he being a man and knowing of her shame.

However, once he assured her he thought no less of her, she now looked forward to his visits.

She turned towards the back door, but as she did she heard a cry. It couldn't be Mary, she thought, and wondered if it had been Matthew she'd heard.

Then she saw them; Matthew was holding Mary's sob-wracked little body in his arms, and he, too, was sobbing. What on earth was going on? she wondered. And then she caught on. There were riders in the lane. Mary must be terrified again, she decided, and Matthew was upset because of it. Shaking her head in anger, frustration and sadness, she went on inside.

Matthew came again the following week, looking to reassure Mary, it seemed, although he didn't mention to Flo anything about what had upset her so, and she thought it best not to mention it. She knew men could be touchy about being seen crying. Besides, Matthew had enough to think about. Although he was glad to have a position, she could tell he wasn't at all happy at the manor. In his retelling of the circumstances of how the Lady Leonora had run away with Colan Underwood, it was obvious he already loathed the squire, and she didn't think it would make for a very happy working life. Again, she felt really sorry for the nice young man, and cursed Harriet Bennett for being such a foolish woman. But then, she thought, she was Sarah Underwood's sister after all, so what could anyone expect?

Matthew told her all the details of the lady's escape, and said things might have gone very smoothly for her and Colan too if only they hadn't tried to take Thomas with them. But this had resulted in Colan and the squire brawling with a knife between them, Colan's arm being slashed, and the squire's leg being injured.

"The little boy screamed the place down when the squire took him from his mother," Matthew said, his voice choppy with emotion. "Then the squire grabbed the boy, held the knife to his throat, and threatened the lady that if she didn't stay he would kill her son. The lady went maze. Colan called him a coward and a bully to hide behind his son like that, and then the squire threw the boy aside and went for Colan. That's when Colan got his arm slashed. But Colan struck the squire who fell on the knife. Now the wound's infected and the doctor says he'll be lucky if he can save his leg. At the least he'll be left with a limp."

"Dear God in heaven, what a to-do," Flo said.

"Pity he hadn't stabbed his wicked heart," was Matthew's reply.

"Yes, well, there are a lot who might think that, Matthew, but it would be Colan who'd be hanged for it, and the squire is hardly worth giving up his life for."

"Well, they're well away now. He's got all and sundry out looking for them, but nobody reckons he'll search past Bristol. He's got what he wants, the boy, and her money. At least, that's what everyone is saying."

"And they probably aren't far wrong either. I say more power to the lady, if only she hadn't had to leave the boy behind. How is the poor little mite?"

"Proper perplexed. Although the squire reckons he'll be all right once he forgets his mother."

Flo shook her head sorrowfully. Although she knew that in time Thomas might forget that terrible moment, she reckoned that it was wishful thinking on the squire's part that the boy would ever forget his gentle mother. "And there you are all in the midst of it," Flo said. "I'm sorry you had to be there at this time, Matthew."

His eyes narrowed. "As far as I'm concerned there could be no better time, Mrs. Endacott, and I'll outlast the lot of them, you'll see."

ꕥ

After Matthew left, Flo went over to Furze. She had received a letter from Margery to say that Blanche le March would be delighted to have Felicity visit Whitmouth House, and she and Enid, an artist friend, would fetch her the following week.

"I can't tell you what a relief that is," Leah said, when Flo imparted the news. "Things are at breaking point around here and I don't know how much more I can stand."

Flo could see the situation was taking a toll on her friend and suspected there was much more she wasn't telling her, too. "I bet your mother will perk right up when she knows she's going. It'll help things here for a while," she said.

Leah was just about to say she wished she were going to Whitmouth instead, when she looked through the window and saw someone coming down the lane. "Why, that looks like Joshua Underwood. What can he want? He never comes over here."

As yet Flo hadn't said anything to Leah about Colan's escapade. Her friend's pregnancy wasn't going along as well as she would have liked, and she was reluctant to impart such volatile news. She watched anxiously as Leah went to the door, hoping her insensitive father-in-law wouldn't impart the news without at least some polite preamble.

But when Leah opened the door and asked if Joshua would care to come in, he said, "I haven't come here to socialize, where's Hern?"

Leah was taken aback by his brusqueness. "He's down at Barn Cottage," she said. "That's down the yard and through the gate, but can't I offer you a cup of tea?"

Joshua gave her a look as if she had offered him poison, then stomped off.

"Well!" Leah said, closing the door. "Whatever's got into him?"

"You'd better sit down," said Flo with a sigh. "It might as well be me who tells you. There's been a bit of bother at the manor."

ꕥ

Although Hern vaguely remembered his brother saying something about his plans the last time they met, he found it hard to imagine Colan actually having the gall to run away with the squire's wife. And even though Hern thought it served the squire right, because everyone reckoned Gordon was getting a dose of his own medicine, he was nonetheless shocked when Joshua told him about it.

Part of his reaction was indignation, because his father reckoned he and Leah had known about it all along. Leah had been seen going to the manor at least once,

Joshua said, and Sarah reckoned she had been acting as a go-between. Joshua didn't appreciate it when Hern laughed in his face and said how bleddy ridiculous *that* was.

However, Hern's curiosity was tweaked, and after his father left, he confronted her, wanting to know if what Joshua said was true. Leah denied knowing anything about his brother's affair, but admitted going to the manor on business.

"What business?" Hern demanded.

"It was to do with Mother," was all she would say, no matter how he cursed her.

That night Hern couldn't sleep for wondering about what she hadn't told him. He kept wondering what business his featherbrained mother-in-law could have had with the squire. And if Leah were lying, what other reason would she have for going to the manor? Did the father of that bleddy bastard live there? He scowled into his pillow. He would have to keep a better eye on her in the future. Once she'd got *this* bun out of the oven he would have to hurry up and get her seeded again. That would put paid to her bleddy gadding about.

With that thought in mind he turned over and put his hand on her breast.

"Not now, Hern," Leah said, who felt dog-tired, but who also couldn't get to sleep for worry. "I've told you, it isn't doing me any good. I don't want to lose the baby."

"I don't care if you bleddy lose it. Come over here."

She pushed him away. "Leave me alone. Saying things like that doesn't help our marriage."

"And what you did doesn't either," he growled, turning over and passing wind.

Leah closed her eyes. His cursing and foul manners irritated her beyond belief. If he wasn't belching, he was spitting, or puffing out the other end. God in heaven, she thought, what had she done to deserve this? It was no wonder she had cramps and bled a little, what with the worry of the farm, the bewilderment over the last night of her father's life, and now Colan going off like that.

Although Flo had told her as gently as she could, and said that according to gossip the affair had been going on for some time, Leah was still really shocked. She felt unreasonably annoyed with Colan for not having timed it better. After all, if he had taken off with the squire's wife before she'd married Hern, who was to say the squire's attitude regarding her pregnancy might not have been different?

Now she was stuck with this foul-mannered, disgusting oaf, who further depressed her after Joshua's visit by saying, 'look out for anyone with the Underwood name now,' extinguishing all hope that the squire might have second thoughts about their tenancy at Furze. How much longer could she contend with it all?

ꟾ

Just when Leah felt she had reached the point where she might lose her sanity, she went into the village and found a letter waiting for her at the post office, postmarked Whitmouth. At first, she thought it was from Margery, writing to her personally to confirm the arrangements for collecting Felicity, but when she broke the seal she found it was from Justin le March.

When she got home, she ran upstairs and closed her bedroom door where she could read the letter in privacy.

Justin began by explaining why he had been standing outside the library on the day of her visit, and apologized for having overheard her conversation with the squire. Leah willingly accepted his apology, and was grateful to him for preventing Maddox's tongue from wagging afterwards, which it indubitably would have. Neither did she doubt Justin's word that he could be relied upon to keep the matter to himself.

He went on to say that she would be pleased to learn the squire had signed an affidavit to the effect that they would not be evicted, and that the legal document now rested with Coldswill the solicitor, in Moretonhampstead.

Leah lowered the letter to her lap and closed her eyes with relief. This was nothing less than a miracle. She didn't think to ask herself why Justin had become involved in the matter; uppermost in her mind was the squire, who, she decided, must have been teaching her a lesson for her indiscreet handling of their affair. After her visit, he had obviously regretted his unkind behavior and decided to resolve the matter. Although it had been vindictive and cruel of him, she consoled herself with the fact that he had, eventually, felt compassion for her. She smiled to herself. It was even possible that he cared for her after all.

She hid the letter under a loose floorboard in her mother's bedroom where she had, as a child, discovered a small hiding place, and where she now kept her diary.

Feeling much happier than she had in a long while, she went downstairs to tell her mother that Furze was theirs again, and was safe. And she made Felicity promise she would never speak of the matter again.

Chapter 14

The following week was a flurry of activity while Leah helped Felicity prepare for her departure to Whitmouth. Hern was delighted that his mother-in-law was going away, as he said she was next to useless anyway and he didn't care if she never came back. Although Leah felt cross with him for saying such a thing, in some ways, she had to agree. However, she felt guilty in doing so and made a special effort to be kind to Felicity before she left.

Felicity was looking forward to the change. Relieved about the outcome at Furze, she now looked on her visit to Whitmouth as a fresh start. She hadn't been anywhere in years, she said, and would use this event as an excuse to clear out all her drawers and wardrobe.

"Perhaps you can sort those out while I am away," she said, indicating Peter's clothes. "I just can't bring myself to. And perhaps you would like to have this room now; it's bigger and suits a married couple. When I return, I will take yours."

ꕥ

At Forde, Mary helped prepare for the arrival of Margery and Enid. They cleaned and baked, and aired the bedding, and even though the days were chilly, opened up windows to freshen the rooms. Flo commented that with all that work one would think they were expecting royalty. But although Mary smiled and worked willingly she fairly dreaded meeting Margery. Flo had told her she was Sarah Underwood's daughter, and Mary worried Margery might be like her mother.

She was relieved to find her worries were unfounded, however. On their arrival, she found Margery's temperament, although boisterous, quite different from Sarah's. She was treated very kindly, and Margery even showed some sympathy and understanding for her predicament.

However, it was to Enid that Mary gravitated. Mysterious, dark-haired and dark-eyed Enid, who didn't appear to adhere to any conventional form of fashion, but wore her curls tied back with a scarf and seemed to float, not walk about the place, in long flowing robes of bright colors, the likes of which Mary had never seen before. When Leah commented humorously that Enid reminded her of a traveler who had once come to the farm to sell pegs and tell fortunes, Mary smiled. She wouldn't have been a bit surprised if Enid hadn't taken her hand and insisted upon reading her palm. As it was, her way of almost devouring a person when she looked at them was rather disconcerting.

Enid was just as fascinated with Mary. "What a beautiful young girl," she kept saying. "What a *beautiful* young girl." And on the second morning after their arrival she declared, "I must paint her, Flo. I intended to paint scenes of the moors; they are so splendid in color this time of year with the dying bracken and the heather, but compared to Mary… Her inner beauty takes my breath away. And the portrait will be for you, my dear, for taking her in."

"That's a lovely thought, I must say," Flo said, but she looked doubtful, and added, "I'm not sure that Mary will agree to having her portrait done, she's very shy."

But to their surprise and Enid's delight, Mary did agree, because Enid told her how it would be a gift for Flo.

"She knows she owes you her life," Enid confided. "I am sure she feels it is the least she can do for having been given a home and some happiness before she leaves you."

"Oh, we don't intend her to stay in Plymouth forever," Flo said. "She'll come home again, with the child." She laughed. "At last, Acheson and I will hear some laughter and childish patter around the place."

When Leah knew about the portrait, she rushed home to fetch her wedding gown and persuaded Mary to wear it, although Enid would have to imagine the fit, she said, because of Mary's expanding figure. "It's perfect for the occasion," she said, remembering her reluctance to use the wondrous gown for her own miserable wedding, and thinking sadly that Mary would bear a child without having had a wedding at all. "And it'll be such a thrill for Mary to wear it."

Mary's hair was arranged, the gown put on, and the women stood back, gazing at her in amazement at her transformation.

"I told you," Enid murmured, as she took up her brush.

"I wonder who the poor girl really is?" Margery said to Flo, looking at Mary curiously. "She's no guttersnipe, I'd warrant that."

"We'll probably never know," said Flo. "But she looks like a princess now."

During the next few days, Flo saw a new light in Mary's eyes, and glimpsed the carefree girl that Ronald had reminisced about, the day he visited Forde. Once again, she grieved the loss of the person Mary might have become, had not so much tragedy struck her young life. And she cursed afresh the man who had helped to ruin it.

ꙮ

There was giggling and laughter, gossiping and intrigue about this and that for several days. Acheson made them all laugh when he stuck a notice on the back door that read *The House of Women*, and good-naturedly stayed out of the way except to keep the fires stoked for their comfort.

By the middle of the following week, however, when the skies turned an ominous gray, although Enid would have stayed longer, Margery became anxious and said they must leave.

Enid had captured Mary well enough, but hadn't enough time to complete the gown. So she asked Leah if she might take it with her to Whitmouth and return it later.

Leah didn't mind at all. She was only too pleased it was being put to good use at last, even though her mother put a damper on it when she said she didn't think it was good luck for anyone to wear someone else's wedding dress. Leah dismissed her opinion as superstitious twaddle, and both it and the portrait were carefully wrapped and taken to Whitmouth.

Enid was quiet on the journey home, and when they were alone, Margery ascertained that her mind was on Mary. "I've been thinking of her too, the poor little thing," she said. "Such a tragedy. I'd like to get my hands on the man who did that to her. He must be a monster."

"He will, in the end, reap what he has sown," Enid said quietly.

"Oh, Enid," Margery said enthusiastically. "What have you seen?"

"It's all very vague," Enid said evasively, knowing she couldn't tell Margery the vision that had come to her, just in case she said something to Flo: that kindly woman, who loved Mary as if she were her own daughter, would never be able to bear it.

Chapter 15

It was early December, and Flo, Leah and Mary were huddled around the fire at Forde, trying to keep warm while they darned socks.

Flo hadn't been able to persuade Mary to stay with her cousin May in Plymouth, and now it was too late, her pregnancy was too far advanced and the roads were impassable. Flo wasn't entirely displeased. At least now she could see the child born safely, and she'd decided they would just have to try and resolve the matter once the spring came. Although she and Acheson would be used to the baby by then, and would miss them terribly.

"Hern will be pleased," Leah said, cutting into Flo's thoughts. "I could even go for his suggestion that Mother should live in Barn Cottage when she returns. I don't know how I'm going to put up with them both living under the same roof again."

She was speaking of the letter that had arrived from Margery, in which she stated Felicity would not be returning to Furze until the spring.

Flo brought herself back to the moment, and thought about what Leah said. She could sympathize to some extent, she supposed. She had lived for six months with Acheson's mother, and even though they'd got along rather well, she knew what a strain it could be sharing a house. She hardly thought it appropriate that Felicity should be banned from her own home, however, but that was Leah's business and she didn't say anything.

Leah sensed Flo's disapproval and changed the subject. "So, I hear Colan is doing well?"

"Yes, apparently so," Flo said. "He's working for the lady's cousin in the mines. He was always keen on engines, and he's helping with machinery. Margery says things are working out very well between him and the lady."

Leah jabbed the darning needle into Hern's sock. "I'm glad somebody's happy."

"Well, not all marriages are the same," Flo said tactfully. "Let's hope it will be easier for you once the baby is here. It's difficult for a man, I dare say, watching his wife swell up when he didn't have the pleasure of making it. It'll be different when you have one of Hern's own."

Leah looked at her in dismay. "I can't bear the thought of having any more children. I only want this one."

Flo tried not to feel resentment at Leah talking about children she would rather not have; for some reason her lack of a family was harder to bear at this time of year. She was also bothered that Leah seemed to have little idea how difficult it was going to be to raise someone else's child in Hern's household, and that it would be in her own interest to give him one of his own as soon as possible.

ꕥ

It was clear and cold on Christmas Day, but clouds rolled in again overnight, and on Boxing Day it began to snow and didn't let up. It was the worst winter for a long time, and Hern cursed when two newborn lambs froze to death. Then towards the end of January, the snow turned to rain. There wasn't the flooding of the previous year, but everywhere was like a mud bath. It was damp and cold and miserable. The fires hissed in the grates and gave no heat.

After Hern took a chill he was left with a bad cough, and to throw him into further consternation, Jones, the man Joshua and Sarah had hired, came over from Lower one morning with his snotty-nosed little boy, Parky, to tell them that Joshua had collapsed and Sarah said he must go over right away.

At first Hern refused. His parents hadn't bothered with him he said, so why should he bother with them? But Leah said if he didn't go he would only further the rift, and it was bad enough as it was. So off he went, grumbling that he didn't know how long it would take him to get there owing to the mud, and not to expect him home for a few days.

ꙮ

The morning after he left, Leah awoke with an ache in her back that didn't resolve as the morning went on. She also felt restless and unable to settle to anything. She prowled around the house, picking up this, putting down that, and ended up in her mother's room, which hadn't yet been turned into their room because Hern was procrastinating as usual and hadn't got around to it. She sighed with frustration, and on impulse decided to make a start by sorting out her father's clothes. She took each item from the wardrobe and folded it into a pile she intended to take to the church, where they could be distributed to others who were not as well off as themselves.

The last item she looked at was the coat her father had worn on the night he died. She had been going to throw it away all those months ago, but her mother wouldn't hear of it and the sodden, muddy thing was hung in the wardrobe with the rest of his things. Now Leah could see it was completely ruined and didn't even warrant being added to the pile. However, she decided the buttons might be useful and she fetched her scissors to cut them off.

Before she discarded it, as a matter of habit she felt in the pockets. One of the linings had a hole in it, and out of curiosity she felt beyond. Down inside the fluff and debris of years of wearing was what at first she thought to be a coin. When she took it out, she found it was a ring. Her curiosity turned to dismay. Her heart began to pound: she would have known that crest anywhere. *What was it doing in the pocket of her father's coat?*

She thought back a few months to when she had gone to the manor; she could still see it now, that filthy, water-stained note. And then, in contradiction to what the squire said it proved, Ronald Bennett's comments echoed in her mind.

Now, she wondered, what if Ronald had been right? What if her father had *won* that evening and been set upon by thieves? *Or a thief?*

The ring was heavy. Heavier still was the burden of this new suspicion. Because… what if that thief hadn't found the ring he'd gambled away, but in any case had stolen back the note that had been settled earlier that evening?

Leah whimpered at the dreadful scenario in her mind. Her poor father. The *treachery.*

But what was she to do about it? A woman such as herself stood no chance against a man like the squire. He was powerful and wealthy, and protected in every way. The only person she could possibly turn to for help would be Justin le March. Even so, he was one of them too, and would be unlikely to turn against his brother-in-law to such an extent as to accuse him of such a heinous crime.

And then there was Hern to think about. If she did make any accusations he might get to know whose child she carried, the only child she would ever have that wasn't his. She put her head in her hands. May God forgive her, but she found easier to loathe her husband than the squire.

She gasped suddenly as a knifelike pain shot through her body; for what seemed an eternity, all thoughts, except how to bear the excruciating pain, fled.

When it passed, breathing rapidly, she placed her hand upon herself. *My child must be coming,* she thought. *His* child too, she reminded herself, her heart fluttering wildly with fear and consternation. *Now, quite possibly a murderer's child. Oh, God. Oh, dear God.* And she bent her head in misery to weep for herself, and for her foolish, foolish heart.

ꕤ

When Flo came over and saw the state Leah was in, she ordered her to bed. But although Leah and her body willed the child to come, it seemed not to care about coming into the world at all.

"I don't know if I can bear it," Leah said once, between contractions. "What if I should die of it? What will happen to the child? Hern doesn't want it."

"Don't worry, I'll take care of the baby," Flo said. "And as for you, as you'll be out of your misery, you won't have to worry about it, will you?"

"How can you be so callous?" Leah cried, wiping away her tears.

All Flo was interested in was keeping Leah's spirit alive, and she was relieved to see her retaliate. "Well, don't talk such rot. You aren't going anywhere for a start, and secondly, you want to put your thoughts into bringing this child into the world instead of you leaving it."

But Flo stayed beside her that night, because that very fear was in the back of her mind.

ꕤ

Towards the early morning Flo drifted off to sleep, and was woken up by Acheson shouting up the stairs. She stumbled out onto the landing and saw him staring up at her. "What is it?" she said sleepily.

"I think Mary's started to have her baby."

"Oh Lord, what am I going to do now?" Flo said. "I can't leave Leah." She was tempted to ask Acheson to fetch the doctor—not that he wouldn't be able to do anything that she couldn't, and his hands were as large again as hers. So she decided against it; she couldn't bear the thought of causing her friend more pain than necessary, and besides, Hern wouldn't approve of incurring such a cost.

"There's nothing for it," she said. "You'll have to bring Mary down here and I'll put her in the spare bedroom."

"Hern won't like it if he comes back," Acheson said dubiously.

"I don't care what he does or doesn't like," snapped Flo. "It isn't him that's in agony."

Acheson did as he was asked. Unknown to Leah, Mary was carried into the house and put in the bedroom across the landing.

ഌ

Despite Mary's fragile form and constitution, she gave birth to a girl without any complications later that afternoon, and then drifted in and out of sleep, alternately feeling the peace of unconsciousness and, on waking, hearing Leah's unearthly screams. She was thankful when they stopped. Leah's babe must be born at last, she thought, and she kept her eye on the door, anxiously waiting for Flo to come in and tell her it was so.

It was a while before Flo came, however, and when she did she looked exhausted, and very sad. "Leah had a little boy, but she lost him," she said. "She doesn't know it yet, and I don't know how I'm going to tell her."

Tears welled in Mary's eyes. She knew how much Leah had wanted her baby; she'd heard her say so countless times.

"She set such store by that baby, didn't she," said Flo, as if she read Mary's thoughts. "I'm afraid what the losing of it will do to her. As it is, she's barely conscious. It's only grace that saved her, so we have to be thankful for that."

A tear slid down Mary's cheek. She gazed at the tiny form tucked into the crook of her arm. Her baby had a tiny face like a precious flower, and, thank God, when she cried they could hear her. She tried to imagine what it would be like for Leah, going through those months of discomfort and all that pain without having anything to hold in her arms at the end of it.

ഌ

In the early hours of the morning, when the house slept and all was still, Mary lay wide-awake. She was thinking about Tilly, and how she had once said that every creature that came to the earth had a purpose.

How right she was, Mary thought now, as she gazed lovingly at her daughter. Now it didn't matter how this beautiful, perfect little baby had been made, only that she had. Because now she was here, she could heal a deep wound in someone's life, and through it she would be able to live her own life to its full potential: a life quite unlike the one she, Mary Jay, both unmarried and unable to speak a word, would be able to give her. Now her child would never bear the stigma of being called a bastard, or the embarrassment of having a mother like herself.

Tears rolled down Mary's cheeks as she kissed her baby on the forehead. She took a deep breath of her newborn scent. *I pray you will always make the right choices in the future, and take the right paths to make your life worthwhile,* she thought. *I will love and watch over you always.*

With tears streaming down her face she got out of bed, quietly opened the door and tiptoed across the landing.

ꕥ

Flo was so exhausted that she fell into a deep sleep in the chair beside the fire and didn't stir until Acheson shook her the following morning. When she felt awake enough, she braced herself to go upstairs to break the news to Leah. But when she walked into Leah's bedroom she couldn't believe the vision in front of her. She *knew* she'd taken the stillborn downstairs the previous evening, but Leah was lying in bed with a baby tucked in beside her.

Leah heard the movement and opened her eyes. "Oh, it's you, Flo," she said, her voice slurred and sleepy. "I thought you were an angel earlier. You see, I thought the baby must have died, going through all that, and I couldn't believe it when you placed her in my arms." She looked adoringly at the baby. "It's an absolute miracle she survived, isn't it?"

"Yes, it is," said Flo quietly, barely breathing; feeling as if she had stumbled into a nightmare.

"I'm going to call her Kitty," Leah said, and closed her eyes.

Flo shook herself, pulled herself together and tucked the covers around her friend. "I'll be back in a while," she murmured, before hurrying from the room.

Outside the door she leaned against the wall, her hand clasped to her pounding heart. She looked across the landing to Mary's room. She knew she must go in, yet she dreaded to look inside. It was several moments before she could take the first step.

Acheson looked up as Flo came downstairs.

"Whatever's the matter?" he said. "You look as if you've seen a ghost."

"Mary's gone," she whispered, her voice hardly audible. "I've looked in all the rooms. She must have slipped out during the night. I never heard a thing. Oh, Acheson, do hurry and look for her, will you?"

ꕥ

Filled with foreboding, it seemed to Flo the longest time she had ever waited in her life, before Acheson returned. The back door opened and he stood there, pale and shaken, leaning against the jamb of the door for support.

"I'll have to sit down a minute," he said, wobbling past her and sinking into a chair.

Flo could smell a faint stench of vomit on him. Her heart was pounding so hard she didn't believe she would hear him even if he spoke, which he didn't for a moment or two. She stood helplessly watching her strong, brave Acheson weep. Waiting for him to tell her what she already knew.

Flo gasped and closed her eyes, as he said, "She's hung herself in the barn. I pray I never see anything so terrible again in my life. I went in there thinking she might have hidden in the hay. Something...." His voice caught, and he swallowed hard. "Something dripped on me. When I looked up, I saw her hanging from the rafters."

Each of them stood there in their own torment, and neither said anything for a moment. Thoughts were rushing through Flo's mind like a torrent.

"They'll want to bury her outside the boundaries," she thought aloud. "There's even some that—" She swallowed. Then she cleared her throat with a sob. "There are those who will want to drive a stake through her heart, Acheson. I can't bear them to do that, not to our Mary!"

"We have no choice," Acheson said dully, with a deep, resigned sigh. "My dear, it's what they do."

Flo wept and shook her head from side to side. "But this isn't *her* fault. That maid was an angel. You know she was. I won't have her treated like... like some criminal."

Acheson got up and put his arms around her. Tears were pouring down his face as he stroked her hair and tried to soothe her. "My dear, there's nothing we can do about it. You know that. Come on now."

"There is a way," Flo cried, twisting herself away from him angrily. "There *has* to be." She went over to the window and stared out of it unseeing, her mind working relentlessly.

"Why can't we bury her ourselves?" she said, suddenly turning.

"My God, Flo. Do you know what you're suggesting?"

"Yes, I know. But I will *not* have my dear Mary's body desecrated. I *won't.* We have the perfect alibi. We've already said she might be going to Plymouth. So that's where we can say she's gone. The only people she's really seen in latter months are Leah and Matthew, and they both know we've suggested it. Then later we can say she's decided to stay there."

Acheson looked dubious. "I don't know, Flo—"

"If you won't do it, I'll bury her myself," Flo cried vehemently. "Can *you* bear a stake to go through her heart?"

"No. No, dear God in heaven, I can barely think about it. But what about the baby? How can we explain it?"

Flo looked away from him. "There is no baby," she said quietly.

"You mean it didn't survive?" Acheson followed Flo's eyes to the bundle she had wrapped in the sheeting.

"A stillborn," she said. Then added brokenly, because she had never before lied to Acheson. "I've never been devious in all my born days, but sometimes it's better if people don't know certain things."

Eventually he said, "It won't be an easy thing to live with, Flo, but I do understand your reasoning, and for that I'll do it. The sooner we get to it the better, too. You bring the little one and I'll take Mary up to the house. I'll go ahead and dig the grave, if you'll see to her. There is a place up on the moor side, near the crossroads. The ground should be fairly soft underneath that old beech tree, and no one will ever disturb them there."

"I know the place," said Flo.

After Acheson left, Flo prepared a breakfast for Leah and returned upstairs.

Leah seemed a bit brighter. "Poor Flo," she said. "You must be exhausted. You worked so hard to save us both. I don't know how to thank you."

Flo felt such a pain in her heart. She thought of her hopes and dreams to have a child in the house. She was no longer a young woman, and with each passing year her hope for having a child of her own diminished. Soon it would fade altogether.

But now she had made that choice downstairs there was no going back. If she had been going to say something she should have done it first thing. Besides, wasn't this what Mary wanted? "It isn't me you should be thanking," she said brokenly.

༄༅

Flo returned to Forde and dressed Mary in one of her best nightgowns, and then she and Acheson took her to where their farm ended and where the moor began. Acheson had dug a deep hole and he placed Mary's body beside it.

"Please," Flo said, "give me a few minutes with her alone."

Acheson nodded, and went off to the side.

Flo knelt down and lay Leah's child on Mary's breast. "Forgive me," she whispered. "I know 'tis his, but take him home with you. The poor little mite didn't ask to come into the world, so it isn't his fault." She kissed Mary's cold cheek. "Aw, my dear, you'll never know how much I'll miss you. But I promise I'll look after your own little maid as best I can."

She got up, and turned away as Acheson placed Mary's body in the grave and began to fill it in. As he leveled out the ground and scuffed the leaves around, he commented, "No one will ever know it's been disturbed."

Flo sincerely hoped not. But one thing was for sure; no harm would ever come to her Mary again. "The poor little maid will know peace at last," she said.

Acheson dipped his head in prayer. "I hope so, my dear. And pray God, so may we."

༄༅

Flo didn't know how she managed to get through the remainder of the day at Furze, and she was thankful when Hern came home at the end of it. He seemed relieved things had happened while he was away, although he showed no gratitude for her help. She had the distinct feeling he would have been a lot happier to have come home and found Leah as childless as nature had intended her to be.

Wearily, she trudged home across the field, carrying a lantern to light her way because it was dark by then. A few sheep scattered at the sight of her and she told them not to be so silly.

Finally she sank into bed. That day had been almost too much for her. Leah's agony, the loss of her baby: the loss of Mary, her own agony. It hadn't begun to sink in yet. And there was the greater loss: Mary's child. A child to love and hold. Now she would never hear her running through the house, calling Mary's name. Calling *her* name.

What a capacity we humans must have for pain, she thought, weeping quietly into her pillow. And just as well, because this pain would always be with her. Having to watch Kitty being raised next door. Hearing her call Leah, *Mother.*

The Reverend Pugh's words, those words he loved so well, were the last thing that came to Flo's mind before she finally fell into an exhausted sleep. But if God's mysterious ways meant that Mary had to die so that Leah could have a child, she didn't understand them at all.

What could possibly be the reasoning behind it? she thought. Where was the sense in Kitty growing up at Furze?

Part II

1824

North Bovey

When you are unsure about the future,
do what is in front of you with all your heart and with love
and what is meant for you will find you

Gurumayi Chidvilasananda

Chapter 16

Leah and Hern's second daughter, Ruth, was born barely thirteen months after Kitty. And because Hern refused to acknowledge Kitty as his daughter and Leah persisted in denying love to Ruth, these disharmonies manifested themselves in the girls who grew up disliking each other, though never knowing why.

Kitty regretted that her relationship with her father was not better, especially now when she needed to talk to him about a particular matter: although he communicated with Ruth, and Martha, their youngest sister, he seldom spoke to her unless it was to tell her to do something or to scold. Kitty felt he was tongue-tied and awkward in her company, as if she were a stranger to him and not his own flesh and blood.

Kitty was fourteen years old and about to leave school. Emily Foss, the younger of her two teachers at the dame school, had suggested she should take further education and become a teacher. Emily said Kitty would be on the leading edge of the many changes that were taking place in society, and, although the changes might take a generation or two, she could envisage a time when every woman would have a chance to become educated. This, Emily said, would eventually lead to the emancipation of women.

A witness to her parents' marriage, this idea really appealed to Kitty: she had no aspirations to use marriage as a means of getting away from her mother's almost smothering love and her father's uncouth personality. However, when she repeated Emily's revolutionary prediction to her father he cut her off with roars of laughter and said he'd never heard tell of such rubbish—her teacher must not be all there.

Kitty didn't pursue it further, but asked her mother if she would speak to him on her behalf. "After all, he wouldn't miss me if I wasn't here," she said. "He's always hinting how much trouble I am."

Leah denied this vehemently, and added that she felt insulted to think Kitty would want to leave her. She also gave her a sharp lecture on how important it was to keep both feet on the ground and not let her foolish ideas run away with her.

Kitty thought her mother was blind and had no foresight. As for her denying Hern's dislike, she was unconvinced. She knew for a fact that her father loathed her, and no one was going to tell her otherwise.

After weeks of patience, while she waited for Leah to speak about the matter and nothing transpired, Kitty decided one evening to take the plunge and put it to her father herself. She believed that if he met with Emily and saw how sensible she was, he would change his mind.

It was at the supper table she plucked up courage to say, "I'm leaving school soon, Father. I wondered if my teacher might—"

"Bleddy good job," Hern interrupted. "Now you can learn something *really* useful." He dug something out from between his teeth and wiped it on the edge of the table. "A bleddy waste of time education is for you lot."

"A certain amount of education isn't a waste of time for anyone, Hern," Leah said, frowning at Kitty all the same. "After all, if I couldn't read, where would we be?"

The girls looked from one parent to the other, waiting for the inevitable onslaught. They were surprised when all their father did was swear. When he got up and went out, and they heard him watering the bushes just outside the back door, they realized he intended to annoy their mother in quite a different manner.

Martha sniggered and Leah cuffed her ear. "That'll be enough," she said, giving Kitty a stern look.

"But Mother—"

"You know better than to mention that to him," Ruth hissed across the table to Kitty. "Now look what you've done, you've upset Mother."

Leah's eyes were indeed full of tears; she was expecting a baby and her moods changed like the weather, tears to laughter; laughter to tears. Hern said it drove him mad, and the girls didn't find it much easier either.

Kitty felt awful. "I'm sorry, Mother," she mumbled, shamefaced. "But—"

"Be quiet!" Leah banged her fist on the table. "I don't want to hear any more about it, do you understand? Now all of you, just go to bed."

"But what about the dishes?" Kitty asked.

"I'll do them," Leah said. "Just go upstairs."

"But I was going to help Father outside," Ruth said, pouting. "Why should Martha and I suffer because of *her*?" She shot a venomous look at Kitty.

"Your father can help himself," Leah snapped. "Now, get along upstairs or I'll give you something to complain about."

Grumbling, the girls got up from the table. When they went outside to use the privy, Ruth had another go at Kitty. "I'll get you back for this," she said.

"Why are you so upset, Ruth?" Kitty took little heed of her sister's threats. Ruth was a procrastinator like their father and rarely followed through. "What are you up to that you need to be outside so late?"

Martha chirped, "I know. I know!" Ruth clipped her around the ear and stormed off in a temper. Martha, sniveling, slipped her hand into Kitty's.

When Kitty returned indoors, Hern was still arguing with her mother. "I don't know of any other bleddy woman who couldn't breed a boy," he was saying. "And it can't be my fault, can it? It's not like I was the only—"

Kitty didn't want to hear any more. With her hand over her ears, she quickly ran upstairs and closed her bedroom door. She sat on her bed, wondering and wishing why her parents couldn't be more like Flo and Acheson. She couldn't remember them arguing about anything, and when they made conversation it was about happy things, such as who had heard the cuckoo yet, or how many bluebells carpeted the woods that year. All her father ever did was grumble about one thing or another, usually about the cost of things. She knew the price of tea was skyrocketing and that he got angry because her mother still bought it. She realized how lucky they were to have shoes when a lot of others in the village went without, but she wished her father wouldn't make them, herself in particular, feel so guilty about it.

According to Emily, these hard times were all to do with the war ending, which made for a disgruntled populace. But as far as Kitty was concerned Hern's contrary moods had little to do with trade suffering or the changes taking place; he had always been like it, especially with her.

She wondered if he would say 'good riddance' if she died, as he had when Grandma Felicity passed away. It had infuriated her mother, who retorted it was a pity it wasn't the other one, meaning Grandma Underwood. Although she knew it wasn't very nice of her, Kitty agreed. Grandma Underwood was one of the meanest people she had ever met, at least she was to her and her mother. She couldn't understand it. But when she'd asked her mother why, Leah said it was something to do with the past, and Kitty was too young to understand.

Her mother was often evasive about things; sometimes, when they were over at Flo's, she and Flo would be talking about something interesting, when suddenly, remembering her presence, they would stop talking abruptly and her mother would contrive some errand or other to get her out of the way.

Things had been like this ever since Kitty could take notice. She knew it might be just her imagination, but it was as if they shared a secret.

She sighed, and began to undress. One day, she supposed, she would understand everything. Flo always said things came out in the wash, and no doubt this would, too.

ഗ്ര

The next day dawned dank and tuneless, the air heavy as if there might be a storm later on. Ruth and Martha walked to school in a mood, much the same as on any other morning, reluctantly, and annoyed with Kitty, who walked ahead and called them on.

As the day evolved, the sky cleared a little, but by the time school finished for the day, clouds had mustered again on the horizon and it looked as though a storm was brewing. Kitty grabbed Martha's hand and headed across the village green.

"What about Ruth?" Martha said. "Aren't we going to wait for her?"

"No, Miss Wood's making her stay behind," Kitty said. "And it serves her right. Come *on*, Martha. Don't dawdle so."

They went through the lych-gate and walked as quickly as was respectable past the church. They used to run through the churchyard until the Reverend Pugh surprised them one day by calling after them, "Only *sinners* run past churches."

Kitty thought that was probably a load of crock, but nevertheless took note in case he was right. She didn't like the Reverend Pugh very much, not only because his sermons made little sense and drove her to distraction, but also because when he gazed at her mother he looked like a pathetic old dog whose bone had been confiscated. She reckoned it was pity he felt, for her mother being married to her father. Hern rarely went to church, but when he did the vicar's wife never failed to sidle up to him, as if they shared a common enemy. Kitty didn't like to think it, but she wondered if it could be her mother.

They came out through the churchyard into Church Lane. On one side was a granite wall that had in places crumbled to the ground; the gaps in it, like missing molars. On the other side was a hedge so wide there was room enough to walk on the top of it between the twiggy hazelnut bushes. The hedge bottom was full of bees and insects, and early wild strawberries.

"I don't like this way," Martha grumbled. "Sometimes there are snakes across the path, especially on thundery days like today."

"Don't be silly," Kitty said, nevertheless looking down at her feet before she stepped any further. "They're probably all in their holes seeing as it's going to rain. I bet they don't like getting wet." She gave an involuntary shudder as she remembered how the gravedigger had once told her that snakes went deep into the earth and curled up next to people's bones.

Martha must have heard the same thing because the next thing she said was, "I bet they like curling around the skelontons."

"Skeletons," said Kitty.

Martha shrugged, too intrigued with the snakes to worry about her diction. "You can find girt lickers in the churchyard near the compost," she said. "I've seen them, even *adders*, writhing about each other." She giggled and gave a little squeal as she hopped into the hedge to pick a strawberry.

"You'll have a stomachache if you eat too many of those," said Kitty. "They aren't really ripe yet. And you shouldn't eat those low down either, that's where the dogs pee."

Martha pushed another berry into her mouth and stuck out a red-stained tongue at her sister. "They don't taste as if they've been peed on." She screwed up her face at their tartness. "They taste lovely."

"Well, I'm not waiting for you, I'm going home. Mind the snakes." And Kitty ran down the last part of the steep and gravelly lane to the bridge at the bottom of the hill. However, she did wait for her sister, and bided her time by looking over the wall of the bridge, gazing into the water to see how many fish she could count.

The same river passed through their bottom fields, but they weren't allowed to catch the trout in it because they belonged to the squire. Kitty thought this was silly and once had asked, how could anyone own fish? It had been one of the questions that infuriated her father and he had called her bleddy stupid. Her mother had said nothing, but changed the subject. Kitty noticed how her mother always got a funny look on her face whenever the squire's name was mentioned. She acted even odder when he rode through the farm, trying to keep her out of his way.

Recently, when Kitty hadn't moved fast enough, he had stopped outside their back door and stared at her as if she irritated him in some way. Afterwards, when she asked her mother why that might be, Leah became angry. "I told you to go inside," she said, as if that explained it. Kitty had worried for days that he had somehow found out about the fish that she and Ruth had once caught and taken home for supper.

She had never forgotten how lovely it tasted, nor the pasting she received afterwards from her father, who said if she'd been caught he would have been the one to be punished; they didn't transport children. For once, her mother agreed with him, and told Kitty to stay away from the squire and the manor grounds.

She needn't worry, Kitty thought, she had no intention of going near the man. She had to admit he fascinated her though. She had never known anyone really wicked except perhaps Grandma Underwood, who her mother said was an evil old witch.

Kitty's thoughts brightened as she thought of the squire's son, however. Thomas seemed quite different to his nasty old father. Once he had even chatted to her when he had ridden through the farm. That was when they'd both been much younger though. She hadn't seen him for a good many years now, and believed he spent most of his holidays in Whitmouth near where her Aunt Margery lived, or in Derbyshire with her Uncle Colan.

She had heard Flo and her mother talking about Thomas a while ago, after Colan had written to say that the Lady Leonora had passed away, and how devastated he and Thomas were. After Kitty had asked Emily what the word devastated meant, Emily had given her a dictionary. Kitty now associated that treasured acquisition with Thomas, and thought of him whenever she used it.

As Martha sped down the path towards her, Kitty heard a horse coming around the corner and saw it was Matthew Steer, the squire's man. Kitty regarded Matthew with some awe after once hearing Flo say he must be a saint, and had the patience of Job.

"Why hello, Miss Kitty," Matthew said. "How are you today then?"

"Quite well, Mr. Steer, thank you. How are you?"

"I'm doing all right." Matthew smiled at Martha whose face was smeared with berry stains. "Been enjoying the strawberries, have you?" He chuckled. "There'll be a lot about this year, I do believe." He stayed chatting for a while about this and that, and then he asked Kitty to give his best to her mother, and rode on.

"How does he know Mother?" Martha said, who was now straddling the stile.

Kitty shrugged. "I don't know. I expect it was when they were young or something." She heard a distant roll of thunder. "Come along, Martha, we'd better get home before that starts, else we'll get soaked."

"But I want to go along beside the river, not that way." Martha made a face. "I don't like the steep hill. Walking up it hurts my chest."

Kitty believed her sister had probably got that idea from their father, who occasionally complained of the same thing. "Well, I'm going this way so I can see Flo," she said, setting off. She smiled as she heard her sister coming along behind her.

When they reached Forde, they found Flo polishing the brass sign on her front door: *Flo Endacott: Midwife*. That sign had always fascinated Kitty, and consequently they were the first words she learned to read.

Flo straightened up. "Hello, you two. What are you up to then?"

"Going home before it rains," Kitty said. "But I'll come over later."

"Aw, I won't be here, dear, more's the pity. Fred Barnes just came over to tell me Millie has just started, so I'll be over there all night, I expect. Fred's like a fart in a thunderstorm when she's having a baby."

"Oh," said Kitty, trying to imagine. "Well, I'll come tomorrow then." She waved her hand and hurried Martha along, who was saying, "What does she mean, Kitty? What's a fart in a—" Then yelped as Kitty gave her a pinch and told her to stop repeating everything she heard.

Furze lane began a field's length past Forde. The gate, which Kitty called the Crying Shame—one of her Grandma Felicity's descriptions—was dilapidated and broken off one hinge, and sprawled on its side like a spent scarecrow. The farm sign was askew and dotted with orange fungus. Dandelions grew in yellow profusion down the lane, and when she'd been younger Kitty had picked them and taken them home to Leah. That was before she was told that their other name was piss-a-beds and that was what they'd make her do.

Although Kitty had grown out of the habit of wanting to pick every flower in sight, Martha hadn't. She was dawdling now, bending down to pick something or the other. Taking advantage of the fact, Kitty ran ahead. With Ruth not being there, she hoped to spend some time alone with her mother and see if she couldn't plead with her some more about the education matter.

꧁꧂

Leah was in the best room, where it was cooler. Her ankles tended to swell badly in the hot weather, and she looked up from her mending as Kitty came in and flopped down in a chair. "I'd love a cup of tea, Kitty," she said. "Or perhaps Ruth will get me one, if you ask her."

"Ruth isn't home yet, she's had to stay behind," Kitty said, with some satisfaction. "She made up some lyrics for a skipping game and Miss Wood didn't like it. But I'll get you one."

As Kitty went out again Leah smiled, for once approving of her second daughter. She wondered what Ruth's lyrics were all about. She couldn't stand that Wood woman who had, in the past, tittered that Kitty wasn't her father's daughter. She was a rampant gossip and had probably got the idea for the double entendre from her friend, curse Sarah Underwood's rotten soul.

Esther Pugh was another gossip. She had come around after Kitty was born, on pretense of inquiring after her health, but couldn't take her eyes off the baby. "She doesn't look premature to me," she'd said, in her silly, sweet voice, as if she expected Leah to reveal what she suspected.

To get her own back, Leah had made a point of asking after John, and Esther left soon afterwards looking as if she'd swallowed a sour plum. Leah knew she had done herself no good, of course. Gossips always repeated what they wanted to, and she had no doubt the trio indulged themselves in an ocean of conjectures about her.

That was a long time ago now—fifteen years this coming January. How time flew, Leah mused; it seemed like only yesterday she had held Kitty in her arms for the first time. Her expression tightened as she remembered, with some bitterness, how Hern had come home from Lower and had no compassion for the terrible time she had suffered bringing her baby into the world, but said later during one of their arguments how he wished Kitty had never been born.

Soon after, ignoring her pleas for him to wait, he had foisted another child on her. It was no wonder she found it so hard to feel anything for Ruth, who had been a sickly, troublesome baby and had grown up sullen and irritating. By comparison, Kitty had never given her a moment's worry. Until now that is. Now, this ridiculous and persistent idea of hers about leaving Furze showed she had a tendency towards being headstrong and willful, and Leah felt very uneasy about it.

Although she had never regretted having Kitty—indeed, her eldest child was the one light in her miserable existence—now that she was no longer blinded by her own ignorance and his devilish charms, and knew how ruthless he could be, she did have concerns about her daughter coming from Hartley Gordon's seed. That was why she had to watch her closely and be prepared for any traits she might have inherited. For once, she agreed with Hern: Emily Foss needed her head examined. She was a dangerous woman to be putting such radical ideas into Kitty's head. Why, she had no choice but to keep Kitty close by. It was in the interests of them all.

Leah's stomach roiled as it always did when she thought of the matter, still unresolved after all these years. Their position was still precarious.

After she had received Justin le March's letter telling her about the affidavit, she was under the illusion that the squire genuinely cared for her, and that was why he had forgiven her father's debt. And then, one day, when Kitty was just a little girl, he'd said something to her as he had ridden through the farm that caused her to worry. She had gone into Moretonhampstead to see Coldswill, and discovered that Furze was only theirs while she and Kitty lived.

It was then, and only then, after all those years of being obsessed and mesmerized by the man, that she recognized what a deluded fool she'd been. She knew now that Hartley Gordon was capable of anything. With that in mind, she had to keep Kitty close by until she was wed. Once she had a man to watch out for her, and a family to take care of, she would have little time for fanciful ideas.

Who knew that better than herself?

Chapter 17

Matthew Steer was a bit bewildered as he rode back to the manor. There was something about that older Underwood girl that always made him think, although what it was exactly he couldn't say. He shook his head. Well, no matter, it would come to him one day.

It was his birthday, and he was celebrating with a day off. Not that he had much to do on his days off, for his life revolved around Hartley Gordon now. If Clara and their child had lived it might have been different, of course, but that didn't bear thinking about.

He had just been to see old Ronald Bennett. Why, he must be almost seventy if he was a day, but still sharp, oh yes, still sharp. He rambled on a bit, mind you, and today he'd been going on again about Peter Peardon and the night he died. Matthew had felt uneasy, because although he wouldn't have been a bit surprised if there had been foul play involving the squire, there was nothing he could do about it. When he had gone to the manor, he'd been very naïve and known very little about the ways of the world. If he had hoped to see the squire reap the consequences for all his misdeeds, he'd been sadly disappointed. Over the years, he'd come to the conclusion that the Devil looked after his own and that justice counted for nothing in the world. When Ronald reiterated his fears about the hazards of working for such a man Matthew couldn't have agreed with him more, and was grateful the good Lord had protected him thus far.

Matthew had been at the manor nigh on fifteen years now and lived alone in the cottage he once shared with Clara. After Lady Leonora left, he and Clara had married and watched over little Thomas until the squire sent the boy away to school. Not long after that Clara had died in childbirth, and Matthew's grief was doubled.

He had subsequently spent good times with Thomas in his holidays though. The young man had a way with horses and could make them do all sorts of things, especially Hector who was getting on now but was still a damned fine horse. Mr. Thomas certainly knew his horses, thought Matthew proudly, and he really appreciated the fine gelding he had given him.

In latter years, Thomas had spent most of his holidays either at Whitmouth House or in Derbyshire, and Matthew hardly saw him. He felt sad about this because he really missed the lad, but he didn't blame him for not wanting to come home. His father was always trying to make him into something he wasn't, always telling him to be a man, or deriding him in other ways. Once, when the squire was cleaning a gun, he'd pointed it at Thomas's head and said 'bang.' Matthew had thought at the time it was a strange thing for a father to do, but, after giving it some thought, he suspected it must be because, deep down, the squire didn't like his own son.

Matthew dismounted and led his horse into the stable.

"Want me to do that, sir?" said the young stable lad, running out to meet him.

"No, it's all right, young Tim," Matthew said. "I've had a day off today and I dare say you've got enough to do, even with the master away."

"I have that, sir," Tim said gratefully, and went off to attend to some of it.

Matthew smiled to himself. Funny how life was, he thought. If anyone had told him all those years ago that he would be top dog at the manor one day, he would have laughed in their faces. But, as he once promised Flo Endacott, he had indeed outlasted the lot of them, and had gained a lot of respect on the way.

Funnily enough, he had seen Flo that afternoon. He'd actually felt a bit disappointed, because he hoped she might stop to have a chat; perhaps even offer him a cup of tea and a piece of cake. However, it appeared she hadn't even noticed him and he wondered if perhaps her eyes were beginning to fail.

He liked Flo a lot, and had good reason to be grateful to her, too. After Clara died he had lost control of himself for a while, and, although he knew it wasn't the thing to do, began to drink a bit. One day Flo had seen him drunk in the village and told him it wouldn't solve anything, and that he was to stop it because it didn't suit him. He had done that very thing, and never touched a drop since.

When Matthew had finished rubbing down his horse he stood back to admire his gleaming coat. He patted the animal's shoulder and made sure he had hay and water before he left the stables.

Horses were all right, Matthew thought, as he walked home, but it was a bit of a lonely existence when that was all you had as a friend. Now that the pain of losing Clara had lessened, he often wished Mary had returned to live at Forde. They could have been company for each other.

He had been thinking a lot about Mary lately, he didn't know why. He had even been wondering what would happen if he went to see her, and that was part of the reason he was disappointed Flo hadn't spoken to him that afternoon, as he was going to ask for Mary's address. Ah well, he thought, he would make a special trip over to Forde one of these days to do that very thing. The squire was spending a lot of time in London again and wouldn't miss him for a day or two. This thought cheered him up a bit, and put a bounce into his stride as he returned to his cottage.

ꙮ

Days later, Flo was still shaken up after seeing Matthew: it wasn't like her to avoid people, but when she'd seen him looking at her so intently she'd hurried into the farmhouse until he'd ridden on by. Even after all these years, she had never been able to shake off the fear that one day he would ask her for Mary's address.

When Acheson once said that the circumstances of Mary's death would be hard to bear, he had never spoken a truer word—although, of course, he was referring to her burial. He knew nothing about the complication of the babies. Flo had often wondered since if it wouldn't have been a lot easier on her if she had told Leah the truth, because the outcome had become an almost unbearable burden that carried its own nightmare, and had plagued her for years.

Flo's waking hours had been no easier in the beginning either. Despite assuring Acheson to the contrary, she had worried herself sick that someone wouldn't only find the grave, but that Leah would somehow discover the truth about the baby. As it was, Leah seemed a bit perplexed when Flo told her that Mary had gone to Plymouth, and, once or twice afterwards, Flo's heart fluttered erratically when she had inquired after her. Eventually Flo said that Mary wasn't coming home again, but that she'd gone to a good home; Leah had never asked after her again.

She was sitting quietly by the fire ruminating these things when Kitty burst through the back door.

"Good gracious me!" Flo said, putting her hand to her heart. "Whatever's up? You're like a jumping jack-in-a-box."

Acheson came in behind Kitty, saying the smell of tea and cake had dragged him in from the fields. Flo laughed and moved the kettle over to the hottest part of the fire.

"Oh? But what's that face for?" she said, seeing Kitty's crestfallen look.

"It's Mother," Kitty said, in disgust. "She just *won't* believe I'm *serious*."

"What's this?" said Acheson.

"Miss Foss said I should take further training so I could go on to teach. But it doesn't look as if it will happen. Not yet anyway. Mother says she can't ask Father yet because he's already in a bad mood because of the baby, and I have to be patient. I *know* she's hoping I'll forget about it. Then, once the baby gets here, she'll find me all sorts of things to do so I won't be able to leave."

Flo exchanged a look with Acheson. "Well, give her time. You know how it flies."

"Not at Furze it doesn't," Kitty said miserably. "It's like purgatory and I hate it. She won't even listen to my reasoning." She narrowed her hazel eyes, the green in them glinting like emeralds. "You know what I think?"

"What's that?" Flo said wearily.

"*I* think she can't wait until she gets me married off."

Flo and Acheson exchanged another look. Acheson looked as if he might agree, and Flo warned him not to say anything; he often hinted that the best thing for Kitty would be to *settle her down*, meaning marriage. Although Flo knew that his opinion was born out of loving the girl dearly, and that he wanted to protect her, it came out all wrong. He had in mind what had happened to Mary, she supposed, but he couldn't seem to see that Kitty was of the nature that the more she was pushed into something, the more she would stubbornly resist it. Also, with age he had become more serious and intense about certain things, and Kitty, who was so unlike her sisters, had an air about her that seemed to provoke his irritation. Flo had once heard him tell Kitty that she hadn't better look above herself, as the gentry would only want girls like her for one thing.

Despite her willfulness, Kitty had Mary's sweet naiveté. She hadn't understood what Acheson meant and asked Flo to explain. When Flo had, Kitty's temper flared. She got on her high horse and said it was nobody's business but her own to whom she might take a fancy. Unfortunately, Leah overheard her, and she received a good hiding for it. Which was ironic, Flo thought, considering the morals of her mother when she was her daughter's age. And yet, she supposed, that was the very thing that made Leah so insensitive to Kitty's aspirations. She was incessantly hinting how it wouldn't be long before she would be able to find herself a nice young man. Flo couldn't count the times she heard Kitty say she didn't want one, and how Leah always turned a deaf ear to it.

Flo sighed. It made things worse no doubt, Leah believing that Kitty was the squire's daughter, and she would dearly have liked to put her mind at rest on that score. But she *couldn't.* The secret of the stillborn child had to remain hidden. Dear God, Flo thought, the burden never lessened.

ꝏ

Kitty didn't go straight home after leaving Forde, but went up the hill behind the farm to her favorite haunt beneath the rowan and beech trees, the place she called her grove. She didn't know why she liked it there so much, except it always felt peaceful and calmed her. In spring, primroses came, tucked into the hedges like precious secrets emerging after the long silence of winter. Then in May, there was the purple haze of bluebells that filled the air with their heavenly scent.

She stayed there for a while enjoying the twittering of the birds, who were having their final flurry of activity before going to roost. Then, as it began to get dark, she knew she must go home else she would be nagged. She got up from where she had been sitting and brushed off her skirt. "I'll be back," she whispered to no one in particular, and ran down the lane.

ꝏ

It was from the grove she ran a few weeks later. The evenings were at their longest now and it was so beautiful at that time of year that Kitty always wished that summer could go on forever.

When she got home, she found Martha in the scullery, sniveling, and Ruth scolding her and banging the dishes about.

"Where've you been?" Ruth said. "Mother's been looking for you."

"Why, what's the matter?" Kitty said.

"She's gone and got a man—"

"And he's as mad as a hornet," Martha chimed in.

"Who, the man?" Kitty said.

Martha giggled. "No, silly. Father. He came from a long way away. Not Father, the man." She giggled again, enjoying the game.

"Shut up, Martha," Ruth said. "He isn't *that* mad, he's just a bit put out because this Charlie fellow just turned up an hour or so ago and Mother took him in without even asking him. And you know how he likes to be asked things. You can barely understand a word he says. Not Father, the man." She looked daggers at Martha, who collapsed in fits of giggles. "You're making me say it now."

"Where is she now?" Kitty tried to keep a straight face, but she couldn't resist adding, "Mother, I mean."

"It isn't funny. Wait until you see him, you'll see for yourself. It looks as if he hasn't washed for a week." She looked at Martha. "Don't you dare say it—"

But Martha couldn't resist. "Father *never* looks as if he's had a wash," she shrieked, and then rushed over to Kitty for protection as Ruth threw a cup at her.

"Now look what you've made me do," Ruth cried, as it crashed to the floor.

Kitty took Martha by the hand. "Come on." When they were outside, she giggled. "She has very little sense of humor. Ruth, I mean." And they could hardly walk for laughing.

"Oh, there you are, Kitty." Leah frowned at them as they burst through the door of Barn Cottage, still giggling. "This is Charlie Chase, and he has just arrived from the north. I was just telling Charlie that the cottage could be made quite cozy with a bit of work, and that I was sure you would help him."

"Yes, Mother." Kitty acknowledged the young man with a nod of her head. Her first impression of him was that he was angry. She didn't know why, but it just seemed that way. Perhaps because, although he was tall and quite broad, his face was gaunt, and his eyes, a startling blue, were wary, as if he'd seen a lot of pain. His mouth was tight too, as if he rarely smiled. Kitty didn't exactly take a dislike to him, but something about him made her feel concerned.

Then she remembered the Reverend Pugh's sermon of the previous Sunday and chided herself: 'Judge not lest ye be judged.' She remembered it because at the time she had looked across to the other side of the church, hoping Esther Pugh would take notice. So she smiled, and took his outstretched hand.

Leah, who was watching her daughter's reaction, also smiled. "Well now, Charlie, we'll leave you to settle in then. And we'll go and rustle up something for you to eat, though I won't be coming down again this evening. I don't always feel too well these days."

"I hope I can take a load off your shoulders, Mrs. Underwood. I'm very grateful to you giving me this chance." Charlie smiled at Kitty. "I'm sure we'll all get along."

Kitty followed Leah out of the cottage, unable to shake the strange uncertainty she felt. She only hoped her mother knew what she was doing. When Martha scampered ahead, she asked, "Isn't this too much for you at the moment, Mother?"

"Not at all," Leah said. "I've been telling your father for months to get someone permanent instead of those casual people he has coming in. It's far better value and it means another pair of reliable hands about the place."

"But… do you think Charlie means what he says, that he will be reliable? You don't really know anything about him."

"I know your Uncle Colan, Kitty, and he wouldn't have sent him if he wasn't trustworthy," Leah said firmly.

Kitty had never met her Uncle Colan, although she had heard Grandma Underwood say horrible things about him often enough. She knew he'd run off with the squire's wife, causing a lot of shame in the family. Grandma Underwood reckoned she would never accept Michael, Colan's son, as her grandson.

"According to your Uncle Colan's letter, Charlie hasn't had a very happy life," Leah explained. "He was in a cotton mill and the conditions were dreadful, so he and a few other people began to protest. The owners of the factory didn't like that, so they tried to kill him and he had to run for his life. He decided to make for the coast, but then ran into Colan in Derbyshire, who employed him for a while." She smiled at her daughter. "Everything will be fine, Kitty, don't look so worried. Why, as far as I'm concerned, Charlie couldn't have come along at a better time."

ഇ൦ദ

Later in the week when Kitty was over at Forde with her mother, she was in another room when she overheard Flo say, "You think Charlie will work out then, Leah?"

"I think so," said Leah. "According to his letter, Colan said he was a very hard worker."

"I was wondering why Colan would suggest he come down here if he was so useful," Flo said. "Acheson said something that makes me think it could be something to do with his instigating."

"What do you mean?" Leah said.

"You know he was trying to stir up trouble in the mill. How do you know he didn't start something in the mines?"

"Oh, but surely… wouldn't Colan have said?"

"Colan's soft enough to feel sorry for someone like that, and not want him to get into any more trouble," Flo said shortly. "So I suppose it would be natural to think he would be better off where there weren't any mills, and few mines."

"Yes, perhaps," said Leah. Then she laughed gaily. "And what better place than North Bovey? He can't get into much trouble around here, can he?"

"I hope not," Flo said quietly.

"Oh, Flo, don't put a damper on this. Charlie's the answer to my prayers."

"Aw yes, and how's that then?"

Kitty's ears pricked up, but it was one of those times when the conversation came to a halt. And then, on cue, came the errand.

Chapter 18

The summer was beautiful that year, and September turned into October, almost without anyone noticing. During those golden days, Kitty and Martha helped Charlie whitewash the inside of Barn Cottage, although Martha got more of it on herself than the walls and they had to tell her to stay outside while they finished it.

Leah found some curtains, and once they were hung, the cottage looked a lot cozier. Charlie made shelves, which he said he intended to fill with books as he could read. Kitty was surprised and pleased to hear that. She told him that Emily lent her books and that she would ask her if he could borrow some, too.

The only interest Hern took in all this was to stroll down the lane occasionally to see what was going on; he didn't lift a finger to help. Allowing Charlie the cottage was as far as his benevolence went. Even if his brother had sent him to Devon, Hern wasn't completely at ease with the stranger, and he told Leah that Charlie wouldn't be allowed to come into the farmhouse for his meals but could look after himself. This declaration evolved into a row that Hern won. However, Leah in her stubborn way, sent something down daily from the kitchen via one girl or the other, or sometimes went down with it herself.

During those months, Kitty lost her shyness with Charlie and, when they got to know each other better, he told her something about his life.

He never spoke of his father, and the only thing he ever said about his mother was that she had sold him to a chimney sweep in order to buy food. When Kitty recovered from that shock, she asked him what it was like being a sweep. She had no idea that the chimneys Charlie spoke of were so large that a whole child could be sent up inside. She couldn't believe it at first when he explained to her how most sweeps never lasted much beyond two or more years, what with the soot and the inevitable sores. She winced as he described how their knees and elbows used to get scraped, and how those parts were soaked in brine and put near the fire to harden the skin.

"Some of the boys used to fall asleep and never wake up," Charlie said. "A merciful release, too. Luckily I grew too broad and I was sold to a mill. Mind you, I don't know why I say luckily, working in the mill was worse, if anything could be. You imagine working eighteen hours a day and if you fell asleep, you'd be beaten awake. Some people used to beat their own kiddies to save the overseer doing it. If anyone stopped work to help others, they'd be beaten, too. They called me a troublemaker when I got a bunch of us together and tried to make a difference. An *instigator.*" He spat the last word out and showed her a faint scar on his cheek. "Know how I got that?"

Kitty shook her head in morbid fascination.

"One day the mill owner and his daughter rode into the yard. I thought there might be some compassion, even though others told me different and said I'd regret it if I said anything to them about the conditions. Compassion! They wouldn't know the meaning of the word. The owner told the boss to get rid of me. Wouldn't even speak to me himself. And his stuck-up daughter struck me across face with her riding crop and called me worse than she would call her dog.

"I lived in two rooms with a family of eleven. Sewage used to run down the street outside. The smell was so bad we even had to bung up the keyhole. But it was home and I had to pay my way. I didn't know how to tell them I'd lost my job, but I had no need. That night, men came and dragged me outside. I got beaten up and was left for dead, but through the night I crawled away. I don't know how I survived really, but I did. When I could walk again I got out of there, went west to Castleton, up to the mines and asked for work. That's when I met your Uncle Colan. Mind you, it wasn't all roses working there either."

"And then you came here," Kitty said.

"Yes. Then I came here."

"Mother said you intended to go to the coast. Did you want to work on a ship?"

"I intended to emigrate to America."

"Oh," said Kitty, who couldn't imagine leaving Devon and going to such a far away and unknown place. "You must be awfully brave, Charlie, are you still thinking of going?"

He looked at her. "Not at the moment."

ഌ൙

Acheson took a real liking to Charlie, and after noticing how much time Kitty spent with him, teased her about it. Kitty blushed furiously and Flo made faces to hush him up, but he took no notice of them and persisted.

One afternoon, when he went too far, Kitty retorted, "I'll never marry a man like Charlie, so you might as well stop hinting that I will."

Acheson's expression darkened, and Kitty knew she'd spoken out of place. When he grumbled at her, she burst into tears and ran inside to Flo.

"What on earth did the maid do?" Flo said, when Acheson came in after her.

He told her. "It was about the worst thing I've ever heard her say," he added. "There's nothing wrong with the likes of Charlie."

"I didn't mean it like you think," Kitty said. "It just slipped out."

"There must be something in your mind for you to say such a thing," Acheson said, not appeased at all. "I've spoken to you about this before."

"And I've told you before about teasing the maid," Flo said sharply. "So I reckon you got what you deserve. As for you, Kitty, before you give yourself to *any* man you make sure it's for the right reason, no matter who he is, else you'll regret it all your life. Now, enough said. And you two kiss and make up. I haven't got patience with either of you."

But all the same, when Kitty had gone home Flo looked after her with a concerned look on her face, and an ache in her heart.

ꕥ

October handed over the reins to November, and soon the girls were all excited and making gifts for Christmas. Later in December, Leah didn't dissuade them from asking Charlie into the house to help put up the decorations, and he brought in boughs of fir, ivy and holly.

They had gathered acorns earlier on in the autumn as fodder for the pigs, and now Kitty and Martha fetched a few out of the store and, with sticks and bits of lace and fabric, made angels to sit on the bare branches, fetched in from the woods.

"They don't look like angels," said Ruth. "Do they, Charlie?"

"We see what we want to," he said, smiling at Leah, who smiled back. "And your sister obviously sees angels."

Martha said, "You're only jealous, Ruth, because you're too fumble-fingered to make anything at all."

Ruth was furious and must have said something to Hern because at supper that evening he said, "I don't want Chase coming into the house anymore, do you understand?"

Leah frowned. "Why not? It's nice for the girls to have a man around who enjoys doing things with them, unlike yourself who doesn't join in anything at all."

"You'll be grinning on the other side of your face when it's too late," said Hern. Then added snidely, "Like mother, like daughter."

Leah narrowed her eyes at him and got up from the table, pushing back her chair on the flagstone floor. The sound grated through Kitty's head, just as their continuous arguing did.

ꕥ

Despite Hern's wishes, Leah insisted that Charlie join them for Christmas dinner, and Charlie said it was the best meal he had ever tasted. As Kitty had done most of the cooking, she was gratified to have this compliment, along with her mother's thanks and Martha's nod of agreement.

Hern and Ruth said nothing, but Ruth did offer to make the supper on Boxing Day. Unfortunately, she added too much salt and didn't know, as Kitty would have done, that adding a potato to the stew would have absorbed a lot of the problem.

"What's this muck?" said Hern, poking at it. He looked first at Leah, then at Kitty. "If you had spent more time at home learning how to cook instead of at that bleddy school, you might have something to show for it."

Kitty opened her mouth to protest and looked at Ruth, expecting her to own up. But Ruth's lips were buttoned as tightly as a rosebud, and her eyes shone with mirth.

Leah tried a mouthful. "It isn't that bad. Don't fuss so much."

Hern looked furious, and for a moment Kitty thought he was going to dump the contents of his plate over her mother's head. Instead, he spun it along the table towards Kitty's, got up and went out, slamming the door behind him.

"You could have owned up, Ruth," Kitty cried, her eyes filling with tears. "You're just a horrid troublemaker."

"Cry baby," Ruth sneered.

"That's enough." Leah stood up and gripped the edge of the table. "Can't we have *one* meal when we don't fall out over something?" She suddenly gave a cry and bent over.

"What is it, Mother?" Kitty said, dismayed.

"The baby," Leah whispered. "I think—" But the rest of what she was going to say was cut off as she gasped with pain.

Ruth said, "But it isn't due yet, is it?"

"Oh, be quiet, Ruth," Leah snapped, taking quick, panting breaths. When she could speak again she told Kitty to run and fetch Flo.

When Kitty reached Forde, however, Acheson told her Flo was away to another birthing and probably wouldn't be home until the next day. "I think you'd better tell your father to get the horse ready," he said, "just in case he needs to fetch the doctor."

When Kitty passed this on to her father, he cursed. "What's the use of having a bleddy midwife living next door if she's never there, think I'm made of bleddy money?" he said. "It's bad enough there's going to be another bleddy mouth to feed."

Kitty felt like saying she knew her mother hadn't wanted this baby; she'd heard her say so to Flo. She'd also heard her say he was welcome to take his doings elsewhere.

"When you've finished downstairs, you can go up there with her," Hern said.

Kitty wondered why Ruth couldn't do the washing up for once, but she daren't suggest it. "Yes, Father," she said meekly.

Martha was in the kitchen, sitting at the kitchen table, humming. She looked up as Kitty came in. "You know this isn't so bad if you add more water to it," she said, poking the mess on her plate.

"Isn't it?" Kitty said, distractedly. "Then you might as well eat the lot. After that you can dry the dishes for me. Where's Ruth?"

"Upstairs. Kitty, why isn't the baby waiting until its proper time? Do you think it didn't like the taste of your supper either?"

"It was *Ruth's* supper," Kitty snapped, and went into the scullery where she dumped dishes into one of the sinks and allowed her tears to mingle with the dishwater. How quickly the Christmas spirit had flown from their house, she thought, miserably.

༄

Just before ten o'clock Leah told Kitty to go and fetch Hern. He was still in the best room and had fallen asleep on the settee. Kitty had to shake him hard to wake him up.

"It's come then?" he said.

"No, Father. Mother wants to see you."

Hern grumbled, but followed her upstairs. "What's up then?" he said to Leah from the doorway.

"I'm not sure," Leah said. "It's like the first time, like it can't come."

Hern put his hands in his pockets and rocked to and fro. "Likely be a bit big then, that's what it'll be. A boy, I bet. Yes, it'll just take a bit more time. A bit more effort than girls."

Leah grimaced and caught hold of the bedstead as another contraction came. "Kitty wasn't a boy," she said, through gritted teeth. "You'll have to get the doctor, Hern."

"Cost a pretty penny," he grumbled.

"For God's sake," she gasped. "And hurry!"

Hern scowled at her, pushed past Kitty and went downstairs.

Kitty looked after him, vowing that she would never allow a man to treat her so callously. Then she returned to the bedside and took each of her mother's hands, trying to rub some warmth into them.

It must have been a half hour later, after another contraction, when Leah gasped. "Kitty! I felt something. Have a look for me, will you? Tell me if you can see the baby yet."

Kitty hesitated. "Mother, please don't ask me. I don't know what to do."

"Who else is there?" Leah said desperately. "Besides, you've done it with lambs and kittens. You must help me, child."

Kitty's heart picked up several beats as she lifted the covers. The room was dim and for a moment, she thought it was part of the afterbirth, although of course it couldn't be. *That black mass.*

"Kitty?" Leah's voice was tremulous. "Can you see the head?"

"No." Kitty swallowed nervously. "Mother, I'm sorry, I don't know what it is. But... I think you're bleeding a bit."

Leah cried, "Oh God, oh God," over and over again. "Why does the bringing of a child have to be like this?"

ᘓᘐ

The hands of the clock ticked on, and still Hern and the doctor didn't arrive. Leah seemed to be making little progress, and Kitty began to worry as all the horrors she had ever heard about childbirth filled her mind.

She turned a tearful face towards the door as the latch lifted. It was Ruth, with Martha snuggled against her and looking disembodied, enveloped in Ruth's voluminous nightgown.

"What's happening?" Ruth asked.

"Well...." Kitty looked worriedly towards the bed. "Mother's still having contractions. But she keeps dropping off to sleep."

"Is that normal?" It wasn't often Ruth looked so pale, and Martha's eyes were wide and frightened.

Kitty shrugged. "How'm I to know? Do you?"

Ruth hated to admit she didn't know things. "She looks awful," she hissed. "Can't you do anything?"

"Like what?" Kitty cried, her voice rising. "If you're so smart, why don't you trade places with me?"

"Not likely," said Ruth. "*You're* her favorite. *You* do it." And she pulled Martha away and closed the door.

Kitty returned to the bedside and looked down at her mother. Ruth was right in one thing, she thought, her mother did look awful. She shook Leah slightly to rouse her, thinking it might be better if she stayed alert.

Leah stirred and turned her face towards Kitty. Her eyes looked dull, as if there was a film over them. "Get me a drink, will you?" she whispered. "I'm so thirsty."

"I wish Flo were here," Kitty said, holding the cup for her mother. "She would know what to do."

"Yes, Flo would know," Leah murmured. "She knew before." She reached out and placed her hand on Kitty's cheek. "I almost died having you. Kitty, you must stay here. You *have* to. And promise me you won't do anything reckless. With a father like yours—" She broke off as another contraction took her. But although she strained, it seemed she just couldn't bring the child.

"If the child lives," Leah said later, as Kitty gently wiped the perspiration from her face, "promise me you'll take care of it. You're the only one I can depend upon."

"Mother, don't, please don't say things like that."

Leah put a finger to Kitty's lips. "To think I've been worrying about losing you. I never thought it would be this way around. Such a short time ago… it seems like only yesterday an angel placed you in my arms." Her brow puckered. "No, it was Flo, what am I thinking?"

"Please, Mother, save your strength." Kitty was concerned with how cold Leah was becoming, and pulled the covers up around her.

But suddenly, with a gasp, Leah gently pushed her aside to look across the room. "Mary?" she said, as if she was surprised, yet pleasantly so. Then she turned her head to look at Kitty.

Slowly her smile faded and was replaced by a look of wonder. "Oh, Mary," she said softly. "It was *you*?" She sank back into her pillows. Then she smiled and shook her head. The smile became a soft laugh. And then her laughter died, and she was silent.

"Mother?" Kitty was alarmed and shook her slightly. "Mother? Wake up!"

Suddenly, thankfully, she heard the sound of horses in the yard and she leapt up and ran out onto the landing. The back door opened and shut. Dr. Morrison took the stairs two at a time. Three strides and he had crossed the landing and was in the room.

"She's not moving, doctor. She's not saying anything," Kitty gabbled, as she followed him.

The doctor quickly took off his coat and peeled off his gloves. He went to the bedside and felt Leah's pulse. Frowning, he said, "Quickly. Some hot water." And began to roll up his sleeves.

Kitty rushed downstairs and back again, carrying with her a pan of water.

"Pour it in the bowl," the doctor said, indicating the washstand. He opened his case and took out an apron. "You'd better go."

"Go?"

"Yes," he said impatiently. "If I'm to try and save the child."

He met Kitty's startled eyes. As she fumbled with the latch, she saw him reach for his case and undo two buttons. A flap fell. Just as she closed the door, a sharp blade glinted in the lamplight.

Chapter 19

Downstairs, the three girls waited. All had grim faces, and Martha was crying softly. Hern had come in after tending to the horses, and after telling Ruth to fetch him when the doctor had finished, returned to the best room.

"What will happen now?" Ruth said.

Kitty met her eyes. She was wondering the same thing, and although she hoped her mother would be spared, she had a terrible feeling the doctor had arrived too late.

"What does she mean, Kitty?" Martha asked in a very small voice.

"I *mean* if Mother dies," Ruth said, her face grim with fear.

"Don't frighten her, Ruth, she may not," Kitty said.

"Mother's going to die?" Martha looked at Kitty in disbelief. "Why?"

Kitty didn't know how to explain. Dogs and cats rarely died when they whelped. Cows and horses did sometimes, but it was usually if the calf or foal was in an awkward position, or too big. But as for humans, she just didn't know. "You'll have to ask Flo, she'll explain."

"Mother didn't die when she had us," Martha said, wiping her eyes and smiling tremulously at them, as if she had discovered a solution to the evening's drama. "So perhaps she won't now?" She turned on Ruth. "You're just being beastly again, Ruth."

Ruth, for once, looked hurt, and Kitty put her hands on Martha's shoulders and faced her. "No," she said quietly. "No, she isn't, Martha. It's different each time, and Mother isn't doing very well this time."

Martha's eyes filled with tears. "But I don't want her to die."

Kitty embraced her younger sister in an effort to comfort her. As she did, she saw Ruth's eyes go the stairs. The doctor stepped into the room. In his arms he held a tiny mewling bundle.

He walked over to them, and bent down for Martha to see the baby. "You have a baby brother, Martha," he said. "Will you be a good girl and hold him while I talk to your sisters?"

Martha wiped her tears away and took the baby from him, smiling up at Kitty as she did so. Ruth led her to a chair, made her sit down, and told her not to move in case she dropped him.

"I'm afraid I could do nothing for your mother," Dr. Morrison said quietly to the older girls. "Even if Flo Endacott had been here earlier there is nothing she could have done either. Not in a case like this. Now, can you fetch your father for me?"

"He's in the best room," Ruth said. "I'll go."

The doctor turned to Kitty. "This is a dreadful shock for you, my dear. I'm so sorry. It will be up to you now, of course. Your father and sisters are going to need all the support they can get. As for the little fellow," he nodded towards the baby, "we'll have to wait and see, but in any event I should have him christened as soon as possible."

"Why?" Kitty's heart picked up a beat. "What do you mean? Isn't he all right?"

"He's surprisingly strong." Dr. Morrison's brows puckered. "But you'll have to feed him up. Watch him carefully. As well, there may be some damage."

Kitty's world stood still. "Damage?"

"In cases like this…." He drew himself up. "Well, I don't want to alarm you. Only time will tell. Ah, Hern, my dear fellow." He forsook Kitty for her father, put his arm about Hern's shoulder and led him to the door. As they went, Kitty heard him say, "You'll have to burn the mattress. Sorry, Hern. Truly, you had a good one there." And she wasn't sure if he spoke of the mattress or her mother.

"Is the baby going to be all right?" Martha said in a small voice. "He isn't very big."

"We were all that size when we were first born," Kitty said shakily. She couldn't bear to think of having a damaged child around, whatever that might mean. How on earth would they cope? And as for her giving them all support, who was going to support *her*?

ꕤ

Ruth and Martha went off to bed and Kitty took the baby to her room, but she hardly slept. She wondered at what a difference a day could make. Only last night they'd all been laughing and enjoying themselves. Even her father had behaved more charitably towards Charlie, who'd kept them in stitches with his tales and his funny accent. Her mother's homemade wine had helped, of course. People were always more jovial after a drink, especially after Leah's elderberry wine. Kitty had once heard Flo remark that it was the best she'd ever tasted.

It was as well, Kitty thought, that Charlie hadn't been there tonight after that disgusting exhibition by her father at the dinner table. Now, as her father's luck would have it, he was stuck with her *muck* as he called it, for a long time to come. The doctor's words *it's up to you* echoed in her mind. With them Kitty felt the clanking of a manacle go around her life, trapping her in a place she had no wish to be.

ꕤ

Hern didn't go to bed that night, but huddled beside the fire, hugging his whiskey bottle. He was just as shocked as his daughters at the turn of events.

Memories of Leah crowded his mind: taking in an orphan lamb and complaining, 'oh, not another.' Burying her nose in the washing picked fresh from the line and closing her eyes; looking across the fields and saying in a voice as sad as winter, 'what a god-forsaken place this is.' Well, God had forsaken her tonight, Hern thought morosely. Not that he'd ever set store by Him anyway since He hadn't bleddy cared so far.

But of all the memories Hern had gathered during the years of his marriage, one stood out most vividly. It was the day he had discovered Leah was expecting someone else's child, and he remembered it as clearly as if it were yesterday.

He had another drink of whiskey. He'd come to like it ever since that day his father had introduced it to him, the day they'd toasted his betrothal. "Bleddy old bastard," he muttered. Even though Joshua had passed on, Hern had never forgiven him for making that pact with Peardon. He still believed they'd known about Leah's condition all along and had enjoyed pulling the wool over his eyes.

He remembered it was in this very room he'd first set eyes on her. He could even recall his thoughts at the time. Yet how different things had turned out to be, he thought sourly. Leah had never attended to his needs as he imagined she would. Nancy had done a better job, although she pleased too many men for his liking and sometimes he feared he might bring home something other than the occasional flea. Betsy had told him the last time he was there that she was getting a little tired of her sister's shenanigans, and was going to send her away again.

Bleddy women, Hern thought. Couldn't do with them, and couldn't do without them. There couldn't be a god of any sort who would make a world like this to live in where you fairly depended on them. Because given time he supposed another woman might come along, although he couldn't see where from. It was only a dim idea in the far reaches of his mind anyway. But then another thought occurred to him. Even if there was anyone else he fancied, who would take on an idiot child, if that is what his son turned out to be?

What a bleddy life so far, he thought miserably, and he began to sob. Not for Leah in particular, but for that other time when he hadn't been able to cry; and for all the wasted years in between.

&

Flo came home in the morning and, when she heard the news, rushed over to Furze to see how things were. All three girls clung to her for comfort while she cried herself, as yet unable to fully comprehend that she would never see Leah again.

When she could speak, she told Ruth to take Martha out for a walk while their mother was being attended to. She told Kitty she had done very well in looking after the baby so far. "It was truly a miracle he lived, bless his little heart," she said. "Oh, my dear, what a sad thing to happen. But even if I'd been here, I doubt there was anything I could have done."

Kitty felt like saying she would rather the miracle had been for her mother than the baby, but immediately felt guilty. "That's what the doctor said. He also said when mothers died like that, babies might be damaged. What did he mean, do you think?"

Flo heard the fear in Kitty's voice. "That old fool," she said crossly. "You take no notice of him. He should never have said anything to frighten you like that. The little fellow looks all right to me, and I bet he will be, too."

"He isn't sucking very well," Kitty said, as if that might be indicative to the contrary.

"Well, he'll be looking for the real thing, won't he? But he'll get the hang of it eventually. You mustn't worry about such a thing. Now, what's he going to be called?"

"Edward."

"Edward Underwood, very nice, too. Well then, Edward Underwood," Flo said to the baby, "what do you think about it all?"

"Do you love all babies?" said Kitty, as she watched Flo rock Edward in her arms.

Flo smiled and nodded. "Yes, I do. I'll never know why the good Lord never saw fit to give me one of my own. But there it is. Nothing you can do about it."

"Couldn't you have taken one that no one else wanted?"

A shadow crept over Flo's face and she handed the baby back to Kitty. "It's no use standing here yapping," she said. "I've got stuff to do upstairs and I shall need the help of your father and Charlie. Will you call them in for me? And when I'm done we'll have a nice cup of tea."

As Flo went upstairs, Kitty sighed to the baby in her arms. There was so much to do yet how could she get on with it now she had him to take care of? She wished Flo hadn't sent Martha and Ruth off like that as they could have helped her. Not that they'd helped much so far, for it was she who had done most of the caretaking. Every time the baby squeaked or moved she panicked. And until last night, she had never realized just how noisy little babies could be. She wondered how she would ever get any sleep from now on, because on Ruth's suggestion that Edward should stay in her room, Hern had agreed.

"Kitty?" Flo's voice came from upstairs. "Have you called your father in yet?"

"No, but I will." Kitty put the baby down and went outside.

When the men came in, Hern went on upstairs, but Charlie lingered. A look of pain crossed his face as he put his hand on Kitty's arm. "I'm sorry about your mother, Kit," he said. "Where's the baby then?"

Kitty was about to show him, when Hern called out, "Come on, Charlie. Don't hang about then."

Charlie shrugged. "I'll see him later."

Kitty knew Flo would lay her mother out in the best room, and she could hear them taking her body down the second set of stairs into the front room. A while later they struggled down the kitchen stairs with the mattress and a bundle of sheets. Charlie looked pale and grim, and this time he barely looked at Kitty, who averted her eyes as she began to cry.

ஐ

"I've never felt more like a cup of tea in my life," Flo said later, as Kitty poured one out for her. She fumbled in her pocket and took out a bottle. It was done up tightly and she screwed up her face as she opened it then poured a drop into her cup. "Just keeps me going, this does."

Kitty looked at her dully, wondering what might keep her going from now on. Her stomach began to roll and pitch, and she felt sick, hot and cold all at the same time.

Flo noticed immediately and guided her into a chair. "Put your head between your knees, quickly. That's it. Poor maid, it's been such a terrible shock for you."

When her nausea passed away, Kitty began to cry. "It all happened so quickly, Flo. The first inkling I got... she asked me to take care of Edward. She was talking strange." Recovering slightly, she said, "Flo, who is Mary?"

At first Flo didn't speak. Then she mouthed, more than said, "Mary?"

"Yes. Mother said her name. It was almost as if she *saw* her. She said, 'it was you?' just as if she had suddenly realized something. Then she looked at me, and laughed a bit. I... think that's when she died."

Kitty also remembered her mother's allusion to her father being reckless, but it made little sense, so she hardly thought it worth mentioning. "I didn't really understand what she meant, Flo, do you?"

Flo had been standing beside her. Now she sank onto the frame of the bed. "Hush," she soothed. She could have been talking to herself, because of the rate her heart was beating. "Try and calm yourself now. Sometimes, when a person is dying, someone comes to help them cross over. I dare say it was someone your mother once knew." She managed a smile. "But now she's at peace, and it is that you must be thankful for."

Chapter 20

There were torrents of rain on the day of Leah's funeral. The church was filled with a congregation as damp and miserable as the sodden umbrellas left dripping in the church porch.

Kitty sat at the end of the pew next to the coffin, with Hern beside her. His face revealed no emotion and Kitty wondered if he felt anything at all, although she had heard him sobbing on the night of her mother's death.

Although her mother had only been gone a few days, it seemed an eternity so far. Kitty didn't care to think how she might manage once her sisters returned to school: even though Ruth tended to be lazy, her reluctant help was better than none at all. Hern had shouted at her yesterday, telling her to get a move on. Kitty had been as surprised as her sister, because neither of them could ever remember him doing such a thing before. But rather than being cowed, Ruth said if *that* was the way things were going, she was leaving.

This remark had instantly instigated a row between them. "But I should be the one to go first," Kitty told her; envious because she knew Ruth usually got what she wanted. "I'm the eldest and should have first choice."

"*You* don't count for anything," Ruth sneered.

"What do you mean, I don't count?" Kitty asked, taken aback. But Ruth got that shuttered look on her face, which Martha called her reptile look, and wouldn't say.

The Reverend Pugh stirred Kitty out of her thoughts as he asked the congregation to stand, and then he plodded through the service, stopping occasionally to clear his throat. Kitty glanced at his wife and her expression tightened; she could see no sadness in Esther's face.

When they filed outside, everyone was relieved to find the rain had stopped and the clouds were lifting. The sun was an opaque balloon behind the clouds, as if it too was in mourning, its brilliance veiled out of respect. Diaphanous mists hovered around the graveyard like guardian ghosts as the mourners followed the bearers across the sodden grass.

The coffin was gently rested on the ground before being slowly lowered into its final resting place. Kitty stared at it, unable to believe her mother was inside.

"Forasmuch as it hath pleased Almighty God of His great mercy…."

Kitty tried not to think about it and concentrated instead on the graveyard. How lush the grass. Was it the bodies that made the ground so fertile; the blood, fodder for the green? But in her mother's case, perhaps not. Leah must have been almost devoid of blood when she took her last breath.

"Dust to dust…."

A handful of grit echoed like a shovelful, and it wasn't dust; it was mud to coffin:

coffin to mud. Kitty suddenly felt as if everything was fading; she felt sick and her ears went hot and cold. If a pair of arms hadn't caught her she would have fallen. "It's all right, I have her," she heard through the buzzing in her head.

She was carried into the church porch and gently put down on one of the granite ledges that ran full length along each side.

"Put your head down," Charlie said. "That's it." He held her forehead, then took each hand and rubbed it to try and warm her, which made Kitty cry because she remembered doing the same for Leah just before she died.

When she felt better, Charlie walked her across the green and left her in the hall with Flo, who was with a well-dressed woman Kitty recognized to be her Aunt Margery.

"You're looking a bit peaky," said Flo. "Better have something to eat and a strong cup of tea. Remember your Aunt Margery, do you?"

"Oh yes." Kitty gave her aunt a kiss and a hug. "I will have something, Flo, but I'd better go and help first." And she went off to hand around sandwiches, cakes and cups of tea to the mourners. Sometimes she slopped the tea in the saucers, which didn't really matter because most people slurped their tea from them anyway.

The ladies fussed and strutted around Hern, and Kitty wouldn't have been in the least surprised if one of them hadn't pecked the crumbs from around his mouth as a hen will off a rooster. She thought he looked bored rather than bereaved and noticed him glance at his watch on more than one occasion.

Ruth was carrying Edward around with her, showing him off. Kitty was pleased about that, and hoped the praise she was receiving would encourage her to take a more active part in his care in the future.

"Oh, look at her," she heard Sarah say. "What a perfect little mother she'll make." Sarah's fogies tittered, and Kitty wondered if it was in polite response to Sarah's comment, or because they'd heard the rumors about Ruth. Kitty avoided her Grandma Underwood. She didn't know how she had the nerve to come to her mother's funeral when she had caused so much trouble in her marriage.

She felt someone touch her on the shoulder and saw it was Matthew Steer. "Sorry to startle you, Miss Kitty," he said, twisting his cap in his hand. "I just wanted to say how sorry I was to hear about your dear mother."

"Thank you kindly, Mr. Steer." Kitty suddenly felt guilty for not having remembered him to her mother as he had requested, and tears sprang to her eyes as she realized it was now forever too late.

"I saw you weren't well by the grave. It's awful stuffy in here, why don't you go outside a minute and I'll bring you a bite to eat and a nice cup of tea?"

Kitty gave in and went outside. She wasn't prone to fainting but it was shock, she supposed; the terrible cold shock of finality, knowing she would never see her mother again.

She was grateful that Matthew had sweetened the tea he handed her, and for a while as she sipped it, they stood companionably without speaking.

After a bit she asked, "Did you know my mother well, Mr. Steer?"

"Not really, I only met her a few times. I used to live at Blackthorn and in those days Mrs. Bennett used to dressmake. She and Mary made your mother's wedding dress, and I used to see her when she came over to try it on. After that, I used to see her about sometimes and we would always have a chat."

Kitty immediately thought of the Mary her mother had mentioned. "Which Mary are you talking about?" she asked.

"A workhouse girl that was at the Bennetts' for a while. A lovely maid, she was."

"Tell me Matthew, did she die?"

"Oh, goodness me no." Matthew looked upset at even the thought. "No, she went away though."

So, Kitty thought, it could hardly be *that* Mary who had come to help her mother pass over. "Where did she go?" she asked, out of curiosity.

"Down near Plymouth somewhere. I don't rightly know exactly where."

Kitty suddenly heard Ruth calling her. "Oh dear, I'm sorry, Mr. Steer, but I'd better go. It's probably the baby again."

Matthew knew Kitty's mother had left behind a child. It couldn't be easy for those girls, he thought. And for some reason it reminded him of Mary and how hard it must have been for her once her baby arrived.

"Well, I hope everything will turn out all right for you, Miss Kitty, and I hope we may talk again one day. Perhaps you would like to call me Matthew now you know me a bit better?"

She smiled at him. "Yes, I will do that. Thank you, Matthew."

She ran on in and found Ruth waiting for her. "What were you doing outside?" Ruth demanded, thrusting the baby at Kitty. "He needs changing."

Seeing that Sarah was watching them, without a word, Kitty took Edward to the back room.

This didn't go unnoticed by Flo, who looked thunderous. "You should have told Ruth to do it herself," she said. "She knows how."

"Grandma Underwood was watching," said Kitty. "I didn't want to make a fuss. You know how she favors Ruth."

"Well, come on in here with us and have a breather," Flo said. "Everybody's got what they want by now, and if they haven't they can help themselves."

No one seemed to notice Kitty slip away: they were all too busy getting settled in their chairs as one of the ladies, with a sheaf of papers in one hand and a glass of port in the other, looked about to give a eulogy. Hern was looking distinctly uncomfortable, but was wedged between two hefty women while others settled around him and adjusted their chins into their necks in anticipation.

"Pull that bolt over," Flo told Kitty as she entered the smaller room. "We need some quiet. Bleddy old gasbags. Here, Margery, hand me that again, will you." She took a small bottle from Margery. "Here, have a drop of this, Kitty, it'll make you feel better. You're as white as Acheson undressed."

Kitty tentatively poured a drop of brandy into her teacup and took a sip. It tasted awful, but after it had gone down, she had to admit it did have a pleasant warming effect.

"Have a drop more," said Flo. "It won't hurt you. Pulled many a woman around that has. I never lets on to Morrison though—he thinks childbirth's all in the course of nature, and he's so bleddy measly with his laudanum. I hope he comes back as a woman next time and then he'll know all about it."

Margery smiled at her niece. "I'm pleased to see you looking so well, dear. And how you've grown up since the last time I saw you. I expect you'd quite forgotten what I looked like, and of course I wish our meeting had been under different circumstances, but you know how things have been."

Kitty didn't know anything except her father and her aunt didn't get along very well, and consequently she hadn't seen much of Margery. Her aunt always remembered them at Christmas and birthdays though, and sent them the most unusual, almost luxurious, gifts. Kitty still cherished a pretty chemise, now too small and with the lace fraying, and remembered how special she had felt when those gifts arrived.

"I say, Flo," Margery said, breaking the silence. "This is awfully good stuff."

"Yes, well, this here is Acheson's best."

"What does he say about your stealing his brandy?" Margery said, amused.

"He doesn't know, but he wouldn't say anything if he did."

"He really is a good-tempered man. I always remember how good he was that time Enid and I came to fetch Felicity. He had endless patience with Enid and her portrait fever." Margery tinkled a laugh. "Do you remember how he put a notice on the door that said The House of Women? He must have been sick of the lot of us by the time we went."

Kitty had never heard Flo say anything about this, and she looked to her for further embellishment.

However, Flo didn't elaborate. "Yes, I remember," she said quietly. "Margery lives near the sea, don't you, Margery?"

Kitty would have liked to have heard more about The House of Women, and wondered about the portrait Margery had spoken of, but talking about the seaside was equally interesting. "I've never even *seen* the sea," she said longingly.

"Well, you'll have to come to Whitmouth one day, won't you?" Margery said.

Kitty was about to give an enthusiastic reply when there was a knock at the door and she got up and unbolted it. It was Ruth. Edward, in her arms, was crying lustily. She glared at Kitty. "Why was the door locked? I've been looking for you everywhere. The baby's been yelling his head off. He needs feeding and—"

Flo got up a little unsteadily from her chair. "Well?" she snapped, and Ruth blinked. "You're quite capable of doing it, young lady. You're just as responsible for Edward as your sister, you know. *She* isn't his mother. Come along with me and I'll show you how. *Again.*"

Ruth shot Kitty a wicked look as Flo led her from the room, and Kitty sighed inwardly, knowing how she would pay for that later with threats and accusations.

When Flo had gone Kitty said, "Who was it Enid painted a portrait of, Aunt Margery? Was it my mother?"

"Oh no, dear, it was a young girl called Mary Jay."

"Really? But… what was she doing at Flo's?"

"She used to live there."

Kitty was puzzled, wondering if it could possibly be the same girl of whom Matthew had spoken.

"That really was a very happy time we spent," Margery said, then took Kitty's attention with her as she began to talk about Whitmouth again.

ᘓᘐ

Kitty felt sad after Margery left. Her fine clothes and nice scent had given her a glimpse of another world and the sort of life she dreamed about having one day, although she had no idea how it would ever come about. "Aunt Margery said I might be able to go and stay with her one day," she said wistfully. "At the moment that seems impossible."

"Nothing's impossible," said Flo. "But there's a time and place for everything."

"Well, I can't imagine a time could ever come when *that* could happen. Not only could I not leave Edward, but if Father and Aunt Margery don't get along he'd never let me go anyway. By the way, why don't they get along?"

"They had a quarrel about something."

"What was it about?"

Flo felt she could hardly say, although she well remembered: Margery had grumbled at her brother for his attitude towards Kitty and they had quarreled about it. Leah, though not exactly taking Hern's part, had told Margery there were some things she didn't understand and that perhaps it wasn't her place to say anything. Margery had taken offense at that and had rarely gone to Furze afterwards.

Flo sighed. "It's all so long ago now. Some things are best left buried in the past."

"There's another thing," Kitty said. "Mr. Steer, well, he wants me to call him Matthew now, was very kind to me today when I felt faint. He said something about how he and a workhouse girl called Mary used to live at Blackthorn. And then Aunt Margery said there was a girl called Mary who stayed at your place. Were they the same one? But it couldn't be the one Mother—"

"Oh, for goodness sake," Flo snapped, more sharply than she intended. "You and your questions! Have a bit of respect for the day, will you, young lady? And another thing, you shouldn't go talking about things to strangers, you hardly know Matthew Steer."

"But I wasn't," Kitty said indignantly. She felt hurt and didn't understand why Flo should snap at her, or warn her against talking to Matthew; she had always thought he was the nicest sort of man. Besides, he was turning out to be interesting and would no doubt tell her more about the mysterious Mary Jay if she asked him.

Chapter 21

Flo extricates herself from Acheson's arms and rises like an apparition in her long, flowing nightgown. He tries to hold onto her, but such is Flo's profession that she's often out at night. And being the good man he is, with a sigh he lets her go.

The moon is full and high, but hides behind the sporadic clouds as if it's shy to come out. But Flo doesn't need the moon; she holds a lamp before her. It catches the eyes of a few sheep huddled in the corner of the field, and one or two of them get skittish and make to run away. "Daft things," Flo says, "I won't hurt you," and hurries by.

Now she's in the beech woods, dark and eerie. She can feel the pulse in her neck and she knows she isn't alone. The scent of bluebells saturates the air, for in the dream it's May and not January, when it really happens. She knows this, but in dreams, you have to take what comes.

Out of the copse at last and up onto the moor. She sees a horse. She looks to where the grave is, and someone's there. There's blood everywhere, and Acheson says, "I hope I never see such a sight again."

Flo awoke with a start. Her heart was pounding as if it couldn't keep up and she was soaked in sweat, with everything stuck to her. She managed to untangle herself from the sheets and got up to put on a dry nightgown.

Acheson stirred and said sleepily, "You all right, my dear?"

Flo whispered, "Yes," and he grunted and fell back to sleep.

But Flo, now in her dry nightgown and with a blanket around her, went to sit by the window. The same nightmare had plagued her for years, except that this time there was a difference, and she got goose bumps trying to recall who she had seen lying atop Mary's grave.

Of course, she knew what had brought it on. When Kitty had asked about Mary, she hadn't known what to say and she was sorry now she had snapped at the girl. It was only because she was confused. So much a part of her wanted to tell Kitty about Mary, and now Leah wasn't around that would be possible. But on the other hand, how did she suddenly up and tell her such a thing? It could shake the very foundation of Kitty's life.

Flo buried her head in her hands; why was it that as life went on, it became more complicated? Although she told Kitty later, yes, Mary had stayed with them for a short while then gone away, not only had she lied to Kitty, she'd been fooling herself. Mary had never gone away. Oh, at first she had thought it was tricks of the mind. A whisper here, a footfall there: the scent of bluebells out of season that occurred, not only in her dreams. But now, according to what Kitty said, Leah had quite possibly seen her, too.

She felt chilled and went back to bed to cuddle into Acheson for warmth. She should take her own advice, she thought. As she had told Kitty, there was a time for everything and when the time was right for her to know the truth, it would happen. In the meantime, she would just have to keep her mouth shut and her mind on other matters.

ᘓᘐ

Across at Furze, Kitty was also having difficulty sleeping, not because of ghosts from the past, but because she was thinking about her future.

She had been foolish enough to let Ruth know how much she wanted to get away from the farm, and now Ruth constantly taunted her with her own plans to do so. Kitty knew she would wheedle their father until she got her own way, if only to spite her. Now, not only was she eaten up with envy because of it, she was also resentful with everyone for taking it for granted she would take over from her mother. She felt her dreams had been cruelly dashed; she felt trapped, and like all creatures held against their will, she began to feel despair.

Beside her, Edward was restless and grizzly. Hern had been irritable with her because of the funeral taking up much of the day, and Ruth had loafed around and been next to useless when they got home and had to catch up on their chores.

"Shut up," she said, and turned over and ignored him.

Edward didn't take kindly to his sister's back and began to yell.

Kitty turned over and shook him. "I've just about had enough of you today," she cried. "Shut up. Oh please, shut *up*!" When he began to scream she took hold of him to shake him again, but the door suddenly opened and Hern stood there.

"What's this bleddy row?"

"I... I had a dream," Kitty said, sitting up, startled. "I think I must have rolled on him."

Hern gave her a long, hard look. "Well, see to him," he said, before closing the door.

Kitty, now horrified at her actions, picked up her brother and cuddled him to her. "I'm sorry. I'm so sorry," she whimpered remorsefully. "Oh, Edward, forgive me. I didn't mean to hurt you, but I feel so alone. So frightened."

She buried her face in him and sobbed. Edward, as if sensing her misery was greater than his own, quieted down, giving little shuddering breaths as if he too had been through a terrible ordeal.

When Kitty calmed down and gave it more thought, it occurred to her, sadly and rather regretfully, that life might not have been much different if her mother had lived. Probably much of Edward's care would have fallen to her anyway, and that wasn't his fault. He'd had no more say about coming into the world than she, and if she kept on resenting him she'd be no better than Hern, who had resented her for all her life.

Sobered and chastened by her reckoning, Kitty closed her eyes and eventually fell asleep with Edward in her arms.

The next morning Hern told Ruth that she must take a turn with Kitty in having the baby in her room, and although Ruth protested, he remained firm. Kitty ignored Ruth's jibes afterwards and when she was alone with her father, thanked him, saying she would be glad of the respite. He made no comment, but she was sure from the look on his face that he had only done it out of concern for his son.

ꕤ

At the end of January it snowed heavily, and February came in cold and wet and cheerless. Despite the doctor's recommendation and the Reverend Pugh taking the trouble to trudge to Furze to inquire politely when Edward might be christened, Hern stubbornly refused to set a date. The girls weren't surprised at his attitude. Their father had never shown much respect for religious matters and disliked the Reverend Pugh. But in any case the vicar didn't come again; Kitty suspected he had only tolerated Hern's rudeness in the past for their mother's sake.

It wasn't until April that Hern finally capitulated, and once the date was decided upon, the girls began preparations that included making a new gown—Edward was now too big to fit into the one each of them had worn at their own christenings. This was a great disappointment, because it was a beautiful gown fashioned out of the material their mother had used for her wedding gown. Not that they had ever actually *seen* the dress. Always, when they had asked to, Leah had replied that it was put away and she didn't want to disturb it.

When Hern next went off to market, Kitty and Ruth went upstairs and rummaged around to see if they could find any remnants of the material. At first, their search seemed futile, and Kitty gave up, saying she had too many chores to do, but that Ruth might keep on searching.

Some time later when Ruth hadn't appeared, Kitty returned upstairs to find her preening and parading in front of the mirror in a long, shimmering gown the color of clotted cream.

Kitty inspected the wrapping paper strewn around an open box. It was addressed to her mother, and postmarked Whitmouth. How strange, she thought. It was obviously her mother's wedding gown, but why had it been sent from there?

"I found it tucked away under the eaves," Ruth said. "There are lots of things there, including enough material to make a new gown for Edward."

"Well, thank goodness for that," Kitty said, dismissing her other thoughts because she simply didn't have time to think about them. "We'd better get on with it, there isn't much time."

"*You* can," Ruth said, making a face. "You know I'm no good at sewing."

"You could if you tried. You don't try hard enough, that's the trouble."

"Oh, shut up," said Ruth. "You sound like Emily Foss."

Kitty sighed. Inevitably, their conversation was taking a turn for the worst. Ruth was like a squirrel; she always had to make her teeth meet and wouldn't be happy until they ended up having a full-blown row.

But that afternoon Ruth was too taken up with the dress to pursue the matter. "It's lovely, isn't it," she said, as she twirled around in it. "So rich and royal looking. Look at the detail on it, and how it shimmers. I shall wear this when I get married."

"Do you think it darkened over time, or do you think it was always that color?"

Ruth sniggered. "Well, Mother could have hardly worn white, could she?"

Kitty crimsoned. It wasn't the first time Ruth had alluded to their mother having to be married, and, knowing she was the reason, she always felt guilty. Ruth made no further comment but reluctantly took off the dress and went downstairs, leaving Kitty to clean up after her.

Ruth had made quite a mess, Kitty thought crossly, as she began to tidy up. She knew she hadn't better leave the room like it, else their father would know they had been in there. He wouldn't understand about the new gown and doubted if he would even notice what Edward was wearing on the day.

"Oh, Ruth," she murmured as she looked down at the floor. Her sister had been at their mother's jewelry box again and broken a string of beads. They were all over the place, many of them caught in the crevices of the floor. Sighing, Kitty got down on her hands and knees and began to pick them up. A few were stuck in so deep she couldn't get them out, and she fiddled until she found she could lift up a whole piece of the floorboard.

As she did, she noticed there was a small book wedged in the space beneath. About to take a closer look, she heard the back door go and Martha calling her name. Kitty couldn't believe the time and knew it wouldn't be long before her father returned. Vowing she'd return another time to investigate further, she quickly replaced the floorboard and ran downstairs.

ꙮ

Margery arrived for the christening with a flourish of gifts and hugs. Hern scowled, but held his tongue, and everyone went off to the parish church to persevere with another of the Reverend Pugh's services.

Afterwards, a small of group of people returned to the farmhouse to have tea. Kitty was somewhat surprised, and rather put out, that her grandmother came too, as she could never recall her visiting Furze while her mother was alive; they had always been expected to traipse over to Lower Farm. Consequently, the atmosphere wasn't as good as it might have been. Margery and Sarah regarded each other frostily and didn't speak, and Kitty stayed mainly in the kitchen out of the way. She hoped her grandmother's visit was a one-off and not indicative of the future.

However, her fears were realized when Sarah began to visit them more frequently. She would turn up unexpectedly, and with her she would bring Parky Jones, who had taken over from his father when he retired. While Parky waited for Sarah he would loiter around the yard, leering at the girls if they were outside, which made Charlie scowl.

Parky was older than Kitty by a couple of years, but used to be a skinny little runt who picked his nose. She remembered once going to his birthday party at Lower where they had been giving one another pick-a-backs. She had dropped him on his backside when he peed down her back, and Sarah had sent her home without any birthday cake, in disgrace with a wet, stinking dress. Leah had plucked at the back of it and asked, why on earth a nice little boy like Parky would do a thing like that, suggesting that Kitty was at fault in some way.

Nice little boy? Kitty didn't think so. She could have told lots of things about him; how he had once exposed himself to her, and grinned wickedly. She had shuddered then as she shuddered every time she saw him. Although Ruth might make eyes at him, Kitty avoided him at all costs.

She also avoided Sarah as best she could; the woman was always putting her down in one way or another, comparing her to Ruth, who, Sarah reckoned, was the image of herself. Although Kitty noticed her father wasn't terribly pleased to have his mother there he did nothing to stand up for her, and she despised him for not having the guts.

Flo was beset with sympathy for Kitty, who poured out her woes to her after each visit. Flo knew very well what Sarah could be like, from what Leah had told her. The only comfort she could give Kitty was to tell her that nothing stayed the same, and that things would be better one day. In the back of her mind, she held Sarah's demise, although she couldn't say so.

Kitty heard what Flo said, but she was hardly comforted. Her despair increased when her father announced that Ruth would be going into service at the Coldswills, in Moretonhampstead. She knew she risked a beating, but she protested, saying *she* was the eldest and should go instead.

Hern didn't beat her, but he said firmly that she was the best one to take care of Edward and he would hear no more about it.

ꟾ

The summer sped by, and soon it was August. The evenings were drawing in and although the days were still hot, the nights were becoming cooler as the sun moved farther south.

Ruth helped out during the haymaking and then spent some time at Lower with her grandmother. At the end of August she was taken into Moretonhampstead to begin work. She was allowed one half-day off per week and that was when she generally came home. She began to give herself airs and graces, and told Kitty she was perfectly happy. However, Martha let slip that their sister admitted she wasn't happy at all and wished Kitty had gone instead. Ruth, Martha said, would rather be at Lower with her grandmother.

Kitty related this to Flo the next time she saw her. She was on her way to the village to see Emily Foss, and Flo was going to take care of Edward for a while.

Edward was gaining weight now and was a sturdy baby with large blue eyes and blond, curly hair. He chuckled prettily to Flo and blew bubbles as Flo took him from Kitty and muzzled her face into his middle.

"What a fine boy he's getting," she said. "You've given him a good start, Kitty maid, you should be proud of yourself."

Kitty was gratified to hear that, but she was more interested in talking about

Ruth. "Now she tells Martha that she doesn't like it at the Coldswills, after all. She wants to be over at Lower."

"Humph. Your father's going to need to keep an eye on her if I'm not mistaken."

"He could if he'd let *me* go to Moretonhampstead instead of her," Kitty whined.

"You aren't still on about that," Flo said wearily. "You wouldn't have liked it. The old man's nice enough, but his wife's a shrew. Looks like one, too. And your sister needs firm handling. Your grandmother would be far too soft with her."

"She always has been. She's never liked me; she's like Father. Anyone'd think I'd done them a personal injury." She looked at Flo from beneath her lashes. "Do *you* know why they don't like me?"

"You and your questions, they're enough to drive a person insane," Flo said, stomping off to the best room.

"Well, there are just so many things I don't understand," cried Kitty, running after her. "I *am* the eldest, though you'd never think so the way they treat me."

"Everything comes to they that wait. You *must* have patience and faith."

"Patience? Faith!" Kitty cried disparagingly. "Why should I have faith when I've been abandoned by God?"

"Don't talk such rot," Flo said, getting riled. Despite her own differences with God, she always tried to encourage Kitty to keep faith. "It's always the other way around, only you don't know it yet. It's no good getting in a pout because you can't have your own way over something. He knows best and when the time is right, it'll happen. Now, we'll leave Edward in here where it's cooler, and hopefully he'll sleep."

Kitty didn't care if Edward slept or not; her feathers were ruffled and she glared at Flo defiantly. *Flo* might believe God might know what He was doing, but she was beginning to wonder if He even existed. She was about to say so too, but Acheson came in, and she bit her tongue. Although she and Flo might talk about God as if He was an eccentric uncle, Acheson was far more devout and would have scolded her for even thinking such a thing.

"Hello, Kitty," Acheson said. "What are you doing here?"

"I'm going to fetch books," Kitty said. "Emily lends them to me and Charlie."

Acheson nodded. "Ah yes, Charlie was telling me."

"Too much reading can go to your head sometimes," Flo muttered.

Acheson frowned. "There's nothing wrong with being educated, Flo. And when everyone is, and not just the chosen few, then you'll see some changes."

He went sullen after that, and although Kitty tried to change the subject, he wouldn't respond. He quickly drank the tea Flo made, and went out.

Flo looked upset, almost close to tears. Kitty felt remorseful now for her former temper, and also wished she had never mentioned anything about the books. She couldn't bear it if Flo and Acheson began not to get along, and she apologized.

"Aw, don't take on so, Kitty. It isn't your fault," Flo said. "He likes me to agree with him over everything, that's all, and this is one thing I can't."

"But I thought you believed in people being educated," Kitty said.

"'Course I do," said Flo quickly. "It isn't that."

"Then what is it? Something to do with Charlie?"

Flo denied it, but Kitty didn't believe her. It must be something Charlie was reading, she thought, and the next time she saw him she would ask him what it was all about.

ꕥ

There had been some gossip in the village when Emily Foss first arrived from Scotland, as with her startling red hair and generous figure, the gossipmongers declared she looked more like a woman who might take to the stage than teach in school. However, under Miss Wood's tutelage the hair was curtailed to a bun and the bosom restrained by unflattering neck-high dresses. If there had been any scandal attached to her sudden arrival it was soon quelled by her exemplary daily conduct, and any remaining doubt won over by her soft, charming accent.

Kitty and Emily had always got along well and Emily welcomed her that day with a warm hug. She asked her in and made tea, and asked her how her dear father was coping.

Kitty blanched at the 'dear' but said Hern was coping very well. She felt like adding she didn't see that her mother's death had made any difference to his life; the home ran smoothly, his meals were always on the table; he still went to the inn regularly. In truth, she hardly thought he missed her mother at all. Indeed, thinking about it made her feel so resentful she said, "I think it's we who notice it the most. And then there's the extra work and everything. Oh, Emily. I *did* so want to get away."

"Yes, of course. I understand, my dear. Losing your mother must have been bad enough, but to have to postpone your dream as well, that's really difficult."

"Postpone?" Kitty said dully. "More likely forget it, you mean."

"Och, Kitty, I know the situation must seem hopeless at the moment, but I'm sure this hard work you are doing and the caring you are giving to others will add up to a great deal. Effort you put in is always returned to you, one way or another. Remember, nothing stays the same. Life is like the tides—it ebbs and flows, and if you keep doing what is before you for now, what is meant for you will eventually find you. You just have to be patient."

"I'm not very good at being patient," Kitty said, making a face.

"I know how hard it is," Emily agreed. "However, it's sometimes necessary. Now, come along into the library and we'll see what we can find for you this time."

While Emily looked through the shelves, Kitty said, "Might I ask you, Emily, do you see anything wrong with the books that Charlie borrows?"

"Wrong? In what way do you mean?"

"I don't know. I just wondered." Kitty gave an embarrassed laugh. "I don't even know what he reads really. I mean, I've looked through them, but they seem so stuffy and boring. But... could anyone get upset about them?"

"I don't see why," Emily said. "Charlie is interested in social reform. And we all ought to take an interest in that, knowing the changes that are on the way."

Kitty felt a sudden stab of fear. Emily had spoken to her before of the troubles going on around the country: the riots, the hayricks being burned, the smashing of machinery to draw attention to the farm laborer's lot. She had also told her how the people who did these things were being made an example of. Charlie had once been called an instigator, and Kitty was just about to mention that fact in confidence, when Emily said, "I'm sure there isn't anything sinister in Charlie's interest, Kitty. He's probably just an intelligent young man who likes to keep abreast of the times."

But Kitty wasn't so sure, and she decided she would talk to him about it.

On the way home, she paused in the churchyard to put fresh flowers on her mother's grave, then collected Edward from Flo. Martha had gone with Hern to market so she still had time to deliver Charlie's books.

As she approached Barn Cottage, her heart fell. From it wafted the most delicious smell; one she knew well, and one that made her heart freeze over. "Oh, Charlie," she murmured as he opened the door to her, "what have you got in your pot again?"

"It ran into my trap," Charlie said, grinning at her. "They all do."

Kitty knew his traps were set on manor, not Furze, property, but she was resigned to not saying how dangerous it was to poach the squire's rabbits. She hated getting onto the subject of the squire at all, because Charlie tended to get carried away. Rather than provoke him she turned her attention to the wooden chest he'd made. "Oh, that's nice," she said, running her hands over the polished surface. "You've made a lovely job of it, Charlie."

"I've made a bed, too."

Kitty could feel him studying her, and her cheeks burned. She didn't make any reply, but took the books out of her basket and set them on the table. "I was over at Forde earlier," she began casually. "When I mentioned I was going to fetch these, Flo got upset. She said that reading could go to your head and Acheson got cross with her."

She looked at him curiously. He'd picked up a book and was flicking through it.

"What do you think she could have meant? Why did she get upset?"

He gave her a steady look. "If I tell you something, Kit, you must promise never to tell."

Her heart stepped up a beat. "You know I won't."

"You know how things are around here on the estate and the way the squire runs the parish," he said quietly, but enthusiastically. "Well, it's the working man's *time,* Kit. Time to do something about it."

"But what has it to do with you?" she asked, perplexed. She looked around the cottage. "You've got a nice place to live, plenty of food. I don't even understand why you have to steal his rabbits."

"That's just the point."

"What, stealing his rabbits?"

"*His* rabbits? *No!* Your mindset. And others like you, believing everything you've been told and questioning nothing. Going on in the same old way until you've sunk so low you'll have nothing left at all."

"You're wrong," she cried. "Emily says there are huge changes coming, and women will be able to have independence—"

"But how do you think these changes will come to pass? Out of the kindness of upper crust hearts? It's people like us who will have to *make* them happen."

Kitty was trying to piece it all together. It was all very well Charlie telling her this, but what was his involvement? Why was Flo so worried? And then she remembered how Acheson always stuck up for Charlie. "Does Acheson feel like this?"

"Yes. And as we can both read and write, it's obvious others who can't will look to us for leadership."

"Leadership?" Kitty whispered, aghast. "But... Charlie, what do you plan to do?"

"Nothing," he said, avoiding her eyes. "You asked me why Flo was upset and I've told you."

"You've hardly told me anything at all, except a few things that will set me worrying day and night. And if Father knew you were getting involved with anything like this, he would—"

He turned on her angrily. "You mustn't mention a word to your father, nor to anyone else for that matter. We aren't doing anything, just talking. And perhaps in time there'll be a meeting or two to see how much support there is. But as far as you are concerned, you know *nothing* about it. Do you understand? And you must forget we ever had this conversation."

"But how *can* I forget it now? You know what's happening to those other people who have been doing this sort of thing—"

He put his hands on her shoulders. "Look, it won't come to that. Promise me you'll forget all about it. It'll be all right."

Kitty, already shocked from his disclosure was dismayed even further. He still had his hands on her and was looking at her in a very different way from just seconds ago. This wasn't the way in which she wanted things to go. Oh no, not at all. He might like her, and she liked him too, but she had meant what she said to Acheson; she really didn't want a man like Charlie. There was just something about him, an intensity that frightened her. Not that he would ever hurt her; she knew that, she just didn't like this... brooding resentment he had. And she certainly didn't want him to be holding her like this.

Gently, she extricated herself. "Father will be home soon," she said quietly. "He'll kill me if he finds me down here, so I'd better go."

She picked up her basket and, without looking at him again, went out and closed the door.

Chapter 22

Emily Foss stood at the window of Miss Wood's house looking out over the village green. She had a smile on her face as she watched the children playing in the late summer evening. They were young and carefree, just as she had once been. And she was reminded of how the years were flying by, her life pouring down the drain of time along with them.

She heard footsteps behind her, and heard Gardenia's tongue cluck with disapproval. "I saw the eldest Underwood girl was here again."

Emily gritted her teeth, preparing herself for the inevitable jibe. "Yes," she said, as lightly as she could. "She comes for books."

"A lot of good that'll do her now. From what I hear I should think she's got more than enough work cut out for her. And what on earth are you staring at, Emily? Put the curtain back at once—I don't know what people will think."

Emily sighed. There was no peace in this household. No time to stand and stare. "I was merely watching the children," she said tiredly. "They will hardly care."

"Fiddlesticks." Gardenia's face puckered, creating an expression that reminded Emily of Ruth Underwood's famous lyrics. "It doesn't do to stand around in idle thought. You know what the Devil does with such minds. And look at the time."

Emily sighed again. Ah yes. Time. Time for this, time for that, time for hot chocolate, day in, day out, month on end, winter or summer, year after year. "Yes of course," she said dutifully, and went into the kitchen.

This ritual had gone on for seven years now. Seven dreadfully long and boring years of a life, where everything had its place, where there was no spontaneity and if there was, one word or gesture could be mistaken, repeated and embellished upon. Gardenia's lips might appear to be as buttoned up as those stays of hers, but in truth she was a fearful gossip. Emily loathed gossip and whenever one of Gardenia's fogies arrived, in particular Sarah Underwood, she would always make some excuse to be elsewhere. It was of course a rendition of herself to their vicious tongues; she knew full well that no one was exempt from their repertoire.

When first coming to Gardenia's abode, she had overlooked a lot more than she could now. Of course, she had been much younger and still hopeful that living there was merely a stepping-stone and that someone would rescue her. There had been one or two, but—

"Emily?" Gardenia's voice rang from the front room.

"Coming," Emily called.

"But you've only brought one cup," Gardenia said, as Emily walked in.

"I'm not having any," said Emily. "I don't feel like it. I'm going out for a while."

"Going out? Where on earth are you going at this hour? Who will read to me?"

"I'm going for a walk," Emily said quietly, but firmly. "It is far too nice an evening to stay in. And I don't feel like reading." And she left the room before Gardenia's astonishment could turn into a torrent of abuse. Although she heard her name called, she ignored it, threw a shawl around her shoulders, and ran out of the house and down the road, past the few children who remained on the green.

At the top of the hill, she paused to catch her breath. Her heart was pounding, not only from running, but also from her daring. Laughter bubbled from her lips and she listened to it returning faintly on the echo, thinking how strange it was to hear herself laugh; these days she so seldom did.

She had laughed a lot, once, long ago when she lived in Scotland. The staff had told her she was like a ray of sunshine when she first went to the castle at the age of twelve. She was skinny then, undeveloped, so she didn't see the laird looking at her until much later. She felt it an honor to be desired by him, even though she knew how precarious her position would be. So while he was still in the heat of the chase she bargained with him; in return for herself, he must teach her to read and write.

He had been honorable in that and taught her well. She blessed her foresight afterwards when she became pregnant with his child. Although he was quite willing to have her stay and bestow on his child some recognition, his wife had other ideas. That cruel and barbaric woman, herself barren, intended to deny her husband any sort of heir and insisted he get rid of Emily.

Emily's mother had called her a slut and beaten her, because the end of her employment at the castle meant no more treats and favors for the family. After her mother finished with her, it was her stepfather's turn. Emily knew that part of his anger was his jealousy because her child wasn't his own.

Emily lost her baby girl. As she watched the small coffin go into the ground, she felt a part of herself go with it. She had been told she would never bear another child, and for months her spirits dwindled. Despised by her mother and continually abused by her detestable stepfather, she eventually ran away to England, and her journey brought her to Devon. She thought it a miracle when she heard that Gardenia Wood was setting up a dame school in North Bovey and needed another teacher.

Shrewdly, Gardenia had guessed Emily was desperate to accept any position and offered her a trial period. Afterwards, Emily discovered that three other young ladies had been given this *trial*: Gardenia didn't only want a teacher to help her, but also a maidservant to wait on her hand and foot.

Emily bit back her resentment as she walked down across the meadow to the brook. She sat for awhile on the bank, closing her eyes and allowing the chuckling water to soothe her. She only wished she could flow away as easily and live a different life. But the chance of finding a husband at her age wasn't very good. Not only was she aging, but also she was unable to have a child, and she would never pretend to someone that she could.

When the sun finally set, Emily began to walk home. She went slowly, dreading her return because she knew what sort of atmosphere would await her: Gardenia's tongue was vicious, and she would pay dearly for her show of rebellion.

As she passed through the churchyard, she paused at Leah Underwood's grave. There were fresh flowers on it, and she supposed Kitty must have placed them there that afternoon.

She was regretful that her last encounter with Kitty's mother hadn't been a very pleasant one. Leah had asked her to stop putting fancy ideas into Kitty's head because she said she would need her at home when the baby came. When Emily pointed out that Kitty was extremely gifted and that it was a shame to keep her back, Leah reacted strongly and threatened to complain to Miss Wood if she persisted with her foolish ideas. At that point, Emily backed down. She realized that no amount of persuasion would ever change Leah's mind; that because of her own circumstances, she must begrudge the freedom that further education could bestow on her eldest daughter.

She had heard plenty of rumors to the effect that the Underwoods' marriage left much to be desired. Emily had even heard Sarah say that it had been doomed from the start, although she hadn't said why. Gardenia had surmised afterwards it was because Leah was far too good for the man; why, hadn't he been seen in the company of Betsy Berry's wayward sister? And didn't *that* prove the old adage that muck clung together?

Although Emily didn't hold with infidelity she had always thought Leah to be a rather cold and heartless woman, and she couldn't find it in her heart to blame Hern for seeking comfort elsewhere. God knows, she knew only too well what it was like to be sexually frustrated. It was one of the things that ate away at a person; diminished the stuff of them until they turned into one of the living dead, which is what she would become if things didn't change. That is why, perhaps, she felt so poignantly for Kitty. She quite understood the girl's frustration of not being able to get on with her own life because she was caught up in the web of others'.

The thought suddenly occurred to Emily that she could give Kitty private lessons to keep up her skills. Although the girl might be trapped at the moment, things could always change. In doing this, she would help Kitty stay prepared. Goodness knows why that hadn't occurred to her before, Emily thought, as, now inspired, she quickened her pace. Why, she could have mentioned it to Kitty that afternoon; that might have put more bounce in her step.

Then Emily had second thoughts and decided perhaps it was as well she hadn't. She sensed some incompatibility between Kitty and her father, so perhaps she should be the one to suggest it to Hern. Even then, indirectly, because Leah had once hinted that her husband, being uneducated, thought it a waste of time for others of their station to be. She didn't want to cause trouble for Kitty.

With this in mind, despite Gardenia's wrath, Emily began to walk out and about more often. And those walks sometimes took her on the right-of-way through Furze Farm.

ဢဢ

By the time Edward was toddling, everyone was relieved to find he seemed to be developing into a healthy enough child, except he spoke little and depended upon his sisters, who doted on him, to know what he wanted by his grunts. And because he was fairly adored, he liked to have his own way and showed a fierce display of temper when he didn't get it.

One afternoon, when they had all been out in the fields, he screamed when Kitty picked him up to bring him in.

Hern shouted across to her to leave him there. "When he has to walk home himself he won't do it again," he said, having had enough of the unruly toddler for one day.

"But what if anything happens to him?" Kitty said. "I can't just leave him."

"Nothing will happen to him. Do as I say, else you'll feel my hand yourself."

When they got indoors Hern went down to the best room, where Kitty knew he would probably have a whiskey, as was becoming his habit, and she hovered at the kitchen window trying to keep an eye on Edward while she prepared supper. He was still scaring the birds away with his screaming.

"Whatever's wrong with Edward?" Martha said, coming in with a pan of berries.

"He's having a paddy and Father's had enough," Kitty said. "He says he has to stay and find his own way in from the field."

Martha's eyes filled with tears. "But he'll get lost. That's really mean of him."

Kitty agreed. Her father's moods were blacker than usual these days and she wondered if it was anything to do with the gossip she'd heard about Nancy leaving the inn after having a row with her sister.

"Listen." Edward had stopped screaming, but although Kitty stood on tiptoe to look through the window, she couldn't see him. "Perhaps he's down by the barn. Martha, quickly, run out and have a look, will you?"

Wide-eyed, Martha ran outside, but not long after rushed back inside. "He's not there," she cried. "I can't see him anywhere."

"Well, he can't have gone far on those little legs of his," Kitty said, wiping her hands and running outside.

Edward, meanwhile, was having a grand adventure. Since his family had deserted him, he decided to visit Flo. He crawled under the gate out into the lane, but once there, he lost sight of both farms and began to whimper with fear because now he didn't know where he was.

Emily was on one of her walks and she saw the small shape in the lane as she turned the corner. As she got nearer she recognized it to be Edward. "Edward," she cried. "What on earth are you doing here alone?"

He turned his small, tearful face towards her. "Uh?" he said, and held up both arms.

"Your sisters will be worried sick about you, you naughty boy," Emily scolded as she picked him up. "Don't you ever roam off like that again, do you hear me?"

By then, Kitty had got everyone into a state. Even Hern looked sheepish, and when he saw Emily struggling down the lane with his heavy son he hurried towards her and took the boy out of her arms.

Standing so close to her, Hern noticed how blue Emily's eyes were, and how golden-red her hair. And because he had taken so little interest in his girls' education, it only vaguely registered that this was one of the schoolteachers he had so often cursed.

"Och, but you must have been worried sick, you poor man," Emily said. "The naughty little monkey."

Hern was enchanted by the lilt of Emily's soft Scottish accent. He caught a whiff of her lavender scent and his nose twitched. He opened his mouth to speak, but didn't know what to say, and he shut it again.

Emily turned to go, but Edward began to yell and held out his chubby, grubby hands to her. "Uh," he cried. "*Uh.*"

Hern was flummoxed. "Be quiet, boy," he said, shaking him slightly.

"Perhaps… if I walked with you to the door?" Emily held Edward's hand as they walked towards the farmhouse.

"You could have a cup of tea," Hern suggested, standing at the back door.

"Och, I wouldn't want to intrude," Emily said. But when she turned to go, Edward screamed again, and Hern, who could take no more from his son, said quite desperately, "Please, Missus, er... um... won't you come in?"

"Miss. Miss Emily Foss." Emily gave him a quick smile. "Thank you, Mr. Underwood, it would be a pleasure."

Anything Hern might have previously thought of Emily slipped from his mind as he showed her inside. He handed Edward over to Kitty and asked her to make them a cup of tea, then he ushered Emily down the passageway to the best room.

Kitty's mouth gaped as she looked after them. To coin her Aunt Margery's phrase at Leah's wedding all those years ago, someone could have knocked her down with a feather.

ഌ

The next day Kitty couldn't wait to run up to Forde to tell Flo what had happened. "He actually invited her to come again," she said excitedly. "And Emily said she would be delighted. And afterwards Father looked funny. Oh, Flo, it's like it says in the Bible—"

"Oh, you're back on God again, that's a relief. Which bit's that then?"

"About His mysterious ways."

"I'm blowed if you don't sound like the Reverend Pugh," Flo said. "You been listening to his sermons at last?"

Kitty laughed and helped herself to another piece of cake. "He was always so dead set against anything to do with school, Father I mean. He even once said that Emily must not be all there." She giggled. "Not that I'll ever remind him of *that.* Now he's agreed that she can give Martha extra help with her lessons because Emily says she's falling behind out of grief for Mother. And she's going to tutor me, too."

"Well, it's nice to see you looking happier for a change. And this is what Emily will do on Saturdays then?"

Kitty nodded. "And in the evenings, if she can come. And we can give her eggs and things in payment, of course."

"'Course," said Flo, smiling.

Kitty's face took on a conspiratorial look. "You know what Charlie said?"

"What's that then?"

"*He* thinks she's out to get him. Father, I mean."

"My word," said Flo. "Whatever would give him that idea, I wonder?"

Kitty shrugged and laughed gaily. "I don't care if she is. He's like a different person when she's around. He even whistles."

"Mysterious indeed."

"Mind you, I don't know what she sees in him. She seems *far* too refined."

"You can never judge a book by its cover," said Flo. "But, my dear, it is good news, I must say. And I'm very glad to hear it."

Emily didn't miss going to Furze on any occasion she could during the following weeks, and the atmosphere at the farmhouse felt lighter because of her presence. Martha gained weight and was happy again. Edward was doing well and loved Emily, but most of all, Kitty could see the change in her father. He often had a smile on his face, and he didn't curse as much.

All of a sudden, Kitty thought things were falling into place and she no longer resented her responsibilities. For the while, her dream to get away took a back seat and she was quite happy to leave it there.

ꕥ

The autumn flew by and in no time at all Christmas was upon them. A time of mixed emotions, what with it being Edward's birthday, and the anniversary of Leah's death. Somehow, Emily's vibrant spirit among them helped to ease the memory. Hern agreed they could put up a few decorations, and for the first time in Kitty's life, he helped them.

Christmas Day broke clear and bright but there was a watery look to the sky and red streaks on the horizon that signaled a change in the weather. Just after Emily arrived, clouds rolled in and it began to drizzle with rain. However, this didn't detract from their enjoyment, and the farmhouse witnessed more fun and laughter within its walls for as far back as Kitty could remember.

It was mid-afternoon and raining hard when they heard the dog barking. Hern frowned and looked out of the window: his mother had arrived and he didn't look too pleased about it.

"I thought you were over with Harriet and Ronald for the day, Mother," he said to Sarah, taking her cloak and shaking the water from it.

Sarah glanced at Emily, who had risen from her chair. "I did do the rounds with

Harriet and Ronald earlier," she said. "But I was so near I thought I would call in to see you."

"Would you like a cup of tea, Grandma?" Ruth asked, looking expectantly at Kitty.

Kitty was only too pleased to have an excuse to leave the room: she thought the look on her grandmother's face didn't bode well for any of them.

She had intuited correctly. Before long, Sarah's conversation deteriorated to its usual level. She began making barbarous comments about this person, that person; and more than one or two were aimed, not so subtly, in Emily's direction. Kitty could feel the atmosphere deteriorating quickly, so she offered more tea. She hoped her relief wasn't too obvious when Sarah nodded her acceptance as if she were royalty.

Unfortunately a fresh pot of tea did nothing to change Sarah's tack. It soon became clear why she was there.

"I must say, Miss Foss, Gardenia was very disappointed to think you would leave her alone on Christmas day," she said when she ran out of other victims.

Emily knew how vicious Sarah could be, and hadn't missed the malicious gleam in her eye when she arrived. To begin with, not wanting to create a scene, she had been able to control her temper and ignore the jibes. Now she was fast tiring of this woman, who had little sensitivity and who seemed to take pleasure in causing trouble wherever she went.

She suspected that Gardenia had put Sarah up to firing one of her arrows. So, against her better judgment, she decided to fire one back. "Och, Mrs. Underwood, I have spent seven long Christmases with Miss Wood. This year I decided I would enjoy myself for a change."

Sarah put down her cup and saucer. "That isn't very gracious of you, Miss Foss." Her eyes flickered to Hern. "I mean, not everyone would have taken you on knowing of your dubious background."

Emily realized then what a terrible mistake she had made. Once, and how she regretted it now, in a moment of weakness she had revealed her past to Gardenia. It happened after Gardenia had compared Emily's spinsterhood to her own, and foolish pride and indignation caused Emily to speak carelessly. When she told Gardenia how she had been the laird's mistress and borne him a child that she lost, there had not been one iota of sympathy or compassion in that woman's face; just a flicker of interest in those small, mean eyes that told Emily the information would be stored away and wouldn't be forgotten.

"Gardenia has no right to talk about me behind my back," Emily said now. "Whatever we may have discussed about my past is no one else's business."

Sarah was gratified to see her jibe had struck home. Not only that, she now had Hern's full attention. "Oh, but from what I understand, it could *become* my business. God alone knows what I suffered through Hern's first marriage," she said. "It never entered his head in that instance to look into Leah Peardon's background to see what *she* was. I wouldn't want him to make another dreadful mistake."

Sarah was like a pod that had burst its seeds, and everybody sat still while the words germinated.

Emily stirred first, looking at Hern, hoping for support. She had planned to tell him about her past when the opportunity arose, and now regretted her delay in doing so. But surely, *surely*, he could see what his mother was trying to do? And surely he wouldn't stand there and allow her to insult his dead wife?

She gave him ample time to speak, but when he remained silent her own disappointment and frustration exploded.

"I can assure you, Mrs. Underwood," she said tersely, "you have absolutely no cause to worry. No matter what you consider Hern's late wife to have been, I pity that poor woman for having had you as a mother-in-law. No woman in her right mind would want to take her place." Twitching her skirts angrily, and with as much dignity as she could muster, Emily excused herself from the table.

Martha cried, "Emily!" and, ignoring Sarah's orders to stay put, ran after her. But Emily sent her back to her father.

With tears running down her cheeks Martha clung to him, crying, "Stop her, Father, *stop* her!"

Edward began to cry and also ran after Emily, and Kitty had to retrieve him, screaming and kicking all the way. She wished she had enough courage to shout at her grandmother, that her mother, no matter what she had *been*, was correct in saying she was an evil old witch, and that she hated her for spoiling their Christmas and driving Emily away.

Only Ruth showed no emotion as she picked up the teapot to pour her grandmother another cup of tea.

Hern pushed Martha gently away from him. "Leave the tea alone, Ruth," he said gruffly. "All of you leave."

They all looked at him in surprise, including Sarah. Ruth knew when her father meant it, and she went outside. Kitty herded the weeping Martha and the still screaming Edward upstairs.

ഇഗ

Hern had an ache in his chest that he thought must be indigestion, but wasn't sure. During the last few months, he had come to know a woman who wasn't like his mother, or his dead wife. She was good with the children, lent a willing hand around the place, and furthermore, she had never repulsed any hints he'd dropped that they might become more than friends.

"No good looking at me like that," Sarah muttered, brushing imaginary crumbs off her chest. "*Everyone* is talking about you. The last thing you want is a woman like that, or any woman at all, for that matter. I should have thought you'd have learned by now. If you don't believe me, why don't you ask her what happened in Scotland?"

"Shut up!" Hern cried. "I don't want to know about it."

He had for years bitten his tongue while he had been forced to listen to his vicious harridan of a mother lash anybody and everybody with hers. She had twisted his gut with her cunning and malicious ways, made all their lives a misery; now, coming between him and Emily, she had simply gone too far. Even if what she said had some truth to it, he had never forgotten those things Colan told him, and the day he'd been storing them up for, had come.

"I don't know how you've got the neck to say anything to anyone after what you did to Joshua," he said now. "You're as much of a bleddy slut as Leah Peardon ever was. Probably even worse." He saw a flicker in Sarah's eyes; a certain way she set her jaw when she was unsure of her next move. "I know why Joshua made that arrangement with Peardon," he continued bitterly. "But the farthing's worth of revenge he had on you was nothing to the miserable bleddy existence I had for years. And now, just when things begin to look up for me, you put your bleddy spoke in again. You've never thought of anyone but yourself, only I've never had the guts to say so before now."

Sarah pursed her lips and stood up. "So, that's the way the land lies, is it?" She went into the scullery to fetch her cloak. By the time she came out, she had recouped some composure.

"You're right in one thing," she said, curling her lip, "you don't have guts, boy. And my one consolation is, you'll never have enough guts to go after *her*."

Hern watched her leave then, as she left, he exploded with rage. "Damn you," he cried, running to the door and kicking it. "God damn your bleddy soul!"

Chapter 23

"Is that you, Emily?" Gardenia's voice rang out from the drawing room.

Emily gave a shudder as she shook out her umbrella. She was soaked, absolutely soaked. In her hurry to leave Furze she hadn't changed back into her other skirt or boots, and now she had ruined a good pair of shoes and likely her skirt, too.

She went into the kitchen and saw the glasses from the morning's drinks were still on the side, unwashed. No doubt, it was expected she would do them. Bristling with indignation, she felt like smashing them all to the floor, and she reached into the cupboard, took out a bottle of port and poured herself a good measure.

"Emily," Gardenia said from the doorway. "You're back."

Emily ignored her. She tipped back her head and drank a whole glass of port.

Gardenia frowned. "What *are* you doing? You'll become tipsy... or perhaps you are already."

"Well, it's Christmas, isn't it?" Emily said. "Although from the scene I've just left you would never have guessed it. Your friend Sarah Underwood visited Furze while I was there." Gardenia's color rose a notch as Emily glared at her. "Ah yes, I'm sure you can imagine what happened. I knew it was a mistake to confide in you about my past, Gardenia. But I did it before I knew how malicious you could be. However, if you recall, you promised you would never tell a soul. And of all people, you told her. Why, in heaven's name, did you do it?"

"I did it for you," Gardenia said stoutly.

"For me. And how did you think it would help me?"

"I've seen what's been going on. And I think you would end up being dreadfully unhappy."

Emily laughed. "I see. And that would be a pity, wouldn't it, to spoil my deliriously happy life?"

"Don't be facetious, Emily, Sarah's son is an awful man. He's an uncouth oaf. I didn't want to lose you to that."

"I'm sure you don't want to lose me," Emily said. "Who would want to lose a slave? But Gardenia, *I'm not yours to lose!*" She banged her hand on the counter and a glass jumped off and smashed to the floor. "It's up to *me* to decide what I do with my own life."

"And make a mess of it, like the last time you were involved with a man?"

"I know very well you've interfered before," cried Emily. "There was Joseph Smith, and Leonard Pike. I wonder what little evils you whispered in *their* ears to make them go away."

"I've only been trying to protect you from your own nature, Emily. Women like you—"

"Women like *me*? Women with real blood in their veins instead of ice, you mean? Women who want a *real life*?"

Gardenia's face became ugly. "I was trying to be tactful, but you're nothing but a slut, Emily Foss. I thought that the first time you poured out your pathetic story to me. I don't care *who* the father of your misbegotten child was. It was a mercy it died, if you ask me."

"You wicked, vicious old woman," Emily cried. "May God forgive you for saying that; I never will." And she smashed her glass on the floor to join the other, and went upstairs to pack.

Pulling things out of drawers and taking her few clothes out of the wardrobe Emily was thankful she had been prudent enough to save most of her meager earnings and only spent a little on books: at least she would have something to sustain her for a while.

Gardenia was nowhere to be seen when she went downstairs, but all the same, she called out that someone would collect her books later. Then she let herself out of the front door.

She stood for a moment, looking back towards the house. Her explosive anger had given away to a kind of numbness now. What a Christmas, she thought. Out of a home, with no prospects of a job. Still, she mustn't panic. She had been in far worse places and survived, and she knew from experience the way to do anything was to take a step at a time. Now, the first thing she must do was to find a room for the night.

ꙮ

Tom and Betsy had entertained their family for most of Christmas day and looked forward to a quiet evening, as there were no guests staying at the inn. Tom frowned when he heard someone banging on the door and was prepared to do battle if necessary in order to have Christmas night alone with his wife. He got the surprise of his life when he found the young schoolmistress standing there.

"Well, I never!" he said. "Whatever's happened to bring you here of all places, my dear?" He helped a rather shaken Emily in and shouted for his wife, who came running to see who it was.

Emily began to bever and couldn't speak for a moment until Betsy led her to the fire and gave her a bracing drink. When she felt better she explained that she and Miss Wood had quarreled, and asked, as there was no chance she could return there, could they put her up for the night?

"Well, did you ever, Tom?" Betsy said. She had never liked Miss Wood, believing her to be pompous and affected. To tell the truth, she didn't like educators in general because they reminded her of her own inadequacies. Still, Miss Foss was different somehow, and she had a way with children. Betsy knew that from what her own daughter told her.

"I'll only need to stay for a night or so. I will look for something else."

"I'll get you another drink," said Betsy, frowning as she touched Emily's forehead. "Tom, bring a blanket, Emily's steeved through with the cold."

During that first night, the dreadful reality of what had happened sent Emily into a state of panic. If it hadn't been for Betsy, saying that she knew more about the minds of the people of North Bovey than God, and reassuring her she would have a lot of sympathy and support, she might have gone crawling back, begging Gardenia to reinstate her.

As it happened, she couldn't go anywhere because she fell ill and it took until the end of January for her to recover. Then, because Betsy took a real liking to her, they came to an amicable arrangement. Emily began working in the kitchen in return for her board and lodging, and a little more besides. As Betsy told her, "If I could pay my good-for-nothing sister, I'm darned sure I can pay you."

ജ്ഞ

The events on Christmas Day were not spoken of openly, nor was Emily's name mentioned at Furze. Hern became bad-tempered, banging doors and cursing. Kitty felt that this was one of the bleakest times of her life. Despite Martha praying constantly that Emily would return to their lives, she didn't see how it could happen.

The weather didn't help matters. Snow began the day after Boxing Day and the temperatures plummeted. The only room they could keep warm was the kitchen and Hern slept beside the fire for a few nights to keep it going. Kitty shared her bed with Martha and Edward, and, between them, they managed to keep warm. That was the best of the arrangement; Martha would often awake crying during the night, and Kitty knew it was because she missed Emily.

During January, Hern hardly left the farm owing to the bad weather. Although he could have gone to the Blackbird if he had wanted to, hearing Emily was there served as a double deterrent. Not only was he embarrassed for what had happened on Christmas Day and for not standing up for her at the time, but also his mother's reference to Emily's past irked him, and he needed time to think about what the insinuations might mean. Once bitten, twice shy.

Towards the middle of February, Mr. Coldswill sent word to Furze, and despite the threat of another snowstorm, Hern set off to Moretonhampstead to see what he wanted. On his way home, the wind changed and it began to snow. It came down as thick as goose feathers, and although his horse tried his best, it was almost impossible to see the road ahead. By the time Hern reached the village he doubted he would make it any further. Even though he knew he wouldn't be able to avoid seeing Emily, he left his horse in the Berry's stables and went into the Blackbird to have a whiskey and thaw out. He had never felt so cold and miserable in his life.

As Emily hurried to and from the kitchen, Hern couldn't tear his eyes away from her. Her hair was no longer in those tight braids at the back of her neck, and what he had imagined about her figure, previously concealed by those unflattering dresses, was now revealed to be everything he'd once hoped. He had always suspected that under her calm exterior was a woman fit to burst and he'd hoped to be the one to catch the full force of her explosion.

But Sarah's taunting voice still echoed in his mind and he was almost driven mad with jealousy, wondering just who and how many Emily had been with. What sort of woman must she be to stay at the inn, he asked himself? After all, she could have got herself decent lodgings. Not that Tom and Betsy weren't decent folk, mind you. And, he reasoned, it had been difficult getting around in the snow.

His mind revolved and somersaulted as he had another whiskey, and another. And with each one his desire was fueled, not doused as he hoped. He kept looking towards the kitchen door, hoping and dreading the next time Emily might appear, until he was too drunk to focus at all.

Later when everyone had gone home, Emily watched Tom try to get Hern to his feet.

"Och, Tom, look at the weather," she said. "You can't put the poor wee man out in this."

Tom huffed with exertion. "He doesn't *feel* like a wee man," he grumbled. "Well, what do *you* suggest I do with him then?"

"Put him over here by the fire. I'll keep an eye on him."

"Aye well, I'll leave him in your tender care then," Tom said, giving her a wink. He and Betsy had heard rumors of how much time Emily had been spending at Furze in recent months and thought it would be a jolly good idea if she and the lonely farmer got together.

Emily blushed. Although she had more or less said she would have nothing to do with a family who had Sarah in it, it had been her pride and temper talking, not herself. Because when Hern had surprised her by walking into the Blackbird earlier that evening, she knew she still wanted what he could give her; the family she wanted with all her heart. And because she had an idea of how stubborn he could be, she also knew it would never happen if she didn't make the first move.

During the night, Hern stirred and opened his eyes. He had a splitting headache and a horrible taste in his mouth. The first shock was that he wasn't at home but was still at the inn. The second was that Emily was sitting on the floor in front of him, in the glow of the fire she had kept going.

She handed him a mug of water. "I dare say you feel like this?"

Without taking his eyes off her, Hern gulped it down greedily. She was in her night attire. Her hair, red-gold in the firelight, tumbled almost to her waist. He could see her full breasts, pressing against her nightgown. She looked very desirable, and he could feel his passion rising.

"Hern, I would like to put things straight." Emily smiled tremulously and reached for his hand. "After all, if we're to be close again I think you should know everything there is to know about me."

Hern didn't pull his hand away. He was powerless to fight against what he knew he wanted.

When Hern rode away from the inn the next morning he was in a much happier frame of mind. Emily had told him about the laird, and wept about the loss of her little girl. She said there had been no other man since, and although it went against the grain of his nature Hern had decided to give her the benefit of the doubt. He didn't know why. He needed to believe her, he supposed. It wasn't as if *they* didn't have something in common: seven years, she said, she had spent in purgatory living with Gardenia Wood, and he blurted out that so far his whole life had been one long purgatory.

Emily had put his hand on her breast. "Well," she'd said in her lovely soft accent, "there'll be no more of that now, will there?"

It was a bleddy miracle, he thought, and despite the weather and what Coldswill had told him about Ruth's escapades, he whistled as his horse slipped and stumbled all the way home.

ഌ

Kitty was thrilled when Emily began to visit Furze again and was even happier when she saw the affection growing between her and Hern.

"I only hope she remembers that if a horse can get his oats in the field it's hard to get him into the stable," Flo said, when she knew.

Kitty blushed at Flo's insinuation but she hoped the same. She'd noticed her father, always the procrastinator, hadn't yet mentioned a wedding date.

Chapter 24

Hern might never have taken the plunge if Sarah hadn't suddenly taken to her deathbed, although it wasn't her actual death that finally bound Hern and Emily together, but the events that followed her funeral.

It was one morning in April when Parky Jones lathered his pony by riding hard to Furze, carrying the news that Sarah had slipped and fallen and was now very ill, and asking Hern to come right away.

Kitty didn't think her father had been to Lower since the argument at Christmas, and wasn't surprised when he grumbled that it was the last place he wanted to go. She felt just as reluctant, but as Hern wasn't feeling well she was bidden to drive him on the cart.

It seemed to take forever, and all the while Parky rode behind them, his eyes boring into Kitty's back. Hern said not a word, but sat beside her with a tight, grim look on his face.

When they reached Lower, Hern looked almost with dread towards the farmhouse, and Kitty felt a twinge of sympathy as she followed him to the back door.

As he opened it, he stopped dead in his tracks. "Bleddy hell!" he said. "You're the last person I expected to see."

"Bleddy hell, indeed," a voice chuckled. "By, Hern, you haven't changed a bit."

Hern ran to his brother and clapped his arms about him. "Aw, Christ, Col. Am I pleased to see you."

Within a week, Sarah was dead. Although Kitty felt guilty, she couldn't bring herself to mourn a grandmother who had never once shown her one grain of affection. Ruth, however, took Sarah's death very hard, as Kitty might have expected, and consequently the Coldswills gave her leave until after the funeral.

Embittered by her current lifestyle, Ruth's temper hadn't improved, and she was almost unbearable to be with. She did as little as possible around the farm, grumbled about everything and everyone, including Emily: because of her, Ruth said, her father and grandmother had become estranged. If that hadn't happened and he had visited Lower more frequently, Sarah might still be alive.

"That's rubbish, Ruth, and you know it," Kitty told her. "It isn't Emily's fault at all, and you'd better be nicer to her. Father's far more even-tempered when she's around and I'm fed up with your tantrums about it. I'm the one who has to live with him. He may have been all right to you, but he never has to me."

Realizing she was fighting a losing battle as regards to Emily, Ruth changed tack. "And do you know *why* he doesn't like you?" she said slyly.

Kitty was caught off guard. "I suppose it's because he had to marry Mother," she replied, annoyed with her sister for bringing up that most unpleasant subject. "But they must have loved each other once, else I wouldn't be here, would I?"

"That's where you're wrong," Ruth cried vehemently. "He *never* loved her! He only married her for the farm, although he wouldn't have even done that if he'd known she was already expecting you, because he isn't your father."

Kitty didn't speak for a moment, but stared at her. "How do you know that?" she said, eventually.

"Grandma told me. She told me lots of things."

Kitty could hardly take it in. Her mother had been with someone else before marrying her father? And then she remembered her mother's words on her deathbed: *promise me you won't do anything reckless. With a father like yours…*

It was on the tip of her tongue to ask Ruth what else she knew, but her sister's comment had been made out of spite and Kitty decided not to give her the pleasure of gloating further. Ruth was considerably taken aback when she lifted her chin and said, "Thank you for that information, Ruth. It's such a pity he's *yours*, isn't it?"

Kitty didn't know if Ruth regretted her outburst, or whether she was disappointed she hadn't got the reaction she hoped for, but she was subdued after that and neither girl raised the subject again.

However, Kitty couldn't stop thinking about it, and kept going over things Leah had said that might indicate who her father was. She tried unsuccessfully to pump Flo: hoping to lead on to the question of her paternity, she asked what her mother had been like when she was young. But Flo didn't take the bait—she just said quietly that Kitty's mother had been an angel, too good for the world, and there were those who had taken advantage of her. Kitty almost retorted that *that* didn't sound much like Leah, then realized she might not have known her mother as well as she thought, so she kept silent.

ꕥ

On the day of Sarah's funeral, the girls rode to church with Hern and left Edward with Flo in the hall, where she and some other ladies were preparing a tea for the mourners. In truth, Kitty would have rather waited there too, but Hern insisted she go with them. She was relieved when the service was over and made a beeline for the hall.

As she went across the village green, an elderly gentleman caught up with her. "Hello, my dear. I had no idea you had come back. How is your dear mother?"

"Well, my mother just passed away, sir," Kitty said.

Ronald's face fell. "Oh dear, I am sorry. 'Course I don't get out and about much now, so I don't get to hear these things. Are you at Mrs. Endacott's again then?"

"No," Kitty said, bewildered even further. "I live at Furze."

"Ah, Furze. I must say I was so sorry to hear of young Mrs. Underwood passing like that. Such a young woman. So terribly sad. And now her mother-in-law." He clucked his tongue. "But, oh well, comes to us all eventually, I suppose." He chuckled. "Except the good Lord's giving me a long run, I must say."

Kitty realized by then that he was mistaking her for someone else. "I do know who Mrs. Endacott is, sir," she said kindly. "And I see an awful lot of her."

"Well, I'm glad to hear that. She was so good to your mother, you know." He lowered his voice. "I'm glad it turned out all right in the end. So nice to have met you, my dear." He was about to move away when Matthew happened along. "Well, Matthew," Ronald said, clapping him on the back. "And how are you, my dear boy?"

"Very well, Mr. Bennett, thank you. Good afternoon, Miss Kitty."

"Oh, you know each other?" Ronald said. "Aw, Matthew, our maid would have liked that now, wouldn't she?" He glanced over to his wife. "But I'd best be going." And he hurried off to join Harriet, who was looking at Kitty in a most startled fashion.

Kitty looked after him. "I think he's confusing me with someone else," she said.

"Well, Mr. Bennett's getting on now," said Matthew, who was also a bit puzzled to know what Ronald had meant. "He tends to wander a bit. May I walk you to the hall, Miss Kitty?"

"Please. My, what a lot of people turned up for the funeral."

"Well, there's always those who go to funerals out of relief, not regret. And in this instance I fear that may be so." Matthew smiled at her and they shared a look of mutual understanding. Once again Matthew felt briefly puzzled, because in Kitty's face was that elusive something that he recognized, but just couldn't put his finger on.

Margery was standing at the door and greeted Kitty with a warm hug.

"How nice to see you again, Aunt Margery," Kitty said, "although it always seems to be at funerals or christenings, doesn't it?"

"Lord, that's a sobering thought," said Margery. "Let's go in and find Flo. I could do with one of her special cups of tea."

"Before you do, allow me to introduce Matthew Steer."

Margery gave Matthew a wide smile as he took her hand. "Well, Matthew, I've heard of you through Colan. Come along in, I know he'd like to see you."

A few people came to offer Margery their condolences. "Hypocrites all of them," Margery muttered under her breath after they moved away. "I'll warrant not one person in this room cares how I feel any more than they liked my mother. Oh, here's Colan. Hello Col, how are things going? Weathering the storm?"

Colan's sudden arrival had surprised many people and caused considerable consternation. To begin with, people said, it was an amazing coincidence he should arrive when he hadn't even known Sarah was failing. Others said that it was probably his arrival that probably caused her to fail. And then there was the opinion that Colan was a fool to have returned at all. This gossip had trickled through to him bit by bit.

"Memories like elephants; brains like peas," he said with a crooked grin. He shook Matthew's hand as Kitty introduced him. "I feel I know you so well, Matthew. I've heard so much about you from Thomas over the years, and how good you've been to him."

"I haven't done much." Matthew colored with embarrassment. "But he's been good to me, too. Gave me a nice horse, he did."

"And you well deserved it, from what I hear," Colan said solemnly. "It was a great comfort to the Lady Leonora to know you were at the manor watching out for him."

"I did my best, sir. And I must say I'm gratified and honored to know she thought that. I only regret I never had the pleasure of knowing that fine lady. From all I have heard from Master Thomas, he thought the world of her."

"We both did," said Colan sadly. "Losing her was very hard on all of us."

"And you are here to stay, I hear?"

"Yes. I've left my son Michael in my stead." Colan paused as a sudden hush fell over the room. The squire, and a tall, blond, young man, who was Thomas, had just walked through the door.

The squire bellowed out Colan's name. Everyone stopped eating, and one or two glanced anxiously at one another. But Thomas managed to get his father outside, and apart from a few curious onlookers who were standing near the door, conversations and the chink of cutlery on china gradually resumed.

Thomas was arguing with his father, trying to persuade him back to his horse, but Hartley Gordon was raving. "I'm not going anywhere until I've seen that bally man. Is he too yellow to come out and face me?"

Colan came outside at that moment. "I've never been yellow, Gordon," he said. "What is it you want with me?" He saw Thomas's alarm. "Don't worry, Thomas, I would never fight a man who can barely stand on his feet."

Hartley's face turned into a mask of hatred. "You've got a nerve, Underwood, coming back here." He slapped his riding crop against his leather boot. "You always were a man who needed cutting down to size."

"You've nothing on me," Colan said quietly. "Your wife left you of her own accord, and was justified too from all she told me."

"Why, you—" Hartley lifted the crop, but Thomas wrestled it from him. "Come along, Father, have some respect. This is a funeral."

Hartley reluctantly turned away. "You're an arrogant bastard, Underwood," he shouted, partway to his horse. "You've been a pain in my arse for long enough, and something will be done about it."

"You'd better stay off my land," Colan growled, seeing the squire's eyes slide over to Kitty, who was standing beside Flo and Margery. His expression tightened further. "And you'd better keep away from Furze, too."

"Oh?" Hartley said arrogantly. "But you can't keep me off my own land."

It was as if the picture froze. And it now included Hern and Ruth, who were standing in the doorway of the hall. Colan frowned and looked at his brother, as if to say *what does he mean*? But Hern shrugged.

The squire saw their consternation and smiled. "Yes," he drawled. "That's got you foxed, hasn't it?"

Thomas hadn't yet mounted up. He was standing beside Colan. "I'm so sorry. This is unforgivable, but I'm afraid I couldn't stop him."

"It isn't your fault, Thomas," Colan said, then added quietly, "Come over and see me while you're here, will you?"

"I will." Thomas nodded to those around him and gave Kitty a quick smile before he mounted his horse and rode after his father.

"What the hell did he mean?" Hern said to Colan. "What did he bleddy mean, *his* land? Does he mean the right of way?"

"I've no idea," Colan said.

Hern was holding his chest. Suddenly he gave a cry. As he crumpled to the ground Flo cried, "Quick, someone fetch Morrison."

ﬆ

In the quietness of the back room where she had once sipped brandy with Flo and Margery, Kitty bore witness to the most shocking news she could have heard. After Colan questioned him again and Hern swore he didn't know what Hartley Gordon was talking about, Flo stepped forward.

"But this has to do with Peter Peardon, Hern," she said. "His gambling. Surely Leah must have mentioned what happened?"

Hern looked at her blankly. They all looked at her blankly.

"What's this then, Flo?" Colan said.

"I understood from Leah that her father once lost the farm to Gordon in a card game, but later she heard from Mr. le March that the squire changed his mind, and forgave the debt."

"If he had a bleddy change of mind, what the hell's he on about?" Hern shouted, then began to rant and rave, and called Leah every name under the sun. He wanted to know just why le March was involved, and when he said this, looked accusingly at Kitty, as if she would know. They had to give him some laudanum to calm him down.

"*What* a to-do!" Margery said, as she and Kitty drove home together. "I thought the squire and Colan might fight again. At least we were spared that, the beastly man. My goodness me, what a day. And fancy. *Fancy* your grandfather doing such a thing. I can't get over it."

Kitty couldn't get over it either. No wonder her mother and grandmother hadn't spoken of Grandfather Peardon very often—she had often wondered why. What a week of revelations, she thought. She felt as if her world had turned topsy-turvy.

Margery patted her arm. "Look, dear, you must try not to worry. I'm *sure* the squire has no grounds on which to say such a thing. Colan will no doubt contact Justin and see what it's all about, so *do* try and put your mind at rest."

Kitty nodded, hoping she could believe her. In truth she was as confused as everyone else, wondering why Mr. le March would have got involved with the matter. Now, *that* opened up a completely new set of possibilities, and she felt almost dizzy with the thought that her mother could have been a rich man's mistress.

"You'll have to come and visit me while I'm at Lower," Margery said, interrupting her tumultuous thoughts. "Things are in quite a state, so I'll be there a while, I imagine."

Suddenly, she startled Kitty by bursting out laughing and tossing her head in such a way it reminded her of Duffy.

"Oh, I'm sorry," she said. "I know it's far from a laughing matter. But really, I can't help think what a send off today has been for Sarah. She couldn't have done better than if she had planned it herself, could she?"

Chapter 25

Dr. Morrison's opinion was that Hern had a heart condition and must rest as much as possible. This meant that once Ruth returned to the Coldswills, Martha was kept home from school to look after Edward and generally help out.

Emily left instructions with Kitty how to tutor Martha, if she had time. It would be good practice, she said. But although Kitty appreciated Emily's unwavering faith in a future in which she would use these skills, with the added burden of her father's failing health she doubted she ever would.

Margery came over to help out whenever she could, although that wasn't very often because she had enough work cut out for her at Lower. Sarah had let things go, she said, and the farm was in a dreadful state. Parky Jones had barely kept the place running, so the first thing Colan had done was to get rid of him. Parky had, apparently, slunk home to his father in a sulk and with a huge grudge. "But it can't be helped," Margery said. "One just cannot afford to employ a lazy scoundrel who won't pull his weight."

One afternoon while Margery was visiting, Emily arrived. Hern was particularly morose that day and refused to budge from the best room, where he sat hugging his whiskey bottle. When Emily went to see if she could coax him out of it, Margery whispered, "I don't know why he doesn't marry her and be done with it. You could certainly do with an extra pair of hands around the place."

Kitty agreed, and wondered if her father's dilatoriness had anything to do with Flo's horse and oats theory. However, it was hardly the sort of thing she could mention to her Aunt Margery.

Emily was with Hern barely five minutes before she came rushing back into the kitchen. She wouldn't say what had upset her. Nor would she stay and have a cup of tea, but gathered up her belongings and said tearfully that she must go.

After she left, Margery sighed deeply. "Oh dear, I'd better go and see what's up, I suppose," and she went down to the best room to confront Hern.

"Your father's a fool, Kitty," she said when she returned. "And I don't know what's to be done about it. Because of this Furze affair he reckons he has nothing to offer Emily, and has more or less told her not to come here any more."

"But that's ridiculous," Kitty cried. "He doesn't know that for a fact. And Emily wouldn't care. It's him she loves, not the farm." Disappointment washed over her like a giant wave. She couldn't bear the thought of carrying on without Emily in their lives. "Oh, Aunt Margery, I was hoping they would get married."

Margery sighed. "Don't give up, dear. Perhaps once it's sorted out and your father feels reassured he will change his mind."

"He's awfully stubborn," Kitty said woefully. "I can't see him ever going to see

Emily again, let alone asking her back."

"Stranger things have happened. Remember you thought that after Sarah put her spoke in. Don't fall into despair, my dear. Things will work out."

But without Emily's visits to look forward to Kitty became so miserable she hardly knew how to get out of bed each morning. Martha was unhappy also when she knew her father had asked Emily not to come to Furze, and wouldn't speak to him. Kitty knew if she had ever behaved in such a way she wouldn't have got away with it, but Hern was fond of his youngest daughter and seemed genuinely hurt by her contempt. Still, even that wasn't enough to make him relent over the matter.

Meanwhile, Colan went to Whitmouth to see Justin, who reassured him that Hern had nothing to worry about. Justin didn't mention specifics, or how he had become involved, and Colan didn't ask him, having the distinct feeling that he didn't wish to talk about it further. However, knowing Justin wasn't the sort of man to say something was all right when it wasn't, Colan rode right away to Furze to tell Hern the good news.

Although Hern was pleased to hear it, he still scowled. "Bleddy bitch," he said of Leah. "She was a deep one all right. Never told me any bleddy thing."

"But all that's in the past, Hern," Colan said. "You have Emily now."

"No, I don't." Hern's voice was strangled with regret. "Emily won't be coming here again. I asked her not to."

"What? For goodness sake, *why*?"

"What use was it to encourage her and then find we may be homeless?"

"Damn it, Hern, you'd never *be* homeless." Colan felt exasperated with his elder brother. "You've got Lower to come to any time you want, didn't you think of that? You should go and see her right away."

"I don't know that I can," Hern said sheepishly. "I said some things to her. It was my pride, Col. I couldn't tell her the real reason why I didn't want to see her. I said it was because of her past."

Colan thought his brother a fool, but he could see Hern was feeling miserable enough without telling him so. Instead, he decided to impart the tidbit of gossip he had heard, hoping it might stir him to overcome his pride. "Well, I know of one person who isn't bothered by her past. By all accounts the squire is frequenting the inn because he has an eye on a certain redhead." He was gratified to see he had Hern's immediate attention. "Well, I must be off. Send Kitty over sometime, will you? Margery has dug up some things from the attic she might like."

Hern hardly heard him, for his mind was running riot with images of the squire running after his Emily.

ഌശ

Emily was sitting in her room, miserably contemplating her situation and knowing full well she would have to resolve it. She was grieving over her loss; she felt so bereft without her family, as she now thought of them. To make matters worse, the squire kept pestering her. Even when she had given him a blatant *no*, and a stinging slap across his face, he had merely laughed, and his eyes had glittered like shiny coal.

Betsy and Tom had witnessed this and were very concerned. They were fond of Emily and had been hoping things would work out with Hern. Now, Betsy was distressed to know they had become estranged, especially since the squire was showing so much interest in her. Tom was also worried, and had even gone so far as to hint that she might leave the inn, to get out of the man's reach.

Emily knew what a difficult position he was in because he didn't want any trouble there. Now it was fast becoming a habit that whenever she heard the squire coming she would leave her duties and flee to her room. This was very awkward for all of them, and she knew it couldn't go on. The problem was, she doubted anyone in the village would take her in because it might incur the squire's displeasure, and for the first time in years, she was forced to consider returning to Scotland, although she blanched at even the thought.

She started when a knock came to her door, and she hesitated to answer it for fear of who it might be. It came again, this time a little louder. "Is that you, Betsy? Tom?"

"No, it's Hern."

"Hern!" Emily's hand flew to her mouth in surprise and she quickly got up and unbolted the door.

Hern stood there, looking like a little lost boy. Emily's heart melted: what else could she do but hold out her arms to him? She hadn't really believed his excuse for not wanting to see her, simply because her past hadn't bothered him up until then. However, because of his heart condition she hadn't wished to contradict him, and had accepted his decision.

He fell into her arms. "Oh Emmy," he said, over and over again. "Oh Emmy, will you have me?"

Emily, who thought that could be considered a proposal of marriage, drew him inside and bolted the door.

Flo and Kitty need not have spent any time worrying about the horses and oats. Although Emily had permitted Hern some liberties, they hadn't yet enjoyed each other fully. But after ensuring Hern's proposal was for real, Emily asked him to stay with her that night.

She had a way with Hern that made him feel able to let down all his defenses. He admitted he had lied to her about being bothered by her past: his chagrin, he said, had been partly because of the discrepancy over Furze, and his frustrations and jealousies from his previous marriage.

"Some man must have pleased her," he said miserably. "But I never could. Sighed like the wind in the bleddy trees, she did."

When morning came and Emily asked him coyly if she'd sighed like the wind, he replied, "More like a bleddy hurricane, if you ask me." And had sounded very pleased about it, too.

Relieved that a solution had been found to Emily's dilemma, Tom and Betsy closed their eyes to Hern having spent the night in her room. They were delighted to hear their news, and although Betsy said she would miss Emily, she also said she thought their engagement would more than likely stop any further pestering by the squire.

"Nort but trouble he is," Betsy grumbled, as she dished them out a hearty breakfast.

"Aye," Tom agreed. "He would turn his own mother's milk sour."

ꕥ

Hern rode away from the inn in a happy daze. He had melted into Emily's softness again that morning and become lost in a place he hadn't even known existed. It was as if Emily held a key to him, because for the first time in his life he felt as if he was working properly.

On his way home, he called into Forde. He agreed with Tom and Betsy that Emily might be safer away from the inn. However, he didn't feel it appropriate for her to move into Furze until they were married, so he intended to ask Flo if she could stay there meanwhile.

He hadn't spoken to Flo since she had imparted the bad news about the farm, and he knocked at the door a little sheepishly, hoping she wouldn't remember how he had sworn at her.

Flo did, but she wasn't one to bear a grudge. Although she didn't particularly like Hern, she could feel for him in many ways. She thought that having parents like Sarah and Joshua, and a wife who despised him, hadn't been an easy load to carry, and she could understand how disappointed he must be with life.

"Emily's very welcome, Hern," she said, knowing what it must have cost his pride to come to her door that morning. And for Kitty's sake, she was genuinely pleased to hear his news. "We have plenty of room, and she can stay for as long as she likes."

Kitty and Martha were speculating where their father might have been all night, and their suspicions were joyfully confirmed when he admitted he had stayed at the inn because of an important matter he had to discuss with Emily.

He actually smiled at Kitty when he said, "I want you to take a message over to the Blackbird. You can tell Emily that Flo Endacott says she can stay there."

Martha's face fell. "Oh, why? Is she going to live there, Father?"

"Only for a time." Hern paused. "Until we get married."

Kitty and Martha squealed with delight and hugged each other. Martha ran over to her father and gave him a kiss.

Kitty shook his hand. It was a strange gesture, she supposed, but felt it was the only appropriate thing to do. "I'm very pleased for you, Father. Perhaps you'll be happy now."

Their eyes met, and for the first time in her life, she saw a glimmer of something in them that wasn't loathing. It was amazing, she thought, what love could do.

Chapter 26

By the end of the week, Emily was safely installed at Forde, and Acheson said he would be waiting for Hartley Gordon if he dared set foot on his property.

On the Saturday morning, Hern went into Moretonhampstead, and, as Emily was there to take care of Edward, Kitty and Martha decided to ride Duffy over to Lower to see their Aunt Margery.

It was May now and bluebell time. Their purple-blue blossoms were everywhere in the hedgerows, and they carpeted the woodlands and filled the air with their fragrance.

"Can we stop at that place, Kitty?" Martha said, as they were going up the hill behind Forde. "You know, where all the flowers grow?"

"On the way back," Kitty said. "Else we'll never get there."

Martha pouted. "But I want to take Aunt Margery some flowers."

"Oh, very well, but you'll have to hurry and not pick too many."

When they reached the grove, Martha slid off the pony and ran over to beneath the beech tree. The wizened crabapple beside it was in blossom, and many of the petals had fallen to the ground. Martha picked up handfuls and threw them into the air around her. "Look! I'm getting married."

Kitty smiled to herself, and tied the pony to a branch. Duffy wrapped her soft muzzle around a mouthful of grass and flowers and tugged it from the hedgerow, roots and all.

"Look, Kitty. There are violets, too. How do they come here, do you think?"

"I don't know," said Kitty, pulling the clods of earth off the stalks of grass in Duffy's mouth. "There have always been flowers here."

"Perhaps it's the birds that bring the seeds," Martha said, her eyes growing wide, "Or perhaps it's *pixies*."

"It doesn't really matter, does it, it's just a lovely place, that's all."

"Is it your most favorite place in the whole world?"

Kitty smiled. "I've never thought about it. But I suppose it is the one place I can come to and have a bit of peace. That is, except when you're here."

"Oh, you." Martha charged her, and they both fell to the ground, time and flowers forgotten while they rolled and tickled each other.

ꕥ

Thomas Gordon was also on his way to Lower that morning to see Colan.

He had argued with his father about what happened outside the hall, demanding to know what he'd meant regarding the Underwood's property. Not that he got anywhere, except to get depressed. And he had ridden off in a temper to

Whitmouth, where he knew he would find some consolation, understanding and information from Justin.

Justin explained that the squire had a claim on Furze because he had won it in a card game, but later had a change of heart and secured the farm for Leah and Kitty's lifetimes. In the future, he said, Thomas would have the power to return the farm to the Underwoods for good. Thomas agreed wholeheartedly, and on his way home had called into see Coldswill, where he signed a document to that effect, to be held until the appropriate time.

In doing so, he hoped he would cancel out any evil deed his father might have committed in the past, because he felt that Justin's explanation was barely adequate. However, he hadn't pressed him for details. In truth, he had heard quite enough about his father's past, and didn't think he could take much more.

When he was younger and more impressionable, he had adored his father and was impressed with the power he wielded. But that was before he had seen the true man. After his father had stood over him one day and forced him to drown some kittens, to 'make him be a man,' Thomas was so sick at heart he had taken each kitten afterwards and held it in his hands, willing it to live. But of course none of them had. What was worse, the squire had found him doing it, and called him a sissy.

Things had changed between them after that. The squire found little time for him and demeaned him, and Thomas stayed out of his way as much as possible. When he wasn't away at school, he spent his time at Whitmouth House or visiting his mother and Colan in Derbyshire. At least in those places he was able to be himself without the squire's crude comments about what an excuse he was for a man.

Justin and Colan never tried to influence his thoughts, but remained close by and had supported him through what he considered to be a very dark childhood. Even though he knew he probably didn't know the half of it, what deeds of his father's that did reach his ears, sickened him.

However, that wasn't his only distress. When he rode around the estate he was ashamed to see the misery and poverty. He longed to change it all, and in doing so drive out the resentment from the tenants' faces. He felt the only meaningful purpose to his life was his ideas for the future that he would implement once certain aspects of his training were over. In this way, he hoped to somehow repair the damage his father had done.

When he reached the crossroads, he heard the giggling and reined in. He sat quietly on Hector watching the two girls rolling around among the bluebells and rusty beech leaves. He smiled wistfully, remembering how he had once rough-and-tumbled in a similar way with Matthew.

Suddenly, Kitty became aware they were being watched. "Hush," she told Martha, and got up, brushing off the moss and peat, and spitting out bits of leaf that had found their way into her mouth.

Thomas dipped his head politely. "Good day, ladies."

Martha ran over and curtsied. "Good day, sir. I'm Martha, from Furze."

He smiled at her broadly. "I'm very pleased to meet you, Martha from Furze. And I'm Thomas, from the manor."

Kitty lifted her chin haughtily and didn't curtsy, even though she knew she should. "I know who you are," she said, and not very nicely.

"Ouch! Being the squire's son doesn't make me the squire, you know."

Kitty suddenly felt embarrassed. She remembered his former kindness to her, and now felt ashamed for her coolness. She walked over to him. "I beg your pardon, sir. I'm Kitty, also from Furze."

"I remember you well, Kitty," Thomas said, giving her a warm, and rather stunning, smile.

Duffy, who nickered, interrupted them. Her ears were pricked forward and she was tugging at the reins.

"That's Duffy," Martha piped up. "We're on our way to Lower Farm."

"What a coincidence," Thomas said. "So am I."

"Hooray! We can go together."

"Martha." Kitty frowned at her.

Thomas looked at the pony. "You're sharing?"

"Yes," Kitty said defensively. "Duffy may be old but she's quite capable of carrying us both if we take her steady. Come on, Martha, else we'll never get there."

"But I haven't picked any flowers yet," Martha said.

Kitty sighed. "You don't have time now. Aunt Margery won't mind."

"Why don't you let your sister pick the flowers and I'll wait and let her ride with me?" Thomas offered. "You can take Duffy ahead."

"Oh please," said Martha. "*Please* can I, Kitty?"

Kitty looked at Hector dubiously. "Is he safe? He looks a bit spirited."

"He has spirit," Thomas said. "But he's as old as I am, and he's quite safe."

"Oh *please*," Martha said again.

"Which way do you go?" said Thomas.

"The quickest way is by the tor," Kitty said. "I'll meet you up there if you like, and then we can go down together."

"Then the tor it is. Hurry, Martha, else we'll have to gallop like the wind to catch your sister, and I don't think she would like that."

Kitty mounted Duffy and trotted off. She looked behind her and smiled as she saw Thomas patiently watching Martha as she gathered as many flowers as quickly as she could.

She had just reached the top of the tor when she heard them coming up behind her. She felt more kindly towards Thomas when she saw he wasn't galloping, but held his horse at a steady canter.

They rode around to the south side together and before descending, paused in the lee of the wind to look at the view.

"Down there are remains of stone hut circles," Kitty said. "I don't know if you knew they were there. And further on, if you go along the ridge and through the gate you can walk down into the valley and along to the falls. This time of year the whole moor that side and the valley floors are covered in bluebells. It is so beautiful and smells divine."

Thomas gave her long look and said quietly, "You're almost part of the moor yourself."

Kitty felt embarrassed under his gaze. She was unsure of what he meant, except she thought it might be a compliment.

They enjoyed the view for a while longer. It was such a clear day they could see the outline of the English Channel on the far horizon, many miles away. And then they began to descend, down and along to Lower Farm.

ഌ௸

Margery was still turning out and making the farm a proper place for Colan to live, as she put it, before she returned to Whitmouth. Colan had been busy mending fences, securing the gates and making new ones where required. He had also trimmed the hedges and cut the verges.

Margery had been tending the garden, weeding the paths, and had bought a few perennials from the plant sale at the local May Day celebrations. That morning she had turned out the attic, and found rugs and wall hangings, a silver tea service and china, too.

"Just look at all this," she said to Colan. "It must have been our grandmother's, I wonder why they never used it."

His reply was grim. "I doubt Joshua would have wanted Sarah to have had the pleasure."

"What a marriage they had," Margery said. "I'd say you're better off being a spinster than living like that, although it's easy for me to say, I suppose. Without Edwin's generosity I might have found myself in similar, or even worse, circumstances."

"I'm glad it worked out for you, Margery," Colan said. "Justin always spoke very highly of you when he came to see Leonora, and said how you'd given his father a few years of happiness."

"Well, his parents' marriage was more of a business arrangement, because of their dual fortunes. But Edwin respected her and was very sad when she died. Poor man, he never really got over losing his daughter at the same time. He was such a kind man, and Justin is just like him." Margery looked out of the window as she heard horses coming into the yard. "Well, look who's come to see us."

Colan walked outside, and lifted Martha down from Hector. She said it was the highest perch she'd ever had on a horse, which made them all laugh. She thrust the bedraggled flowers into Margery's hands, who said they must hurry and put them into water to save them. Martha snatched them back again and ran over to the horse trough and dunked them in.

Kitty laughed, and said to Thomas, "I bet she never stopped chattering."

He shook his head and chuckled, and then went down the yard with Colan, leaving her with Margery.

"How did you come to be riding with Thomas?" Margery said curiously.

"We met at the crossroads," Kitty said. "I'm ashamed to say he caught us romping on the ground. I still feel embarrassed about it."

Margery chuckled as she took a small piece of moss out of Kitty's hair. "Yes, you might like to tidy your hair. But you don't have to worry about Thomas. I wouldn't be surprised if he hadn't secretly wanted to join you. You don't know him."

"No, I don't," said Kitty. "I keep remembering who he is though."

"Well, that's understandable, but I suggest you just relax and take him as he comes. Now, what news from Furze?"

While Kitty looked over the things Margery had kept out for her, in the background she heard Thomas and Colan discussing the new farming practices Thomas hoped to implement on the estate in the future, and in the long run benefit themselves and the tenants. As Kitty listened to his pleasant, cultured voice talk so enthusiastically about his ideas she wished Acheson and Charlie could be there to hear about them.

When the afternoon light began to show signs of fading, Kitty reluctantly said they must return home. Thomas said he would go with them and Martha could ride with him to the crossroads if she wished.

As they rode along side by side, Kitty felt herself really liking Thomas, who seemed to be a very kind person. He must take after his mother, she thought, not only in his looks but in his nature, too. He was good with horses too, although when she openly admired Hector, he was very modest and said Justin had trained him.

She couldn't help but think how similar their lives were. They both had fathers who had little time for them and for whom they had scant respect. It was on the tip of her tongue to tell him how Hern had treated her, and how it must be because he wasn't her real father. But then she remembered Martha was with them and kept quiet.

When they reached the crossroads Thomas lifted Martha down from Hector. "I bet Hector can go a long way," she said, patting the horse in admiration. "Thank you, Hector, for the ride."

"Yes, indeed he can, Martha," Thomas said. "I have ridden as far as Plymouth."

"That *is* a long way," Kitty said. "Wasn't it dangerous to go so far alone?"

Thomas shrugged. "Hector is a wily creature. He seems to remember all the short cuts, especially if he's heading in a homeward direction."

Kitty laughed and said Duffy tended to be like that, and perhaps it was the same with all horses. He smiled and reached for her hand. His lips brushed the back of it. "Farewell for now, but not forever, I hope," he said, looking into her eyes.

He also took Martha's hand. "Fare ye well, kindred soul."

Martha shrieked with pleasure and clapped her hands. "I *like* you, Thomas. But I *love* your horse."

Kitty and Thomas burst out laughing, and then he gave Hector a gentle rein and they set off. No spurs for him, thought Kitty, watching him go. He would have no need. It was obvious what a fine horseman he was: a kind and gentle rider.

When Kitty and Martha reached Forde, they called into see Flo, but it was Acheson who came to the door.

"Flo hasn't been feeling too good this afternoon, my dears," he said, "she's lying down. Can you come back later?" He ruffled Martha's curls. "How's my beauty then? My, you're getting a big maid."

"I just rode on a *big* horse, Acheson," Martha said.

"Did you now, and whose might that have been?"

"It was Thomas Gordon's. And he's called Hector."

Acheson's expression changed immediately. "You go along home now," he told her. "Your sister will catch you up."

When Martha had gone he said, "What's this then, Kitty?"

"We met Thomas Gordon and he let Martha ride with him on Hector. He was on his way to Lower, too. That's all."

"That's all?"

Kitty looked at him in surprise. "Well... yes. She was quite safe."

"*Safe*? When has anyone ever been safe with one of the Gordons, for crying out loud? Have you gone mad, Kitty maid?"

"No, I haven't," Kitty said indignantly, upset with him for getting cross with her.

"I've never forgotten what you said to me once, my girl. And it's worried me ever since."

"What was that?"

"About how you would never marry anyone like Charlie. If you're having thoughts—"

"Oh, Acheson, don't be so silly."

"Allow me to finish, my dear. I know what it's like to be young, but if you take my advice, you'll keep well away from the likes of Thomas Gordon. You'll find nothing but sorrow there."

"But I wasn't even thinking—"

"No, you weren't thinking at all."

"But you're wrong about him, Acheson, I know you are. He really cares about people."

"When did one of his sort ever care about the likes of others? The likes of you and me, Kitty? I won't hear of this, do you hear?" And he turned and went indoors, closing the door firmly behind him.

Kitty's heart was pounding, her breath coming in gasps. Never in her life had Acheson lost his temper with her. "It isn't what you think," she cried after him. "It *isn't*." What a stupid, prejudiced old man he was, she thought. How could he say that about someone he didn't even know? As for *those sort* bringing sadness to people, Uncle Colan had lived with one of *them*, and *he* hadn't been unhappy.

In a temper, she stomped home across the field.

As she passed the barn, she looked in to make sure the pony had been properly taken care of. "She was ready for her oats this afternoon," Charlie said, laughing. "The weight of you two, I suppose."

Normally Kitty would have laughed along with him, but today angry tears came to her eyes.

"What's wrong, Kit?" Charlie asked, looking concerned.

"Nothing," she said sulkily. "Well, Acheson said something."

"Oh? And what was that?"

"He's making judgments about someone he doesn't even know. Thomas Gordon gave Martha a ride and he's just blown my head off for it."

"I'm not surprised," Charlie said quietly. "Have you gone mad?"

Kitty looked at him in surprise. "Why, you're no better than Acheson. What makes you think you can judge someone when you don't even know him? I can't stand this prejudice for no reason."

"No reason? You know what the Gordons are like."

"No, I don't know what *all* the Gordons are like. And nor do you!" Kitty stormed towards the door. "Now both of you have ruined my day. I was going to tell you about the things I heard Thomas speak of to Uncle Colan. He's different, I tell you. He's *kind.* I don't care what you say."

"Well, you certainly seem to have made up your mind about him," Charlie said tightly, his eyes like flint. "By the way," he shouted, as she ran out of the door, "your father's all steamed up about something, so I shouldn't say anything to him about your precious Thomas Gordon if I were you."

Hern was sitting at the table with a cup of tea in front of him. Ruth was sitting in the corner wearing her reptile look, and Martha was hovering between them. What a sight to come home to, Kitty thought.

"Where've you been?" Hern grumbled.

"We went to see Aunt Margery, Father," Kitty said. "Martha and I went. Where's Emily?"

He grunted. "Upstairs."

Kitty went up and Martha followed her. "Don't you say anything about seeing Thomas, do you understand?" Kitty whispered.

"Why?" Martha whispered back.

"Because Father will be angry and he'll beat you."

"All right," said Martha, her eyes becoming wide.

Emily was trying to settle Edward, who was fretful. "He has earache, I think," she said. "He keeps rubbing one side and it's very red."

Kitty had a look at him. "He keeps getting these infections. I'll put an onion on to boil. What happened downstairs?"

Emily glanced at Martha. "Martha dear, would you go and check for the eggs? I quite forgot to do it earlier, what with Edward not feeling well, and we wouldn't want those naughty chickens pecking at them, would we?"

"Most definitely not," said Martha, and skipped out of the room.

"I'm afraid Ruth is very angry with me," Emily said quietly. "I don't know if you knew but there have been complaints about her from the Coldswills and now she's been dismissed. She's taken up with Parky Jones of all people. He'll only use her and quite possibly leave her in trouble."

"Oh dear. I suppose that's why she always liked going to Lower."

"Your father received word this morning that they'd had enough, and he went into Moretonhampstead to fetch her."

"So that's why she's downstairs sulking." Kitty's heart sank at the thought of having Ruth at home again. "What will happen now?"

"Your father thinks that rather than have her here, he will find her another position, and I came up with an idea. Ruth is so angry with me for suggesting it." Emily sighed. "Well, she'll hate us both for a while, I imagine, but if we can only get her past this stage, when she's older she'll understand why we did it. Perhaps you'd run an errand for me tomorrow, Kitty, but now I really think I'll go back to Forde if you can take care of Edward. It might help the atmosphere if I disappear for a while."

"Acheson said Flo wasn't very well today. Do you know what was wrong with her?"

"No, I've been here for most of the day."

Kitty looked sheepish. "Acheson isn't very happy with me, I'm afraid. We met Thomas Gordon on the way over to Uncle Colan's, and he gave Martha a ride on his horse. Oh please, don't say anything to Father about it. It really was all right, but Acheson said I was mad."

"I don't think you're mad, Kitty, but we will have to talk about it another time. Don't worry, dear, Acheson will come around. He loves you dearly."

"Yes, I know." Kitty made a rueful face. "That's what makes it worse."

Emily kissed her and went downstairs.

"Good riddance," Ruth muttered from the chair when Emily told Hern she was going.

"I'll bleddy give you another one if you don't shut your mouth!" Hern shouted at her. "You're just like my bleddy mother; always have to have the last word don't you?"

Supper was eaten in silence. Hern accompanied Ruth to the outhouse then followed her upstairs. Kitty and Martha heard him hammering. He came down and went outside, and they heard him hammering again.

Martha peeked out of the door. "He's hammering something outside Ruth's window. It looks like a piece of wood. He's nailing it across her window so she can't get out. Oh, Kitty, what do you think she's done?"

"Something she shouldn't have, I dare say."

Hern came in afterwards and sat down. "That should keep the slut in her place for a while."

ஐ

That was the word Gardenia Wood used, not so quietly that Kitty wouldn't hear, when she read Emily's note the following morning. Kitty didn't know if she referred to Emily or Ruth.

"You'd better come in a moment," Gardenia said, looking Kitty up and down.

Emily had told Kitty that no one worked for Miss Wood for very long, so although she might put up a bit of resistance she would probably agree to having Ruth; not only was she probably quite desperate for help, but she also enjoyed a challenge.

"I think it's rather a nerve," Gardenia threw over her shoulder as she went down the hall.

Kitty said nothing, but followed her into the front room, where Gardenia sat down at her bureau, snatched up a piece of paper and began to write.

"If they were proposing you, Kitty, it would be a different matter," Gardenia said. "But your sister was always a minx."

"I'm sure if you take her she will behave herself, Miss Wood. I heard Father say if she didn't he would—"

"Thank you, Kitty, but I'm sure *I* can deal with your sister. Now, you're to give this to your father, do you understand?"

Kitty nodded as she took the sealed note. She didn't bother to say he couldn't read and would probably hand it over to Emily.

When she got home he did just that, and Emily read that Ruth could be taken over to Gardenia's at any time. Hern went to fetch the cart. When it was ready, he hauled Ruth outside, where he told her in no uncertain terms what he would do to her if she didn't behave herself. Then he shoved her up onto the cart and drove off.

Chapter 27

Acheson hadn't been lying to Kitty when he said Flo wasn't well. Something dreadful had happened: Matthew Steer had come over and asked outright if he could have Mary's address because he felt like going to see her. Although Flo had wondered many a time what she would say if that ever happened, she'd been unprepared to know what to do, and her head had gone all fuzzy with panic.

"Do you think that's such a good idea?" she'd said, hoping to stall him. Matthew had looked at her, perplexed. "After all, it's such a long time ago Mary went away." But he'd been so persistent she hadn't been able to think straight. And so she had revealed where her cousin May lived.

Since doing so, she kept asking herself, *why* had she done such a thing when she could have told Matthew the truth? Oh, he would have been shocked, there was no doubt about that. And he would have been mighty angry with her for deceiving him for all those years. But wasn't this worse? It was like putting her head in a noose and waiting for someone to open the trap door. And what would her cousin May say when he turned up on her doorstep?

To try and ease her troubled mind, Flo decided she would set about some spring-cleaning. Housework had a way of calming her down, and afterwards she always felt the satisfaction of having made the effort. Upstairs in the spare room was a cupboard she hadn't tidied for years, and as Hern and Emily were getting married she thought it would be a good idea to clear it out and find some oddments she could give to Emily. But it was the worst thing she could have possibly done. There, buried with the paraphernalia, was the portrait of Mary.

When Enid had first sent it to her, the incident of Mary's death was so raw that Flo hadn't even been able to bring herself to untie the string that bound it. Acheson had never questioned her about it, suspecting it would be too painful for her, she supposed. Nor had he ever mentioned it since and she believed he'd probably forgotten all about it. Now, as her heart thumped mightily and her fingers fumbled with the string and peeled off the last layer of wrapping, she was thankful he had.

She had often wondered if her memory was true; that perhaps it was only in her imagination that she thought Kitty looked so much like Mary. But when she stood back and looked at it, she knew anyone would have to be blind not to see Kitty smiling out of that canvas.

She'd had to lie down afterwards, and that's when Acheson had come upstairs to tell her how Martha had ridden with Thomas Gordon on his horse.

He had caught Flo in a very fragile state of mind and she'd got quite cross with him for having gone on to Kitty about it. "The fastest way to drive any maid into a boy's arms is to tell her no, she can't," she said. "She's only a young maid and she's going to meet all sorts before she's ready to settle down."

"Why Charlie doesn't say something to her and be done with it, I don't know," Acheson said, grumbling about young people these days. "Why is it that some women are as blind as bats and can't see a good thing staring them in the face?"

"I thought it was only men that had that problem," snapped Flo. "And I'm not sure he *would* be good for her. He's a troublemaker, I don't care what you say."

"Oh, I knew you'd bring that up," Acheson shouted. "And you mark my words, Flo, a Gordon's a Gordon, and I don't care what you say about that either."

Flo had felt awful ever since. Usually they could compromise over things, but she could see that as far as Thomas Gordon was concerned there would be no compromising on Acheson's part.

Nor would she change her mind about Charlie. She felt he was leading Acheson astray and she felt helpless to do anything about it.

Chapter 28

Ruth had only been at Miss Wood's for a few weeks before she was able to bribe one of the delivery boys to take a message to Kitty.

Kitty was surprised to receive the mysterious note that asked her to fetch a package Ruth had left at the Coldswills. She knew her sister tended to be scatter-brained, but she was a bit suspicious, especially as Ruth said to keep quiet about it. However, the next time Kitty was in Moretonhampstead she made time to call into the Coldswills' residence and asked to see the mistress.

Prunella Coldswill had a sharp little face, and did look rather like a shrew, as Flo said. In a voice that went with her physique she made it quite clear she didn't take kindly to being bothered. Ruth had caused them no end of trouble, she said, and she wished to be finished with the girl. Kitty felt more than a little embarrassed and hoped Ruth hadn't sent her on a wild goose chase just to be spiteful.

However, after searching upstairs, Prunella found a package hidden behind the wardrobe. She handed it to Kitty, and said she hoped she wouldn't be troubled again.

Gardenia happened to be in her garden and didn't look at all pleased when Kitty arrived and asked to see Ruth. "She's very busy," she said, "and has no time for idle gossip." Her eyes went to the parcel Kitty held. "I certainly don't feel she deserves any gifts."

"Oh, this isn't a gift," Kitty said. "It's just something Ruth will find useful in her work."

Gardenia sniffed. "Then I suppose you'd better give it to her. She's in the kitchen."

"Thank you so much," Kitty said, smiling sweetly as she swept past her.

Ruth must have seen her arrive, because the back door opened as Kitty approached, and she stepped out and swiped the parcel out of Kitty's hands without even a word of thanks.

"I expect this is the last time I'll be seeing you," she whispered slyly.

Kitty could hardly save herself from laughing. "Oh, and why's that? Going somewhere, Ruth? I thought you'd just arrived."

"If Father thinks I'm staying here, he's out of his mind," Ruth hissed, and slammed the door in Kitty's face.

Kitty chuckled to herself as she went down the path and woke Duffy up from her pony snooze. As she mounted up she made sure the bag that held her mother's wedding gown was tied securely to the saddle ring. The village shop had been very obliging in giving her a couple of old sacks she'd wrapped up for Ruth. Now her sister *really* had something to hate her for.

When Kitty reached the bridge at the bottom of the hill, rather than go home by way of Forde she went through the gate by the stile and rode along by the river. The day was oppressively hot and the flies were bad. Duffy shook her head irritably, and Kitty knew the old pony would be glad to get home to a cool stable.

She looked longingly at the river and thought how inviting it looked. Around the corner, there was a swimming hole: a tree had fallen some years ago, partially damming the river and creating a deep pool. On impulse, she reined Duffy in and dismounted. Not intending to be long, she didn't bother to tether her. Duffy immediately thrust her nose into the succulent grass, and then wandered off into the bracken to get away from the flies.

Kitty took off most of her clothing and slid down the grassy bank into the water. It was leg-achingly cold and it took her a while before she could bring herself to plunge into the deeper water. Eventually she did and paddled around for a while until she felt cooler.

She was just about to get out when she was startled by voices coming along the path. She tried to hurry, but had no time to reach the bank before Parky Jones, together with another boy from the village, came into sight.

"Well, look'ee here," said Parky. "Caught ourselves a big one, looks like."

The other boy sniggered as Kitty ducked under the water. "I was just about to get out, Parky," she said, folding her arms across her breasts. "Would you mind going on, so I can? You know what Father'll be like if I'm late home."

Parky dug the other boy in the ribs. "What's it worth then? You come as cheap as your sister?"

Kitty glared at his detestable face. "You know better than that. Go on, leave me alone, it's freezing in here."

"We'll soon warm you up," Parky said. "Won't we, Roy?"

Roy looked uncomfortable. "Aw, come on, Parky. Let her get out, that water's perishing, I bet." But Parky ignored him.

Minutes passed and Kitty began to bever. Parky never took his eyes off her, and occasionally he whispered something to Roy and dug him in the ribs.

Suddenly Roy stood up and said, "Quick! Someone's coming."

"Who is it?" Parky grumbled, still in no hurry to go.

"Charlie Chase," said Roy. "I'm off!"

Parky got up then and, taking one last look at Kitty, ran down the path.

Endeavoring to make her way to the bank, Kitty tried to pick her way across the stony riverbed by stepping on the soft weed. She was so cold she couldn't place her feet properly, and twice she slipped and splashed back into the water.

Suddenly, she saw Charlie on the bank. "Oh, Charlie," she cried. "Thank goodness you came. Parky Jones came along and I couldn't get out."

Charlie swore and looked down the path. "I was in the bottom fields when I saw Duffy," he said. "I thought you might have taken a tumble. Here, let me give you a hand."

"No, no," she said quickly. "Just turn around, I'll manage." But she lost her balance and fell again.

"Christ, Kit, this is no time to be modest." Charlie plunged into the water and lifted her out onto the bank. "You ought to know better than this," he grumbled roughly. "You aren't a child any longer."

"I was hot," she said defensively. "*I* wasn't to know anyone would come along. Especially anyone who would—" She shuddered at the thought of what Parky and Roy might have done to her. "Oh, Charlie, I was so frightened. And now I'm so cold I can hardly feel anything. I was in there for *ages.*"

He tore off his shirt and wrapped it around her, and then he pulled her into his arms, wrapping as much of himself as he could around her.

"I couldn't bear it if anything happened to you, Kitty," he said, nuzzling into her hair. And he held her for a long time, rubbing her body to try and get some warmth into her. But it seemed only to fire his own heat. He held her so tightly she felt he would crush her. "I love you so much," he murmured. "Oh, Kitty, I wish you would say you love me too."

"Oh, Charlie," she whispered, thinking *not now, Charlie, please not now.*

"It's all right," he said. "I mean you're only just waking up, aren't you? A slow starter. But I could wake you up all the way if only you'd let me."

Please, she begged silently. *Please don't.* But she could feel him rising, hot and hard against her. "Please," she whispered. "Oh, Charlie, please don't hurt me."

He stood back from her. "*Hurt* you?" His face crumpled. "Kit… I would never hurt you. I'm sorry, I didn't mean to frighten you." He looked puzzled. Most of the village girls fell over themselves to get to him. He didn't fully understand why Kitty was so reluctant. "No one has ever done anything to frighten you, have they?"

She didn't get his meaning at first, and then she understood. "No, no it's nothing like that." She looked at him, knowing he would never understand how she felt. She didn't understand it herself really. She knew Acheson was right in a way; Charlie was a good man. He was strong and handsome, and he would take care of her. But if he should touch her and she responded, why, she might end up like her mother; trapped in a marriage with a man who wasn't right for her.

"I'm sorry," she said lamely. "I'm just not ready. But you're such a good friend, Charlie. That's twice you've come to my rescue now, and I do appreciate it."

"Let's hope there's never a third time," he said gruffly. "Although you don't have to worry about Jones. I'll make sure he never goes after you again. Come on, let's get your clothes on and get you home."

He helped her put her clothes on then he carried her all the way back to the farm. Emily took one look at her, and put her straight to bed.

Although Kitty felt as if only a small flame of life flickered inside her, by evening she was burning up with a fever.

Chapter 29

Kitty felt cosseted in a warm, soft quilt. All was velvet, dark and soft and there were no edges.

Someone sat with her day and night. They lifted, patted and fussed, and sometimes she could feel her wrappings being removed and the air felt cool to her skin. Something cold and hard would be pushed beneath her and she would hear the tinkle of water.

Numbness paralyzed her limbs. She wanted to speak, to say she was still there, able to hear too, but something glued her eyes shut, her lips wouldn't move and she couldn't feel her voice.

There was a scent. A lady with her mother. They had their arms about each other and were smiling. Surrounding them were the most beautiful flowers, and birds sang in the branches above.

Kitty was overjoyed to see there was only the span of a shallow river separating them from herself, and she flowed towards the pretty-colored stones, willing to cross. But they turned and saw her and waved her back.

The lady drifted nearer. "You must go back," she said. "I'm always watching over you. I'm always here."

And then Kitty heard Margery's voice quite clearly. "I'm here now, dear. Isn't it time you went home, Flo? You're looking peaky. If you don't rest, you'll be ill."

"If I don't see her get well," Flo said. "I'll die."

Once there was Charlie asking, "How is she Flo?" His voice full of love and concern. And Kitty remembered how he had held her: his urgent whispers.

"Goodness knows what would have happened if it hadn't been for you," Flo said, and Kitty heard a sob and Charlie comforting her.

The next time she surfaced, she heard a clatter of china. "I've milked the cups, my dear," Flo said. "Do have yours while it's hot."

"I had no idea Charlie was so fond," Margery said, and Kitty could detect something disagreeable in her voice.

"I think he's cared for a long time," said Flo. "And Leah was encouraging it. She didn't want to lose her, you see. And there'd be nothing wrong with Charlie if only he could get certain things out of his mind."

"And what's that, Flo?"

But Flo didn't answer. All Kitty could hear was the chink of a cup against a saucer.

ꙮ

Suddenly, without warning or contemplation, Kitty opened her eyes.

She was in bed, the sun streaming through the window. Someone was near the window. Was it Mother, or the lady? Perhaps this time they wouldn't send her away. But when the person turned around Kitty saw it was Flo, and she felt a fleeting disappointment that she was at Furze.

She must have uttered a sound because Flo flew to the bedside. "Why, maid," she said, bursting into tears. "Oh, don't mind me. It's tears of relief. Oh, thank the blessed Lord. You've come back." She felt Kitty's forehead. "And by the feel of you, you're back for good this time. My, you've been coming and going like summer for weeks."

Kitty's lips trembled. *Weeks?* But it seemed only hours ago.

"Aw, Kitty, I'm as pleased as punch you're back," Flo said, wiping her eyes.

"There was a place...." Kitty whispered, her voice hoarse. "I saw someone with Mother."

"Dreams, maid, that's all. Dreams. I'll go downstairs and tell Emily, and heat a drop of broth. Killed a chicken once a week I did, in case you came around."

Flo closed the door and Kitty looked around her. Suddenly, she knew how a newborn must feel when arriving in the world. No wonder babies cried so much, she thought, as she burst into tears.

ꕥ

As Kitty's physical health improved, Flo ceased the daily treks to Furze and left the care of her to Emily. She was very concerned about Kitty's emotional health, however, and when Margery suggested that Kitty might benefit from a visit to Whitmouth, Flo agreed. She didn't know if Margery's suggestion was on account of Charlie, who had been showing an inordinate amount of interest in the girl, but in any case, she felt it would be better for Kitty to go away, rather than feel obligated to make a decision she would later regret.

It wasn't that Flo didn't like Charlie—he was a nice enough fellow and a very good worker—but if he continued on in the same vein she knew he was bound to get himself and others into trouble, and she didn't want Kitty to be among them.

As if the worry of all this wasn't enough, she had something else on her mind. Matthew had been away for a while and was now home. The noose tightened; the trap door trembled.

One afternoon, a knock came to the door and she opened it to find Matthew on her doorstep.

For a moment, they stood looking at each other. Then Flo sighed and said, "I've been expecting you, Matthew. Won't you come in, and I'll make some tea?"

"I don't want any tea, thank you all the same," Matthew said curtly. "I'd just like you to tell me what happened to Mary. Your cousin said they'd never set eyes on her and they couldn't think what had got into your head. Why did you do it, Mrs. Endacott? Why did you send me all that way for nothing?"

"Oh, please come in, Matthew. It isn't something we can talk about on the doorstep. I'll make tea all the same, and then we'll go where we can be private."

She took him along to the best room and closed the door behind them, grateful that Acheson was out for the afternoon. The last thing she needed was for him to come back and interrupt them.

"I've had an awful time lately, Matthew," she began, her hand shaking so much she could hardly pour the tea. "Young Kitty's been very ill, you know. She got a chill from the river and it turned inward. I thought we were going to lose her, to tell you the truth."

"Oh dear, I'm sorry to hear that," Matthew said, some of his anger dissipating. He thought how ill Flo looked, and this explained it.

"She's going to be all right now, but that, on top of everything else ..." Flo buried her face in her hands. "Oh, Matthew, I'm so sorry. So very sorry."

Matthew shifted uncomfortably. He hated to see a woman cry and he didn't know what to do. "If only you'd tell me—" he began.

"I will, I will Matthew. Just give me a minute or two."

When she could gather herself, as quietly and as calmly as she could, Flo told him what had happened the night of Kitty's birth. Finally, after she made him swear he would never tell, she revealed who had fathered Leah's child, and how she and Acheson had buried the stillborn with Mary.

"I've often wished since I'd called the doctor and let him deal with it," she said, "but at the time whoever has time to think? You act on impulse and mine was to prevent Mary's shame. And then Leah already thought the baby was hers. How *could* I ever have told her? But oh, my dear, the nightmares I've had since have been enough to make a person go mad."

"The times I've looked at Kitty and wondered who she reminded me of," Matthew said. "I never once imagined it was my dear Mary."

"Well, why would you, my dear? You had no reason to even think it. Leah never knew herself, although, in latter years when Kitty began to grow up, I was often tempted to tell her. At least it would have put her mind at rest over one thing. Thinking Kitty was his, of course, she was so fearful the girl might have some of his traits."

Matthew stared into his cup then placed it in the saucer. He put his head in his hands and began to sob.

"I know it's been an awful shock," Flo said, placing a hand on his arm. "Oh, Matthew, I hope you can forgive me."

"Of course I do," he said, when he could speak. "I understand now why you were so reluctant to tell me. And perhaps, when I've said what I have to say, you'll show me a bit of understanding, too. You see, you aren't the only one who's been carrying around a secret."

"What do you mean, Matthew?" Flo asked.

"I'm loath to tell you this, Mrs. Endacott, but you couldn't have put Mrs. Underwood's mind at rest at all." He met her eyes; his own were filled with pain and anguish as he said in a dead, low voice. "The squire's the one who ravished our dear Mary. That bastard fathered Kitty."

Flo paled, and grasped her throat. "But… how do you know this?"

"I found out the day I told Mary I was going to work at the manor. It was the horror in her eyes. The fear. I knew something was up, and I pressed her. That's why I've been so determined all these years to stay there. If it's the last thing I do, I don't know how, or when, but one day I'll see that bastard gets his just deserts."

ꙮ

It irked Hern to see Kitty lying around so uselessly, so when Margery suggested she should return with her to Whitmouth to convalesce he didn't object. Margery was delighted and, as a courtesy, wrote to Enid to make sure she had no objections to having Kitty at May Cottage.

Enid replied that she would be delighted to have Leah's daughter to stay with them for a while, as she remembered Leah with great affection. And she said she would ask Justin to provide a carriage for their return.

By the time Margery received Enid's letter it gave them four days in which to prepare to leave.

"Four days," Kitty said. "But I can't, it isn't enough time."

"And what do you need time for?" Flo said. "You don't have a thing to do except get into the carriage."

Kitty avoided Flo's eyes. She didn't feel like saying it was because Charlie had put seeds of doubt into her mind. He had been very disappointed when she told him she might be going to Whitmouth for a holiday, and said that if she did, things would never be the same again. There were other things he had said also, and now Kitty echoed some of them.

"But what if I don't fit in?" she said. "And what about Enid?"

"What do you mean, not fit in?" Flo asked tiredly. "And what about Enid?"

"What if she doesn't like me?"

"You silly maid," said Flo. "Of course she'll like you. And you'll love her." She had no difficulty in remembering the sprightly woman she'd met all those years ago. "Your mother did. She and Enid—" She stopped mid-sentence, realizing what she'd just said.

"Did she? Do you think Enid will remember her?"

Flo nodded, unable to find her voice. Until then she'd quite forgotten how Enid and Mary had hit it off, and now she was dismayed. What if Enid, so keen on looking into faces, saw the resemblance?

Emily was in the scullery and overheard the conversation.

"There's nothing to be afraid of, Kitty," she said, coming into the kitchen. "*Everyone* will love you, dear, and Whitmouth isn't so far away you can't come home if you don't like it. You'll have a lovely time, and I think it's the best thing that could happen to you. Don't you, Flo?"

"Yes," said Flo, although in truth, she was now quite uncertain what to think.

ஐ

The day before Kitty was due to leave, she went down to Duffy's field to say goodbye to the pony. While she was there, Charlie came over. He looked very downcast when she told him she was definitely leaving the following day, and as a result, she felt cross with him for being so much against it. "Why can't you be pleased for me?" she said. "After all, it's only a convalescence."

"I can't help think there's more behind it," he said, prodding a tuft of grass with his foot. "Your aunt probably wants to get you away from me. She never has been that friendly when I've come into the house to see you." He gave a short laugh. "She probably has it in her mind to find you a rich husband."

Kitty's cheeks burned because he wasn't far from the truth in one thing: although she hadn't heard Margery say anything about finding a husband, she had overheard her say to Emily that all she would get from Charlie was a passel of children. She had been hurt at the time, and disappointed that Margery would say such a thing. But after giving it some thought she decided her aunt was probably right; she'd heard the girls in the village giggle about the probabilities of Charlie's virility.

"I don't think it's you in particular, Charlie," she said tactfully. "I just think she wants me to have some other experiences before I settle down."

"But do you *really* want to go?" he said, desperately searching her face.

Don't do this to me, she cried inside. She was so grateful to him, for he was the best and dearest friend she'd ever had, but ever since he had hauled her out of the river he had become almost unbearably possessive.

"Yes, I do," she said gently. "Aunt Margery says the sea air will do me good, and Emily and Flo agree. So I feel I shouldn't throw kindness in their faces."

"Well, I think there's more behind it," he persisted. "Your aunt in particular is probably as ambitious for you as she was for herself."

"What do you know about Aunt Margery?"

"I've heard your father talk about her. Look, Kitty, girls like you—"

"What do you mean, *girls like me*?" Kitty's eyes blazed. Of course she knew very well what he meant: someone like herself, without title or money. Someone with little hope to advance in life unless she sold herself, like her Aunt Margery was supposed to have done. She knew very well what her father called his sister.

"I just meant... remember who you *are,* Kitty."

"That's a fine thing for a man with your convictions to say, isn't it?" she cried. "Someone who believes anyone can become anything, given half a chance? Well, just as you have your dreams, so do I. And at the moment they do not include being here with you!"

Instantly regretting her words because they'd come out all wrong, she ran away from him; stumbled back to the farmhouse and fell sobbing into Emily's arms.

Emily could make little sense of her incoherent mumbling except it was something to do with Charlie, and she looked heavenward and thanked God for Margery.

ঌঌ

When the time finally arrived for their departure, Margery had to guide Kitty to the door. Margery assured her it was only because she hadn't gained her full strength that she felt reluctant to go, and that once she was in Whitmouth she would feel entirely different.

Emily hugged her tightly and Martha clung to her waist and told her to come home soon. Edward pointed to the horses that drew the carriage and said, "Horthie. Horthie," and bobbed his head away from Kitty's kiss, more interested in the matching grays than his eldest sister. Kitty blinked back sudden tears, not daring to think about how much she would miss him.

Flo put her arms about her and hugged her tightly, but she couldn't speak, and all Acheson could say was, "Be a good maid."

Kitty's eyes so swam with tears that she hardly saw Hern as she shook his hand for the second time in her life. He grunted awkwardly, and looked as if he would be glad when her departure was over.

As Margery did her round of farewells Kitty got into the carriage and Charlie stepped forward to help her.

"Take care," he said softly. "Don't go jumping into any more deep water." And he brought his face close. Suddenly so close, and his lips brushed hers gently.

It seemed to happen so slowly and yet it was over so quickly. And before she knew it, he was gone. A face outside a window; a man outside her life.

"Oh, Charlie," she whispered, feeling as if she should run after him and get things straight before she left. But as Margery got into the carriage and Kitty saw Charlie's expression she knew there would be no reasoning with him. The frustration of it tore at her and she began to sob uncontrollably.

Margery patted her. "It's all right, dear," she said. "A good cry will get it all out of your system." And Kitty noticed she glanced back towards the yard as she said it.

Part III

Whitmouth

Our souls sit close and silently within,
And their own webs from their own entrails spin;
And when eyes meet far off, our sense is such
That, spider-like, we feel the tenderest touch.

John Dryden 1631-1701

Chapter 30

On the way to Whitmouth, Kitty's emotions alternated between being excited with all the new sights and sounds and the thrill of what might await her, and her guilt and regret at leaving Charlie, who so obviously wished her to stay. There was his kiss too, and when Margery wasn't explaining where they were, or describing something of interest, Kitty closed her eyes and recalled the feeling of it. Just a feather's touch really, that was all, but she felt as if he'd put an invisible brand on her.

Because of her inner turmoil, she gave very little thought to her final destination, until they began to descend the long hill into Whitmouth and drove through the maze of streets. Flo had once told her you could never tell from a person's outward appearance what their circumstances might be, and now Kitty began to feel anxious, wondering just where Margery might be taking her.

However, when the carriage pulled up outside Margery's home, all her fears were assuaged. May Cottage looked like a dream, at the least enchanted. It sat back from the road nestled in beds of perennials, its diamond-paned windows glinting in the late afternoon sun. Over the gate was an arbor, smothered in climbing roses, and Kitty took deep breaths of the delicate floral scent as she walked beneath it.

The front door opened as if by magic, and a young woman, introduced by Margery as Lilly, their cook-general, bobbed a curtsy. No one had ever curtsied to Kitty before, and she felt embarrassed.

The inside of the cottage was as quaint as the exterior. The flagstone floors were covered with thick, bright rugs, and a blood red carpet with patterned edges ran the length of the hall. The windows were deep set with seats, upon which were cushions that matched the brightly colored curtains. There were nooks and crannies everywhere filled with interesting objects, and pictures on the wall. Kitty's eyes couldn't gobble everything up fast enough.

She heard a cry of joy, and turned to see a woman in a long, flowing gown of many colors, gliding down the stairs.

"Enid!" Margery cried, rushing to meet her.

Enid caught Margery in her arms and after a deep embrace, held her away to take a look at her. "Oh, Margery," she said at length, "how pleased I am to have you home again. It's seemed such an age."

"It has indeed," Margery said.

Enid turned her all-devouring eyes on Kitty. "My dear," she began, "well, how lovely to—" She paused mid-sentence. She took Kitty's hand, and looked into her eyes. "Why… my dear, how wonderful to meet you."

There was a strained silence. Margery, frowning slightly, gave Enid a curious glance, then said, "Lilly, would you be a dear and show Kitty to her room? We'll freshen up and then have a bite to eat, shall we?" And then she placed her arm in Enid's and they went upstairs together.

Lilly took Kitty along the sumptuously carpeted hallway to the back of the cottage, and opened a door into a large, low-ceilinged room. Kitty had merely expected to be led into a bedroom, but besides a bed there was a small bureau, shelves with a collection of books, and a drop-leaf table with a chair. There was also a small settee by the glass doors, through which she could see the back garden.

"This is just lovely, Lilly," she said, genuinely and pleasantly surprised. "I had no idea what to expect."

"It is a lovely room," Lilly said, without envy. "Shall I help you change now?"

"Oh, but I usually do it alone."

"Oh, I see," said Lilly, who obviously didn't, and Kitty blushed, realizing how gauche she must seem. "Well, when you are ready," Lilly said all the same, "you pull that bell rope there, and I'll come and take you to the dining room."

When she'd gone, Kitty sat on the bed, mortified at her faux pas. She should have known better and accepted Lilly's help, she supposed. Although, she next thought, surely, once she was better she would be expected to help her, so wouldn't they be on a par?

Hoping she would redeem herself, although in truth she felt it was a bit silly because she could have found the way on her own, once she had tidied her hair and changed her dusty and crumpled clothes, she obediently pulled the bell rope and waited for Lilly to show her into the dining room.

It had been a sunny day but a fire was lit to take off the evening chill. Enid was sitting beside it in one of the armchairs, and Kitty sat down opposite her. While they waited for Margery to join them, they chatted about her life at Furze.

"So you see a lot of Flo?" Enid asked.

"Oh, yes," Kitty said. "I always have."

Enid smiled. "I'm pleased to hear that."

Margery came in, looking more refreshed, and shortly afterwards Lilly announced that supper was ready.

Kitty was surprised at how hungry she was. When they had stopped along the way at an inn, she'd eaten a huge lunch. Now, after she ate her portion of the delicious chowder and accepted another, Margery chuckled and said that the sea air must be having an effect already, and that she was pleased to see it.

When Lilly cleared away the plates, Margery followed her to the door and closed it firmly. "It fails to catch sometimes," she said. "I would hate Lilly to overhear me say this, she's such a good girl, you understand, *and* an excellent cook, wouldn't you agree? But she does tend to gossip, so keep that in mind, Kitty. However, when you're stronger she can chaperone you around the town—she'll be a perfect companion when I can't manage it."

When Kitty expressed her appreciation for her surroundings, Margery said, "I'm glad you like May Cottage. We've been so happy here, haven't we, Enid, and I think it always tells in a house. Oh, I'm so excited to have you here in Whitmouth, my dear. There's so much to see, and do, and it'll be fun showing you around—I shall see it all anew." She frowned. "Although we shall have to get you a new wardrobe before you do. And do something about your hands."

"But I thought... won't I be helping Lilly once I'm feeling stronger?"

"Good Lord no. Whatever gave you that idea?"

Kitty looked from one to the other. "Surely I have to earn my keep?"

"Not at all. You've come here to convalesce, not work. You aren't at Furze now."

"I'm sorry to hear you were so ill, Kitty," Enid put in. "The change in air will probably do you a lot of good."

"I hope it will," Margery said. "She's far more fragile than she looks—she almost died."

"I think I did die… in a way," Kitty said.

Enid inched forward in her chair. "Why do you think so, Kitty? Do tell us."

"While I was in the sort of coma, I saw Mother with a lady. They were in a garden, across the other side of a river. It was simply beautiful." Kitty closed her eyes, trying to recapture the feelings it had given her so that she could better describe it. "It was so peaceful. The colors so… so brilliant… as if painted with light. There was a blue light. A soft blue light. Loving, almost."

She opened her eyes to find both women staring at her. "I wanted to be with them," she continued shyly, "but the lady told me I couldn't, it wasn't time."

"The lady," Enid said softly. "What did she look like, can you remember?"

"She was beautiful. Her hair was as dark as mine; her eyes of the deepest blue. She seemed very gentle." Kitty blushed. "I know it may sound silly, but that's why I wondered if I had died. I wondered if it was Mary."

"Mary," Enid echoed, her eyes alive with interest.

"Well, yes. The Mother of Christ. You see, Flo is always telling me to have faith, and I wondered if it was perhaps a sign. Because she did say she was always there, watching over me."

Enid gave a strange smile. "Did… Mary say anything else?"

"If she did I can't remember," Kitty said disappointedly. "And what I can remember is somewhat vague, as if it never really happened. But I know it did."

"It sounds as if you had a very wonderful experience, Kitty. What a lovely feeling, to know someone is always looking out for you from the other side."

Kitty smiled at her, then at Margery. At first she had instantly regretted her outburst; she didn't know what had made her say such a thing really. Now, seeing that both women weren't ridiculing her for her comments, she felt relief, and a great deal more comfortable in their presence. "It is," she agreed. "Although… I wish I knew who she was."

"I'm sure you will one day," Enid said. "Meanwhile, you must continue on with your earthly journey, until everything becomes clear."

"Yes," Margery said. "And part of that is to enjoy your new life in Whitmouth."

"But what will I do all day if I'm not working? I like to be busy."

"Oh, don't worry, I shall think of things," Margery replied. "In fact I have thought of something already. You can catalogue our library of books, if you like. Emily told me you like being industrious that way."

"I do," Kitty said enthusiastically. "I should love to do that for you."

"Good. That's settled then. And you may begin any time you feel like it. But don't overdo it—they're in a terrible muddle and it'll take time. People keep borrowing them and don't replace them properly. We need them in some sort of order, don't we, Enid?"

Enid smiled. "Margery must have order. She's a wonderful antidote to myself who must be the most disorderly person alive."

"Yes, you should see her studio," Margery said, rolling her eyes. "Paints and brushes and whatnots all over the place."

"I take it you haven't seen the portrait I did for Flo," Enid said suddenly. It wasn't a question.

"No. I'm sorry, I don't know...."

"Remember I told you about it?" Margery said. "The one of Mary Jay."

"Flo did mention that Mary lived with them for a while," said Kitty. "But I've never seen a portrait of her."

"I wonder what she's done with it," Margery mused.

Enid glanced at her. "Kitty will see it when it's the right time," she said, and changed the subject.

It wasn't long before Kitty found it hard to keep her eyes open, and when Margery suggested she should have an early night, she agreed. On her way, she went into the kitchen to seek out Lilly, to thank her for the delicious meal. Returning along the hallway, as the dining room door was slightly ajar, she heard Enid say, "I'm telling you it *is* so, Margery. You know I never forget a face."

"But how *could* she be?" came Margery's reply, as she closed the door.

Kitty hurried on down the hallway. She didn't want to be thought eavesdropping, but she wondered if they were referring to her, and if so, what they were talking about. It seemed fanciful, she knew, but she'd noticed Enid's occasional meaningful looks to Margery throughout the evening, and it occurred to her that the secret that existed at Furze between her mother and Flo had followed her to Whitmouth.

Then, thinking more about it, she told herself not to be so silly. She was tired, that was all, and reading things into something that wasn't there. She climbed into bed and fell asleep immediately.

She slept so soundly that when she first awoke she couldn't believe it was morning already, or even think for a moment where she was. And then she heard the seagulls outside her window and remembered she was in Whitmouth.

Hearing gulls wasn't totally alien to her. Although Furze was miles from the coast, often in spring the birds would fly inland when it was said to be rough at sea. It was a lovely sight to see them swooping and flying around Charlie or her father at the plow behind the big horse. Remembering this made her think of Edward, and she wondered if he missed her yet. A wave of homesickness washed over her and she might have resorted to tears if Lilly hadn't knocked upon her door at that very moment and brought in a tray of tea.

As Lilly pulled back the curtains and chatted away cheerfully about what a lovely morning it was, and how once Kitty was up she could join her aunt and Miss Enid in the garden for breakfast, she began to feel better. She took a deep breath, and vowed from then on she would try not to think too much of Furze, but enjoy her time in Whitmouth for however long she was there.

ꕥ

As the days flew by, Kitty's health improved in leaps and bounds, and she quickly grew used to her new surroundings. As she did, the pangs of homesickness dissipated.

She was also delighted with the new clothes Margery provided. "They say you can't judge a book from its cover," Margery said, "but I'm afraid in Whitmouth that tends to be the case and I won't have you going around looking like a ragamuffin."

Kitty was a little affronted at that comment, but in the act of replacing her old things with the new, she had to admit they were rather the worse for wear, and she forgave Margery who, although she could often be tactless, had a heart of gold.

Not only was Kitty's wardrobe changing, but Margery also provided her with a jar of beeswax hand cream that she used twice daily. This had the remarkable effect of softening her roughened hands. And after her nails were neatly manicured and her hair arranged in a more fashionable style, Margery told her she was beginning to look like a lady.

One morning, Margery announced that Emily had written to say that she and Hern had decided to have a quiet wedding without any fuss and if Kitty preferred she need not attend. "I tend to agree with her," Margery said. "I think a visit home could be rather disruptive at the moment. You're just beginning to settle in and really get well again."

Although Kitty would like to have seen Emily wed, she was a bit anxious about leaving Whitmouth. She feared that once she was home again her father might not allow her to return. And then there was Charlie, who must be angry with her because she had never written to him directly. She knew her aunt wouldn't approve of it and so she had asked Emily to pass on her letters to him, hoping it would compensate for her silence.

"You're probably right, Aunt Margery," Kitty said, relieved in a way that the decision had more or less been made for her. However, as Emily's wedding day approached she became rather subdued. Although she knew Hern wouldn't miss her, she hoped Emily wouldn't take offense by her absence.

Margery perceived this, and one morning while they were walking along the promenade she said, "You know, dear, Emily really won't mind you not attending her wedding. I'm sure she'll miss you, but she will understand."

"I hope so. She's been so good to me, I would hate her to feel insulted."

"She won't be." Margery patted her hand reassuringly. "Far from it. Emily is a very unique person in that she often puts others' interests before her own. I know how ambitious she is on your behalf, so she wouldn't want you to throw this opportunity away."

Remembering what Charlie had said, Kitty looked at her sharply. "You mean... in finding a rich husband?"

Margery let out a peal of laughter. "Oh, Kitty, I meant the opportunity of having a more interesting life. Whoever put that idea into your head?"

Kitty was now furious that she had listened to Charlie, even more so to think she'd just repeated what he said.

At her non-reply Margery leaned closer to her. "But if it does happen—the husband, I mean—I can assure you, you'll have far more choice in Whitmouth." She took no notice of Kitty's flaming cheeks, but added enthusiastically, "Look where we are, the Beach Cafe. What do you say about going in and having a nice cup of coffee and a fancy cake or two?"

They were welcomed into the cafe by a pleasant young waitress, who seated them by the window. As they were sitting down, Margery waved discreetly to a man who was seated across the other side of the cafe.

"Well, well," Margery said, raising an eyebrow.

"Who is that?" Kitty whispered.

"That's Justin le March," Margery said, in a pleased tone of voice. And then, not so pleased, added, "And Suzannah Carrington, his artist in residence." And she explained Justin's role as patron of the arts in Whitmouth, and how he, as his father had done before him, opened his home to artists who benefited from his sponsorship whilst developing their career.

Kitty glanced at Justin and saw him say something to Suzannah before getting up and approaching their table. Suzannah's eyes followed him. She looked right at Kitty, but she didn't smile.

"How pleasant to see you, Justin," Margery said, as he took her hand. "This is Kitty, of whom we have often spoken."

His eyes twinkled in a smile as he bent over Kitty's hand. "Enid told me you were coming, and I am delighted to meet you, my dear." He glanced over to his companion. "But if you will excuse me I mustn't be rude. I wished merely to introduce myself. You must bring Kitty over to Whitmouth House for lunch, Margery. We will arrange something."

"Well now," Margery said, as he returned to his own table. "That's two outings for you to look forward to, dear, because I've been thinking, perhaps Lilly could take you to the beach with a picnic on Saturday if the weather holds? Would you like that?"

"Oh, I would," said Kitty. "I could never spend enough time on any beach." Especially on Saturday, she thought, when it would help keep her mind off Emily's wedding day and what Charlie would say when he knew she wasn't going to be there.

Saturday dawned a mellow golden day, the sun giving its last before the onset of winter. After breakfast, Kitty and Lilly took a hansom cab down to the sea front. From there they crossed the bridge over the river and began to climb away from the town, up through the scrubby, windswept copse of trees to the top of the cliffs. Such a long walk gave them an appetite and they had no problem devouring all the food Lilly had prepared. They lay on the grass afterwards and chatted about their lives.

Kitty was surprised to learn that Lilly had come from a workhouse and she instantly thought of Mary Jay with whom she had been so intrigued only a short while ago. But that particular curiosity had faded now, seeming far removed from her new life. "Did you ever know your mother or father?" she asked.

Lilly frowned. "My mother died. Don't think I had a father. Well, you know what I mean. I never *knew* him."

Kitty was tempted for a moment to tell Lilly she had no idea who had fathered her either, but then remembered Margery's warning and kept quiet. But she did ask, "How do you feel, not knowing who he is?"

Lilly shrugged. "Don't know. Don't care. Never think about it really."

I wish I didn't, Kitty thought, bearing in mind the amount of time she brooded over the matter of her paternity. She listened to Lilly chatting on about other aspects of workhouse life. "Well, thank goodness you got out of there," she said, when Lilly finished. "How did you?"

"Miss Blanche, that's Mr. Justin's deceased sister, used to go around doing good. She took me out of the workhouse to Whitmouth House and then I went with Miss Margery to May Cottage."

Kitty recalled Flo saying that Margery had lived at Whitmouth House for a number of years and then had gone to live in Whitmouth itself, but she had never told Kitty why. Her father had hinted enough times that Margery was nothing less than a fancy whore, and Kitty bristled to think he'd gone so far as to suggest such a thing to Charlie.

"How did my aunt come to be at May Cottage?" she asked now.

"Well, Miss Blanche and their mother got killed in an accident," said Lilly, obviously still rather shocked by the event. "Miss Margery was the only one who could bring old Mr. Edwin around—that's Mr. Justin's father. When he got better, he gave May Cottage to Miss Margery because he was so grateful, and I went with her. Then when he died Mr. Justin thought she might be lonely and Miss Enid came to live with us."

"Really?" Kitty said. Although Lilly hadn't given her many details it did seem her father had been wrong about his sister, and she made a mental note that if the opportunity ever arose she would tell Charlie.

"I suppose there might have been a *bit* of how's your father," said Lilly, having further thoughts. "But that's normal for the gentry, isn't it. Many go along quite happily with a wife *and* a mistress because some women don't like doing, well, you know, *that,* because they're afraid of having children. So off the husband goes and takes out his, *you know what,* on his mistress, and everybody's happy." She thought for a moment. "If Mr. Justin had taken it out on somebody else then perhaps his wife would still be alive. The doctor said she should never have no children, but she did. She died a few years ago having their son."

Kitty felt a sudden sadness. In a flash, she saw Leah's pain. The blood. Always that soaked mattress. It was a memory that would never leave her. "How awful," she said, thinking more of the mother than the child.

"I never want to have a baby and go that way," Lilly said, shuddering. "But it isn't likely, considering I don't even have a sweetheart."

"I've seen the baker boy making eyes at you," said Kitty mischievously. "Isn't *he* your sweetheart?"

"Gawd no. Miss Margery would kill me. Don't allow no followers, she don't. Anyway, Miss Enid once told me I would never have a husband. Not that it worries me. When the likes of me gets married all you have to look forward to is poverty and a baby every twelve month. I'm quite happy as I am, thank you very much."

Kitty suspected Enid had probably just said that to stop Lilly hankering after one. "Oh, you'll change your mind one day, Lilly. I mean, how can you never fall in love? And anyway, how could Enid possibly be sure of that?"

"She has the sight, doesn't she? Don't half give me the willies I don't mind telling you. You do know what I'm talking about?"

"Of course I do."

"She's always seeing things."

"Goodness, I wonder what she's seen for me. When I first met her she looked at me as if she had seen a ghost, and she didn't take her eyes off me all evening."

"If it's nasty she won't tell you," Lilly said knowingly. "Until it's over, and then she'll say something like, 'yes, of course,' or, 'ah, so *that's* why….'"

"You haven't heard her say anything about me, have you?"

Lilly looked thoughtful. "Not really. Except… I did hear her once say to Miss Margery, 'well, you have a look the next time you're there, you'll see' when your name was mentioned. But that's all."

"Not much to go on, is it?" Kitty said.

"No, not really." Lilly stood up and looked out over the cliff. "I bet the tide'll be out by now. Do you want to go down? The land dips again a bit further on and there's a path to the beach where the cliff's fallen in. It's a bit steep, but we can manage it, I think."

"Oh, yes, let's," Kitty said enthusiastically. "I can't wait to run along the sand." She held out her hand and they ran down the cliff path together, laughing with glee. She felt a little guilty having gossiped, but on the other hand, this one conversation with Lilly had told her far more than all those weeks spent with her aunt and her polite circle of acquaintances. She was also gratified to think her father was so wrong; Lilly made Margery's relationship with Edwin sound quite respectable, unlike Hern's crude comments, which suggested she had taken on half a regiment of soldiers.

The beach was deserted and the girls took off their shoes and stockings and raced each other out to where the first wavelets trickled in and crossed on the slick, hard sand. Kitty held onto Lilly and shrieked with joy as the cold water trickled over her feet, then they looked for shells that Kitty said she would send home to Martha.

When the heat of the sun faded and they'd had enough, they went home. There they found Margery quite excited; Justin had sent word and they were to go to Whitmouth House the very next day.

Chapter 31

"Stop fidgeting," Lilly complained as she struggled with Kitty's hair.

"It looks good enough," said Kitty. "I'm not going to see the king." Nevertheless, she giggled nervously—she *was* going to Whitmouth House and her Aunt Margery was making such a big fuss about it.

"First impressions are important. I've heard Miss Margery say so."

"He's already seen me and will have formed an opinion," said Kitty, who had felt Justin's eyes on her frequently while they were in the cafe.

"Yes, but that wasn't formal, and this is. So keep still else I'll never get done. They've already called you once."

Eventually Lilly stood back and said Kitty looked a picture. As Kitty walked out into the hall Margery also looked at her with approval and said, now could they go? The carriage had been kept waiting long enough.

ꕥ

Whitmouth House was set in acres of rolling land encompassed on the roadside by a high granite wall.

They turned in through wrought iron gates set beside a granite lodge, and drove along between rows of trees. Before sweeping up and around manicured lawns, they passed over a bridge that spanned the tail end of a small lake. The carriage came to a halt in a courtyard and Kitty stared in awe at the expanse of house before them.

They were warmly welcomed at the door and shown down the hallway. As they passed a wide, curving staircase, Kitty could hear someone playing a piano upstairs, and wondered if it was Suzannah.

Justin was delighted to see them, and as they chatted away Kitty could tell he was very fond of the two women. He regarded Enid most indulgently while she described her latest work of art, and he asked Margery, who was an avid reader, to give him her opinion on a book. When the conversation came around to what Kitty had been doing with herself since she arrived in Whitmouth, Margery explained with some pride how she was sorting and cataloguing all the books in their library.

"That's wonderful, I might actually be able to find what I'm looking for now," Justin said, looking mischievously at Enid, who scolded him humorously, saying he was the worst culprit for replacing their books incorrectly.

When it was announced that lunch was ready, they all went into a large conservatory where a table had been prepared. "I thought we would eat in here," said Justin. "It's far more informal and so pleasant with the sun this time of year. We can also enjoy the view."

Kitty gazed out of the window. She hadn't realized how far they had climbed from the road, and it quite took her breath away to see the whole town of

Whitmouth nestled between the east and west hills, like a child's model. Beyond was the sea, glinting in the sun. Why, she thought, it was almost like sitting on top of the world: Justin must feel like God.

Indeed, he had a heavenly cook, she decided, as she enjoyed each delectable dish set before her. And her mind wandered off thinking what Charlie might have said about how many mouths their extravagant lunch would have fed.

She came back to herself to hear them talking about Justin's son, Reave.

"I noticed he was with one of the gardeners as we arrived," Enid said.

Justin sighed. "He's supposed to be having a music lesson."

"No governess again?" asked Margery, exchanging a look with Enid.

As if mentioning his name conjured him up, there was a rumpus outside the door and Reave ran in, pursued by a maid. He was grubby and his shoes were covered in mud. Oblivious of anyone else in the room he ran straight to Justin, knocking his knife off the table.

Justin dismissed the maid who hovered uncomfortably in the background. "What's happened now?" he asked Reave.

Reave sobbed into his father's arms. "Father, Miss Carrington shouted at me."

Justin sighed. "Did she. Well, perhaps she was justified because you were supposed to be having a lesson. But look at you. What have you been doing?"

"Digging worms," Reave mumbled.

Justin groaned. "Excuse me for a moment, will you, ladies?"

Margery and Enid heaved their chests in unison and continued to eat in silence, but moments later started in their seats as they heard one almighty chord resounding on the piano. Then they heard Reave crying and Suzannah's angry voice.

"Discord. It's in her aura," murmured Enid, and then looked at Margery, who smiled.

Justin returned a while later, minus his small son but accompanied by Suzannah Carrington. Looking at her, Kitty couldn't imagine her having a thing to do with any child, let alone the ruffian Reave. Her blond hair was swept up into an elaborate style. Her figure and dress were perfection. She was like a fine bird with every feather preened immaculately into place. But when Suzannah was introduced to her and looked into her eyes, Kitty recoiled: Suzannah might say she was pleased to meet her, but Kitty knew just the opposite was true. She hadn't lived with Ruth all those years not to recognize dislike.

From then on lunch progressed awkwardly. Suzannah made little attempt to converse with any of them except Justin, and before long she appeared to become bored and even yawned once or twice. In the end, Justin seemed to give up trying to make a go of the meeting, and said he had no objections if she wished to return to her piano; he was sure the ladies would excuse her.

Margery and Enid nodded, perhaps a little too enthusiastically, because Suzannah shot them a venomous look from beneath her long lashes. Nor was Kitty left unscathed; Suzannah said it had been interesting to meet a farm girl who could hold a conversation. Kitty didn't respond except to incline her head slightly. She hadn't enjoyed meeting the mean-hearted woman and had no intention of saying she had. She didn't care how rude anyone thought her.

After Suzannah left them, Justin suggested they all go for a stroll in the garden but Margery declined, saying she had done enough walking that week and would prefer to sit in the sun and read a book. Enid said she would stay with Margery, as she was feeling sleepy after what had been, for her, an unusually large and very rich lunch.

Kitty imagined Justin might change his mind if neither of them wished to accompany him, but he said, "You aren't going to turn me down, are you, Kitty?" And before she could demur he took her arm and led her outside onto the terrace, and down the steps to the garden.

As they meandered through the shrubbery, Justin apologized on Suzannah's behalf and said she often spoke unthinkingly. He blamed it on her artistic temperament. "She really is very gifted," he said. Then he changed the subject and began to ask Kitty about herself. But his many questions were unlike Suzannah's that had been in the main to belittle her.

Justin kept hold of her arm, and occasionally patted her hand as if to reassure her. Quite often, he laughed at her replies, and called her refreshing. So few people spoke their mind in front of him, he said, although he always tried to seek out those who did. In that moment, Kitty realized just how lonely a man he could be, and she felt genuinely sorry he had lost his wife.

They walked on until they came to a swimming pool. Surrounding it were tall evergreens to the north and rhododendrons to the south, well pruned to allow the sun to warm the water. At one end of the pool was a small wooden changing hut. Kitty marveled at it, saying how she envied anyone who could learn to swim in there, rather than in the freezing waters of the River Bovey.

"Margery was telling me you were quite ill after swimming this summer."

"Yes," Kitty said, blushing at the memory. "I stayed in overlong."

"Rivers can be very tricky," Justin said.

"It wasn't the river's fault," said Kitty, and suddenly she found herself telling him what had happened.

"Thank goodness Mr. Chase came when he did," Justin said, when she finished. He was quiet then, as if her experience reminded him of something else.

As they had been talking about the River Bovey, Kitty wondered if he was thinking about the drowning of her grandfather, and she said shyly, "I'd like to thank you for being so kind in helping our family in the past. I didn't know until recently, but my grandfather appears to have been rather a foolish man, and I understand you had a hand in sorting the matter out."

"I wish I could have done more," he replied. "But regarding your grandfather, Kitty, don't think too badly of him. Although I don't approve of gambling, sometimes circumstances are not always what they seem."

He might have said more, but they were interrupted as Reave came thundering around the corner. Neither of them had heard him coming and were quite startled. "What are you doing here?" Justin said crossly.

Reave grinned mischievously. "Miss Carrington said I could come."

"I'm sure she did not."

"She did, Father. Honestly, she did." Reave looked at Kitty. "This lady isn't my new governess, is she?"

"No, she isn't. Kitty is my guest, and you will treat her with respect."

Reave looked at Kitty solemnly. "But Miss Carrington said she *looked* like a governess."

"I'm sure you have that wrong," Justin said. "And you know what happens to little boys who tell fibs."

"But I'm not telling fibs," Reave protested.

"Come along," said Justin. "Back to the house for that lesson."

"I don't want her to teach me."

"I've spoken to you about this before," Justin said sharply.

"But I don't *like* her." Reave looked at Kitty. "Can *you* play the piano, Miss Kitty?"

"A little," Kitty said.

"Can Kitty teach me?" said Reave, dancing circles around them. "*Can* she, Father?"

"Be quiet, Reave," Justin said irritably. "If you barrage Kitty like this you'll frighten her away. Don't take any notice of him, Kitty. He may be little, but he can be quite intimidating."

Reave gave his father a look that tore at Kitty's heart. Poor, motherless little soul, she thought. He obviously loathed the Carrington woman and who could blame him. Kitty didn't believe he'd fibbed either. Suzannah most likely had said she looked like a governess, although the cheek of it made her quite cross, considering how much time and effort she and Lilly had put into her appearance.

ꕥ

Going home in the carriage, Kitty closed her eyes. She wanted to relive her conversation with Justin and try to analyze the feelings she experienced whilst being with him. It was like nothing she'd ever felt before, as if something had caught inside her and wouldn't let go, but was so elusive she couldn't quite grasp it. The only thing she knew for certain was how regretful she had felt when he said goodbye.

She also wanted to mull over those things he had said about her family and wished they hadn't been interrupted, as she might have been able to discover just why he'd helped them. Despite what Lilly had said, she wondered again, *could* he be her father? And was that why she felt so comfortable with him? Comfortable enough to have told him what happened at the river, anyway.

Through her reverie she heard Margery say, "Is she…?"

"I think so."

Kitty felt Enid prod her, but she didn't open her eyes. Although she had no wish to deceive them, she wanted more to be alone with her thoughts. But then, Margery had her full attention when she said, "He'll have to be careful. I'm so worried she'll snare him. Poor Linnet would be mortified, the woman's nothing but a piranha."

"He's a man emerging from a very lonely place, but he isn't a fool," Enid said. "Don't worry, my dear. Truth will out the other in the end."

Kitty's heart fell. Suzannah wanted Justin? Oh, but she hoped for Reave's sake it wasn't true.

ꕥ

On their return to May Cottage, Lillie couldn't wait to get Kitty alone so they could talk about the visit. Kitty told her how enthralled she had been with Whitmouth House, and described in great detail their splendid lunch and how she had enjoyed walking in the garden. However, she omitted to say that Justin alone accompanied her, wanting to keep those few special moments to herself.

She tried to settle herself back down to completing her task in the library, but now and again she would find herself longing to be back at Whitmouth House. She scolded herself for it though. It was presumptuous of her to think of it even; no one had mentioned another visit.

She was rather surprised therefore, and her heart beat rather erratically, when Justin called a few days later and said he wished to speak to her alone.

After a polite preamble, he said, "You've made a real impression on my son. He's been pestering me constantly to know when you might be coming again." He paused then smiled self-consciously. "It isn't often I find myself lost for words, but I can think of no other way to say this except to ask you outright, Kitty. Would you consider coming to live at Whitmouth House, to tutor Reave in the rudiments and generally keep him company?"

Kitty wasn't sure she'd heard him correctly. She stared at him blankly.

Justin continued. "He will need a more experienced tutor later on, but for now I think you would be more than adequate. You wouldn't be considered a servant, or for that matter a governess, but be treated as a member of the family. You would have your own apartments and take your meals with us. I shall allow you time off—if and when you require it. And I will provide you with a gentle mare I have in my stables." He paused. Kitty had an incredulous look on her face. "You will receive a salary," he went on hurriedly. "I shall write to your father, but first I need to know how you feel about it."

"I... I hardly know what to say," she whispered.

"I'm sorry, Kitty, I realize I have sprung this upon you, and I shall, of course, allow you time to think it over, but for pity's sake, please don't take too long." He smiled as he glanced at his watch. "I ask you to forgive me, but I cannot stay. As usual I have a devil of a lot to do." He took her hand and his lips brushed the back of it. "I suppose I should warn you, it will be no small undertaking on your part if you accept my offer. I'm afraid I would be less than honest if I said Reave was an easy child. But please give it some consideration. I shall look forward to your decision, and if you decide not to accept, I shall be disappointed but I will understand. Au revoir, my dear."

Moments later the door opened and Margery came in. "Oh, Kitty," she said. "He *told* me! Oh, how wonderful." Her eyes twinkled. "I think from reading between the lines Reave has been making himself a little pest ever since he met you. So it's that little monkey you have to thank for this."

Kitty smiled, imagining the persistent Reave bouncing up and down waiting for his father's return, wanting to know her answer. She also thought of what Suzannah Carrington would say about the possibility of her presence at Whitmouth House, and her smile faded.

Margery looked at her anxiously. "Kitty... you aren't going to turn him down, are you?"

"Of course not," Kitty said. "I'm just rather shocked that's all. I never imagined anything like this might happen." *But it was my wildest dream.*

Chapter 32

Two weeks later, Kitty took her rather emotional leave of May Cottage. Lilly cried and said she would miss her. Margery told her not to be so silly; Kitty wasn't going to the other ends of the earth and they would see her often. Enid devoured her with her eyes, and smiled mysteriously.

When Kitty reached Whitmouth House, Justin assembled the staff together. He introduced her as Reave's companion and said she should be treated as one of the family.

Kitty looked around her at the sea of faces, but saw no resentment or dislike in any of them. Only afterwards, when she realized the full extent of Reave's mischievousness and became aware of the reasons why his other governesses had left, did she think back to that time and wonder if the staff's smiles hadn't been concealed humor and cynicism.

She had, in part, intuited correctly. On her arrival, although it was nothing personal but the way things had evolved, they'd taken bets to see how long she would last. When word got around a few weeks later that she had spanked the boy and was in before the master, the coachman sighed and prepared for the inevitable.

Cook, who had taken to Kitty from the start, was particularly concerned and decided that before the master dismissed the girl, she would have a word with him. She'd been with the family almost as long as old Nanny, who was now retired, and she didn't feel like standing by and watching an injustice done. In her opinion, Kitty wasn't an upstart giving herself airs because she was at Whitmouth House, but an earnest young woman with a wise head on her shoulders.

But whether she had acted wisely or not, Kitty now had to face the consequences of her actions, and made her way to Justin's study. She knew she had behaved impulsively, but spanking Reave was no more than she would have done to Edward had he been such a pest.

"Ah, Kitty," Justin said, looking up from his desk as she came in. "What is this I hear about Reave being spanked? I thought I made it quite clear that any punishment would be dealt with by myself?"

Kitty suspected that Suzannah, who had witnessed the event, had tittle-tattled to Justin, no doubt hoping to discredit her. "Forgive me, sir. I did indeed spank him, but only twice on his behind because he was so naughty. And not at all hard."

"Oh? And what did he do this time?"

"I found two snakes in my bedroom," Kitty said. "Grass snakes," she added quickly, because by his expression he looked dismayed, as if she might be talking about adders. "But even so, I am quite terrified of the creatures."

"Well, quite." Justin sighed. "In truth, Kitty, I don't know what to do with the child. Perhaps I ought to send him away to school, after all."

Kitty knew who was promoting that idea. It was one of Suzannah's ploys not only to get rid of Reave, but herself as well.

"If I may say so, Mr. Le March, I don't believe that would be a very satisfactory solution," Kitty said awkwardly, knowing she was treading on difficult ground. "What I mean is, although it would rid you of his pranks, I believe it would only make Reave more unhappy."

"Reave is unhappy?" He looked genuinely surprised.

Flo had said once that people became defensive when they were told something they would rather not hear, and Kitty feared this might now be the case. Fair master or not, if she spoke out of turn Justin would probably dismiss her.

But all the same she lifted her chin. "You gave your son into my care, and so I wouldn't have him think I would be shy of speaking on his behalf. Perhaps there are children who can thrive quite happily without being with their parents, but I believe Reave needs you very much. I don't know how to say this in any other way, but I think… I *know* he feels that you are often too busy." She paused. She wasn't making a very good job of this. But how did she tell him? The staff gossiped about it all the time; how their otherwise kind and understanding master had no time for his unruly son because he resented him being alive when his wife had died.

"Go on," Justin said, his voice tense.

Kitty's courage faltered. "In truth, I do not know how to, sir, without… without being bluntly truthful, and thus offending you."

He relaxed slightly. "Above all, Kitty, I hold the truth most precious." He sighed. "No matter what it is, please, go on."

Dear Lord, she thought. Why did this have to fall to her? Why couldn't one of the others have told him? Of course she knew it was because they were afraid for their jobs. Nevertheless, she loved it at Whitmouth House and would rather not leave.

But then she thought of Reave, and his little tear-streaked face as he cried himself to sleep because he thought his father hated him.

"You cannot fool children, sir. They know when they are not wanted, or are resented."

The clocked ticked on the mantelpiece, loud in the silence of the room.

Justin eventually spoke. "I was devoted to my wife, Kitty. When she died…." He gave a deep sigh. "I simply hold myself responsible for her death."

"And," Kitty dared to add quietly, "Reave is a daily reminder of your guilt."

He looked at her, his eyes searching her own. After a moment he said, "You are wise beyond your years, Kitty."

"In some ways, perhaps I have felt pain beyond my years," she replied. "I believe there is no worse thing on earth than feeling rejected by those closest to you, or being told they love you when you know very well they don't. But besides my personal grief, after my mother died I felt trapped, and I resented my baby brother's existence. One night, when I felt particularly angry about it, I suddenly realized it wasn't his fault he had come into the world, and if I didn't change my attitude towards him I would be no better than my father, who has begrudged my existence for all of my life. I know that the circumstances are different, but can you understand what I am trying to explain?"

Justin looked stricken, and Kitty, now feeling awful, searched for something to say that might soften the blow of her words. And then something Flo had once said came to mind. She remembered it, because Flo had said she wished she could abide by it, and Kitty had pondered on it for a long while, wondering in what context she meant.

"I was told once that you cannot carry guilt for someone else's choice," she said tentatively. "You cannot blame yourself for something that was—"

"But it *was* within my control! If that is what you intend to point out."

She knew what she was risking to pursue the matter. "But you *didn't* know. You had no idea your wife had been told that she should never bear a child."

He stared at her. "And how do you know this?"

Kitty blushed. It was Cook who'd told her, but she didn't want to get the kindly woman into trouble. "It isn't that I know it, *exactly*," she said, averting her eyes. "It's just that I've heard Aunt Margery and Enid speaking fondly of your wife...." This was even a stretching of the truth since they'd only actually mentioned Linnet's name once or twice.

"They have no right to discuss such matters." he said crossly.

"Oh, but they haven't," Kitty said quickly, praying he wouldn't quiz them over it. "It's just what I have deduced. And then, through my own experience—"

"Deduced."

She swallowed. "Yes, sir. You know. Read between the lines of conversation."

He gave her a dubious look.

"You won't...." she began, worriedly.

"You've no need to worry. I shall say nothing to them."

Relieved, Kitty said, "They care for you so deeply, sir, and hate to think of any disharmony between yourself and your son. As do I."

Justin sat quietly for a while. Then he gave a deep sigh. "Nor would Linnet be able to bear the thought that I resent our son. It was not a conscious act, you understand. But how can I begin to change things? Where do I begin?"

"All Reave needs is a regular amount of your time," Kitty said, her enthusiasm picking up. "One idea might be for you to come into the schoolroom every morning, just for a little while. And the other would be to look in on him at night when he is in bed. I believe this would make all the difference, and then along with this might come a better understanding between the both of you. I know once I changed my attitude towards my brother, I began to really enjoy him."

"You miss him," he said, regarding her closely.

"Yes, I do, sir. But Reave helps to make up for that loss."

"Then you are happy here?"

"Oh yes," Kitty enthused, tears springing to her eyes. "I will hate to leave."

"Leave?" Justin looked taken aback. "You are going to leave?"

"I... expect you to dismiss me for speaking so plainly. I didn't mean to sound above myself."

"Oh, Kitty." He visibly relaxed. "My dear, I would far rather you speak—as you put it—above yourself and tell me the truth, than grovel and lie. In truth, I cannot imagine what Whitmouth House would be like without you now, so you can put that idea from your head immediately."

He stood up and walked to the window, where he gazed out. He took a deep breath. "She never did tell me, it's true," he said quietly. "And because I loved her so much, it...." He cleared his throat. "When you are one day in love, Kitty, you will understand how hard it is not to touch or caress the object of your desire."

I know that now came the unbidden thought, startling her.

"Now, where is the Rascal Reave?"

"He... he's waiting outside, sir, believing you will call him in to punish him."

"Waiting will probably be punishment enough," he said dryly. "We'll let him sit there for a while longer."

"Indeed, I do believe I punished him sufficiently, for I've never even shouted at him before."

"Snakes," Justin mused. "Why on earth would he bring *snakes* indoors?"

Kitty had asked herself the same question; she was quite sure Reave hadn't meant to frighten her. He seemed to bear her no resentment at all.

"Well," he said, "the matter is dealt with now, and I believe something positive has come out of it. At least I hope so. I will do my best, and we will see what happens. We will review the situation as it goes along. Now you may go, I'm sure you have a lot to attend to."

"Yes, sir," she whispered.

At the door she glanced behind her and saw he was still looking at her. She smiled quickly, and let herself out.

Outside the study Kitty saw a forlorn-looking Reave gazing down at her from between the banisters. "Is Father going to send you away?" he whispered.

"No," Kitty said.

"Does he want to see me?" he said, his lips quivering.

Kitty shook her head. "No, everything is all right. But you must wait there a while." And she hurried into the kitchen where she threw her arms around Cook's neck and burst into tears.

"Oh lor," Cook said. "He hasn't dismissed you has he? Because if he has—"

"No, no, it isn't that."

Cook removed Kitty's arms. "Then what is it, my dear?"

"I don't know. I don't know. But... oh, Cook, he did love her so." And she knew then without a doubt, loving his wife in such a way wiped out any possibility that Justin had philandered with Leah and was her father. But her sudden outburst was nothing to do with that. In truth, she didn't know why she was so upset.

"Aw, it will be relief, I expect," Cook said. "And you'll be in shock. Because I'll tell you now, it took courage to do what you did, my dear. But it needed to be said, and it's done now, so let it go and forget it. I'm sure the master will." Her eyes twinkled. "The boy will also be pleased that you aren't leaving. He's most fond of you, anyone can see that, despite the snakes, which I hear were for her, by the way."

A ghost of a smile played around Kitty's lips. "So, that's why he brought the snakes in."

Cook nodded. "They were to go under her piano lid, but the young tacker was storing them in your room. Meanwhile they wriggled away. He was most put out to think you could find them and he couldn't."

Kitty could see Cook was trying to keep a straight face, but then she had to chuckle at such a thought, and they both burst out laughing.

"You're a very brave girl," Cook said. "And you'll see quite a difference after this, you wait. And my goodness me, won't everyone be pleased about that."

Praise from Cook was praise indeed. And when it became obvious that Justin had listened to Kitty, with the result that Reave saw fit to lessen his plague of pranks, the staff began to relax. So did the coachman, and was even heard to whistle on occasion.

It seemed everyone was much happier except Suzannah, who openly stated that Kitty was spoiling the child. Once, when they were alone, she even told Kitty that when she became mistress of Whitmouth House she would be the first to go.

ꕤ

As promised, Justin provided Kitty with a reliable mount called Bliss, an apt name for the gentle mare who gave her a very smooth and pleasant ride. Weather permitting, she rode every day with Reave, whose Dartmoor pony was called Toad, Reave's own christening. Toad seemed to like his small master and behaved himself fairly well except to canter off from time to time in protest if Reave showed inappropriate behavior. But the boy was an excellent rider and Toad rarely managed to unseat him, if that was his intention.

Because of the clement weather, Kitty and Reave continued to ride right up until mid-November, when suddenly it turned sharp and unkind. Then only the grooms exercised the larger horses and Toad was given his winter's rest. Now Kitty turned her attention to indoor matters and spent her time helping Reave, who said he wanted to make everyone he knew a Christmas gift.

Justin was amused when he was banned from the schoolroom, in case he walked in on something he shouldn't see, although Reave, unwilling to relinquish the time he had gained with his father, went downstairs to Justin's study every morning to see what *he* was doing. Kitty either waited for him in the schoolroom or went into the kitchen and had a gossip with Cook. She missed her morning liaison with Justin, and knew she wouldn't be sad when Christmas was over and they resumed their normal routine.

Margery and Enid came over on Christmas Eve, and they brought with them Lilly who went off to the kitchen to visit her old friends.

There was a flurry of excitement as the other guests arrived. Kitty was delighted to find amongst Justin's circle of friends and acquaintances an element of the unusual. Artists and musicians whom the family had patronized over the years called in during the day to wish him well or ruffle Reave's hair, and a few of them stayed for dinner. She imagined many of them had come from quite obscure or insignificant backgrounds, and because of this didn't feel quite so out of place as she might have done. It seemed to her that Justin was quite selective with whom he mixed and she seemed to be accepted warmly, although not without some curiosity, by his friends.

She was disappointed when Thomas decided not to return to Whitmouth House for Christmas. Apparently, he was with friends on the Continent, and although Justin commented that it cheered him to think Thomas was having fun, she thought he was rather disappointed, too.

The celebrations went on through Christmas Day until the following evening, when many of the guests left for other commitments. Others went out the next morning after breakfast for the hunt. Suzannah was one of them and made a show of disappointment when Justin declined to join her. It was the anniversary of Linnet's death and those who remembered that Justin liked to spend the day quietly, commented privately on her insensitivity.

"Let's hope it puts her off, the hard-hearted so-and-so," Cook said, and told Kitty that, according to Suzannah's maid, her mistress had said she was 'bored and rather put off' by Justin's show of grief. She reckoned it was an insult to herself, who was alive and entertaining, when he couldn't forget a dead wife.

Reave was subdued later that day, no doubt on account of all the excitement of his birthday and the late nights, and perhaps because it was also the anniversary of his mother's death. Poor little mite, Kitty thought, although she had to admit he did seem a lot happier these days, and she hoped his shaky beginnings would one day fade from his memory.

He lolled in front of the fire, while Kitty sat beside him quietly reading a book. It wasn't long before she saw his eyes droop, and he got up onto the settee beside her, put his head on her lap and fell asleep. Kitty lowered her book and closed her eyes. She listened to the fire crackling and thought about Furze and what they all might be doing. Emily and Martha had sent her gifts for Christmas, but she had received nothing from Charlie, not even a letter. Today was also the anniversary of her mother's death. That particular pain was a little easier this year, and she hoped her mother was happy, wherever she was.

She thought of Edward's birthday and the preparations Emily might have made for it. She knew if anyone could make it enjoyable Emily would, and not for the first time, silently blessed her for coming into their lives.

The door opened and Justin came in. She placed a finger to her lips to indicate

Reave was asleep. Justin smiled. He had brought a book with him, and sat down opposite her and began to read. Feeling comfortable and secure, Kitty closed her eyes again and thought there was no better way in which she could have spent the afternoon.

ꕥ

The winter was short and mild in the New Year, and everyone was happy to see such an early spring. Kitty and Reave resumed their riding, and sometimes, to Reave's absolute delight, Justin rode with them around the estate. Kitty came to know the tenants, and subsequently when she and Reave rode out alone they were greeted cordially. She glowed with pride when comments were made on how well the boy was doing.

Suzannah, however, didn't express this opinion and criticized Kitty whenever the occasion arose. When Kitty said one evening that she intended to teach Reave to swim that summer, Suzannah retorted, "Stuff and nonsense. Why would *anyone* want to learn how to do that?"

"It can save lives, Miss Carrington," Kitty said confidently, knowing Justin shared her views, because it had been something they had discussed and agreed upon.

"Really, Miss Underwood, you have the strangest ideas," Suzannah persisted.

Justin overheard the exchange. "I think you would do well to remember why you are here, Suzannah, and leave the management of my son to Kitty. As far as I am concerned, she is doing an excellent job and no more will be said about it."

Kitty was astonished that Justin had spoken so brusquely. Embarrassed, she made the excuse she would check on Reave, and excused herself to get away from Suzannah's venomous glare. She was surprised when Justin followed her upstairs.

"Kitty," he said. "I wish to speak to you."

"What is it, sir?" she said, alarmed. "I haven't spoken out of place, have I?"

"In no way at all. I only wanted to say that you really are doing such a good job with Reave."

"It is very good of you to reassure me."

"Yes, well, I wouldn't want you to be hurt by any criticism."

His words warmed her. Enid had been right, she thought. He could see through Suzannah's wiles. And how relieved Reave would be about that. He was most upset after overhearing the servants gossiping that his father intended to marry her.

Justin smiled down at her. She loved it when his eyes crinkled like that. "So everything is all right?"

"Yes," she whispered. "Everything is."

After he closed her apartment door she stood, staring at the back of it. She put her hand to her flaming cheeks. What had happened in that moment? For something had, there was no doubt. That pull, that attachment she'd felt when they first met. And lately, enjoying his company so much, longing to hear his voice.

She shivered. What invisible thread had been spinning that now threatened to catch her in its web?

Chapter 33

From that moment on, Kitty's life at Whitmouth House changed. It was as if she had come out into the light after being in a dark place. Never before had she felt so happy to be alive. She awoke each morning eager for the day ahead. And at night she was happy to fall asleep so she might perchance dream of her beloved. Yet alongside this was love's cruel sting; falling in love with Justin le March, master of Whitmouth House, was a very futile thing to do, and she spent the following months in a dizzy euphoria, both in ecstasy and agony.

The ecstasy was easy to endure. Swimming with Justin in the pool where, amidst much laughter and only a few tears, they taught Reave to swim. Suzannah lurked and sulked either by the edge of the pool or stomped back to the house and took out her frustration on the piano. Those strident sounds carried all the way down the garden, and Kitty smiled to herself one afternoon when she saw one of the gardeners conducting with his spade. Cook told her the staff were delighted to see the master having so much fun, and tickled pink by Suzannah's musical tantrums.

When Justin was able to, he rode with them, and he told Kitty she was ready to move up to a more challenging mount. He suggested she ride Thomas Gordon's horse, Hector, who was stabled at Whitmouth while Thomas was away. Reave, he said, could then try Bliss and they would be more evenly paced. Both Kitty and Reave were thrilled, and Kitty found she could manage Hector quite well; although he was old, he was still spirited, but behaved politely when she was on his back and nickered when he saw her approaching the stables.

The agony was harder to bear. She knew it was a hopeless, hapless love, but like Leah before her, Kitty was discovering that love knows no boundaries, and desire has little common sense.

At the end of July, Kitty had to relinquish Hector for a while when Thomas arrived. She noticed Suzannah tried to monopolize him just as she did Justin. However, he managed to avoid the woman most of the time, and consequently they spent a lot of time together. Kitty couldn't say she was entirely displeased. They got along extremely well; just as they had the day they had ridden to Lower together. Indeed, that was something Thomas had never forgotten: he told her the memory of that day would remain with him forever.

One evening, after Kitty put Reave to bed, she returned downstairs to find Justin and Thomas on the terrace deep in conversation. Normally she would have joined them, but as their conversation sounded particularly intense, not wanting to intrude, she went to her favorite seat by the potted palm in the conservatory and began to read.

From there she could hear them talking quite clearly, and she smiled at Thomas's enthusiasm as he talked about the changes he would bring to the manor as he gradually took over from his father. He had spoken to her often of these matters, and while Kitty knew he feared his father and would find it difficult to oppose him when the time came, she applauded his courage. She thought he was an earnest young man, and she hoped for the sake of all concerned he would succeed.

Engrossed in her book, she didn't notice when the conversation took a turn, but she lost interest in her paragraph when she heard Justin say, "It is important in your position to have a wife who is capable and has some intelligence. You know what that situation demands."

"You have any doubt I would choose any other?" Thomas said.

"No, Thomas," Justin said solemnly. "I trust your judgment."

"If only my father did," Thomas said dully. "He will have his own ideas. But I am determined to have my way over this matter."

It sounded very much to Kitty that Thomas had plans to marry, and she was surprised. Although they had become close in recent weeks, often sharing intimate thoughts as one friend to another, he had never mentioned it to her, and she felt a little hurt. But then she reminded herself: of course he wouldn't discuss it with her. She was a mere farm girl and she must never forget it.

Deciding it might be better if she didn't overhear anything else that wasn't intended for her ears, she uncurled from her seat. She had barely taken two steps, however, when she heard Justin say, "I hear there's been trouble in North Devon, and I fear it might spread south. It is on estates like your father's where these things are happening, and although I warned him years ago unfortunately he didn't heed me."

"It's his own fault if anything does happen," Thomas said bitterly. "Yet he has made it clear if he finds any dissension he'll, 'string them up himself,' or, 'send them to the colonies.'"

Kitty's mouth went dry. The matter of Thomas's mystery sweetheart fled from her mind, to be replaced by what Charlie and Acheson had been up to before she had come to Whitmouth. Dear God, she thought. What if they had taken things any further? She hurried upstairs, deciding that she must write to them without delay.

Kitty had written the letter, but not sealed it, when she heard voices in Reave's room, which was next to her own. When she opened the adjoining door she found Suzannah ordering him to get into bed.

"I caught him sneaking down the stairs," Suzannah said.

"I wasn't sneaking," Reave said tearfully. "I had a bad dream and I was looking for you, Kitty."

Kitty sighed inwardly. She wished Suzannah would stop interfering. "I came up early to do some correspondence," she said. "I'll be in my room for a while longer and will leave the door open between us. You try and go back to sleep now, Reave."

Reave looked unhappy, but made no protest and got back into bed. Kitty returned to her room, followed by Suzannah who was about to leave when Reave cried out again.

Susannah gave Kitty a disparaging look as Kitty returned to his room, and closed the door between them.

Kitty took Reave into her arms and soothed him until he settled down. When he was fast asleep, she returned to her room and sealed her letter.

She never had the need to send it, however, because the next morning she heard from Emily saying Hern had suffered a stroke. Although Emily made no suggestion she should return home, Kitty decided she would, knowing then she could speak to Charlie directly. It was arranged that she would travel to Furze with Margery, and they would leave the following day.

Margery wasn't particularly pleased to be going to Furze, but called it an unavoidable necessity. She was preoccupied all the way there, and consequently conversation was sparse. But this gave Kitty a chance to think about what she would say to Charlie when she saw him. She felt uneasy about talking to him at all, as she was afraid he would still be sore about her living at Whitmouth House.

When the carriage turned into Furze lane, Margery's nose curled with distaste. Kitty was embarrassed to see how poor everything looked. The Crying Shame was almost buried now by the undergrowth. The hedges were unkempt and the carriage had difficulty negotiating the lane. She wondered, had it always been like this? Or was she comparing it to the standards of Whitmouth House?

She felt nauseated by the clutter and old dog bones in the back porch, and it smelled as if a tomcat was visiting. Something in a bucket covered with a cloth stank, and Kitty pinched her nose as she passed it.

She pushed open the back door and a small boy, who was Edward, began screaming when he saw them. He ran, petrified, to the stair door, shouting, "'Me! 'Me!"

Kitty felt hurt to think he didn't know her: little Edward whom she had nurtured and cared for during the first fragile months of his life.

They heard Emily call out, "Yes, I've seen them, I'm coming," and moments later she came downstairs. Kitty was rather shocked to see her; she had lost weight and looked exhausted.

"Och, I am that pleased to see you," Emily said, rushing towards them. "*That* pleased." She pushed a strand of hair out of her face. "You'll have to excuse the mess. I haven't been well myself, and have had no time to see to things. Charlie has his hands full. Hern can't do anything you see, he's paralyzed down one side and needs constant care."

"Oh dear," said Margery. "I had no idea it was that bad. Poor Emily."

At Margery's sympathy Emily became tearful. "It was such a shock, I can barely get over it."

"There, there," Margery said stoutly, guiding her into a chair. "We're here now, and we'll do whatever we can to help. Is the doctor hopeful he will recover?"

"Well, somewhat," Emily replied. "He says he should regain use of his limbs, but he'll never be the same." Tears threatened again. "I know there's nothing you can do. Nothing any of us can do, except hope and pray, but it means such a lot to me to have you here." She looked at Kitty in particular, and Kitty felt a twinge of guilt, knowing her ulterior motive for coming.

The door opened behind them and they turned to see it was Martha. In the short time Kitty had been away her youngest sister had shot up inches and lost her little-girl look. "Goodness, I hardly recognize you," Kitty said.

"I wouldn't have recognized *you* at all," Martha said, standing back to look at her. "You look such a grand lady now."

Edward was getting used to his visitors by now and decided to let his presence be known. He jumped up and down beside Emily, shouting, "Gand aidee! Gand aidee!" And they all laughed to see his antics.

"Well," Margery said, with a sigh. "I suppose we ought to go up and see Hern."

"He's probably sleeping," Emily said. "But you may as well take your things upstairs and get settled in. Perhaps Kitty could share Martha's bed, and, Margery, you can have the spare room. I'll air the bed for you."

"I can't wait to hear all your news," Martha said, as Kitty followed her upstairs. "Whitmouth sounds a lovely place. I bet you didn't really want to come home, did you." She sounded as if she wanted Kitty to deny it, so Kitty evaded the answer altogether so as not to hurt her feelings. But, in truth, she was feeling very strange to be at Furze again.

"Look," Martha said. "Here are those shells you sent me. Charlie made a small box and I stuck them on the lid. Aren't they pretty?"

Kitty turned the box over in her hand. "He's made a lovely job of it. But then, he's clever that way."

"Do you like the way I've stuck those shells on?"

"Oh yes, you've arranged them beautifully." Kitty could remember quite clearly the day she had found them. Such a lot had happened since then, and suddenly she felt as if her life was moving along in leaps and bounds, a little too fast for her.

"I would like you to keep it. I bet Charlie would like you to have something of his too—he's always talking about you."

"Is he?" Kitty turned, surprised. "What does he say?"

Martha shrugged. "Oh, this and that." But she didn't elaborate, and after a while she left Kitty alone and returned to her outside chores.

When Kitty began to unpack, she realized with some dismay that the clothes she'd brought with her were quite unsuitable. She was thankful no one had thrown out her old things and hoped she could still fit into them. She wondered what on earth she had been thinking of. How could she have forgotten so quickly?

Suddenly, she longed for Reave and the sound of Justin's voice. As she returned downstairs, she had to stifle the urge to run out of the door, up the lane and away towards Moretonhampstead, where she could catch a coach to Whitmouth.

"It seems a bit strange I expect, doesn't it?" Emily said, looking at her closely. "But look at you. When you left here you were a girl, and now you've come back a young woman."

Kitty chuckled. "At times Reave would age an angel." She sat down and Edward clambered onto her lap. He'd got over his initial shyness and now seemed fascinated with her.

Emily smiled. "But you are happy, dear?"

"Oh yes, Emily. I'm so glad I went now. I really love it at Whitmouth House."

"I'm so happy for you, Kitty. I can tell by your letters that you make the most of every moment. I do so enjoy getting them, you know."

"Do you still pass them on to Charlie?"

"Yes." Emily frowned. "Why, don't you want me to?"

"Well, yes… but he's never written to me."

Emily sighed. "You know Charlie. He didn't want you to go away in the first place, and I suspect he hopes it's just a temporary situation."

"I almost dread seeing him," Kitty admitted.

"I thought you might. That's one of the reasons why I suggested to Margery there was no need for you to return for the wedding."

"That was very thoughtful of you, Emily."

"To be honest, I'm surprised that you came this time. Though I appreciate your kindness, there was no need."

"There was every need," Kitty said quietly. "Please don't misunderstand me, Emily, it is so good to see you again, and I am concerned about what happened. But I also came for another reason." She knew she had once promised Charlie she would never say a word to anyone, but now she felt there was no choice; she had to trust someone. "You must promise not to say anything, but just before I received your letter I overheard something I thought Charlie should know about. There have been troubles in North Devon, and—"

Emily put her finger to her lips. "No need to say any more," she said quietly. "I am aware where Charlie's sympathies lie."

"Of course, I may be worrying on no account," Kitty said quickly, searching Emily's eyes.

Emily shook her head. "I fear not. There's good reason to be concerned. Flo tells me they are holding meetings at Barn Cottage. She's beside herself, because Acheson won't listen to reason."

This was the worst news Kitty could have possibly heard. Not only were they carrying on, but on Furze property. "But that's madness! What is to be done to stop them?"

But Emily never had a chance to reply, because just then the door opened and Charlie came in with a bowl of eggs. His eyes flickered over Kitty then settled on Edward, who slid off Kitty's lap and ran over to him, putting one arm around his legs.

"Martha gave me these to bring in," Charlie said, putting the bowl on the table.

"Egs," Edward said, grinning from ear to ear. He pointed at Kitty. "Aidee. Gand aidee!"

Kitty tried to laugh it off, hoping Charlie would join her, but a smile didn't cross his face. He ruffled Edward's hair. "That's no lady, Edward. That's your sister, Kitty." He looked defiantly at her. "I saw the carriage arrive. Did you come on your own?"

"No," Kitty said. "Aunt Margery came, too."

"Hadn't better hang around here then," he said tightly, and turned to leave.

"Charlie—"

"I'd change your shoes if I were you," he said without looking at her. "That's if you have anything left that's suitable."

After he'd gone Kitty looked helplessly at Emily. "I hoped he wouldn't be like this, but I must still talk to him."

"You can but try." Emily hadn't the energy to tell Kitty she had pleaded with both Charlie and Acheson, and was now treated less kindly because of it.

By the time Kitty had found a pair of her old boots, Charlie was in the barn. He must have known when she walked in because the door creaked, but he didn't acknowledge her presence until she spoke.

Disappointed, Kitty said, "I thought you'd be pleased to see me."

"I hardly recognized you," Charlie said curtly.

"I've had to change my outward appearance to fit into where I live," she said defensively. "I can hardly wear a woolen shawl and heavy boots in a drawing-room."

"There's changing to fit in and changing so as you don't fit in anywhere."

"I fit in quite nicely where I am," Kitty said lightly. "I'm very happy and they respect and like me." She mentally excluded Suzannah, of course.

"While you're of use, they will," Charlie said shortly.

Kitty opened her mouth to make an angry retort then thought better of it. "I'm not here to argue with you, Charlie. I can't change the way you think, or behave. Although I would ask you to reconsider it."

"And what is that supposed to mean?"

"You know what I'm talking about. You once told me to forget it. Well, I never have."

"Oh aye?" He sounded indifferent, but his expression was keener.

"I realize perhaps you think you are doing the right thing, but it's so terribly dangerous. Can't you wait and see what happens when things change at the manor?"

He pushed a lock of hair out of his eyes. "What do you mean, when things change?"

"I know they're going to."

"It's Thomas bloody Gordon, isn't it," he growled. "You're on about him again. Isn't filling the pages of your letters about him enough without you coming back here to rub my nose in it?" Kitty stared at him. She took a step back as if he'd struck her when he added, "Why don't you stick to your search to find a rich husband and stay out of my life?"

Her voice shook as she fought back tears. "I'm not searching for anyone! The only reason I write about Thomas in my letters is so that you'll realize he isn't like his father, and that things will change if only you'll give it time. Then there'll be no need for you to get into trouble. His father will have no mercy on anyone he finds. He'll *transport* people, or," her voice caught in a sob, "or *hang* them. Oh, for pity's sake, Charlie, *why* won't you listen to me?"

"For the same reason you don't listen to me. I'm telling you, Kitty, you're treading on very dangerous ground. They'll use you and then—"

"What I do with my life is my own business. I don't need your help. But it's obvious you need mine. I heard them talking about what the squire intended to do to any troublemakers, and I came home to warn you. I *know* I'm right."

"Yes, and I know *I'm* right too, on both accounts. About you and the bloody gentry. And about what has to happen around here so that people have something to live for!"

They stood there, staring each other down like two angry roosters.

Kitty was exasperated. "Is there *nothing* that will stop you?"

He looked at her for the longest time then said quietly, "In all this world there is one thing." He moved closer. His breath was warm on her cheek as he added, "If you would come home and marry me, Kit."

He pulled her to him, and before she could protest, he'd taken her into his arms and was kissing her deeply.

Part of her responded to him; that female part of her, aroused so many times in her dreams when longing for Justin, felt very comforted to have a man's arms around her. But she forced herself away from him, knowing that to fulfill her need in the wrong way would just create another problem, not resolve one.

"I'm sorry," she said, her voice ragged. "I care for you very much, but—"

"You want me," he said. "I know you do. I can tell."

"I do find you attractive," she said, blushing. "But I'm sorry, Charlie, I don't believe that marrying you would be the right thing to do." She knew how those words must hurt him, and unable to look him in the face, she picked up her skirts and ran to the door.

He didn't try to stop her, but shouted after her, "I pity you, Kitty Underwood, when you can't tell real love when you see it."

Kitty burst into tears as she went across the yard. When she got in, she hurried through the kitchen, mumbled an excuse to Emily, and ran upstairs.

ꕥ

The next morning, Kitty avoided looking at Charlie when he came in. She felt him hover behind her, but when she didn't acknowledge him he went out again without saying a word.

"Do you want to talk about it?" Emily said, noticing how miserable she looked.

Kitty glanced towards the stairs. Margery was helping Hern with his breakfast, but the stair door wasn't closed.

Emily went over to latch it. "She'll be up there for a while yet," she said quietly. "Come on, tell me all about it."

"Charlie asked me to marry him," Kitty said. "He more or less said if I did he would be different." She blushed as she remembered how her body had responded to his kiss. "I do find him attractive, but… I said no. And now I feel guilty because if I had accepted him, I might have saved him getting into trouble."

Emily noticed Kitty's embarrassment and felt cross with Charlie, wondering just how far he'd gone to try and persuade her. He was considerably older and more experienced, and would know just how to get his own way.

"You know, Kitty, sometimes we make promises we really mean to keep. And for a while we often do. But I think in Charlie's case your instinct was right. Oh, I'm sure he meant what he said, and he would try his best to keep his word, but whether he could is another matter. I mean, when you think of it logically, how could he deny the very principles he lives and breathes by? They've accompanied him through his whole life so far."

Tears stung Kitty's eyes. "That's what I thought. But not only that, there are other reasons."

"If you feel that strongly about it then you must not then. I'll tell you something now and you must never forget it. Marrying someone for the wrong reason only brings you misery. Don't misunderstand me; I'm not talking from experience. Despite what has happened here, I'm still happy to be at Furze. But I have seen enough during my lifetime to know that fact to be true."

Kitty heard a movement from upstairs. "I ought to go and relieve Aunt Margery now, oughtn't I?"

"Have a cup of tea first," Emily said. "Your aunt is quite capable of managing on her own for a while longer."

They drank their tea in silence then Kitty went upstairs. Emily felt saddened about what had happened. She knew how much Charlie thought he loved her, and perhaps he did in his way. But love meant giving someone space and respecting their wishes, and if he couldn't see that Kitty was happy where she was and didn't want the life he could offer her, he ought not to cause her to feel so torn.

If only he didn't have this particular point of view, she thought, but she knew the circumstances of his childhood and she feared he would never get over them. She didn't know what, if anything, he had ever told Kitty about his past, but she was aware that after being taken advantage of by the master of the house in which she'd been a servant, when it was discovered she was with child, his mother had been kicked out to fend for herself and had become a prostitute. It was obvious to Emily that before she sold Charlie in order to survive, she had passed on to him all her bitterness and hatred for the rich.

It was not an uncommon story, she was sure, but Charlie's beginning had scarred him for life, perhaps even set him on the path of self-destruction. At least Kitty's decision would prevent her from getting towed along with it.

ഌ

Hern was awake and looked around as Kitty came in the door.

"You remember Kitty?" said Margery, as she picked up his breakfast tray.

"'Course I bleddy do," he said, scowling at Margery. He spoke with difficulty, because the stroke had paralyzed the left side of his face.

"I shall tell Emily you're starting to be more like your old self," Margery said tartly, and went downstairs in a huff. Hern cursed under his breath, and Kitty felt sorry for Emily who must have to put up with this, day in and day out.

"Hello, Father," she said.

He grunted. "You came too then."

"Yes, I came. I'm sorry you're ill, but you'll be better again."

"Never be the same."

Kitty drew up a chair and sat beside him. Hern didn't say anything more; he didn't ask her how she was, or what she had been doing. She didn't know what to say to him either. Nothing had changed.

When his eyes closed, she went downstairs to find that Margery had gone over to Forde to see Flo. This gave Kitty some time alone with Emily in which to catch up on other news, and she learned that Ruth was now at Lower, keeping house for Colan while waiting to be married to their cousin Michael.

"Are you going to see her while you are here?" Emily said. "She comes over quite regularly now. We get along quite well."

"She might have forgiven you," Kitty said wryly, "but I bet she still hates me because of the dress."

"Och no, I don't think so," said Emily. "If it hadn't been for that she wouldn't have met Michael. Since she fell in love with him, she's been quite different. Why don't you go over to Lower to see her? I really think she would like that, and it would give you a break from here for an afternoon."

"I must admit I would like to see Uncle Colan again," Kitty said. "But today I'm going to help you, Emily. And when Aunt Margery returns, I'll go and see Flo."

ഌ

Margery had gone to Forde with intent. She also had an ulterior motive in coming to Furze, albeit a small one, but there was a certain curiosity she wanted to satisfy before going home, if only to prove she was right.

Ever since Kitty had arrived in Whitmouth, Enid had insisted she was the image of the workhouse girl whose portrait she had done all those years ago. Of course, Margery knew it had to be nonsense, and thought perhaps Enid was remembering Leah instead. Not that Kitty really looked like Leah, come to think of it, but anyway now she was here she would be able to look at the portrait and see for herself.

Flo was delighted to see her and said it was just as well Margery hadn't come sooner because she had been out the previous day, and up a good deal of the night to a delivery.

"Kitty will be relieved about that. She was worried you'd be upset she hadn't been to see you, but she was so tired last evening she went to bed early."

Flo knew very well why Kitty had retired early, because when she came home, Charlie's proposal of marriage was the first thing Acheson told her about. Charlie had, apparently, come over to Forde in a real state because Kitty had turned him down. But Flo didn't say anything to Margery; the last thing she wanted was to hear her friend's opinion about that!

"I'd better get a cake on if Kitty's coming," Flo said, with a chuckle. "Now tell me all about everything, Margery. How's Enid doing?"

"Very well. She commands a high price now for her portraits—the one of Mary will be worth something one day. Where did you hang it by the way, Flo?"

Since Kitty had gone to live in Whitmouth, Flo had hung the painting in the room Mary had occupied, and had placed her Bible on a small table beneath it. Acheson rarely went in there and Flo figured if he did, now that Kitty was far away and he had nothing to compare it with, he wouldn't see the resemblance.

"It's upstairs in the spare room," she said. "It was the only place I had really."

"Would you mind if I looked at it?"

"'Course not. Go on up. It's the first door to your left."

Flo considered Margery's request a bit odd, but then she thought Enid might have asked her to have a look. Perhaps, she mused, as Enid had no children of her own, her paintings filled that space, and she liked to keep an eye on them from time to time to see how they were doing. In any case she was pleased she'd hung it now. She would have hated Enid to think she had thrown kindness in her face. As it was, Margery might wonder why it was hung on a wall in an unused bedroom rather than in the front room. Oh dear, Flo thought, always complications, and the nightmare never completely went away.

When Margery came downstairs, Flo caught her breath. Margery was clutching Mary's Bible in her hand.

Margery didn't say anything for a moment. Then she said, "When Kitty arrived at May Cottage, Enid said she recognized her. I didn't believe her, of course. That's why I wanted to see the portrait of Mary for myself." She paused. "She's Kitty's mother, isn't she? Lord, Flo, whatever happened?"

Flo put down the mixing bowl, and sighed. "You'd better sit down, Margery."

❧

When Margery returned to Furze, Kitty was in the scullery. Kitty heard her murmur something to Emily, then go upstairs.

Emily looked around the door. "Margery's back, dear, are you going up to Forde?"

"Will you be all right, Emily? What about Father?"

"Margery says she'll keep an eye on him," Emily said. "She says she has a headache and would rather be quiet upstairs."

"Why don't you take advantage of that and have a rest?" Kitty said. "I'll take Edward with me."

At one time Kitty would have taken Edward across to Flo's just as he was, but now she tidied him up and wiped his face. "It seems such a short while ago I did this," she said, buttoning up his little jacket. "Oh, Edward, I have missed you. If it hadn't been for Reave I don't think I would have been able to bear it."

"Wreve?" he said, hardly able to get his mouth around the new word. "Play wiv Wreve?"

"Perhaps you will be able to one day," Kitty said, having in the back of her mind a plan to one day invite him and Martha to Whitmouth House, if Justin would permit it. And of course, she thought with an inner sigh, if Emily would ever be able to spare Martha.

Acheson opened the door to them and Edward scampered on inside, eager to find Flo. But Kitty stood there, feeling awkward and unsure because of Acheson's expression.

Flo saved the moment as she came to greet her warmly, tears in her eyes as she hugged her and drew her inside. "You're looking proper grown up, isn't she Acheson?" she said.

"I hardly recognized her," Acheson said.

Kitty exchanged a look with Flo, and Flo shook her head slightly, as if to say, don't mind him.

But Acheson was feeling in a provocative mood. "Charlie's been over."

It was all he needed to say. By the expression on both their faces, Kitty knew they were aware of Charlie's proposal and her refusal, and her temper rose a notch, angry that he would get to her dearest friends before she had a chance to.

"I thought you would have jumped at the chance of settling down and having your own family, instead of looking after someone else's child," Acheson went on. "He's a good man, Kitty, and he'd take care of you."

"I know he is, Acheson, and I'm fond of him. But I don't think it's right to wed someone you don't love. Besides," Kitty looked him square in the eyes, hoping that what she was about to say might hit home, "I would not be a widow so soon."

"And what do you mean by that?" Acheson said, frowning.

"I'm sure if Charlie has told you one thing he's told you another. And he will have told you why I came home."

"What business you think it is of yours I don't know," Acheson grumbled, glancing at Flo. "Interfering in things that don't concern you."

"I don't call warning someone about to do something foolish, *interfering*," Kitty retorted. "I've also told him that Thomas Gordon has definite plans for the manor. When he's of age next year he—"

"If you think Thomas Gordon has the guts to stand up to his father you're as much of a dreamer as he is!" Acheson snapped.

"He doesn't sound as if he's dreaming. I've heard him talking about this ever since I've known him, and I know he intends to use the inheritance he receives from his mother. He can do what he likes with it, and his father won't be able to stop him."

"You're too young to know what the hell you're talking about," Acheson shouted. "To think you would trust the likes of Thomas Gordon. You're still setting your sights above you, aren't you, my girl?"

"This has nothing to do with anything but wanting to save you from getting into trouble, Acheson! Oh, *why* are you and Charlie being so stubborn?"

"I could ask the same thing of you, my lady."

Flo, having had enough for one day, cried for them to stop it. Her head ached abominably, and hearing the two people she loved most in the whole world argue in this way was just too much.

"Kitty was only doing what she thought was right," she said wearily. "And as far as I'm concerned you'd do well to heed her, Acheson."

"I suppose it was you who told her about all this," Acheson said accusingly.

"Don't you ever blame Flo," Kitty said. "I found out about it some time ago. Then just recently, when I heard Thomas and Justin le March talking about what the squire would do if he has trouble at the manor, I thought I should warn you."

Whether Acheson believed her or not she didn't know. He didn't say, or ask any more about the matter but drank his tea in silence then went outside. Kitty could see the frustration and hurt in Flo's eyes. "Oh, Flo, I'm sorry," she said. "I didn't mean to cause trouble."

Flo shrugged helplessly. "Aw, Kitty, my dear, it isn't your fault, you only said what you thought was right. Acheson's got this bee in his bonnet and nothing I can say makes any difference. I don't understand it really; he's always been such a sensible man. But this passion, there's no reason to it."

Kitty thought of her feelings for Justin. She was rapidly coming to the conclusion that where passion was concerned there *was* no reason.

She held out her arms and Flo fell into them. How things change in such a short time, Kitty thought. It wasn't long ago that Flo had held and comforted her like this. But now it was as if she was the parent and Flo the child. "Oh, Flo," she sighed. "I wish there was something I could do."

Flo shook her head sadly. "There's nothing either of us can do, my dear. Things have to take their course. All roads lead to somewhere though. It's just that sometimes, well, the way's a bit hard, that's all. We just have to keep plodding on, and we'll get there in the end." She looked anxiously into Kitty's face. "There *isn't* anything between you and Thomas Gordon is there?"

"No, we're just good friends. He shares his thoughts with me and we get along so well." Kitty laughed softly. "I suppose you could say I love him like a brother." She felt Flo stiffen. "But that's all right, isn't it? I mean, there can be no harm in having such a friendship? I know he's a Gordon, but—"

"No, no harm in that my dear. But...." Flo took a deep breath. "There are some things that come to us in life that we have to deal with. Some things we don't ask for, and then at the time, we do what seems to be the right thing. Kitty, there's something I must—"

But just as Flo might have told Kitty what had been on her mind for so long, Edward screamed. No one had been taking any notice of him for quite a while and he had been delving into the coalscuttle, and now had pulled it over on himself. By the time they had sorted him out, cleaned him off and comforted him, the moment for Flo to unburden herself had passed.

Chapter 34

Kitty arose early the next morning and bid her father a cheerful good morning, to which he made no response. She went downstairs, where Edward ran towards her then climbed up onto her lap while she ate breakfast. Kitty cuddled him close, pleased to think that he had lost his shyness with her.

"I've decided I would like to go and see Ruth," she said, "but are you sure I can't do anything around here today, Emily?"

"No, you go along and enjoy yourself," Emily said. "It's going to be a beautiful day, especially for a ride over the moors, and the exercise won't hurt Duffy." She glanced towards the stairs. "Your aunt hasn't said anything to you, has she?"

"About what?"

"I'm not sure. It's just that last night she seemed somewhat subdued, not herself at all, but she wouldn't tell me what was the matter. I just wondered if your father had said something to upset her and she'd mentioned it to you."

Kitty shrugged. "No, there's been nothing like that. But perhaps his illness upsets her more than she likes to say?"

"Yes, perhaps," Emily said, still looking puzzled. She smiled. "But you go along, dear, and make the most of the day."

Kitty hugged her, gathered Duffy's bridle from the porch, and walked down to her field. Duffy nickered softly when she heard her name being called, and after snatching a few more mouthfuls of grass she came across to the gate.

Kitty buried her face in the mare's neck and stood there for a moment, inhaling her sweet pony smell. Then she played their old game that her mother had taught her long ago. She stood back and said, "I don't suppose you feel like traipsing over the moors with me today then, old girl?" After a moment Duffy snorted and nudged Kitty with her nose. Laughing, Kitty slipped the bridle on and led her from the field.

She rode up the lane past Forde, and paused when she reached her grove. She remembered how happy she had been the last time she was there. That is, until Acheson and Charlie had ruined it for her by saying those horrid things about Thomas. She shook that unpleasant memory away and cantered on up the lane.

When Kitty reached the top of the tor, she could see way beyond the woodlands and the valleys and patchwork fields to the English Channel. Whitmouth was somewhere further along the coast and she wondered what Reave and Justin might be doing at that moment. It comforted her to think she would soon be returning home to them.

She encouraged the pony on, and they began to descend until they reached Lower. Colan was in the yard and looked thoroughly pleased to see her. He put one arm about her as they walked to the farmhouse, inquiring after Thomas and Justin.

Ruth came to the door to greet them and stood aside as they went inside. Her sullenness had been replaced by a brightness Kitty had never seen before.

Colan looked from one to the other. "I'll leave you two to get reacquainted then," he said. "I'll be up later for tea and have a chat with you then, Kitty."

"Sit down," Ruth said. "I'll make us tea. Are you all better now then?"

"Oh… yes. Thank you." Kitty was quite dumbfounded at her sister's politeness; Ruth had never cared one whit about her before.

"Sorry I didn't come to see you when you were ill. I should have."

"I didn't expect you to, under the circumstances."

"Even so… like it, do you, in Whitmouth?"

"Yes, thank you." Kitty was reluctant to talk too enthusiastically about her new life for fear of rousing the old enmity between them. "So when's the happy day to be?" She was sure her sister would be happiest talking about herself.

"Next spring, around May. It's the best time for Michael to come, and then I'll go back up north with him. He's working at the mine and he's doing well. He's like his father, likes machines and things and they can't do without him."

Kitty couldn't get over this change in her sister and thought Michael must be one mighty fine man to have wrought it. "How did you meet him?"

Ruth laughed. "I was going to elope with Parky, then you took the dress and I could have killed you. Oh, don't worry, I don't feel like that any more, you did me a real favor. Anyway, I went looking for it on my days off. Few and far between they were, I might add. One day I was over at Furze and who should come by but Uncle Colan and Michael. We got talking and I told him what you'd done—"

"You didn't."

"I was hoping he would side with me, but he said you had probably saved me if only I could see it, because Uncle Colan had told him all about Parky."

"What happened to Parky?" Kitty couldn't say so, but she well remembered how Charlie said he would get rid of him after that episode by the river.

"I don't know exactly. Even Uncle Colan doesn't know where he is. He must have gone away somewhere. But in any case, when I saw Michael again, he said he wanted me for himself. 'Course he never has. Had me, I mean. I've pretended, well, that I'm still pure. I shall have to pretend it hurts on my wedding night." Ruth sniggered. "Men can be so funny about that sort of thing. It's all right for them to go with who they like, but they expect us to be different."

"It's only because we have the babies and they have to make sure—" Kitty blushed, suddenly realizing she was drawing attention to her paternity. "Well, you know what I mean."

"Yes, I know." Ruth smiled slyly, making Kitty's heart turn as she was reminded of Sarah. "No wonder Father used to say butter wouldn't melt in Mother's mouth. We didn't know the half of it, did we?"

"I hardly know any more about it now," murmured Kitty. "I suppose Sarah never let on who my real father was?" She looked around her uneasily, feeling as if her deceased grandmother still hovered in the room somewhere. Although Ruth might like it at Lower, she never had: it was a cold, unpleasant house.

Ruth shrugged. "The only thing she ever told me was that Mother was seen going to the manor more than once, and she wouldn't have been surprised if it hadn't been someone from there."

Kitty looked up from her cup. A thought, unbidden and too shocking even to consider, came into her mind, and she dismissed it immediately.

"I should forget it if I were you. There's nothing you can do about it now." Ruth sniggered again. "Like my precious virginity."

Although Kitty's conversation with Ruth went smoothly, she was thankful they lived miles apart. They had little in common and Kitty still found her too much like Sarah to feel comfortable in her company. However, at least now they were on better terms and had even discussed the wedding dress, which could have been a sore point. Ruth asked her if she would alter it for her, and Kitty said that although she couldn't promise, she would try and be there at least a week or so before the wedding the following spring.

For the remainder of the week, Kitty avoided Charlie as best she could, and spent her time helping Emily.

When it was time to leave, Emily wished her well and Martha cried, while Edward looked on with wide eyes, his dirty little thumb in his mouth. Kitty went to the door of her father's room and said, "Goodbye then, Father." But he didn't acknowledge her, even though he was looking straight at her.

Margery sighed with relief as the carriage drove out of the yard, and Kitty gave a last wave to Martha and Edward, who were still standing in the porch waving to her.

As soon as they got under way, Margery said, "You aren't sad to be leaving this time, Kitty? At least not as before."

"No, not as before," Kitty agreed quietly, who couldn't wait to return to Whitmouth House. "I'm glad we went, though. Emily was glad to see us, wasn't she, and she seemed more cheerful when we left. And it was so good to see Martha and Edward. I hate to think of him forgetting who I am. So our visit served a purpose of sorts."

"Yes, the visit certainly served a purpose," Margery said, closing her eyes.

How anyone could sleep whilst being so jostled about, Kitty didn't know, but she was grateful not to be scrutinized as she took out the small box Martha had pressed into her hand. She was disappointed and hurt that Charlie hadn't come to see her off. Although Martha said he regretted their quarrel, Kitty thought his absence on her departure hadn't been a very good way of showing it.

Martha said there was a note inside and Kitty opened the lid and took it out. She smiled; it had been folded and refolded until it was small. Typical of Martha, she thought, wondering what her sister had written.

She was surprised when she saw that it wasn't from Martha at all, but from Charlie. Even more surprised to read his message. *I'm sorry, Kit. I still want to be friends.*

Tears sprang to Kitty's eyes. *Oh, Charlie,* she thought. And she pressed the piece of paper to her lips before she folded it and replaced it in the box.

Thank you, she said in her heart. *Thank you for releasing me.*

Charlie's note did much to lighten Kitty's mood, and she hoped his gesture might be a sign that he was thinking over her warning and would take heed. Knowing there was nothing more she could do about the matter, she did her best to put it from her mind, and enjoyed the journey home. Once or twice, she caught Margery looking at her rather speculatively, and wondered if Flo had mentioned Charlie's proposal. She knew her aunt, of all people, would be pleased she had turned him down.

After dropping Margery off at May Cottage, Kitty went on alone to Whitmouth House. She was hardly able to contain her eagerness to get there, and was delighted to see Reave rushing out of the house to greet her. Kitty quickly climbed down from the carriage and bent to hug him.

As she straightened up, she saw Justin walking briskly towards her. "Welcome home, my dear," he said, kissing her on both cheeks.

Madeline, the maid who was rapidly becoming her own, was pleased to see Kitty too, and bobbed a curtsey. She had, Justin said, been responsible for Reave while Kitty had been away, and done very well too.

"That's because I behaved myself," Reave said, puffing out his small chest like a robin redbreast and making them all laugh.

Upstairs, while Madeline shook out Kitty's clothes and hung them in the wardrobe, she told her there had been ructions while she was away.

"The master laid out his plans for Miss Carrington," she said. "And apparently they didn't include marriage. You should have heard the tantrums. She's made our life a blooming misery."

I bet she has, thought Kitty, and was glad she hadn't been there to witness it.

"She's to be gone by Easter," Madeline confided. "Mr. Justin has been trying to find someone to manage her affairs and he's been interviewing them all week. 'Course, she doesn't like it one bit."

Kitty sighed. Although she was delighted that Suzannah would be leaving, there were still several months to go, and Kitty knew she would probably make each moment as uncomfortable and difficult as she could.

However, in the weeks ahead, because Kitty had experienced Ruth's ploys she could almost tell what the bitter young woman's next move would be, and was able to parry quite well to foil her ungracious attempts to belittle her. Suzannah might be able to play the piano exquisitely, thought Kitty, but she couldn't be all that bright: anyone with intelligence could see that she was making a complete fool of herself.

In late December, Kitty helped Cook pack the hampers that would be distributed to the tenants on the estate, filling them with puddings and pies, fruits and chocolates and many other delicacies, all of which were luxury items for a laborer's family. She fleetingly thought of the tenants on the manor estate in North Bovey. One day, she thought; if Thomas's hopes and plans came true, they would be treated like this.

On Christmas Eve, the guests began to arrive for dinner. Among them were Margery and Enid, and Lilly, who, after greeting Kitty with a huge hug and a smacking kiss, went downstairs to help, and catch up on all the gossip, as she had done the previous year.

Thomas was expected this Christmas, although he didn't arrive until mid-way through supper, and he apologized for his lateness owing to the state of the roads. Before sitting down at the table, he searched for Kitty and smiled at her. Madeline had helped her choose a gown of the deepest violet, and even Kitty had to admit the color looked quite stunning against her dark hair. She felt Thomas's eyes on her quite frequently during the meal and felt flattered because of it.

After dinner, a rather agitated Margery drew her aside. "Really, my dear, it was very unbecoming of Thomas to be so openly demonstrative," she said. "People might interpret such behavior incorrectly. Unless there is something *to* interpret?"

Kitty hugged her aunt affectionately. "Oh, don't look so worried, Aunt Margery. We are just really good friends and glad to see each other. Besides," she lowered her voice, "I do believe Thomas is smitten by a maiden to whom he intends to propose. If you speak to Justin he'll tell you the same thing, no doubt." And she repeated the conversation she had overheard some weeks ago in the conservatory.

When Margery looked relieved, Kitty realized her aunt had only wished to remind her of her station. Sadly, Kitty thought, it was something she could hardly forget.

She turned away to return to the drawing room. The library doors were wide open, and as she passed she heard voices. It was Justin with Enid, and she was saying, "Age, Justin! What has that to do with anything? Especially love. How many times have I told you? You must—" Then she saw Kitty, and stopped.

"I... I was just passing and heard voices." Kitty felt embarrassed, for she didn't want them to think she had been eavesdropping.

Enid patted Justin's arm. "I'll see you later, dear. Have a nice evening together."

Justin beckoned Kitty into the room. "I'm glad you came along, Kitty. I was just on my way to find you, because I want you to help me to deliver the hampers."

"Oh, but I thought Miss Carrington would be going with you." Kitty knew it had been Suzannah's intention. She had apparently informed Cook, and then upset the kitchen staff by expressing the opinion that Justin was far too generous to those beneath him, and when she was mistress of Whitmouth House things would change. "The cheek of her," Cook had said to Kitty. "She never gives up, does she?"

Justin smiled and touched the tip of Kitty's nose. "I don't believe so. Suzannah will stay here to entertain and dazzle. She's already collared poor Thomas. Come along, the carriage will be ready by now."

Outside, Reave scampered ahead of them to the carriage that was waiting, already loaded with the hampers. The horses' breath billowed in the cold night air. The wind was brisk, and scudding clouds crossed the starlit sky.

"It's clear now," Justin said, looking skyward, "but I've seen the clouds on the horizon, and once the wind dies down I think it may snow by morning."

They set off down the driveway and turned off by the bridge towards the farms. While Reave openly expressed his views over the prospects of it snowing, Kitty kept her excitement to herself. She also wished it would snow. Right now, and heavily. And she lost herself in the fantasy of being stranded with Justin in the carriage all night long.

At each cottage, the Christmas cheer was pressed upon them. A piece of cake was eaten here, and a mince-tart there, and elderberry and parsnip wine flowed until Kitty felt quite giddy. On the way back to the house, Justin laughed along with her as she recalled the events of the evening. He held her securely against him, and in her slight inebriation, Kitty imagined she felt him plant a kiss on the top of her head. She felt as if she was wrapped in a cocoon of happiness, and wished the ride could go on forever.

When they arrived in the courtyard, Reave ran in ahead of them and Justin took Kitty's arm and escorted her to inside the front door. "I have so enjoyed your company this evening, Kitty," he said.

There was no one about in the hall; everyone was in the drawing room and sounded to be having a rollicking good time. He glanced to above him where a piece of mistletoe dangled from the chandelier… but suddenly Thomas came bounding towards them down the hall like a boisterous puppy, joking that Justin had monopolized Kitty for long enough and now it was his turn.

As he led her away, Kitty looked behind her and threw up her hands in a helpless gesture. Justin frowned for only a moment, then took it in good spirit and laughed.

Those who were going to the midnight service at the church left in plenty of time. Kitty had hoped to ride with Justin, but outside in the courtyard, in the excited confusion, Thomas took her arm and ushered her into a conveyance of their own. As she got in, she saw Justin being swept along by Suzannah and her friends, and she felt a twinge of envy, even though Thomas had sought her out.

When she went to the altar to take communion, she found herself kneeling between the two men. Justin was so close she imagined she could feel the heat of his body through her layers of clothing. She took a larger gulp than usual of the wine to steady her emotions and felt the heady glow of it as she returned to her pew.

When the service was over, everyone quickly left the church. It was late and they wanted to get home to their beds. But when she and Thomas went outside, he led her not to their waiting carriage, but around the side of the church.

"Thomas!" Kitty exclaimed. "What are you—?"

He put his finger to his lips indicating for her to be quiet, but Kitty was alarmed. "But surely Justin will wonder where we are?" she whispered.

"I wish to speak to you without interruption, Kitty. I have asked our driver to wait, and we won't be long."

They waited until the congregation left, and the vicar had walked down the path to the vicarage and closed the gate. Thomas led Kitty out of their hiding place and back into the church porch.

Kitty was shivering with the cold and glanced at the driver who was hunched on his seat. He must be absolutely freezing, she thought, feeling a twinge of guilt.

She gasped as they went inside the church. The main lights had been extinguished but the few candles around the nativity scene had been left to burn down. There was barely half-an-inch left to most of them; soon the church would be plunged into total darkness.

"Isn't it magical?" Thomas said.

"Yes," she murmured, because she knew what he meant and she appreciated him sharing it with her. It was magical—but it also felt eerie. She told herself not to be so fanciful. But while the wind howled and buffeted the ramparts of the tower, the still, stagnant air inside made her think of what it must be like to be inside a tomb, and she shivered.

Walking with her down the aisle, Thomas took her arm. "Christmas Eve is the most special night of the year," he said quietly, but excitedly. "A hopeful, expectant time." He stopped by the nativity and turned to face her. "I have been plucking up courage to speak to you. I have thought things over very carefully and you must make no protest about its feasibility. I only wish to know how you feel, my dearest Kitty." He took her hand and knelt in front of her. "As the young Christ is my witness, I do truly adore you. Will you do me the honor of becoming my wife?"

Kitty stared at him. Thomas wished to marry *her*? *She* was the one he had spoken of to Justin?

He asked if he may kiss her, and she was too shocked to demur. His lips were soft and warm, and Kitty responded inquisitively. *A far cry*, a voice said in her mind, *to how you would have reacted had it been Justin.* She pulled herself gently away from him; thinking, what am I doing? What *am* I doing?

"I shall need time to think," she said hastily. "I mean, I never imagined…." She knew very well that she, of all people, couldn't marry a Gordon. And she should tell him right now and nip this madness in the bud.

"Of course you must have time to think about it," Thomas said. "I wanted to keep it to ourselves until the spring anyway, after I have had a chance to speak to my father." He smiled and touched her cheek. "My dearest. From the very moment

I saw you, I *knew* you are the only one I will ever want for my own."

He fumbled with his finger for a moment, and took off a ring, which he then pressed into her hand. "This was my mother's, and I want you to keep it as a token of my love. There are two of them. My father has the other, though he hasn't worn his for years." He frowned for a moment then said desperately, "We *will* make it happen, won't we, Kitty?"

The way Thomas was looking at her would have inspired anyone to believe anything, Kitty thought. Yet, she had many other thoughts clamoring to be aired, and suddenly she longed to be alone to be able to think them. She knew she should refuse him right now, but he looked so earnest, and she cared for him too deeply to dash his hopes on Christmas Eve. She would wait until Christmas was over, beg for time, and then gradually withdraw herself and let him down lightly.

"I will ponder everything," she said carefully. She looked into his face and touched his cheek. "But know this, Thomas, I *do* hold you, and have always held you in the highest esteem, and you have honored me greatly by your proposal."

"At least tell me there is no other in your affections?" he said anxiously, taking her hand and clasping it to his breast.

She longed to be truthful, to say, *there is Justin. I love Justin,* but of course she couldn't, and she shook her head.

"That Suzannah," he mused as he led her down the aisle.

Kitty was taken aback, and paused in her tracks. "Suzannah? What has she to do with this?"

"She has this idea you have affection for your man, Charlie Chase."

"Charlie? Well yes, we have been friends for many years, but I do not wish to marry him."

"I was sure of it. We have spoken of many things, yet you have rarely mentioned his name to me."

And never to Suzannah, Kitty thought with a chill.

They reached the door, and as Thomas opened it, a sharp gust of wind blew into the church and the remaining candles were extinguished. Kitty cried out as the door was blown out of his grasp and slammed shut behind them, and she hurried with him to the waiting carriage and got in quickly.

They were both quiet as they drove back to the house. His expression was blissful, but Kitty's mind churned wildly, trying to think how Suzannah could have even known Charlie's name.

It wasn't until she walked into her sitting room that she remembered the night she had been writing the letter, and how Susan had interrupted her. Now she realized that when she had closed the adjoining door into Reave's room, Suzannah must have lingered and read what she had written. Now, with dismay, she tried to remember exactly what she had said, and how incriminating it could be to Charlie and Acheson.

With this on her mind, she felt too anxious to sleep, and she sat by the fire in her sitting room until the early hours of the morning, worrying about the disaster Suzannah could wreak if she cared to. She was also still stunned by Thomas's unexpected proposal. Eventually, when she couldn't keep awake any longer she went to bed and fell into a troubled, restless sleep.

She awoke later from a horrible nightmare. She was in a forest, waiting for her lover. Both excited and happy, she waved to him as he approached her. But as they kissed, she found herself kissing a statue, its face as still as stone and with lips so cold, they stung her.

On Christmas morning, the horrid dream lingered, and Kitty couldn't conjure up the frivolous mood everyone else seemed to feel. She declined to go outside with Thomas and Reave to frolic in the snow that had fallen during the night, and watched them from the library window.

Justin found her there, alone and deep in thought. "Is everything all right, Kitty, my dear?" he said. "You don't look well."

"I am tired, that's all," she said with a wan smile.

"I was worried about you last night. You were so late back."

"We stayed to look at the candles around the nativity. Thomas wished to share that with me."

"He shouldn't have kept you out so late." Justin looked troubled and put his hand on her shoulder. "Are you sure everything is all right?"

Kitty suddenly had a great longing to confide in him. And perhaps if the door hadn't opened at that moment she might have, because he did look so terribly concerned. But it was Suzannah, and when Kitty saw her glacial look because Justin was still touching her, she slipped from beneath his hand, and quickly made an excuse to leave the room.

ꟃ

A few days after Christmas, Thomas left, and Kitty came down with a chill. Then Reave became ill, and through January and into February half the staff went down with influenza. Suzannah, who couldn't stand illness of any kind, made an excuse to escape and said she would return when they were all well again.

The evening before Suzannah left, Kitty decided to try to make peace with her. Justin had announced that he had found someone capable of managing her affairs and that she would begin a tour in London in May, then go on to the Continent. Kitty said, as tactfully as she could, that she was pleased Suzannah was making strides in her career, and wished her all the best.

But Suzannah had only one thing in mind and was not at all pleased to be leaving Whitmouth House. She twisted everything Kitty said, and they parted on bad terms.

Despondently, Kitty realized that Suzannah regarded her gesture of friendship as a weakness on her part, and now she felt more vulnerable than ever.

Chapter 35

As Easter approached, Suzannah's moods worsened. Kitty often bore the brunt of her temper, and always when they were alone. Although she tried to avoid such confrontations, one evening just prior to Suzannah's final departure, she lost her temper.

"You are a bad-tempered shrew, Suzannah," she cried. "No matter how talented you may be, your treatment of others is intolerable, and all of us will be pleased to see the back of you!"

"You think you're so clever, worming your way in here, don't you? Little miss prim and proper." Suzannah's eyes narrowed and she smiled nastily. "But everyone will be changing their tune about *that* before I'm finished. Nobody gets the better of me."

Kitty had no idea what Suzannah meant by that spiteful remark, although it did occur to her that the sneaky woman might suspect Thomas had designs on her and go tittle-tattling to Justin. Kitty felt somewhat deceitful in that she hadn't told Justin of Thomas's proposal, but reasoned she would soon have nothing to tell: Thomas had written to say he wouldn't be lingering at Whitmouth at Easter, and would only be calling in briefly to fetch Hector before returning to North Bovey. This would be around the time she was at Furze for Ruth's wedding, so she would be able to talk to him before he had a chance to spend any time with Justin.

On the day Suzannah left Whitmouth House, the staff gathered to say their farewells, as was the custom. Nor could any of them been more pleased to have been disturbed from their duties. As Suzannah went from one to the other, 'giving them the evil-eye,' as Cook commented later, Kitty saw many a hand making the sign of protection as she passed.

When Suzannah reached Kitty, she took her hand, and then kissed her on both cheeks. Kitty was more than startled, but was pleased to think that Suzannah might have overcome her chagrin and decided to part as friends. When Suzannah drew away and looked into her eyes, however, Kitty felt a chill pass through her: the woman was mocking her, and in the worst possible way.

Suzannah walked on, lingering an embarrassingly long amount of time in front of Justin, but finally he managed to get her into the carriage. As it pulled away, Reave whooped with joy, but although everyone laughed and Justin didn't scold him, Kitty didn't smile.

Cook noticed this and sidled up to her. "What was all that about?" she said.

"I'm not sure," Kitty said uneasily.

"God save us from such souls," Cook muttered. "Because there's a dark one, if ever I saw one. The place is well rid of her."

That unpleasant event took days to fade from Kitty's thoughts, and she lost some sleep over it, worrying about Susannah's motives. But then, when the next few weeks became the most pleasurable she had ever spent at Whitmouth House, she was able to put it to the back of her mind.

With Suzannah gone, Kitty felt as if a great cloud had been lifted from their presence, and marveled at how the absence of one person could change a whole atmosphere. Justin seemed much happier too, and he became very attentive to her, drawing her more into discussions of matters regarding the estate, and inviting her to accompany him on an evening's entertainment. His fogies kissed Kitty's hand and looked at her in the most speculative manner, saying they were enchanted to meet her and that they found her interesting and refreshing.

All this bemused Kitty. Even though she felt her responses and opinions were probably immature and of little value, Justin seemed to appreciate her input and encouraged her. He even made their social differences seem as if they didn't exist.

ϨϿ

Kitty's bubble of happiness burst one morning when Madeline brought her a letter from Emily, begging her to come home.

It must be important, Kitty thought, for Emily to do that, even though her first reaction was to make an excuse not to go. But then she remembered her promise to Ruth that she would alter the wedding dress, and decided she couldn't let her down. She considered also, that as her father hadn't regained his former strength, Emily might feel overwhelmed with the impending wedding and need her support.

However, her doubts returned again on the morning she was about to leave. When she was told the carriage was at the door, such a feeling of foreboding came over her that she didn't even want to leave her room. And when Justin was helping her into the carriage and pressed a sovereign into her hand she cried, "Oh, Justin, I don't think—"

Justin thought she was protesting his gift. "No, take it, please," he said. "Buy yourself something pretty to wear." And he gave the signal for her to leave.

As the carriage pulled out of the courtyard, Kitty's heart began to race and she to whimper. She almost called for them to stop. She knew her feelings were irrational, but she didn't want to let Justin out of her sight.

On her way, she was to call in at May Cottage; Margery had a gift for Ruth that she was to take with her. But when she arrived, Margery was out, and she only saw Enid.

When Enid saw Kitty's tearful face, she looked most concerned. "Did Justin not speak to you before you left?" she said.

"About what?" Kitty replied.

Enid bit her lip, but didn't say anything. She simply hugged Kitty close to her, and said, "Oh, Kitty, do be careful."

This didn't help ease Kitty's disquiet. As the carriage plowed on along the muddy and rutted roads, many still suffering from the ravages of winter, her feelings of impending doom increased. The day was dull with drizzle. It was gray and unwelcoming. As they neared the moors, the fine mist gave way to torrential rain and Kitty's heart felt as heavy as the mud that cloyed and dragged at the carriage wheels.

When they finally arrived at the farm even the driver seemed reluctant to leave her there, and said, "Come home again soon, Miss Kitty," before driving off.

Kitty bit back tears as she waved to him then turned her attention to Emily, who was running out to greet her. When she saw Emily's face, she knew instantly that something more than Ruth's wedding had brought her home.

Emily wouldn't tell her what it was until she had ushered her inside and given her a strong cup of tea. And then, quietly, she told Kitty their worst fears had happened; Charlie and Acheson had been arrested and were awaiting trial.

For a moment, Kitty was too shocked to speak. "But how did it happen? Were they caught having a meeting?" she whispered. "*What*, Emily?"

Emily shook her head. "They weren't doing anything. The squire's men came all out of the blue and took them away without any explanation. The only thing we can think of is that someone informed on them."

Kitty had to drop her head into her lap to avoid fainting. She couldn't speak for several minutes as nausea overwhelmed her and the blood zinged and rushed through her head. She saw her letter lying open on her bureau. She saw that look in Suzannah's eyes: heard once again her threat.

"Your father is afraid of reprisals, of course," she heard Emily say through the buzzing in her head. "I wouldn't mention Charlie's name in front of him if I were you. Oh Lord, Kitty. What a thing to happen. What with Ruth's wedding...."

Kitty could only nod. This was all *her* fault. She might as well have gone to the squire and told him what Charlie was doing, as to write that letter. And her next thought was: what am I going to do about it? What *can* I do to put it right?

"Nothing can be done," Emily said, "except hope and pray for a miracle. I am so sorry to bring you home like this, but I knew you would want to know. I didn't think it prudent to write a letter."

"You were quite right," Kitty said. "Letters, if they get into the wrong hands, can cause no end of trouble."

She had always felt so close to Emily, and in that moment was so tempted to tell her what she believed had happened. But the weight of guilt was too heavy. How could she admit to doing such a foolish thing? People would only think she had betrayed her dearest friends, and wouldn't understand how it had all come about.

❧

"I'd like to catch who tattled," Flo said angrily, when she saw Kitty.

Kitty's guilt increased, not only because she had written the letter, but also because Flo had aged years in months.

"I don't wish to live if Acheson goes away," Flo said miserably. "He's my life."

Kitty spent much of that night awake, pacing her room. After much thought, she finally concluded that she would have to write to Thomas and ask for his help. Either Acheson and Charlie would be proven right in their opinion of him, or he would help save them. She did briefly consider bypassing Thomas altogether and going straight to Justin. However, although she was sure he would seek justice, she knew Justin didn't get along with the squire and would probably have little authority in the matter.

So, in the morning, while the others milled around downstairs, Kitty found paper and ink, and sat down to write the letter.

Knowing how to word such a letter proved difficult. How did she persuade Thomas to take such a blatant stand against his father? Because she knew that despite all his bravado, he was terrified of the man. As well, how could she ask this enormous favor of him, and then later break his heart by telling him she couldn't marry him?

Finally, she took up the pen and began to write.

She told Thomas what had happened to Charlie and Acheson, and said that she believed they had done no real harm, but that more trouble in the parish might erupt if they were hanged or transported. She kept it short and to the point, telling him where they were being held.

She ended her letter: "Thomas, my dear, I know you must have been waiting for my reply on the other matter. If you can find it in your heart to help release these men, I will willingly and gladly accept your proposal. If, however, you feel otherwise, then I must tell you that a marriage between us would not be right. Indeed, it would not even be possible."

Kitty put down her pen, and for minutes sat staring at the letter, held spellbound by what she had written. *She'd offered to marry him. To become a Gordon.*

A sob rose to her lips. What would her family say when they knew? And Justin. *Oh, Justin.* However would she be able to lie in the arms of one man while she longed for another?

Her fingers flinched, as she was tempted to tear the letter into shreds. Yet really, she had no choice but to send it. Shutting away all other thoughts, except conjuring up an excuse that would take her into Moretonhampstead that morning where she could meet the coach, she quickly folded the letter and sealed it.

It was done.

ꕥ

If Kitty had thought her agony would be over once she wrote the letter, she was sadly mistaken. What with her father's foul moods, Flo's depression and her own anxiety about whether her letter would reach Thomas in time, if at all, and what his reaction would be, she felt as if she was caught in some sort of hellish maze. She fumbled through each day, barely putting up with Ruth's incessant chatter about her wedding day, and trying to concentrate on altering the dress. How Michael put up with his future wife's effervescence Kitty didn't know, but he seemed to take her in his stride. He seemed such a polite young man, and reminded Kitty of Thomas in so many ways. Yet, he was larger, and far livelier, than his more studious and serious half-brother. He possessed the same northern flavor that Charlie had; a stronger vein of life.

He said he was pleased to meet her and inquired after Thomas's health. Kitty said she hadn't seen him since Christmas. She didn't mention that she had written for his help over the matter of Charlie and Acheson. As each day passed and no word came from him, her hope dwindled that he was even going to reply, and she became almost as demented as Flo, and definitely as irritable as Hern.

It was the day before the wedding that Kitty finally had word. Emily and Hern had taken Martha and Edward into Moretonhampstead for some last minute shopping, and she was alone in the house. Having been so busy attending to everyone else's needs she'd had little time to see to her own. Now she was frantically trying to put a costume together that would be suitable for the wedding.

Searching through her mother's jewelry box, she came across the necklace that Ruth had broken all those years ago, and thought how perfectly it would go with her outfit. She was about to lift the floorboard to retrieve the loose beads, when she heard the dog barking. She looked out of the window to see a boy running up the yard. Beads forgotten, she sped downstairs.

The boy was from the manor and he held out a letter to her. When Kitty saw Thomas's handwriting on it, she gave him a whole penny, and he scampered off in delight. With trembling fingers, Kitty unfolded it.

"My dearest love," Thomas wrote. "I left as soon as I received your letter and I am at the manor. I stopped only briefly at Whitmouth House to collect Hector and didn't see Justin, who was apparently in Whitmouth for the afternoon. Considering the circumstances I decided not to dally there. Of *course* I will do all I can. Your friends will obtain their freedom tomorrow. I shall also speak to the squire regarding the other matter. Can we meet by the crossroads (where I first fell in love with you), tomorrow afternoon?

"This place is like hell. I long to see you again, my beloved. You are my destiny. I will love you forever, Kitty, my love."

Kitty burst into tears with sheer relief. She read the letter over and over again then put on her boots and quickly ran across the field to tell Flo the good news. She kept telling herself she mustn't even think about the marriage until Thomas had released Acheson and Charlie and spoken to his father. Then their betrothal could be announced. How it had come about would remain a secret she would have to keep from her family forever. Just as she would have to pretend to love Thomas in that way, forever. A sob caught in her throat. She mustn't think of it now. *And she must try not to think of her love for Justin ever again.*

If Flo had been her normal self then quite possibly she might have seen the anxiety lurking beneath Kitty's brightness, but her mind was too focused on Acheson and the news Kitty was giving her. She expressed some doubts as to why Thomas

Gordon would help the likes of them, but Kitty assured her it was true and that Acheson and Charlie would be freed the following day.

"They won't be able to stay here though," Flo said. "Once that squire knows what his son has done there will be hell to pay, you mark my words. I'd best pack up a few things and they can go to my cousin in Plymouth. We'll have to take the cart, though, more's the pity because it will take longer, but I doubt Acheson would make it on horseback."

Kitty hadn't thought beyond Acheson and Charlie getting out of jail and realized that Flo was right. "But better they have to hide for a while," she said, "than face a hangman's noose or go to a God-forsaken country never to be seen again."

"Too true," Flo said. "I'll ready the cart with some straw and comforts. Oh, my dear, you don't know how happy this makes me."

Kitty's burden of guilt lifted a little as she heard the enthusiasm creep back into Flo's voice and impulsively she hugged her. "I love you so much, Flo," she said. "You've been like a mother to me. I wish—" She stopped. She wanted so much to confide in her, but she *mustn't*. She couldn't.

But Flo took her at cross-purposes. She hugged Kitty close to her. "So do I, Kitty. It was a trick of fate, that's all. And when this is over I will tell you all about it." And left Kitty puzzling about what she meant.

However, there was so much else on Kitty's mind that the moment passed and lay forgotten.

Chapter 36

Ruth's wedding day dawned clear and crisp.

Kitty had been so busy helping Emily, she found no time to rescue or restring the beads, and now wore something entirely different from what she had first planned.

Emily was still busy with last minute details, and Kitty and Martha scurried around from early morning until Colan brought Ruth over to Furze mid-day, as it was from there she was to leave for the church.

Later, as Ruth descended the stairs in her mother's glorious shimmering gown, Emily burst into tears. This set them all off, and Hern, who remembered Leah wearing the same dress, scowled and told them, in his almost incoherent mumble, not to be so bleddy daft.

The church was packed full of people who came to see Peardon's rather wayward granddaughter get married, and some looked for tell-tale signs that might reveal why she was doing so.

After the ceremony, Michael took Ruth's hand and led her across the green to the hall, where they were adorned with flowers and blessed with good wishes. As the guests gobbled up the food and drank the ale and homemade wine, the jocular and dazed expressions that always accompanied such celebrations gradually crept over everyone. Then someone struck up some music and the dancing began.

Margery had come down for the wedding, but she had only arrived that morning and said she didn't plan to stay long after the service. She told Kitty she was going to visit someone in Newton Abbot and would be gone for a few days, but would call for her on her return, when they would return to Whitmouth together.

Although Kitty was tempted to tell Margery that her plans might have to be changed, she decided that until she saw Thomas she ought not to say anything. With her heart in her mouth, she bid her aunt farewell, and hoped that when Margery knew about her betrothal she would forgive her for not mentioning it.

Everyone was having a whale of a time so no one noticed Kitty leave the celebrations to sit by the village pump on the green. Soon, she planned to make her way to see Thomas, where she would hear what had happened to Charlie and Acheson, and any other news he might have. Just thinking about it made her stomach roll, but it was too late now to go back on her word. She willed herself to think of the positive effects their marriage could have, once her family and the squire became used to the idea. Of Justin, she did not allow herself to think at all.

She suddenly looked up as she saw Matthew coming across the green towards her. She had no idea that Mary Jay had sat in the same place so many years ago, contemplating the primroses at her feet.

But Matthew did, and that was why his expression was so pained when he said, "Have you seen Master Thomas, Miss Kitty?"

"No," Kitty said. "Is anything wrong, Matthew?"

"Oh, dear God, Miss Kitty, someone should have told you. Someone should have told you both."

A feeling of dread uncurled inside Kitty like a loathsome snake. "What do you mean? What are you talking about?"

Matthew looked away. "I have to find Master Thomas. If you can think of where he might be, please tell me."

"I was going to meet him," she said hesitantly.

"Where? Tell me quickly, where?"

"Above Forde. By the crossroads."

Matthew's face went ashen. "*That* place?" Without another word, he set off across the green towards his horse.

"Matthew!" Kitty cried. "Wait for me."

ჽ◯ᲀ

Down the lane and over the bridge they went, along the bottom and up the hill, and Matthew was silent all the way.

How many times Kitty had walked or ridden this way before, yet never did it seem to take so long. They hurried up past Forde towards the moor, heading for the crossroads. But when they came up around the hill, before they turned the corner, Matthew's horse balked and would go no further. Kitty slid off, but although she tried to lead him on, the horse showed the whites of his eyes, threw his head up and refused to budge.

"Why won't he go forward?" she asked fearfully, looking up into Matthew's face.

Matthew dismounted. "I don't know. I'll have a look."

The horse wouldn't stand still so Kitty led him down the hill and tied him to a gate. Then she went up and around the corner to see what might be wrong.

She stopped in her tracks when she saw Matthew bent over something on the ground. Something. A body. She went closer, and then she recognized who it was. It was Thomas. *Thomas's* body.

Her hand to her heart, she stumbled. Whispered, "Oh no! Oh, Thomas, *no!*"

Her voice hardly registered with Matthew; it was her scream that turned him away from his beloved master, and he stood up, hands outstretched. "No, Miss Kitty! Oh dear Lord, no!" he said, trying to prevent her going closer.

But Kitty pushed past him and fell upon Thomas's still, cold body.

ჽ◯ᲀ

Afterwards, memories of that moment were elusive. Only fragments danced in Kitty's mind; their vivid shards of pain....

She could remember Hector snorting with fear, his reins dragging on the ground as he stood beside his master. Yet, because he was well trained, he waited faithfully for Thomas to get up from the ground. He must have been as bewildered as she when he didn't.

She remembered looking into those lifeless eyes. Those deep pools of gray were vacant now, his spirit gone. Those lips that had once spoken her name were growing cold, his voice stilled forever.

Those bluebells. That carpet of crushed amazing blue, his sweet body's grave, cushioned her also. And they, along with his blood, stained her dress when she fell upon him. Matthew had to tear her away and lead her home like a little child, where he handed her over to Emily, who couldn't hide the shocked expression in her eyes.

Later, while Matthew and Emily hovered restlessly at her bedside, Kitty heard them talking. They thought her unable to comprehend, and most of it afterwards she couldn't recall, it was true. But she did remember Matthew saying that she was Hartley Gordon's daughter.

It was true then; that unbidden thought she'd once had in Sarah's kitchen and chased away so quickly. A year ago, when she had seen Ruth. And she thought, *Oh, Thomas. There was no need to take your life for sake of me. However am I going to bear it?*

She was left alone on the day of the funeral because it was thought she was too far gone to even get out of bed. But she'd heard the whisperings and knew it was his day.

When all of them were gone, she slipped out of bed. Like an apparition, she went down the hill, over the bridge and up Church Lane. She knew the way so well she could have walked it in her sleep.

When she reached the church they stood aside and let her through.

Was that her name she heard spoken? Was that Justin she saw?

Oh, Justin.

Too late now. All misty, foggy. Faces blurred and voices slurred.

She stood crushed between bodies at the meeting of the aisles, north to south; east to west; the very center of the church where she intended to thrust the knife into her heart. As Thomas had taken his life for the sake of her, she would take her own, unable to live with the knowledge it had been *her* fault, *her* acceptance of him that had caused his death.

A sharp little knife to do the trick, she cunningly told herself. *A quick pain that is all,* and then she could join him. She had given him her word and wouldn't break it. Death would not part them; she to him; dust to dust….

And then through the crowd she saw his coffin.

"*Thomaas! Thomaas!*" Was that her voice, that sobbing scream?

The congregation parted like a wave. Eyes on her like hawks, accusing.

A voice. Deep and resonant. "Who is that?"

It was the squire. Her *father.* And she cried, "Did you hear him, Thomas? Did you hear what he said? Who *is* that? Who *am* I?" And she could hear someone laughing hysterically.

His detestable voice came again. Nearer this time. And suddenly, she was face to face with the man who had sown the seed: sown *her,* in her mother's womb.

She raised the knife.

"She's got a knife," someone said. "Look out!"

There was a shadow behind her in the doorway. Someone screamed. The shadow bounded forward and the squire was knocked to the ground. Kitty felt the knife fly from her hand. There was a buzzing in her head. And Charlie. It was Charlie, who lifted her through them all, and carried her away.

Part IV

Plymouth and Beyond

Children begin by loving their parents;
As they grow older they judge them;
Sometimes they forgive them.

Oscar Fingal O'Flahertie Wills Wilde 1854-1900

Chapter 37

Charlie took Kitty to Plymouth where he hoped they could stay hidden until they saved enough money to book passage to America. Thomas had given him a horse on which to get away, and when they reached the city, Charlie sold him. The man who bought him looked Kitty up and down as well as the horse and gave some indication where they might find lodging. It was also a place, he said, leering at Kitty, where the lady might find employment.

They discovered that the Crab Catcher was a brothel, thinly disguised as an alehouse, and owned by one bosomy Mrs. Hoskins. Charlie gritted his teeth as he begged for employment; he needed a place where he could both earn money and keep a close eye on Kitty until she was well enough to work.

Mrs. Hoskins drove a hard bargain. She said she would only take him on if she could later employ his sister. Charlie pointed out that Kitty was in fact his wife and that she'd suffered a tragedy that had rendered her incapable of work for a while.

"Well, she can't stay 'ere for free," said the disappointed Hoskins, her expression reminding Kitty so much of the awful Sarah.

Charlie now had the sovereign Justin had given to Kitty and he held it out to her. "She *will* work, Mrs. Hoskins," he promised. "I'm sure she'll be very useful to you in the future, but for now this should take care of her keep."

Mrs. Hoskins took the coin and bit down on it. "You'd better make sure she is," she said, and with a swish of her skirts, bade them follow her upstairs where she showed them into a filthy attic room. Charlie could begin work immediately she said, and she would give his *wife* a while longer to recover.

"I want to die," Kitty moaned when they were alone. "And why did you give her all our money? You've only got to earn it back."

"For goodness sake, Kit," Charlie said impatiently, "what choice do we have? Those who seek us are hardly likely to look for us in a place like this, are they? I'll be close by too, until you can pull yourself together."

Kitty bit back an angry retort. She was ungrateful that he'd saved her; resentful because she knew he'd only done so for his own selfish ends. Now Thomas was gone he wanted her for himself.

But Charlie never laid a hand on her except to hold and comfort her while she wept, something that she did frequently. It wasn't because he didn't want her—he slept on the floor beside the bed for many a torturous night—but he wouldn't take her until she was ready. When she felt better, she would feel differently, he told himself. And when they arrived in America he would make her his wife.

It would be the fresh start that Thomas Gordon had talked about when he released him and Acheson, and suggested they find a safe haven until he could reason with his father. When Charlie asked him why he was helping them, to his amazement Thomas said he loved Kitty and was going to marry her, and, because he intended to do things differently to his father and wanted to create goodwill in the parish, he felt this gesture would prove his sincerity.

"Always the dreamer," Acheson said afterwards, but was grateful all the same, and he, as well as Charlie, were forced to grudgingly acknowledge that Kitty had been right all along, even though they were both shocked by Gordon's intention to marry her.

Charlie was so beset about it he did not go with Acheson and Flo. Kitty had always sworn she had no interest in marrying Gordon, and yet that was what she was about to do. The thought of it gnawed at him like an ulcer, and he didn't intend to leave the vicinity, squire or no squire, until he'd confronted her.

Then he learned of Thomas's death and Kitty's collapse. Subsequently, because of her emotional state, his question seemed irrelevant and was never asked.

Charlie had no idea that Kitty was Hartley Gordon's daughter, and thought Thomas had taken his life because his father wouldn't give him permission to marry an Underwood. To Charlie's mind, that was the sort of thing a rich, spoiled brat would do. As for Kitty, he felt she'd brought this misery on herself by not listening to him and by setting her sights too high. But he never spoke of those things. He felt the sooner Kitty could forget what happened, the sooner she would recover.

Not being able to talk about the past caused Kitty a lot of pain. Sometimes she would look at the ring Thomas had given her. He'd called her his destiny. *Oh yes,* she would think, overwhelmed with grief and guilt, *I was that, all right.*

The worst of her guilt was his needless death. Both Flo and Emily had warned her never to marry for the wrong reason, but that's exactly what she'd planned to do, blindly believing that everything would turn out all right. Now, all the self-recrimination in the world wouldn't bring Thomas back. She'd made a terrible choice, and Thomas had killed himself because of it. Her constant question to herself was: how would she live with it? How *could* she live with it?

Besides trying to come to terms with the death of Thomas, Kitty had to bear her other losses. She missed Justin and Reave terribly, and she longed to see Flo and the rest of her family.

She also loathed the way the girls were treated by the horrible Mrs. Hoskins. There were no depths to which that unscrupulous, compassionless harridan wouldn't sink for monetary reward. She worried too that, although Charlie kept on about how wonderful America would be, he didn't really know that life would be any different over there for the likes of them. What if he couldn't get work, and her fate lay in a similar place to the inn? Now she knew what those girls had to do, the thought terrified her.

Despite her longing to curl up and die, life went on. Kitty was young and healthy and over the next few weeks, her lethargy diminished. Mrs. Hoskins was pleased to see her up and about, and gave her a job in the kitchen.

However, one of the girls warned her. "You'd better watch out, she's after you. She knows you aren't Charlie's wife, and she's bet any money you're a virgin, too. Once she's got 'er claws into you, the gutter or the workhouse are the only way out of this place."

When Kitty told Charlie this, he said Mrs. Hoskins didn't worry him; he would protect her, and by the time the woman did get her claws out they would have sailed. To this end, he took another job in the dockyard. He hoped to do a deal with one of the captains and subsidize his own fare by working his way across the Atlantic. Kitty never argued with his plan. His idea about going to America, still months away, seemed so remote as to be impossible.

ᘓᘐ

Although Kitty loathed Mrs. Hoskins, she got along well with the girls. She discovered that a couple of them, after being abandoned by their lovers, had been thrown out by their families. They had come to Plymouth where Mrs. Hoskins had taken them in, found homes for their babies, and thus they were trapped, working off what they supposedly owed her.

Kitty was infuriated. "You don't owe her anything. Did you ever stop to think she probably sold your children? Why don't you just leave?"

"And where would we go?" one said. "There are far worse places we could be."

Kitty repeated this to Charlie one evening when they were out, and expressed the opinion that it was wrong that women had so few choices in the world, but could become trapped in such situations.

"What have I been trying to tell you?" he said. "Things have to change, and it's people that have to *make* them change. But you wouldn't listen, living with the privileged. After all, you'd never see the likes of a Hoskins girl at Whitmouth House now, would you?"

Kitty was incensed. It wasn't the first time he'd hurt her by saying such things, and she didn't like it. Usually she ignored him, as it was the easiest thing to do, but that particular evening she struck back. They began to argue until one of Charlie's new friends, Jack Scrap, intervened. He'd been listening to their exchange. "Aw, come on, Charlie," he said, handing him a jug of ale. "Drink up and forget it. There's good and bad in all the classes."

"You haven't seen what I have," Charlie grumbled. "Living down here in the south-west you're sheltered and don't know what life is about."

"Oh, is that so?" Jack said. "Well, before you make that assumption go out to one of the tin mines and talk to the miners."

Charlie grabbed his tankard and walked away; he hated to be caught out like that.

"The man's fanatical," Jack muttered.

If only you knew, thought Kitty.

She discovered Jack's last name was Collins. *Scrap* was just a nickname, and according to his reputation, he'd earned it. She was quite fascinated by him and thought how much he reminded her of Enid. His skin was swarthy and his eyes were the color of ripe hazelnuts. He was tall and lean, but he was, apparently, very strong. His mates, and there were many of them, attested to that. He reminded her a little of Charlie when he'd first come to Furze, except he didn't seem as angry.

It was only in Jack's company, strangely enough, that she could forget her guilt. He was funny and made her laugh. He was a handsome devil, and he knew it. He was also a shocking flirt, and that evening when Charlie left them alone, he winked at her and murmured, "Are you really his missus then?" When he saw her dismay he apologized, but he was still cheeky enough to add that if Charlie ever let her down, she could count on him.

Charlie was still so stewed up that when he returned to sit with them, he never noticed Kitty's flaming cheeks. And just as well. He was becoming very possessive of her, and kept saying he couldn't wait until they were married. Although Kitty felt cross with him for ignoring the fact she had already once refused him, she kept quiet when he said it because she felt beholden. She couldn't find the courage to tell him that her feelings hadn't changed. She just hoped that he would open his eyes one day and realize it.

However, as the months progressed there seemed little chance of that happening. Consequently, as their sailing date approached, Kitty became more irritable and impatient.

By the time April arrived, she really began to panic. And when April was almost gone, with May approaching, and their sailing date only two weeks away, although Charlie had told her to put the past behind her and she'd sworn she would try, thoughts about her family would not go away. They rose like bubbles in her mind, and eventually they burst, fervently demanding attention.

Until now she had contacted no one since coming to Plymouth for fear they would be discovered, but one afternoon she decided not to wait until they reached America as Charlie suggested, but to write to Emily right away.

Weeping, and smudging the ink, she constructed a letter. In it, she mentioned the ship on which she and Charlie would be sailing, and asked Emily if she would pray for their safe passage to America. She went out to mail the letter, not knowing if she had done the right thing, but feeling relieved that at least her family would know she loved and thought of them often.

On her return from the post office, she froze in her tracks. Coming towards her down the street was none other than Parky Jones! In a flash, Kitty recalled what had happened the last time they'd met, and she turned and fled.

She never said a word about it to Charlie—he would have been cross enough with her for having gone out alone, and if she told him she'd seen Parky, she didn't know what he might do. The last thing they needed was for him to get himself into some sort of trouble and bring the authorities down on them.

ꕥ

Only days before they were due to sail, Kitty felt an urgent need to go into the countryside, and begged Charlie to spend one or two pennies of their savings and take her outside the city limits. They rode out to the heath, and then walked to the top of a tor and down the other side to a stream.

It was a beautiful spring day. The air was fragrant with the earthy, sensual scents of warm peat and young bracken. Larks trilled in the air above them. Although the surroundings didn't seem to affect Charlie in any way, Kitty's heart began to ache unbearably. She could hardly grasp that she would never see her beloved Dartmoor again.

While they ate their picnic, Charlie chuckled over what the harridan Hoskins might say, once she learned they'd left. "It's as well she's never known who we really were," he said.

Kitty agreed, pushing the uneasy memory of seeing Parky from her mind; after all, he might not have recognized her.

After they'd eaten they felt sleepy and Kitty lay down beside Charlie in the warm, afternoon sunlight. For a while they chatted, and then fell asleep for the first time in each other's arms.

Kitty dreamed she was in Justin's carriage. It was cozy and warm, and his arm was around her. His other hand strayed to her breast, and she moaned softly as he caressed her and told her how beautiful she was. He began showering her with kisses, her face, her neck, and further still... And then the rug around her knees slipped and she felt his hardness, hot against her. Her body flooded with desire and she opened her legs so that he could move between them. She felt him touch her, and slip his finger to her tenderest part. His lips were on her breasts, nuzzling gently, and then she felt him poised at her very opening.

"Oh yes," she murmured as her passion rose; her climax only seconds away. "Oh yes, oh Justin...."

Yet, even in her dream she prepared herself, knowing that despite her desire, her first time might hurt. It was this thought that woke her up.

When she opened her eyes, her arousal fled. She wasn't in a carriage with Justin, but on Dartmoor, lying in Charlie's arms, and she immediately shrank away from him, disgusted with his cunning.

Charlie recoiled too, and made no further move to touch her. "I don't understand," he said angrily. "All set to marry Gordon, yet there you are calling out le March's name. Were you his, then? Did you go with both of them? What the hell's been going on?"

"I haven't been anyone's," Kitty snapped. She felt resentful that he'd been about to take advantage of her, and yet now was accusing her. "I've *never* been anyone's." And she couldn't resist adding, "Nor would Justin le March have done what you just did."

"He obviously didn't fancy you then," Charlie said nastily.

Kitty felt a stab of pain in her heart and looked away, her eyes brimming with tears.

"Why marry Gordon then?" he persisted. "Was he second best?"

"Oh, *damn* you, Charlie Chase!"

"Why then?" he demanded. "Come on, tell me!"

"I'll tell you this only once," she said, her voice tight, her eyes bright with tears. "Don't you ever ask me again. Yes, I loved Justin, but I knew nothing could come of it because of what you said once, about who I am. I never sought out Thomas. He sought *me.* I intended to turn him down, but because of your foolish persistence and my stupid interference, you were arrested. I only agreed to marry him if he would first release you and Acheson." She held his eyes with her own. "I did it for *you,* Charlie. And because of that, Thomas is *dead*!"

She got up and ran away from him in the direction of Plymouth, although in truth she would rather have taken the other road; the one Charlie told her led to home.

He caught up with her. "Don't run away from me, Kit," he begged. "Don't do that." He was distraught, and he apologized for pushing her so far. The whole afternoon had gone wrong, he said, and he was sorry.

Although Kitty said she accepted his apology, inwardly she felt miserable. The afternoon's events had happened, and words once spoken can never be taken back.

They rode back to the inn in silence. Charlie muttered that under the circumstances he would be staying aboard the ship. He made arrangements where to meet her on the day they were to sail, but he didn't kiss her goodbye, and Kitty went upstairs alone to the stuffy attic room, where she sat on the bed and wept.

ꕥ

On the morning of their departure, Kitty crept out of the inn with her bundle of belongings. She was to meet Charlie at their designated spot, and to that end, she made her way through the busy streets towards the docks.

She was surprised to find so many people there, and couldn't imagine they would all be embarking on what seemed to be such a small ship.

She stood beside a little boy, her heart leaping for a moment as she simultaneously thought of Reave, then Edward. She glanced at his mother who bore a striking resemblance to Ruth. She was smiling and talking excitedly to a tall, bearded man, who then pointed at the ship and bent to speak to the small boy. The child seemed distracted and was unresponsive to what was being said to him. He was far more concerned with what he held in his hand.

Sensing Kitty's stare, the child's father glowered at her and moved his wife away, but the child lingered long enough to thrust out his arm towards Kitty and give her the few bluebells he held; their mismatched, wilting stems already twisting for lack of water. "They'll only die," he whispered, looking towards the ship.

Kitty stared at the flowers. Then she looked at the ship. She knew she would die, too, if she boarded it.

Charlie came then, pushing his way through the crowd. As soon as he saw her face he knew something was up. "What's wrong, Kit? What's happened?"

"Nothing. Nothing, but... Oh, Charlie, I just can't do it. I can't come with you."

He laughed. "What? Aw, come on, Kit. It's nerves, that's all."

"No, it isn't. I mean it. I can't go."

His expression changed. "Who's been talking to you?"

"No one. I don't know what you mean."

He looked around them and frowned. "Someone's been nosing around making inquiries."

"What, asking about us?"

He nodded, and swore. "I've always worried that bastard would find me and prevent me from leaving."

"You mean the squire?"

"Who else would be looking for us?"

"I don't know," Kitty said uneasily. She looked past him. "They're starting to load." And she was dismayed. She'd thought perhaps as many as half of the crowd had come to see the others off, yet the whole throng began to mill forward.

"Come on, Kit," Charlie said. "You'll be all right once we get there. We'll be married and have a fine life." He tried to take her hand but she was holding the bluebells. "Where did you get those?"

"A little boy gave them to me." Kitty's eyes filled with tears. "Oh, Charlie, I mean it. I really can't go."

"Christ, Kit! Oh Christ!" He ran his fingers through his hair. "But I can't let you go. Not now."

"You must. It's for you to go, but not me. I know that now. It isn't that I don't appreciate what you've done for me, but—"

He pulled her into his arms. "If this is about the other day, I'm sorry, Kitty. Truly sorry. It's just that I'll never love anyone like I love you, and it's been so hard not to touch you. Christ, I'm not a bloody saint." He looked exasperated. "I promise to give you a good life; can't you do this for me?"

"That's just it, it would be for you," she whispered. *I made that mistake before. I mustn't do it again.* "Please, Charlie, let me go."

His grip tightened. "I can't," he whispered, his voice pure agony.

"You must," she begged. "Please."

Eventually, after what seemed an eternity, she felt him relent. "But what will you do?" he said. "You can't stay here in Plymouth on your own."

"Don't worry about me. I shall be all right." She put her hand to his cheek. She remembered how she had done that to Thomas in the church that fateful Christmas Eve, and her voice caught in a sob. "Oh, Charlie, I know now there are many kinds of love, and mine for you is unique and special, my dearest. Please try and remember that." She looked towards the ship. "You must go now. That is your future, Charlie, and may God go with you into it."

"I thought you didn't believe in Him," he said sullenly, still hesitating.

That was another thing, she thought. Charlie had little faith, which made it harder to keep her own. And, yes, she had expressed her doubts over the past twelve months, just as she'd always expressed her doubts to Flo all her life. All the same, she still said her prayers, just in case.

"I changed my mind," she said lamely. "I do believe there's something. And that it's telling me—"

"*God* is telling you not to come with me?" He snorted in disbelief.

"No. It isn't like that. I just know—"

But he wouldn't let it go. His disappointment at the turn of events was turning to anger. "That you must go and find your precious Justin, I suppose? Aye, I expect he can offer you far more than I can."

"Charlie, stop it," Kitty cried. "Please, don't let's part like this. Nothing could be further from my mind." But she could see he didn't believe her. His expression was a mixture of torment, regret and anger. She knew she would never make him understand.

"I don't believe this is happening," were the last words he ever spoke to her, and then he was gone, taken by the hustle and bustle of the crowd.

She lost him then. Even if he'd waved to her, she wouldn't have seen him because she turned her back to the ship, no longer able to watch the loading of all those people.

She walked up onto the Hoe and waited. Later she saw the ship out in the Sound, its sails now proudly swollen by the wind that took it, and she watched it glide away until it was a speck on the horizon.

A surge of regret washed over her. What *had* she done? She'd thrown away her chance of a new beginning when she could have gone and forgotten….

No, something said inside her; *you aren't the sort of person to forget.*

She watched the ship a little longer, and then raised her hand and waved farewell.

With a shuddering breath of resignation, she began to walk back to the inn. And as she walked, although her heart was aching and felt it would never mend, with each step her conviction grew stronger that, this time, she had made a right decision.

Chapter 38

When Kitty returned to the inn one of the girls said, "There's been a gentleman 'ere askin' about you and 'Oskins was in a right tear when she couldn't find you." She looked at Kitty's bundle and realization dawned on her. "You should never 'ave come back 'ere, you stupid ninny!"

"The man, Maisie, what did he want?" Kitty said urgently. "Who was he?"

"I dunno." Maisie shrugged.

Kitty's skin crawled. What had she been thinking? Mrs. Hoskins would realize by now that she and Charlie had deserted her and would probably be waiting for her with the rolling pin the girls dreaded. She should go right now before—

Suddenly, as Maisie squeaked and scuttled away, Kitty looked behind her.

Looking very pleased with himself was Parky Jones coming out from the taproom. And behind him was Hartley Gordon. Kitty swung around. Mrs. Hoskins was coming down the stairs towards her, grinning all over her face. "I thought my birds had flown," she said. "But I see *one's* returned to the nest."

Kitty bolted for the passageway, only to collide with a man coming through the front door. He held her by her arms, as without looking at him she began to kick and pummel him, demanding to be let go. But then she heard him say, "What's up? What's the matter, Kit?" and looked up to see it was Jack.

"They're after me," she cried. "Oh, Jack, please help me!"

Jack thrust her away from him towards the front door and stood to face her pursuers, even though they were three to his one. Kitty tore outside into the street. Not looking where she was going, she ran full tilt into a man leading a horse. The man fell, the horse reared and pulled his reins out of the man's hand and cantered up the street. People were diving out of the way and shouting, and this gave her the diversion she needed.

She ran down one alley then another, never daring to pause and always heading for the docks. What she would do when she got there she had no idea. In the back of her mind, perhaps, was the hope that Jack might find her later.

It wasn't Jack who found her, however, but Parky, who, after he caught her, boasted about what he'd done to Jack. He pulled her along with him, saying what he'd do to her too when they got back to the Crab Catcher. However, they hadn't even got out of the dockside before three burly fellows stepped into their path. Charlie had always told Kitty about the dangers lurking in that area. But there is honor among friends, and these were friends of Jack's.

"We believe you got somethin' belongin' to our mate," one said, nodding towards Kitty.

Parky pulled Kitty closer to him and drew a knife. "Come any closer, and she's done for."

Another laughed. "There's nothin' to be gained by that. We'll get you afterwards."

"Whereas," the third man said, "let her go and we'll let you go, too."

Parky's eyes darted from one to the other. He'd sought revenge on Kitty ever since Chase had beaten him up and threatened him with something worse if he ever bothered her again. After learning about that fracas in the church at Thomas Gordon's funeral, and hearing what the squire offered to get his hands on them, he'd taken it upon himself to find them. He'd almost given up until he'd seen her that day, rushing away from him, back to the Crab Catcher.

Although Chase had given him the slip, Parky thought with a scowl, he had *this* bird in his grasp now, and he wasn't going to let her go! Dead or alive—and by all accounts the squire wouldn't mind the former—he'd take her with him. His grip tightened. "Out of my way," he growled, as he held the knife closer to Kitty's throat.

He didn't hear the stealthy footfall behind him, so he wasn't prepared for Jack, who hit him in such a way that the knife flew from his hand.

Now freed, Kitty fled into the arms of the first burly fellow, hiding her face in his great sweaty, smelly chest, unable to watch as the others went for Parky. They scuffled and shouted, and with each punch she heard, she winced. Parky was a heavy man, but three to one was a bit much even for him.

Eventually she heard Jack say, "That's enough, boys."

She winced again as she heard a splash. She couldn't bring herself to ask what had happened to Parky. Although she'd wished him away, she hadn't wished him dead.

Jack took her home with him, where Kitty bathed his face as gently as she could, and gave him a compress to hold against the worst bruises.

"So who were those blokes after you then?" he said, through his swollen lips.

"You don't want to ask me that," Kitty said.

"Why? Murder someone, did you?"

The grin on his face faded as Kitty said, "I might as well have." He put her gently from him, fetched two mugs and poured a measure of rum into each of them. He pushed one towards her. "Tell me. Even though I don't believe you could hurt a fly."

In all the time she had been in Plymouth, Kitty had never spoken of the past. Now, once she began, she found she couldn't stop. She supposed the rum helped her flow of words. It certainly helped to dull the pain of her guilt. Weeping, words tumbling out one after the other, she told Jack everything.

"Blimy," he said, when she had finished, "Charlie was a dark horse, he never said a word. And I thought I was a mate of his."

"He didn't like to talk about it," Kitty said. "So he didn't know everything. He certainly never knew the squire was my father."

"I've just remembered, there was a fella asking about you and Charlie a day or so ago," Jack said.

"Other than Parky?"

Jack nodded.

"Perhaps Parky had someone helping him," Kitty said, puzzled. "I feared he saw me that day when I went to post a letter. He probably followed me back to the inn. But why did you come along to the Crab Catcher, Jack?"

"I saw Charlie just before he got on the ship, and he told me you weren't leaving. I thought I might look in and see if anyone knew where you'd gone. I never expected you'd be there."

"I don't know what I was thinking, going back there. I should have got along out of Plymouth. I was just so upset at leaving Charlie, I just wasn't thinking. But, oh, Jack, I'm so grateful you came along. I only wish you hadn't got beaten up."

Jack looked sheepish. "Well, I must admit my intentions in coming to the Crab Catcher *might* not have been all honorable."

Kitty blushed, embarrassed as she realized how precarious her position was, being alone with him.

Despite his sore lips, Jack cracked out laughing. Then he groaned because he really was in a lot of pain. "You're safe enough this evening, but in all truth, my beauty, you'd better be gone from here by tomorrow night. I never was a man to curb my appetites and I have no intention of starting now." He went over to the bed and flicked a blanket from it. "I'll tell you something else," he added, grinning wickedly. "If we ever meet again, I won't be sleeping on the floor. Now, get into my bed and sleep as well as you can. You've a long journey ahead of you tomorrow."

Kitty burst into a fresh set of tears. "You are a very fine and gentle man. I shall never forget you."

"Oh, I'm sure you will," he said.

The next morning, Jack woke her at dawn. He held her close and kissed her. "I must be mad to let you go, but God speed, my beauty."

He left her then and went off to work, but not before giving her his coat with a pocket full of loose change. Before Kitty set off through the streets, she took note of his address. She didn't know how, but one day she intended to repay him for his kindness. Jack might think she would forget him, but she knew she never would.

The streets were deserted when she first set off, but by the time she had walked through half of Plymouth, the city was waking up. Pie sellers and other vendors were stirring and shouting out their wares. People were scurrying to work or to do business; others were scavenging. Kitty felt ravenously hungry and with the few of the coins—she blessed Jack again—she bought several pies to sustain her. She knew she mustn't be tardy in getting out of the city and began to walk in that direction.

To begin with, Kitty didn't pay too much attention to the shouting just ahead of her, but as she got closer she saw a crowd gathering around a horse: he was saddleless, his reins dangling on the ground.

"He won't be caught," said a man, as she came up behind him.

"No wonder, poor thing," said Kitty. "Look at his sides."

"Curses on the man who did that," said another, "but what's to be done with him?"

Kitty looked at the horse more closely. Goodness, but he reminded her of Hector, except he was in very poor condition and his sides were cut and scarred with being spurred. "Let me through," she said. Justin had told her once that she had a natural affinity with horses and she hoped now that he was right.

The horse pricked his ears up when he saw her approach, and he nickered. Kitty ignored those who tugged on her coat and warned her to stay back, saying he'd lunged at those who tried to catch him and might be dangerous. She focused on the horse instead, and when she stood in front of him, reached out with her hand. He blew on her fingers, and then muzzled the flat of her hand, nibbling up the remainder of the piecrust she had there. "You're hungry, old fellow, aren't you?" she murmured as she took up the reins. "Poor boy," she murmured. "Poor old fellow."

Now the horse was caught, the crowd turned away to attend to their daily affairs. All except one man. "He yours then?" he said, creeping up behind her.

Startled, Kitty looked around and the horse jerked his head up sharply.

"He's worth quite a bit, I'd say. If he *isn't* yours, you'd be had up for stealing, wouldn't you? Now, why don't you hand him over to me eh?" the man persisted.

The pie seller, who'd followed Kitty up the street, laughed. "Don't take any notice. He only wants to take him to the knacker's yard."

"I'll tell you what," whined the man, ignoring the other, "*if* he's yours, then he'd let you mount him, wouldn't he?"

Kitty knew what she risked if she tried to mount a vicious horse. Even this man's presence was upsetting him and he was snorting and pulling on the reins. But neither did she like the man; he was the last person to whom she would hand over an animal.

"Stand back," she said, as she led the horse towards a doorstep.

The horse stood quietly enough while she mounted, but as soon as she was on his back he set off up the street. She heard the knacker's man exclaim, "Well, I'll be—" And heard the pie maker chuckle.

And then they were gone, out of her life.

As she rode out of the city, Kitty decided it was nothing less than a miracle the horse had turned up. To walk home would not only have taken her days but also would have been highly dangerous. And although she felt guilty for having more or less stolen him, it would have been nigh impossible and wasted precious time to find his owner. And anyway, she reasoned, anyone who treated an animal like that didn't deserve to have him back.

She stopped at a livery stable, and with her last few coins paid for the horse to have a good feed. She also strung a small bag of oats across his withers. She decided for safety reasons she should take the more frequently used and direct route across the moor to Moretonhampstead. However, when she reached the division in the road, the horse had different ideas and refused to go that way. No matter what she did, including dismounting and attempting to lead him, he wouldn't budge. In the end, she gave up, remounted and let him have his head.

Not having senses like the horse, she was unaware of what might have happened had she taken the other road. With the country in such a poor state and so many men out of homes and jobs, many turned to desperate means to scrape a living. Highwaymen frequented all routes over Dartmoor, and not far up the road two men sat waiting for their next victim.

To begin with, as Kitty rode towards home she fought with her mount many times, thinking he might be leading her astray each time he took a particular turning, or once refusing to budge from a grove of trees he'd taken into his head to run into. Afterwards, riders went by and she began to wonder at his sense. She hadn't even realized there were others on the road, and she knew someone such as herself, alone and on such a fine horse, was tempting bait for anyone.

As their journey continued she began to trust him completely, and by the afternoon of the following day, she cried with relief when she recognized where they were. Just as well they had not far to go because she was feeling faint and lightheaded with hunger. Although the horse had cropped grass along the way and eaten the few oats, she knew it was hardly enough to sustain him. "It won't be long now," she promised. "Then you can eat yourself silly."

A full moon lit her way along the lane to Furze and, thankfully, she saw a light shining from the kitchen window. The old dog stopped his barking once he recognized who she was; his tail began to wag and he began to whine.

The back door opened and Emily called out, "Who's there?" When she saw it was Kitty, she gave a cry and rushed out.

The last thing Kitty heard before she slid to the ground and fainted was Matthew's voice exclaiming, "Dear Lord alive! If that isn't Hector, Thomas Gordon's horse."

Chapter 39

When Kitty awoke the next morning, for several seconds she didn't know whether she was in Whitmouth or Plymouth. Then, as her eyes became accustomed to the room and she came to, she remembered it was Furze.

The latch lifted and Martha and Edward poked their heads around the door. They had almost smothered her the previous evening in their excitement, and seeing she was now awake, they bounded across the room to leap on her bed.

"Emily said to see if you were awake," Martha said. "She has something to tell you."

Edward squeezed in front of his sister. "Father died, thath what," he whispered.

"When?" Kitty said, genuinely shocked, and not without a guilty twinge of relief. It had been her one worry, what Hern would say to her.

Martha glared at her brother. "Emily said *she'd* tell Kitty, you naughty boy." She sighed and sat on the bed. "Well, I might as well tell you now. Father went out on Duffy and she fell with him and couldn't get up. He had to walk all the way home and afterwards he died." Her lips trembled. "Duffy died too."

Kitty found it hard to believe she would never see her mother's old pony again. She also felt ashamed, because the tears she shed were more for Duffy than for Hern.

The door opened and Emily came in.

"He told her, Emily," Martha said immediately.

Emily sighed. "Och, Edward... well, go downstairs and make us tea, will you, Martha, dear? I need to talk to Kitty alone. And take this mischievous scamp with you. Go along, Edward."

"I'm sorry, Kitty," Emily said when they had gone. "I wanted to break it to you myself."

"What a dreadful shock for you," Kitty said.

"Yes, it was, but Hern never fully recovered from the stroke. He used to get very frustrated because he never regained his strength. And then when Charlie went, things became difficult. It was fortunate that Matthew left the manor at that time; I don't know what we would have done without him. He works here now and is living in Barn Cottage."

Kitty remembered Matthew carrying her upstairs the previous evening, and his comment that Hector bringing her home was as if Thomas was watching over her from the grave.

Emily plumped up her pillows and gave Kitty a hug. "Och, I'm that pleased you're here, my dear. It was the last thing we expected, especially after we received your letter to say you were sailing to America."

"You did get it then?" said Kitty. "I feared it wouldn't reach you, because I did so want you to know how much I missed you all. But when the time came for me to go, I couldn't. I hardly knew how to tell Charlie. It was quite the hardest thing I've ever had to do. He didn't understand. He thought it was because I wanted more than he could give me. But it wasn't. It *never* was."

Emily sat on the bed and took Kitty into her arms. "I know," she murmured soothingly. "I know, my dear, I understand." She sighed. "Whether he will ever understand is another matter. I can't say I feel too much sympathy for him—it was his obstinacy that brought this about."

"Obstinacy, but for a reason," Kitty pointed out.

"Yes, I agree… to a point. I know he meant well." Emily sighed again. "I can only hope that he will learn to be more forgiving. Perhaps his new life will help him. People can change and grow if they want to."

That was about as generous as Emily could be in her thoughts about Charlie. As Kitty told her what she'd been doing during the past year and how they'd lived at the Crab Catcher, she shrank within herself. She felt it was unthinkable that anyone would have taken a girl like Kitty to a place like that, and that it was lucky she had escaped unscathed. She would never say so, but she felt glad Charlie had gone to America and was conclusively out of Kitty's life.

While they were talking, Edward crept into the room, followed by Martha, carrying a tray of tea. "We prayed constantly that you would come home," Martha said, as she put it down by the bed. "And you did."

Edward climbed on the bed and sat sucking his thumb with his eyes solemnly on Kitty. "Yeth," he said, pulling his thumb out with a pop! "We pwayed like the devil."

They all laughed, which made the atmosphere a little lighter. Because even though Emily had given Kitty a warm enough welcome and chatted away freely, Kitty felt something wasn't quite right.

Her suspicions grew when later she mentioned that she'd like to go over to Forde to see Flo, and Emily became flustered and made all sorts of excuses why she shouldn't. They'd talk about it later, she said, when Matthew returned from Moretonhampstead and after she'd given Edward his lessons. And she left the room before Kitty could argue about it further.

"Doesn't Edward go to school, Martha?" Kitty asked.

"There is no school," Martha said solemnly. "The squire closed it."

Kitty was convinced now that something was very wrong, and she was tempted to disobey Emily, go downstairs and demand to know what it was. But she was still saddle-sore and weary, and when she closed her eyes again, she fell asleep.

She awoke later to footsteps coming up the stairs, and when her bedroom door opened, Matthew followed Emily into the room. "Hello, Miss Kitty." He looked awkward and out of place. "Forgive me for coming into your room like this."

"I asked him to come," Emily explained. "Sit down, Matthew."

"Nothing's happened to Hector has it?" Kitty asked, alarmed.

"No, nothing like that," said Matthew. "He's never been happier. He'll eat us out of house and home though."

"No wonder, he's in terrible condition." Kitty realized now Hector must have been the horse that had got away outside the inn. The squire must have ridden him to Plymouth.

Matthew grunted. "Your handling of him will be the best he's had in twelve months, I can tell you that." He glanced at Emily. "But no, the horse isn't the reason why I'm here."

Kitty looked from one to the other. "Then what is it?"

"We are so pleased to see you, Kitty, you can't imagine," Emily began. "So relieved you are well and have come home. But I'm afraid it's impossible for you to remain here. Justin made it quite clear that if you ever did come home he must be informed immediately, and I shall write to him post haste. You will have to return to Whitmouth House. But meanwhile you will have to stay hidden."

"Hidden? But why? And I... I can't go *there*," Kitty said, even though her heart leapt at the thought of it. "I can't see Justin. I mean, what must he think of me?" Swamped now by the memories of Thomas's death, and once more drenched with guilt, she added, "He must hate me. And you too, Matthew. You both loved Thomas, and because of me you lost him!"

"Of course they don't hate you," Emily said, a trifle sharply. "Quite the contrary, Justin understands a lot more than you think."

"You've spoken to him about it?"

"Yes, on several occasions. He stays in constant touch with us. He tried so hard to find you, so now you've come home I must—"

"No!" Kitty cried. "No, Emily, you can't!"

"And I say I will!" Emily said, raising her voice for the first time since Kitty had known her. "Matthew, talk some sense into her."

"Miss Kitty," Matthew began patiently. "Neither Mr. Justin, nor I, blame you at all for what happened, and I'm sure he'll explain why. But Emily's right, you have to go because you aren't safe here." He shifted uncomfortably. "What do you remember about the day you walked to the church? The day Charlie took you away?"

"Not a lot." Kitty didn't want to think, let alone talk, about it. Charlie had told her she'd looked wild, like one of the legendary Dartmoor witches, and although he laughed, she had a faint suspicion he wasn't really joking. "I do remember what a sin I was about to commit," she mumbled, ashamed now to think she'd planned to take her life. While at the time, it had seemed the only thing to do, now it was unthinkable.

Emily could understand Kitty's embarrassment. "We understand what you might have had in mind, and why," she said gently. "But others, including the squire himself, thought you meant the knife for him."

And then Kitty remembered. An echo of a memory: *she's got a knife.*

"Unfortunately you played right into his hands," Emily continued. "He didn't want his son labeled as a suicide, so, after Charlie took you away, he put it about that you'd killed Thomas. He said that you and Charlie were in it together; Charlie wanted to disrupt the parish, and you wanted to kill him too and take over the manor."

"But that isn't true!" Kitty cried. "People don't believe it, do they?"

"The state of things hereabouts, my dear, is that people believe what they're told to," Matthew said grimly.

"The squire came here," Emily said. "Before Hern died, he walked right in without a by-your-leave and said once he had dealt with you we would all be evicted."

"*Evicted?*" Kitty said. "But I thought all that had been sorted out?"

Emily exchanged a look with Matthew. Justin had explained to them the terms of the affidavit the squire had signed, impressing upon them how important it was to get Kitty to safety if she remained in the country.

"He'll have you tried for murder and attempted murder, Miss Kitty," Matthew said. "It will be no fair trial, and then, with you out of the way, he knows he can take Furze."

Kitty was bewildered. "But I don't understand."

"The affidavit he signed when your mother was alive only covered a certain period of time," explained Emily. "Although Justin managed to persuade the squire to drop his claim on Furze, it went only as far as your lifetime."

"I believe Master Thomas had already signed a paper that would have put things to right," Matthew said bitterly. "But now that's null and void, and that bastard knows it!"

Emily knew what the squire had done to upset Matthew so much. He'd broken down one night and told her. "Don't, Matthew," she said, placing her hand on his arm. "Upsetting yourself serves no purpose."

"But why is the squire doing this to me, his own flesh and blood?" Kitty said. "I had no intent to harm him."

"He's the sort who always looks for a scapegoat," Matthew muttered. "It isn't you, Miss Kitty, he's always been the same. It's his nature."

"And might be mine!" Kitty cried. "I'm part of that horrible man!"

"Thomas was his, too," Emily reminded her gently.

Kitty thought about this for a moment. "Yes, you are right, Emily. And Thomas was as unlike his father as a person could be."

"That's why the squire hated his own son," Matthew said bitterly. "For years I watched him torment that poor boy and I fear Master Thomas never got over it. I know he was upset he wouldn't be able to marry you, but I do believe he'd have got over that eventually. He didn't do away with himself to hurt you, my dear. He'd never have wanted you to blame yourself either, so get rid of that guilt you carry. He just wanted to pay his father back, and he did it in the only way he knew how."

Now they were talking about it, Kitty didn't want to hear it: yet she had to know. "Tell me. Tell me what happened, Matthew."

Matthew glanced uncomfortably at Emily, but she nodded for him to go ahead. She knew Kitty would be tormented by the past until she knew every little detail of it. Only then would she be able to put it to rest.

"The trouble began," Matthew said, "when Master Thomas told the squire he'd released Charlie and Acheson. In all my time at the manor, I'd never seen the squire so angry. He accused him of interfering, and I do believe he would have sent men after Charlie and Acheson right then, but Master Thomas knocked his father to the ground, and while he stood over him, he said he was going to marry you. I couldn't believe my ears. Not that you wouldn't have been a good match for each other if you'd been able to, don't get me wrong, but I knew you couldn't, you see. The squire was still on the ground and rather stunned I do believe. Master Thomas shouted at him, 'I've made up my mind, Father, there's nothing you can do or say to stop me!'

"The squire put back his head and laughed. I could see Master Thomas was bewildered—he didn't know what to think. And then, as the squire got to his feet I do believe Master Thomas thought he was about to shake hands, to make amends like. He said something like, 'I don't expect your blessing, Father. But don't you see this will end this stupid feud, or whatever it is, between you and the Underwoods? She really is a lovely girl, and most intelligent.' But his father laughed again. I knew he was toying with the boy and I was getting riled myself. Suddenly, the squire looked at him and said, all sly like, 'Even if I did agree, the Church would never allow it.'

"Master Thomas was momentarily confused. 'What do you mean?' he said. 'What are you talking about?' And then—" Matthew's voice caught in a sob and for a moment he couldn't speak. Eventually, he cleared his throat and continued quietly, as if the very words pained him deeply. "And then, that bastard said, 'Her mother was one of my whores. The girl is your sister.'"

He looked towards the window, focusing on the dust motes that spiraled and sparkled in the weak stream of sunlight shining through it. It was as if he was reliving the scene. Tears were rolling down his face.

Returning to the present, he wiped his face and continued. "For a minute Master Thomas didn't move. Then he turned to me—I'll never forget the look on his face. 'He's lying, Matthew, isn't he? Tell me he is?' he said. And I had to tell him, me, who loved that boy like my own, I had to tell him, 'No, Master Thomas, he isn't lying to you this time. Though I have to say Miss Kitty's mother was no whore.'

"That's when he turned to his father and he said, 'You'll be sorry for this, Father. Very, very sorry,' and he left. I wanted to run after him, but the squire called me back. Then a while later I heard Master Thomas gallop off on Hector, and it was then I disobeyed the squire and went after him. I never went back to the manor after that day."

"It was good of you to defend my mother, Matthew," Kitty said, into the silence that followed. "And despite the pain your account brings me, I am gratified to know that Thomas stood up to his father before he…." Her voice caught, and for a moment she couldn't go on. "But how did you know about the squire and my mother?"

Matthew looked uncomfortable and shifted in his seat. "I know about many a misdeed the squire has done," he said quietly.

"But you do see now why you can't stay here?" Emily put in. "Once the squire gets on his feet you won't be safe."

"Neither you nor the horse can stay here, Miss Kitty," Matthew said. "You can't keep a horse like Hector cooped up in a barn, and if the squire sees him, you know what'll happen to all of us."

"What do you mean, when the squire is on his feet? Is he ill?"

Matthew nodded. "It's his heart, by all accounts. I hear since he came back from Plymouth he's taken to his bed for the time being. But to my mind there's not an attack strong enough to take the likes of him, and he'll soon be out of it again. I'm sorry, Miss Kitty, I know it is a sin to say things like that—"

"I don't know how it can be so sinful when the parish would be better off without such a fiend," Kitty said bitterly. "But who would take over from him now Thomas is gone?"

"It will fall to Mr. Justin to decide when the time comes, I imagine," said Matthew, exchanging a look with Emily.

Chapter 40

After Matthew and Emily returned downstairs, Kitty turned her face into her pillow and wept. She shed tears, not only for Thomas, but also for her family who had been forced to suffer the squire's wrath on account of herself: misbegotten by that dark and evil man.

When she could cry no longer, she fell asleep.

Emily awakened her later with a cup of tea. "I check on Flo every day, and so I'll be over at Forde for a while," she said. "She's found it very hard without Acheson there, but he'll never be able to return while the squire is in this frame of mind."

"Can't I come with you, Emily?" Kitty asked. "I would really like to see her."

"Och, I know, my dear," Emily said. "But it's far better you stay here. What if anyone should see you? We cannot take that risk."

Suddenly, Kitty had another suspicion. "Flo isn't angry with me, is she?"

"Angry? Why would she be angry with you?"

Kitty told Emily about the letter that Suzannah Carrington must have seen, and how she blamed herself for having written it.

"Och, Flo doesn't blame you for that. She knows very well that when you wrote it, you were only thinking of Charlie and her husband. But you are right. It was indeed Suzannah who informed the squire. At Thomas's funeral he accused Justin of collaborating with you and Charlie to destroy him. He said it was fortunate there was someone in Justin's household who had his interests at heart, and that's how Justin found out what she had done. He went immediately to London and had it out with her, the treacherous witch, and then he cut off her funding. He said he wouldn't support anyone who was so twisted."

Kitty took some satisfaction from that. At least Suzannah had got what she deserved. But as for the squire accusing Justin! "The man is quite mad."

Emily sighed wearily. "Yes, he is. And that is why our efforts must be put into getting you safely out of his way. Now, I won't be too long. And I will see if Matthew can bring Flo over later to see you."

"But can't she walk over?"

"In truth," Emily said. "I do not know if she would have the strength."

"She's not ill?"

"She is just feeling low, Kitty. But knowing you are here will help to cheer her."

ꕤ

After Emily went downstairs, Kitty felt too restless to return to sleep. Even though her body complained, she got out of bed and stretched her limbs, anxious to get some movement back into them.

She padded across the landing into Emily's room, where she sat in the window seat and watched her go across the field to Forde. She yearned to go with her, and was incensed to think she was more or less being kept a prisoner in her own home because of the squire's monstrous lies.

She was also frightened. Although Emily and Matthew might think she would be safe at Whitmouth House, she had her doubts. She was sure that once the squire knew where she was, he'd never leave her in peace. After all, he'd managed to find her in Plymouth, and God knows what he would have done to her if Jack hadn't saved her.

The thought suddenly occurred to her that everyone might be better off if she went away again. She was sure Jack would have no objections if she asked him for help, and he and his friends would protect her and keep her hidden. In which case, as long as there was no proof she was dead, Furze would be safe, and Matthew and her family would keep a roof over their heads.

Kitty decided it was the only thing she could do. It saddened her though, because despite her protests to Emily, she would have given anything to return to Whitmouth House. However, resigned to her decision, she got up to return to her room. She would pack a few things and write a note to Emily explaining her reasons for leaving, and at first light, she'd steal out of the house and take Hector with her.

As she walked across the room, the floor creaked. It was then she remembered the loose floorboard. As she knelt down, she remembered the day before Ruth's wedding; the same afternoon she had received the letter from Thomas: *you are my destiny, Kitty my love.*

Oh, Thomas, will I never forget those words?

Through blurred vision, with tears splashing on the floor, she pried up the floorboard. She was puzzled to find an old diary of her mother's and flicked through the pages. *Probably nothing much of interest was in it,* she thought, although she had to wonder why Leah had kept it hidden. That alone made her hesitate to put it back, and she took it with her to the window seat.

Kitty was surprised, and a little shocked to find her mother had written so openly about her lovers. The first, a Robbie Barnes, to whom she'd been betrothed, had disappeared, and this evoked pages of copious outpourings of misery, with Leah declaring that she'd never get over it.

However, she apparently had, because then she'd dallied with John Pugh. But although he might have satisfied Felicity's idea of being the perfect husband for her daughter, he fell very short of what Leah herself desired, and she'd turned down his offer of marriage.

Kitty rested the diary on her lap for a moment and thought about the looks the Reverend Pugh used to give her mother during church services. She realized now it hadn't been pity in his eyes she'd seen. No wonder Esther had been so eaten up with jealousy.

Yet, Esther had no reason to feel that way, Kitty decided, as she read on. John Pugh's name was never mentioned after Leah took up with Hartley Gordon.

Kitty's cheeks burned with embarrassment as she read the detailed accounts of her mother's passionate encounters with the squire. Leah said he'd stolen her heart and that she was helpless in her need for him. She was therefore devastated when, after promising to take care of her if she should conceive a child, he rejected her.

Shortly afterwards, she described her horror at being betrothed to Hern, and said her wedding day was 'the worst day' of her life.

After Leah's wedding, the entries became mundane, except for the account of her father's drowning, when she stated her contempt for him, not only for forcing her to, 'marry the clod Hern,' but also for being so stupid as to gamble their home away. Kitty read how she went to the manor to plead with the squire to forgive the debt, but to no avail. She also read Leah's bewilderment over the 'strange conversation' she'd had with Mr. Bennett at the manor, although no details were recorded.

There was nothing more of interest until Leah mentioned the letter she'd received from Justin le March, because, on its receipt, she felt the squire did still have feelings for her, and she wrote, 'it will sustain me in my miserable existence.' Kitty unfolded the letter that was with the diary. She touched Justin's fine handwriting, and smiled. Sighing, she refolded it, and put it away.

She read on. Leah's entries were now all about the baby she was expecting, and how it kept her going. Her mother had indeed wanted her very much, Kitty thought, and it warmed her heart.

There was nothing more of interest, except one of the last entries was confusing. Leah wrote, 'I almost died giving birth, and I almost wish I had. Because then I would not have to think about what finding the ring implies.'

Kitty frowned, and flipped back through the pages. She couldn't remember having read about a ring, and she quickly skip read each page to see if she could find a mention of it. But there was nothing. How odd, she thought. How very odd.

She gave a sigh and closed the book. She felt somewhat exasperated with her mother for being so foolish. She also felt intrusive, and in some ways wished she hadn't read her mother's thoughts; they belonged to another time, an era she didn't understand very well. Knowing the squire as he was now, she couldn't imagine how any woman could have been so in love with him. Why, it was almost as if Leah had been under a spell of some sort: she'd certainly seemed blinded to his true nature.

She knelt down on the floor to put the diary away, and while she was there, decided she would restring the necklace. That, at least, was something of her mother's she could take with her. She really had nothing else.

As she was prying out the little beads, she found, wedged in the space beneath, a piece of paper wrapped around something hard. Puzzled, she sat back on her haunches and unfolded it. As she did, a ring fell to the floor.

Kitty picked it up and stared at it.

She would have known that crest anywhere. It was the larger version of the ring Thomas had given her, and must be the one he said his father hadn't worn for years.

She straightened out the sheet of paper. It was a page, torn from her mother's diary. And it looked as if it had been opened and refolded many times.

Surely enough, she read, 'Sometimes I take out this ring and look at it, and I think what it might have meant had he given it to me in love, instead of finding it as I did in the pocket of my father's coat. I had doubts and many suspicions after speaking with Mr. Bennett, but I put them aside, believing I was listening to the ramblings of an old man. I was unable and unwilling at the time to look at what they might imply. But on the eve of Kitty's birth I found this.

'Even then, I didn't want to see what was so clearly before me. *Even then,* my obsession with him still consumed me. But today, after returning from seeing Mr. Coldswill, I realized that if it hadn't been for Justin le March, Kitty and I would have been out of a home long ago. Knowing now what Hartley Gordon is capable of, I know my father never lost the farm to him, nor was his drowning an accident.

'I am filled with despair. Even though Furze may have been claimed by foul means there is little I can do about it. There is no one to whom I can turn. No one on this earth who can stand up to Hartley Gordon and win.'

Deeply shaken, Kitty lowered the sheet of paper to her knees. Of all things, she had never expected this.

But it explained so many things! How their precarious position must have played on her mother's mind. Why she had been so bad-tempered at times. Smothering, too. Now Kitty understood why Leah had been so cross with Emily's suggestion that she should take further education and leave the farm; she must have been worried sick that something would happen to her, and they would have nowhere to live.

Kitty was suddenly filled with an icy rage. Hartley Gordon's cruel selfishness had caused so much unhappiness to others; the injustice of it was insufferable. She'd only ever heard Thomas's ideology, witnessed Justin's behavior. Gordon was the dark side of all they stood for, and Charlie was right: men like him *must* be taken down. It should never be the other way around, where Charlie and Acheson had to fear for their lives, stay in hiding and even leave their country because they had the courage to stand up for justice.

Kitty read her mother's words again: *No one can stand up to him and win.* And they seared her mind.

Others might not be able to fight him, she thought. But others didn't have what she had: *his very own blood in her, the very strength and determination of a Gordon.* And it was a Gordon's own blood who would bring him down.

With this thought, she replaced the floorboard, tucked the piece of paper inside the diary and took it to her room. Her intention of returning to Plymouth fled. Suddenly everything was so clear. She knew why she had come home.

Chapter 41

Emily looked up as Kitty came downstairs, dressed in her old riding clothes. "You're dressed," she said, looking surprised.

"Yes," Kitty said. "I've been thinking about what you said. You're right, Emily, I should go to Whitmouth before the squire gets up and about. And while I'm about it, I'll take Hector."

They looked towards the door as it opened and Matthew came in. "Oh, hello, Miss Kitty," he said. "You're up and about then?"

"Yes, I am, Matthew. I've decided to go to Whitmouth." Kitty glanced at Emily. "I mean now. This evening."

Emily didn't speak for a moment as if she couldn't believe what she had just heard. Then, as she saw Kitty's determination, her eyes flashed angrily. "Are you *mad,* Kitty? This riding around the moors on your own must have gone to your head. Matthew, tell her, she's being ridiculous. Tell her she must wait until Justin sends his carriage."

Matthew looked from one to the other. He could see the set look on Kitty's face. "I'll go and saddle the horse," he said resignedly.

"But Matthew! If she's going to do such a thing, you should go with her. It's far too dangerous for her to go alone. Kitty, please, don't do this," Emily begged. "It's madness. Why, it'll be dark in a couple of hours. And you aren't strong enough."

Martha was looking worried by now, and she and Edward clung together. That sight alone made Kitty more determined to do something to help her family.

"Everything will be all right," she said. "I'm still weary, I'll admit. But I'm strong, and I will easily make Bovey Tracey by nightfall. Tomorrow, I'll go across the heath and make my way to Exeter. I do know where I'm going. I have done the journey several times in the past. The road is well-traveled and generally safe." She looked at her sister and brother. "But Matthew must stay here with you. We haven't another horse who can keep up with Hector anyway."

"You think you're invincible!" Emily cried. "There are all sorts of perils out there."

Martha ran to embrace Kitty. "You will be careful, Kitty?" she said, clinging to her sister.

"Yes, I will, Martha," Kitty said solemnly. "Hector is a wily old horse. Remember, he brought me home across the moors from Plymouth. If he can do that, he can certainly get me to Whitmouth." Over Martha's head, she looked at Emily. "I do understand your concerns, Emily, but the sooner I go the better, you know it is. I cannot bear to see you so on edge. Indeed, I have never known you to be so touchy."

"In truth, I don't know how much more of it I can take," she admitted.

"Then don't hold me back."

Emily gave a weary sigh. "No, no, I won't then. But I pray that God will watch over you. I shall not rest until I have word that you have arrived safely."

ꕥ

Hector was happy to be taken out of the barn. After a good rest and a feed or two, he was now in fine fettle, and Kitty set off at a good pace that he was comfortable with. She avoided going up the hill past Forde. She didn't want Flo to have any idea of what she was doing, else she would only worry further. Besides, she didn't think she could ride past her grove. Not yet.

Soon she was cantering along the lonely moorland road. At the point where it divided, she pulled Hector up, and for a moment gazed in the direction of Plymouth. She thought of Jack and his kindness, and how, if her circumstances were different, she wouldn't have minded returning to him. There was something about him that was so attractive. She smiled to herself. And yes, she thought, something about him that attracted all the other girls, too.

She laughed, shaking her head at her thoughts. "Au revoir, Jack," she said softly. Then she guided Hector towards the opposite direction and urged him forward. "Come on, Hector. Let's take you home."

She arrived in Bovey Tracey just before nightfall, found safe lodgings for herself and a dry, comfortable stable for Hector. The innkeeper looked at her oddly, and indeed, she imagined she must be a sight in Jack's old coat and her worn breeches, her hair tucked beneath a cap. She intended it that way, knowing she would be far safer to be taken for a young man rather than a woman. After a good supper, she was led upstairs to a clean room, miraculously free of vermin. She made sure her door was secure; she slept well and was up at dawn the next day. After a hearty breakfast she set off on the most difficult and dangerous part of her journey.

She was very relieved to reach Whitmouth. Despite her brave words to Emily, she had been nervous crossing the heath and taking the coastal road.

She was cold and soaked through from the drizzle that fell, but she gritted her teeth and rode on. Hector's hooves clattered through the cobbled streets of Whitmouth, and then the houses petered out and, at last, they were making their way up the long driveway to Whitmouth House. By that time, the rain was driving across the lawns in curtains and Kitty could hardly see the house ahead of her.

Hector wasn't a young horse and she'd ridden him fairly hard. He was wet, miserable and tired, and as she rode him into the stable yard he only managed a weary whinny, but the other horses neighed an eager welcome in return and brought the stable boy running out to see who was there. He took the bridle and led Kitty into the covered yard, where she dismounted.

"Why," he said, his eyes growing wide with surprise as he recognized her, "It's Miss Kitty. Oh, Miss Kitty, I can't believe it's you!"

"It is," she said. "And I've brought Hector home."

A shadow crossed the boy's face as he saw the scars on Hector's sides. "Just as well too, by the looks of it," he said grimly.

"He'll be safe here now," Kitty said. "Give him a good feed in a while and a good rub down meanwhile. He's done well today and must be weary." She gave Hector an affectionate pat. "You're a brave horse, Hector. Thomas would have been so proud of you." Then she braced herself and went to the rear door of the house. She was nervous, and shivering not only because of the cold.

The door was opened by the tweeny. Madeline, who appeared behind, almost knocked her over as she pushed past. "Oh, my God! It's her! It's Miss Kitty!" she cried. Both girls hugged and sobbed with joy to see each other.

Huffing mightily, Cook came out to give a piece of her mind to whoever it was kicking up such a hullabaloo on her doorstep, but her expression changed when she saw it was Kitty. "Oh, my dear, my dear, come on in," she cried, throwing her arms around her. "We'd given you up, but here you are, safe and sound and home again." She stood back and looked in disapproval at Kitty's clothes. "But look at you, how wet you are," she scolded. "I don't know what the master would say. Good job we have time to clean you up before he comes home." And she bundled her off with Madeline to have a bath.

"When will he be back?" said Kitty, following Madeline upstairs. "Where has he gone?"

"Just into Whitmouth," said Madeline. She threw open the door to what used to be Kitty's room. Kitty followed her in and gasped at what she saw before her. There was a fire burning merrily in the grate and flowers on the table. She was about to ask if they'd expected a guest when Madeline said, "He asked me to light it a couple of days ago. I admit I thought he'd gone funny at the time. But Miss Kitty, he must have sensed you were coming home."

Justin arrived home a while later. He'd taken Reave into Whitmouth to see Enid and Margery, along with Julia Fulham, Reave's current governess and companion, the daughter of a reverend friend.

Julia had some artistic talent and shared some common ground with Enid. They were going to an art show that evening and were taking Reave with them. Justin, however, had declined.

"Dreadful evening," he said to Madeline, as she took his coat and shook it.

"All depends how you look at it, sir," Madeline said, quite impishly. She was bursting to tell him Kitty had arrived, but Cook had insisted *she* be the one to tell him, else she wouldn't have the pleasure of seeing his face. "Cook would like to see you, sir, if you don't mind."

Justin looked at her curiously. "Is something wrong?" He knew Cook never bothered him with anything trivial.

Madeline was almost beside herself. "Oh, please, sir, do hurry."

Justin burst into the kitchen, now convinced something untoward must have happened. But Cook turned and looked at him quite calmly.

"What is going on? " Justin said.

"I just wanted to tell you I'm preparing a special meal," Cook said, beaming at him. "For your guest."

"We have a guest?" Justin said, perplexed. "That is all?"

"Yes, sir. And she has been put in Miss Kitty's room."

"Why that room when we have twenty others?" Justin said, looking slightly annoyed. "I know it's aired, but surely—"

Cook couldn't contain herself any longer. "Well, sir," she said, trying to keep a straight face. "I doubt Miss Kitty would like any other room but her own." She suddenly burst into tears. "She's here, sir! Miss Kitty has come home." And she looked towards the door, because just then, as Madeline had rushed to fetch her, Kitty came through it.

Justin turned. The world he had resigned himself to, suddenly shifted and another was taking its place. Because there she was, his little love lost.

"Kitty," he said. "Oh, Kitty."

At that point, having seen all they thought was appropriate, Cook and Madeline went discreetly into the hall where they fell upon each other, sobbing and laughing with joy to see their master looking happier than he had for a long time.

"I never expected...." Justin began. But then he stopped. What was he saying? Why the lit fire, the warmed bed, the flowers brought to her room? He let the sentence die and began again. "When did you arrive? Oh, my dear, how did you get here?"

"I came a while ago," Kitty said. She still held his hands. Neither could she take her eyes off his face. "I came on Hector."

"Hector? But how is that?" Justin searched her eyes. Through the mists in his mind he heard her say, "I have so much to tell you. So very much."

"Come along then. Come and tell me everything." He led her into the drawing room. "Would you care for a glass of sherry before dinner?"

"I would," Kitty said. "Thank you, sir."

"Sir?" He raised an eyebrow. "Can't you call me Justin? Are we not old friends?"

"Justin, then," she said.

He handed her a glass. "Why did you not wait at Furze? One word from Emily and I would have come down immediately to fetch you. I would have worried sick had I known you were riding here alone. That is such a dangerous thing to do."

"I couldn't wait a moment longer." Kitty looked shamefaced. "I know it was rash, but, the plight of my family—my own fears, drove me. It seems the squire has lost his mind in his efforts to destroy us. Besides, Hector wasn't safe at Furze. Matthew had him hidden in the barn, but he couldn't stay there. And I couldn't bear to think of him returning to the manor."

"The squire took Hector when Thomas passed away, after he rode his own horse into the ground," Justin said grimly. "How on earth did you come to have him?"

"I rode him home from Plymouth."

"Plymouth!" Justin said. "Good Lord, Kitty—!"

Kitty took a gulp of her sherry. "As I said, I have so much to tell you. Indeed, I hardly know where to begin."

Justin sat down beside her, and reached for her hand. "Start at the beginning, my dear."

Leaving out few details, determined this time that she would keep no secrets from him ever again, Kitty told Justin where she and Charlie had lived in Plymouth, and of Charlie's plans.

"Emily wrote to me as soon as she received your letter," Justin said. "It was then I tried to find you. I had tried many times before, but you stayed so well hidden."

"We had to," Kitty said. "Although at the time I had no idea what price was on my head, Charlie was so afraid he would never get away."

"But here you are. You didn't go. Why, Kitty? Why didn't you sail after all?"

Because I love you, she wanted to say. *Because I have to have you in my life.*

"I couldn't," she said, averting her eyes. "And it was a terrible thing to do to Charlie, after he saved me." And then she remembered what he had saved her from, and when, and her guilt came flooding back. "Oh, Justin," she said brokenly. "And how ever can you forgive me for what I did to you?"

"What did you do to me?" he asked gently.

Her eyes filled with tears. "You must think... if it wasn't for me Thomas would still be alive."

"Oh, Kitty, I understand how you must feel. But cast your mind back a while to the time when you first came to Whitmouth House. When we had a conversation about my attitude towards Reave. Do you not remember what you said to me? How you so assuredly told me how I shouldn't carry the guilt for someone else's choice?"

"Yes, I do remember. But I don't see what that has to do with this."

"Is it so hard to take your own advice? Was it not Thomas's own choice to take his life?"

"Well, yes," she admitted. "But still, if I hadn't agreed to marry him he wouldn't have done that."

"You can never say that. None of us can never say what might not have happened if we hadn't done such and such a thing, simply because we don't know. My dear, don't misunderstand me—I don't wish to speak ill of the dead—but there's something about Thomas you must know, if indeed, you hadn't already guessed it. He suffered from depressions so deep, he had once or twice before hinted about taking his life."

"He had? But why?"

"He was a bright and truthful soul, so he found it very hard being his father's son. Living with such darkness can be very destructive." Justin sighed. "That is why I never told him who you were. I was hoping there would be no need to add to his pain. I had no idea he'd fallen in love with you; no idea who he was talking about when he told me he planned to marry and that his choice would not please his father—"

"But to do it there, where we met," Kitty whispered. "It was where he said he fell in love with me. That is why I thought he did it because he couldn't marry me. Matthew assures me it isn't so, but—"

"Has it never occured to you that Thomas might have felt comfortable dying in a place that held such happy memories for him, and that was the reason?"

"No." Kitty was startled by the thought. "I had not thought of that."

"Do you really think, knowing how much he loved you, that he would want you to carry this burden of guilt? It wasn't you he wanted to hurt, Kitty. As for his timing, he knew if he died before his age of majority, his mother's inheritance would bypass his father and return to the le March estate. It was only days before his birthday. Now, what do you think his father would think of that?"

"He wouldn't be too pleased."

"No, indeed. Because had Thomas lived and inherited that money, the squire would have found a way to get his hands on it—it was his way. So, even though Thomas was not of a revengeful nature as a rule, I imagine this was the one way he knew he could repay his father for all the hurt he had inflicted upon others." He smiled at her gently. "Now, are you beginning to understand the situation a little better?"

"Yes," Kitty said, after thinking about it. "Yes, I think so. And I do understand what you mean about Thomas's emotional health. Perhaps that is why I felt such a great tenderness towards him. Such as a sister might feel for her brother." She smiled sadly. "When he proposed to me I felt honored, but I intended to refuse him." She could still see the candles around the nativity in the church, Thomas's earnest expression. "But I couldn't bring myself to dash his hopes so cruelly at the time. I was going to let him down gently, when I saw him in May. Meanwhile, Charlie and Acheson were imprisoned. I felt, because of the letter I had written, which had unwittingly got them into trouble, I had no choice but to save them if I could. The only way I could think of repaying Thomas for the enormous favor I was about to ask of him was to accept his proposal. Oh, if only—"

"But you acted out of love, Kitty," Justin interrupted. "You *cannot* carry the guilt for that either. It was Suzannah who sinned."

"I suspected her, and Emily confirmed it." Kitty's eyes flashed angrily. "She also told me of the squire's accusations about yourself. It is ridiculous! As ridiculous as the things he is saying about me, his own flesh and blood." Her expression grew harder. "And, yes, I may be his flesh and blood, and as such I will not stand for the way he is treating my family. I have proof of how treacherous he has been in the past! How he has lied."

Justin's face lit up with interest. "What proof?"

Kitty got up from her chair. "I have it upstairs. I will fetch it."

Chapter 42

Kitty slept until almost noon the next day, and even then had to be woken up by Madeline, who brought with her a tray of breakfast.

Disoriented, Kitty sat up. She couldn't believe she had slept so long. "What must Justin think," she said.

"It was by his instructions you were to be left until now," Madeline said. "He said you'd done quite a bit of riding lately." Her eyes twinkled curiously.

Kitty knew very well that Justin wouldn't have mentioned anything to the staff of her adventure, and that they'd probably been conjecturing between themselves. She would have liked to confide in Madeline, but she really didn't want anyone knowing what had happened.

"I have indeed," she said, and as Madeline put the tray on the bed she caught her hand. "But know this Madeline, I didn't stay away out of choice. I missed you terribly. I missed everyone."

Madeline looked pleased to hear that, and didn't pursue the matter any further.

Kitty lay back into her pillows with a sigh. She had worried what everyone's reaction might be to her, turning up like that all out of the blue. But they'd welcomed her so far. And what a delicious breakfast, she thought, as she tucked into it. How wonderful to be so coddled.

She dressed and went downstairs. As she approached the drawing room, she recognized Enid's laughter. She paused, her heart fluttering uncomfortably. Just as she'd feared the staff's reaction, now she worried what Enid and Margery would say.

It was too late to retrace her steps. Justin saw her and came towards her with his hand outstretched and led her into the room. Margery and Enid were there, and Reave was sitting beside an attractive woman, who stood up politely to acknowledge her.

"Oh, my dear!" Margery cried, throwing her arms about her. "What a relief it is to have you safe again and to know you are well."

"And all the richer for the experience if I am not mistaken," Enid said, taking her turn to embrace her.

Julia stood up and offered her hand, as Justin introduced her. "This is Julia Fulham, Reave's present companion."

"I am pleased to meet you, Miss Fulham," Kitty said.

"I am delighted to meet you, Miss Underwood." Julia looked at her closely. "Justin has told me so much about you. And please, call me Julia."

Kitty turned to look at Reave, hoping he might say something to her, but he just gave her a solemn look, and didn't say anything at all.

Justin whispered, "Do not take it to heart, Kitty. He is beside himself with joy."

He has a funny way of showing it, Kitty thought.

Indeed, when they all went outside later into the garden, Reave sidled up to her and said quite petulantly, "Because you weren't here Father might marry Julia now."

Kitty looked sharply at Julia, who at that moment was looking up into Justin's face, laughing over something he was saying. Kitty felt a pang in her heart, but in all honesty she couldn't blame him for being attracted to the young woman. After all, what had she expected after being away for a year?

Julia saw her looking at them and she came over to take Kitty's arm. "Justin has been telling me about your travels," she said. "Would you care to walk with me to the stables and show me your fine mount?"

Kitty wondered if Julia wanted to be alone with her so she could break the news of their betrothal. But Julia didn't mention Justin, apart from saying that he was absolutely delighted to see Kitty again, and he was sorry to see how badly Hector had been treated.

They were standing outside Hector's stall. He'd been groomed and his chestnut coat shone. "He's looking much better than he did yesterday," Kitty said. "Unfortunately those scars on his sides will never completely disappear."

"How cruel," Julia said. "How could anyone spoil such a magnificent animal?"

"I have seen a lot of cruelty in the past year," Kitty said, thinking of the Crab Catcher's girls.

"In Plymouth, you mean. Yes, Justin mentioned you were staying in rather an unsavory part of the city, and I must say it intrigues me."

"It does?" Kitty could feel herself blushing, and part of it was anger that Justin would talk about her escapades to Julia.

Her embarrassment didn't escape Julia's notice. Immediately the sensitive woman was all concern and she placed her hand on Kitty's arm.

"Please," she said, "don't be cross with Justin for discussing it with me. It's only that I have interests in that sort of thing. In my position, or rather, the position I will be assuming, it will be necessary for me to have an understanding of those who are not as fortunate as myself, so that I may help them."

Kitty's heart caught. "Your... position?"

Julia put a finger to her lips. "It is a secret for now. Promise you won't mention it to anyone."

"Of course not," said Kitty as her heart fell even further.

ꙮ

Enid sidled up to Justin. He was looking through the window at Julia and Kitty, who were strolling back from the stables.

"Well?" Enid said softly. "How is she, my dear?"

"Remarkably well, considering," Justin said. "But she is carrying the burden of guilt, as we thought she might."

Enid nodded. "But you did explain about Thomas?"

"As best I could."

"And did she accept it?"

"I think she will grow to. Whatever his reasoning, dwelling on it will not bring him back. I know that only too well. I constantly hover on the brink of guilt myself."

"I could say the same," Enid said. "I could have stopped Kitty from leaving that morning; I knew very well she didn't want to return to Furze. But, Justin my dear, you know well there are so many twists and turns to life, so many possibilities. Where one would save oneself from one menace, there is always another to take its place. Had Thomas learned of your love for Kitty, who knows how it would have played on his mind? At the least, there might have been a rift between you. And without you in his life?" She lifted her hands in a gesture.

"I know you're right. Life is rather like being in a play without a script, isn't it? And at times, rather disconcerting."

Enid smiled. "It is indeed. But it is also somewhat interesting. Look what Margery has turned up about Kitty. You haven't mentioned it to her yet?"

"No. I think it's prudent to wait until I have seen the squire."

"Very wise," Enid agreed. "Yes, better to get him sorted out first. When will you return to North Bovey?"

"I thought the day after tomorrow. I'll give Kitty another day before she travels again."

"She's looking very well, all things considered."

"Yes, she is. There is something else about her, too. A honing. A confidence she didn't have before."

Enid smiled. "We don't go through these trials for nothing. The past year will have strengthened her for what is to come." She put her hand on Justin's arm. "Don't leave her here, Justin. She must return with you to North Bovey. This has to be completed. You know that. But you mustn't worry; she is going to come through it all right."

Justin caught Margery's eyes over the top of Enid's head, and she smiled. "I hope so," he said. "The next few days aren't going to be easy."

"But it has to be done," Margery said. "He has to know who she is, and I'll make my way to Newton Abbot tomorrow and fetch our witness."

Justin nodded. "So be it."

ഌഗ

Kitty couldn't say she disliked Julia, in fact she felt quite to the contrary. But as Julia kept dropping hints about her future plans, Kitty still couldn't help placing them within the context of her being the next Mrs. le March, and she felt envious. Not that Julia ever said directly that she and Justin were going to be married, but it seemed obvious.

That evening after dinner, she excused herself and went to her room, leaving Julia alone with Justin. He'd told her they would be leaving for North Bovey in another day, and she had mixed feelings about it. She was surprised to hear she would be going with him; she'd hoped that now she was at Whitmouth House she would be able to stay there, but he hadn't mentioned the future.

She sat by the fire in her room enjoying the comfort of it. Although it was almost the end of May it was still somewhat chilly at night. It had been a cool, damp spring on the whole, with only the occasional nice day. Like the one she had spent on the moors with Charlie.

She thought about Charlie then, and wondered how he was. It was hard to imagine he would still be at sea in that tiny ship with all those people. A coffin ship Jack had called it, and she shuddered, praying he would reach his destination.

She heard the door open and looked around to see it was Reave. "Why… Reave," she said, surprised. He'd been sulky with her all day. "What are you doing here?"

He looked sheepish. "I came to say I'm sorry, Kitty. I told a lie. I really am very pleased to see you again. I'm not absolutely sure they're going to be married. It's only what other people have been saying."

"Oh, Reave." Kitty held out her arms to him, wondering if he would feel too grown up for her to hold him, but he snuggled close to her. "It's all right. I like Julia, and your father deserves some happiness."

He took a deep sniff. "I've missed you," he said. "Father was really unhappy without you here. Why did you stay away?"

"When you are older I promise I will explain. It's too difficult for you to understand at the moment."

"But it was something to do with Thomas?"

Kitty nodded. "Yes, it was."

"I miss seeing him. I've heard Father crying."

"We all miss him," Kitty said, her voice breaking.

"Julia says he's in heaven and is happy there. Do you think he is?"

"Yes, I like to think he's at peace now."

"I'd better go back to bed now," Reave said. "Julia's going to take me to the beach tomorrow. Do you want to come with us?"

"I don't know…." Kitty saw his face drop. "All right. Perhaps if Julia wouldn't mind, I will."

"Hooray!" He laughed with glee. "We can pick up shells. Julia likes gathering them, and if you do too, then I think you two will get along very well."

Kitty laughed, and kissed him. "You are a dear boy. That is why I missed you so much. Would you like me to accompany you to your room?"

He nodded sleepily, and Kitty took his hand and led him along the corridor. His room was next to Justin's now, she noticed. She supposed that had come about because of her leaving.

She tucked him into bed and stayed with him until he fell asleep. As she walked back to her room, she heard Justin and Julia in the hall downstairs.

"Thank you for being so understanding, my dear," Justin was saying.

"Oh, Justin," Julia said. "How could I not?" Kitty saw her kiss him first on one cheek, and then the other. Her vision blurred by tears, she returned to her room.

The following afternoon, the weather cleared up and it became quite warm. Julia said she would love to have Kitty for company, and clapped her hands like a delighted girl as they got into the carriage to go to the beach. Justin waved them off, obviously happy to see them getting along so well.

They took the carriage to the sea front. The tide was out and Reave scampered off, running as fast as his legs would carry him along the hard, slick sand to the waves.

"I can't tell you how this pleases me," said Julia, tucking Kitty's arm into hers. "I just know we are going to become the closest of friends."

If only you weren't going to marry Justin, Kitty thought. But then felt ashamed of her thoughts. She had to admit she couldn't dislike the beautiful, gentle woman walking beside her, and her conscience made her say, "I think so, too, Julia."

Julia gave her a look that was something like admiration. "Thank you, Kitty. You don't know how happy that makes me."

ꙮ

The next day, Justin set off with Kitty to North Bovey. Reave wanted to go with them, but Justin said he had better stay with Julia.

On the way, he said to Kitty, "I am sorry Reave was a bit off with you to begin with, but I notice he soon came around."

"Yes, he did, we had a good talk. He came to my room."

"Oh, did he? Good. I'm glad to hear it. He missed you terribly, you know, and it was so hard to know what to tell him. It's strange. Sometimes children seem to understand tragedy and deal with it better than adults. When he knew it was something to do with Thomas, he stopped asking."

"I told him I would explain everything when he is older. That's if he still wants to know. Hopefully he will forget the past twelve months as time goes on."

"It will be good to put a lot of things behind us. Including the next few days."

He halted the carriage in Moretonhampstead, where he got out, saying he needed to have a word with Coldswill. He instructed the coachman to go on to Furze and to stop for no one, and assured Kitty he would be in touch with her shortly.

Emily came running out when she heard the carriage arrive. She looked shocked to see Kitty, and not at all pleased. "Kitty! I expected to have word from you, but not you yourself," she scolded. "What are you thinking of, returning here? Someone at the manor told Matthew the squire thinks you must have come back here from Plymouth. It's only a matter of time before he comes looking for you. Och, you should have stayed in Whitmouth. Whatever is Justin thinking of?"

"Shh, Emily, shh," Kitty said, drawing her inside. "I have nothing but good news. Justin is thinking of a great deal. Now, let us have a cup of tea and I'll tell you all about it."

Matthew and Emily listened while Kitty told them about finding Leah's diary, and what was written in it.

"Old Mr. Bennett always did reckon there was foul play the night Peter Peardon died," Matthew said. "He spoke of it many a time."

"It's all very well trying to see justice done now," Emily said irritably, pushing the hair out of her eyes. "But that happened a long time ago, and you know what the squire is like. I hope this doesn't make things worse."

"How can they be worse?" Kitty said, disappointed with Emily's reaction. "You know we can't go on like this."

Matthew looked from one to the other, then stood up and sniffed the air. "I think we're due for a storm," he said.

Matthew was correct. By late afternoon, the sky had darkened. It looked as if a giant purple bruise had crept over the horizon, and while Emily was outside bringing in the washing, she heard the first roll of thunder in the distance. She ushered Edward into the house. "It's going to be a big one, by the look of it," she said. And as she spoke, raindrops as large as pennies began to dot the ground.

During the night, the storm moved right overhead and crashes of thunder shook the very foundations of the house. Martha and Edward ran into Kitty's room and leapt into her bed beneath the covers. By then there was hardly any count between the flashes of lightning and the thunderclaps; flash, boom; flash, boom; on and on it went. Edward was terrified and began to wail.

All of a sudden, there was a huge crack. Kitty shrieked when the flash that accompanied it lit up the room, making it look as if it was filled with ghoulish shapes. She imagined she saw someone standing at the foot of her bed and she dove beneath the covers.

Towards dawn, the storm finally moved away but although Martha returned to her room, Edward stayed snuggled into Kitty. He still sucked his thumb, but soon it slid from his mouth as he fell asleep. Kitty cuddled into him while she listened to the water dripping from the eaves outside. She wondered how Justin was faring. She knew how he must dread the task of confronting the squire, and considered him to be very brave.

In the morning, when Kitty went outside, she found the yard looking like the aftermath of a great flood. Emily's flowers that had previously flounced their brilliance to the world were dashed to the ground. The sky was gray and sullen, and the air was still and humid. When Matthew came up from Barn Cottage he said he felt uneasy. When Kitty said she was going over to see if Flo was all right, he told her not to hang about afterwards, but to come straight home. He thought there was another storm brewing and she shouldn't be out in it.

Flo hugged Kitty as if she might never let her go. "Aw, maid, my maid," she kept saying, over and over again. "Thank God you never went abroad." She held Kitty away from her. "And here you are, a woman grown. But…what are you doing here again? I thought Emily said you'd gone to Whitmouth?"

"I did. But Justin has come to see the squire, and he wanted me to come with him." And Kitty repeated what she'd told Emily and Matthew about the diary, and how Justin was going to confront the squire so they could all live in peace.

"I'd be only too pleased to think that could happen," Flo said. "But I fear the only time anyone hereabouts will have any peace is when he's six feet under. How could a man like Justin le March have any idea of the wickedness in that man's heart? What can he do to change his ways?"

"Well, he has to try. We can't all go on living in fear. And if he makes him promise not to plague us, perhaps Acheson can come home."

"I know you mean well, and I'm sure Mr. le March does, too. But I'm telling you, while Hartley Gordon lives, none of us will ever be able to sleep safe in our beds."

Kitty was disappointed with Flo's pessimism and to change the subject she talked about Reave, and how only yesterday it had been warm enough in Whitmouth to walk on the beach and search for shells. She glanced through the window. "But look at it now. Matthew thinks we may have another storm."

"If we do I hope it isn't as bad as the one we had last night," said Flo, giving a shudder.

"So do I," said Kitty. "Edward was petrified."

"I'm sure I heard a tree come down somewhere."

"That must have been when I heard the crack. You ought to have seen the flash, Flo; it lit up the whole room and made it look full of shapes. I even thought I saw someone at the foot of my bed." She shivered. "You don't think it was a ghost, do you, because—"

Kitty stopped. Flo's face was full of anguish. And then she remembered how ill she'd been, and realized how she was chattering on regardless. Filled with remorse she said, "Oh, I'm so sorry. I forgot you weren't well. Look, if you're nervous here alone, why don't you come over to Furze during the storm? I'll take care of you."

"It isn't that, maid. Though I'll have to admit I didn't sleep well…."

"Look how you're shaking. Let me take you upstairs so you can lie down for a while. I'll make you a nice cup of tea and we'll talk later."

Flo gave in. "Well, just for a while then. I do feel a bit dizzy."

After Kitty steadied her up the stairs, Flo took off her shoes and lay under the covers. She did feel shaken. She knew the time had come when she simply *must* tell Kitty about Mary, and vowed that when Kitty came upstairs she would. Lately, more than usual, the house was filled with the scent of bluebells, and it wasn't from any she brought in. She shivered, despite being cozy in bed. Mary was near, and she knew it must be for a reason.

But as she lay there under the covers, the dripping of the water outside the window had a soothing, hypnotic effect, and she fell asleep.

ঌ৩

Kitty was disappointed Flo had fallen asleep. She put the tray beside the bed with a cozy over the teapot, hoping it would stay warm for her when she awoke.

"I love you so much," she whispered. "And one way or another I'll see that Acheson comes home again. Don't worry." She kissed Flo and tiptoed from the room.

Mindful of Matthew's warning, Kitty knew she should get back to Furze, but when she went outside she thought again about the fallen tree, and wondered if one had come down in her grove. She was still reluctant to go there: she didn't know if she was ready to face the place where Thomas had died. But suddenly she found herself running up the hill, unable to stop herself.

When she turned the corner, she couldn't believe the devastation the storm had wrought; the whole area was strewn with boughs and broken branches, sticks and leaves. It seemed brighter too, as if something was missing. And then she realized part of the canopy had gone. What Flo had heard come crashing down in the night was the huge beech tree, and it had taken the rowan and crab apple along with it. Tree and bluebell roots were exposed, tangled and ugly.

She whimpered: her grove, her beautiful grove where she and Martha had frolicked and met Thomas that day. She could see him now, sitting on Hector, his hand outstretched towards her. A sob caught in her throat as she remembered how foolishly proud she'd been. Then later. When his body had lain crushing the bluebells, how she had been humbled by his death. "Oh, Thomas," she whispered. "Thomas."

She looked at the fallen beech. Beneath its upturned roots was now a gaping hole filled with sticks and debris. She went closer, and frowned as something caught her eye. She couldn't quite make out what it was, so she picked up a stick and began to poke at it. Clod by clod the earth fell away from what Kitty first thought was a smooth rock. She recoiled as she realized it was a human skull.

She shivered. The wind had come up and was moving listlessly among the trees. Their branches rustled almost menacingly. The next storm must be blowing in, she thought, as she remembered Matthew's warning. She should get home lest he should worry. She should tell him what she'd found and let him deal with it.

But as she turned, a grip of steel went around her arm. What with the wind and her fascination, she hadn't heard his approach: she was standing face to face with the man who wanted to destroy her.

"So," Hartley Gordon said, "here's le March's little tittle-tattler." He bent her arm cruelly behind her back, and looked down at the hole. "And what's this but a grave already dug for my purpose?"

"Killing me won't solve anything," Kitty cried. "Justin knows what you did to my grandfather, and he'll see that something is done about it. You'd be far wiser to negotiate with him than to hurt me."

"I'm done with le March's *negotiations*," he growled, wrenching her arm up a notch.

"Haven't you done enough harm? Spreading lies about me, your own flesh and blood!"

He swung her around to face him and raised his hand, but Kitty's fear had been replaced by anger. "I'm not afraid of you," she spat. "I am *part* of you, remember? A Gordon." Her voice was filled with exaltation: because now, seeing him in the flesh, facing her fear and dread of him, she realized he was only a man. *A pathetic old man.*

"You have no power over me," she sneered. "You'll have no power over anyone soon, because you're going to get what's been coming to you for a very long time."

He shook her until her teeth rattled. But still she kept on taunting him; determined to get some revenge on him for hurting her mother, murdering her grandfather, and finally, for driving his son to commit suicide.

But when she mentioned Thomas's name, the squire wouldn't stand to hear it, and he lifted his hand and struck her so hard, Kitty reeled back and he lost his hold on her for a moment. Then, as he reached for her, he gave a cry and clutched at his chest. He seemed for a moment to be grappling with the air then he lost his balance and toppled into the grave.

Kitty heard a shout and turned to see Matthew running towards her, shouting, "Miss Kitty, oh, Miss Kitty, are you all right?"

"I hardly know what happened," she said. "One minute he had hold of me, and then, after he hit me, it seemed he was struggling…."

She turned as she heard a horse coming and saw it was Justin. As he leapt to the ground, she could see his coat was torn, his face cut and bruised, and she ran to meet him.

Seeing the redness where the squire had hit her, Justin touched her cheek. "He has been here. Where is he?"

"We struggled… he fell... Justin, there are *bones* beneath him."

Justin narrowed his eyes to where Matthew stood, talking into the grave. He took her arm.

Matthew didn't hear their approach. But as the wind was blowing from his direction they heard every word he said.

"How long have I waited for this day, when you yourself are held hostage by a nightmare," he was saying. "I've known you to do some things, Squire, but none so foul than what you did to that poor maid, Mary Jay. I know for certain you're the bastard who took her down and ruined her life."

The squire's life was ebbing, but he could still hear, and his eyes flickered towards Matthew.

"All I can say is, it's a pity you couldn't stay like this for nine long months, wondering and worrying what might happen next, like poor Mary did." Matthew grinned horribly. "But now you can go into the next world knowing that she has been avenged. Leah Underwood's son—*your* son—was stillborn, but Mary's daughter Kitty lived, and before Mary hung herself, she gave her to Leah. Aye."

Matthew paused, then added with relish in his voice. "And guess where Mary was buried? Right here. Right here, beneath you. It's Mary Jay's bones you die on, and it's Kitty Underwood who will have your manor now."

Suddenly a gust of wind came up and swept across the grave. And as it did the squire's eyes rolled back and his life passed away.

Matthew stood and growled, "And may the Devil take your soul."

Suddenly, sensing someone behind him, he turned to find Kitty staring at him. "Oh… Miss Kitty! I... I thought you'd gone." He looked in anguish at Justin. "Oh, sir, in all the world I would not have had her hear it this way."

Kitty whimpered and backed away. "But I did, Matthew," she whispered. "I *did.*" And she stumbled away and fled down the lane.

ꙮ

Flo woke up when she heard Justin's horse thundering past Forde. She discovered the tea was lukewarm and that Kitty was no longer there, and she threw a shawl over her shoulders and hurried downstairs.

She met Matthew and Justin coming down the lane, and when she saw their faces, knew something had happened. When Matthew told her, Justin had to steady her back to the farmhouse. He suggested she should rest while they searched for Kitty, but Flo wouldn't have it.

"No," she said shakily. "It must be me who finds her. It was me who did the deed, and now I must tell her everything. Matthew, you go on home to Emily—she must be worrying. You can tell her what's happened. Mr. le March, sir, if you don't mind perhaps you would like to wait inside the house." She looked down the yard. "I believe I know where I'll find the maid."

Kitty had gone, as Mary had many years before her, down the hill into the barn. And just as Mary had stumbled onto the hay, sobbing with exhaustion and shock, so had Kitty.

"Maid?" Flo said, tentatively and rather nervously, for although she was relieved she'd found Kitty, she worried that with her sensitive nature the shock might be too much. She was therefore relieved to see a spark of petulance in her eyes as Kitty said, "How did you know I would be here?"

"I first set eyes on your dear mother in here," Flo said, sitting down beside her. "I heard this commotion in the yard and thought a fox was after the hens. When I came in here, I found her. At first I thought she'd died."

"Better that she had," cried Kitty, bursting into fresh tears. "And then I wouldn't have been born!"

Flo knew Kitty was upset from the shock and only wanted to hit back. "I believe she would have preferred death than to live on after what happened to her," Flo said quietly. "But something must have made her carry on, and I believe it was because she wanted to give you life before she left the world."

"Then why didn't you have me? Didn't you want me? Why did I have to spend my life at Furze with someone who hated my existence?"

Flo put her hand to her heart. "My dear, you don't know what you're saying—"

"And why didn't you ever tell me?" Kitty cried, sparking again. "No one has told me anything. I've had to find it out in the most horrible ways."

"I wish that had been different, it's true," said Flo. "And many a time I wanted to, my dear, but always, *always*, something happened to stop me. So perhaps it had to be in this way."

Her voice caught. "When it happened I never thought of what would happen in the years ahead. But because it was Mary's will there seemed to be little choice. A person can only ever do what they feel is right at the time." She took a deep breath. "And now I shall tell you what happened the night you were born."

ꙮ

"We were so fearful, burying Mary like that," Flo said, finally. "But we couldn't bear to think what would happen to her. You do know—"

"Yes," Kitty said quietly. "Yes, I do know what can happen to suicides."

"Never judge Mary for giving you to Leah," Flo said. "She must have thought she was doing the best for everyone's sake, but mainly your own, because of how you would have been stigmatized after you were born. Think of the torture that poor maid would have gone through. She might have even worried you would judge her. Perhaps even blame her. Poor little maid, she had such a terrible life. The only happiness she ever knew was those days with us, though I do believe Mr. Bennett was kind to her, and Matthew loved her dearly."

Flo's voice broke and for a moment she couldn't speak, but cried quietly, her face buried in her hands.

"How I missed her. And I missed you too, Kitty, because before you were born I lived in the hope that you would be brought up at Forde. It was a bitter disappointment to me when you weren't: a continuous heartache seeing how Hern treated you. Every little pain of yours was one of mine, my dear. Never, ever say I didn't want you."

Kitty gave a sob and flew into her arms. "Oh, Flo, I'm sorry. I didn't mean to hurt you."

Flo took out a handkerchief and first wiped her eyes, and then Kitty's. "I know you didn't. But now you know all about it. And because you are a good, brave maid you must put it all behind you. Mary's sorrow is over now and hopefully she will go to rest. How you came to be in the world isn't important. That you are here is what really counts." She tucked the handkerchief away and struggled to her feet. "There's something else, you see. Something else you have to know."

"There's more?" Kitty cried incredulously, and on her guard again. "What *more* can there be?"

"Come on, there's a good maid," Flo said, taking her arm. "There's no need to be afraid. It's good news this time. The best news you'll ever have had in all your life."

They walked up the yard arm in arm, Kitty more like her old self and pestering Flo with questions; and Flo entirely like herself, telling Kitty to be patient.

Justin was sitting in the best room where Flo had now hung Mary's portrait. Kitty gasped when she saw it, and thought it was no wonder Enid had recognized her when they met: it could have been herself looking out from that canvas.

"I regret terribly what happened to that lovely young girl," Justin said. "But in all honesty, I cannot regret that you were born, Kitty. Enid captured the beauty in her soul, and you are the very image of her." He handed her Mary's Bible. "Look inside, because it will lead to the next thing I have to tell you."

"Go on," Flo said to Kitty's hesitation. "It isn't going to bite you. 'Tis good news, I say."

Kitty opened the cover. She blinked when she saw Celine's handwriting: it could have been her own. "But... who was Celine?" she said, looking inquiringly from one to the other.

"She was Jared Gordon's wife," Justin said. "Your grandmother."

"I told you it was good news," Flo said to Kitty's astonished face. "Tilly Black, that's the person who wrote the other inscription, was Celine's nurse and Margery has found her still alive."

"Margery is at this very moment on her way here from Newton Abbot, and bringing Tilly with her," Justin said. He smiled at Flo. "Would it be asking too much for you to ready a couple of rooms, Mrs. Endacott? I fear the manor is in no fit state to house any guests." His eyes returned to Kitty. "It is in dire need of a woman's touch."

Kitty looked from one to the other, and felt a surge of panic. "But you can't mean me? I can't inherit. There must be some mistake. There must be a male relative *somewhere?*"

Justin shook his head. "There are none, Kitty. I've had Coldswill look into it. And, there is no one in the parish at this moment better than yourself to understand what needs doing around here. You listened to Thomas's plans often enough and I have seen your capabilities. The manor will become yours now."

Kitty stared at him. "But I wouldn't know where to start… I can't do it alone."

Justin longed to put her mind at rest and say she wouldn't have to, but the squire's death had thrown his plans awry and he needed a day or so to think things out. He did have another idea in the back of his mind, one that hadn't been born of these circumstances, but one he'd been considering for a while. It would just mean bringing it forward, that was all.

"You mustn't worry," he said. "I will have an idea shortly of what can be done. My dear, this has been such a sudden, unexpected occurrence. Please, be patient with me while I try to sort it out." He took Kitty's hand and pressed it to his lips. "I know this is a great shock. It all is, but all will be well, Kitty, I promise. Now, I must be going. I have a lot to do, as you can well imagine."

As he walked down the hallway she heard him tell Flo that Margery would probably arrive the following day.

Kitty sank into a chair. Her head was throbbing. She simply couldn't take it all in. It was too much. All too much.

Chapter 43

After some difficulty, Margery had discovered Tilly Black's whereabouts the day after Ruth's wedding. Tilly had been suspicious at first when Margery said she'd come via her sister, Kat, but when she knew what Margery wanted to talk about, she'd asked her in. Through the ensuing year they kept in touch, and shared their grief over the loss of Kitty before Tilly could even meet her.

Tilly was overjoyed, therefore, to find Margery on her doorstep, beaming with happiness and bearing the good news of Kitty's return. She was quite happy to pack up a few belongings and accompany her to North Bovey.

ཀ༄

Kitty waited in Flo's best room with some trepidation. She had no idea what Tilly would be like. Nor did she know how she would feel hearing about Mary. No matter what Flo said, Kitty thought it had been pretty selfish of her to hang herself and cause everyone so much unhappiness.

Rather than feel any joy at Flo's disclosure, the shock, and also the nagging thought that Justin was going to marry Julia, had driven her into a depression. She only just managed a smile as Tilly walked into the room, and was introduced by Margery.

Tilly smiled at her kindly, her eyes filling with tears as she took Kitty's hand. "I would have known you anywhere," she said. "Mary would have been so proud. *So* proud, my dear. But naturally, you're shocked about all this. So much, and so quickly. Margery has explained." She patted Kitty's hand. "I also realize you must be wondering just what sort of woman would give you away? Well, once you hear what I have to say I hope you will be a little more understanding and forgiving. You will be far kinder to yourself if you are."

Kitty blushed to think Tilly had more or less read her thoughts, and she felt ashamed. A tear slid down her cheek, and as Tilly gently wiped it away, tears filled the old lady's eyes. "If only you knew how much you were like my dear girl," she whispered. "It's as if she's come back."

She took a deep breath. "Now come along, my dear, sit down and I will tell you everything I know about your dear mother, and her mother before her."

Feeling a little more at ease, Kitty sat down beside her.

"I was Celine's nurse," Tilly began, "as I'm sure you've been told. She was such a young little thing, barely seventeen years old when they married her off, and she'd always been delicate. She suffered from nerves, you know. More highly strung than the master's stallion, I used to say." She smiled at a distant memory.

"So, upon her marriage to Jared Gordon, I went with her to North Bovey. Kat, that's my sister, was her maid and she came, too. To put your mind at rest about a certain matter I will say now that Jared was Gordon's son from his first marriage. *Hartley* was acquired from Gordon's second wife, and therefore no blood relative to your mother, Mary.

"Mr. Jared was all very well, you know, but he was a dreamer. He and Celine hadn't been married five minutes before he read something out of a newspaper and took the fancy of going on an expedition. Well, that was his excuse, and what a row he had with his father over it. My poor Celine. Proper confounded she was, I can tell you. But she put a brave face on, even took his part against his parents. He wasn't cut out to be a squire, let alone a husband. All of us below stairs knew why he went away. He gave up everything, his wife and his home for his freedom, if that is indeed what he found. No one ever heard from him again.

"Kat's son, Alfred, worked at the manor. A nice young man he was and he'd been taken on as a gardener. After a while, when Jared didn't return, Celine began to spend a lot of time with Alfred in the gardens. It was her consolation, I think, and she told me she was going to learn all about plants so that when Jared came home she could pleasantly surprise him.

"The old squire was a pompous, unapproachable soul, as was his wife. My mistress kept out of their way as much as possible and wasn't as close to them as she might have been. Because of this, she didn't tell them her news. Along with this, Hartley was cock of the roost now his elder brother had gone. 'Good riddance to him,' I heard him say more than once, and his mother encouraged him. He could do no wrong in her eyes.

"Well, my dear, one day he propositioned Celine and she came flying to me, saying she'd told him if he didn't leave her alone she would tell his father what he was up to. But he wasn't the sort of man anyone should turn down, nor threaten, and after that he set about besmirching her name."

Tilly's voice caught. "Of course, me being her nurse and attending to her intimate affairs I knew when she'd conceived her child. But she'd left it so long to tell Jared's parents she played right into Hartley's hands. He accused her of having a liaison with Alfred, and Mrs. Gordon, curse her rotten soul, chose to believe him rather than my dear Celine. She told her since they found her morals intolerable, they were sending her back to her parents." She sighed. "Celine's parents were no better than the Gordons. Mean, unbending sort of people, and they wouldn't take her back because of the perceived scandal.

"Alfred now being implicated sort of thing, and having a kind heart, insisted he would take care of her, much against Kat's wishes, I might add, and Celine moved into his cottage. When that happened, Kat and I were dismissed and we found work in the village for a time.

"Celine had a little girl—that would be your mother—and at least they had a few years of happiness. But it wasn't to last. When Mary was only three years old, Alfred was found drowned in the river. There were never any questions asked, no reason given. Kat almost went out of her mind.

"Now destitute, Celine took Mary to the manor and begged them to help, if not herself, then the child. She told them they owed it to her after what their son had done to Alfred. Of course, that was the worse thing she could have said to them." Tilly took a deep, shuddering breath. "The last time I saw Celine she was very distraught. Hartley had gone to see her and, well, he'd taken her against her will. He was a man who would always get what he wanted."

She took out a handkerchief and dabbed her eyes. "Not long after that Celine took her own life. I'm sure she must have thought it was her only escape from him and hoped that her in-laws would take her daughter in. But the only thing Mrs. Gordon did was to see Mary put in the workhouse. It was kept very quiet, as was Celine's suicide. I left the position I was in and went to see if I could get employment in the workhouse so I could keep an eye on Mary. That poor little girl—she was so shocked at first I thought she would die. She never spoke again, nor did she ever remember me."

"She loved you though," Flo said. "Often she would point to your name in her Bible and smile."

"That's so nice to hear," Tilly said. "The poor little thing had the most dreadfully sad life. But she made the most of what had happened to her by giving you to Leah, Kitty. Knowing her like I did, there is no doubt in my mind she must have loved you dearly to do such a thing. She wanted you to have everything she could never give you." Tilly smiled. "Can you see that now? Can you find it within your heart to forgive your mother?"

Kitty was crying softly. She couldn't imagine how awful Mary's life must have been. And all because of the Gordons. She felt a surge of anger, and it made her more determined than ever to do everything in her power to make the most of the opportunity she was now being given. Her mother had died to give her a chance, and she would do her damnedest to make her proud.

I'll always be there. Those words suddenly came into Kitty's mind, and she realized that Mary must have been the lady whom she'd seen with Leah when she was ill. Leah, now knowing the truth, would also want her to succeed: if she did, she would avenge them both.

As these thoughts came to her, any feelings of anger or resentment for Mary faded. Her poor, dear mother had loved her, as had Leah, and she had absolutely nothing to complain about.

She smiled and wiped her eyes. "I feel truly blessed," she said. "Thank you for telling me all this, Miss Black. I'm sorry you had to see her suffer, but I shall do my best to make up for the past by ensuring that, at least within the manor estate, others like her have a better life."

Pride shone from Tilly's eyes. "Carrying around this knowledge for all these years has been a heavy burden, Kitty. But hearing you say that makes it all worthwhile. They are indeed the best words I could have ever heard spoken." And she gave a satisfied, if rather watery, smile to Margery and Flo.

ꕥ

Outside in the kitchen Margery sighed with relief. "I hoped she would take it in her stride and not bear a grudge," she said. "She's a good, brave girl."

"As was her mother," Flo said. "This was a tricky situation and such a shock for the maid, but she's come through as I hoped she would. It isn't easy for her either, because she's beside herself with worrying about something else. I thought Justin le March was going to make his feelings known to her, and yet he hasn't said a word. He might be a fine man and all that, but, in affairs of the heart, he's sadly lacking!"

Margery sighed. "You may not believe this, Flo, but even a man like Justin has his fears, and one of them is that Kitty will reject him."

"*What?* Is the man blind?"

"He's just afraid. Flo… where are you going?"

Flo was throwing on her cape. "You stay here with Kitty and Tilly. I'm off to the manor. Blow his darned fear—he's driving my Kitty to distraction with his dilly-dallying, and in turn the maid's driving me insane. I've had enough and I'm going to do something about it!"

Chapter 44

On the day of the squire's funeral, the moody, thundery weather moved away. The air cleared, the sun shone brilliantly and the birds began to sing as if they'd never sung before. A good sign, said those who would have nonetheless braved a hurricane to see the squire put safely into the ground, six feet under.

There was considerable consternation among the parishioners. It had been all anyone could talk about since word had got around that the squire had finally had an attack strong enough to stop his wicked heart. But who would be at the manor now? That was the next question. Because sometimes the devil you knew was better than the devil you didn't.

Kitty glanced nervously across the aisle at Justin. He'd told her he proposed to make an announcement to the effect that she would be taking up residence at the manor as Jared Gordon's granddaughter. Although she was excited about her new responsibilities, she occasionally shrank from the thought of living at the manor, and hoped the squire's spirit wouldn't hover as Mary's had done.

She'd voiced this opinion to Matthew who said she needn't worry: he reckoned the squire, who'd been a bottomless pit of greed and self-indulgence, would already be somewhere else paying for his wicked deeds. She glanced at the squire's coffin. A waste of good wood Matthew called it.

Kitty knew Matthew would never forgive the squire for hurting Mary. She also knew that if she'd lived in their time and experienced it firsthand, she would have probably feel the same. But she was a generation removed and couldn't bring herself to hate the means by which she'd come into the world. Still, she wasn't sorry the squire was gone, and from what she could gather, no one else was either. How sad to have lived a life and have no one mourn you, she thought. That was the thing, when nasty people died all they left behind them was relief.

Justin's thoughts ran along the same lines as Kitty's as he waited for the Reverend Pugh to begin the service. Despite what his brother-in-law had been, he thought it sad that no one would miss him. He considered that to have lived a life in such a way was a terrible waste.

He glanced behind him and was pleased to see the church was overflowing. The more parishioners who knew that someone responsible was going into the manor, the less bewilderment and confusion there would be about it afterwards.

It had been quite the week for him. One in which he'd made a monumental decision regarding his family home. But it hadn't been an impulsive one. There was no doubt in his mind that times were changing and that one day it would be impossible to run a mansion like Whitmouth House as he did now. It was always his way to be one step ahead, and he wanted to provide as secure a future as he could for Reave and any other children he might have. He had plans to turn Whitmouth House into an agricultural college, and once it was all arranged he would, God willing, be able to share the remainder of his days with Kitty at the manor.

The Reverend Pugh began the service, but that man of so many words seemed to have lost his eloquence on this particular occasion and he gave a dismal eulogy. People shuffled in their pews, and those standing were restless. But then, when all was said and done, what *could* be said about such a demon as the squire?

When the service was over, before the congregation moved to the graveyard, Justin stood up to make his announcement. He introduced himself to those who didn't already know him.

"As some of you may know," he said. "Squire Gordon has passed on, sadly without an heir—"

At this point there was a disturbance at the back of the church. A woman, clutching the hand of a small boy, shouted something. The congregation looked at one another; turned in their seats. Justin held up his hand for their murmurings to stop. "Come here, please?" he asked.

The woman, her face contorted with rage, dragged the boy up the aisle. "You say he left no heir," she hissed. "But *this* be Squire Gordon's son. *My* son, Nathaniel Creber, fathered ten years ago. Ten long years, I say, and me without a penny still." She pointed a finger at Justin. "And say you there is no heir?"

"No *legitimate* heir, no, madam. Not from Hartley Gordon," Justin said stiffly. "But his elder brother, Jared, left this country some years ago, and I'm very pleased to say that his granddaughter will be taking up residence at the manor."

The woman would have spoken again, but others intervened and hustled her away, out of the door.

Justin waited until the fuss had abated, then carried on to assure everyone that there would be a much brighter future for the estate and the parish. He was about to sit down when he happened to glance at Flo. He'd been quite touched by her sincerity when she had turned up at the manor to lecture him about his treatment of Kitty's heart. Now, on impulse, he held up his hand for the congregation to give him one more moment, and, meeting Flo's eyes with a mischievous twinkle in his own, he beckoned Kitty over to stand beside him.

There was a cough. One or two rustlings. A 'well, I never did' or two. Then there was a hushed silence as all eyes turned on him, wondering what he was going to do next. The Reverend Pugh took off his glasses and made a great show of wiping them on his cassock, no doubt due to the impropriety of things.

Justin ignored Pugh's pointed clearing of the throat. "There is one thing I forgot to mention," he said. "After the burial everyone will be welcome back to the manor for a celebration."

Kitty blinked. Many others did too, and there were a few murmurs of disapproval in the congregation. At a glance Kitty could see the question in her mind reflected on their faces; although it might be the truth, it was quite another thing to describe the squire's wake as a celebration!

And then one woman at the front of the church called out, "He's on his knees!"

Justin was indeed. And afterwards Kitty imagined how that moment would be told for generations. It would be their children's favorite bedtime story: 'Mother, tell us again how Father proposed to you.'

And she would gladly tell it as many times as they wanted to listen, how, standing by the squire's coffin, she said to the man she loved, "Yes, oh, Justin. Yes, of course! *Please* get up." And caused such a riot in the church and consternation among the bearers, who now found it difficult to decide who should take which end of the coffin, or indeed, whether to bury the squire at all before going off to make merry.

But bury him they did, and in fine style too; the Reverend Pugh now having recovered from his chagrin and thinking of the brighter days ahead. It was the best wake a body had seen for years, it was said afterwards, both a good ending and beginning.

ജ്ഞ

After the burial, before they left the churchyard, Kitty felt a hand on her arm. It was the woman who had caused the rumpus in the church.

"You won't get away with this," the woman called Creber said. "You wait, when he's old enough, he'll come to claim his own." Her eyes were a pale blue and seemed to penetrate right into Kitty's soul.

Kitty swallowed. "Justin, that is, my husband-to-be, will see you are all right. There is nothing more to be done."

Justin came up behind her and stepped between them. "I will come to see you another day, madam, when we may discuss this."

The woman glanced at her son, who was cowering behind her skirts, and then narrowing her eyes at Kitty, she walked away.

Kitty clung to Justin. "I hope there is no further trouble with that woman."

"I will take care of everything," he assured her. "Before I do anything else, I am going to do what I have wanted to for a very long time." And he kissed her deeply. "My little love," he whispered. "I have found you and will never let you go until death decrees it."

He saw that she was still looking after the woman. "I dare say," he added dryly, "there is many a woman in the parish that can make such a claim. We could not satisfy them all. However, I will see her and try to settle her down with some sort of offer. You are not to worry any more about it, do you hear me? You are to think instead of how you will be fulfilling Thomas's dream."

Kitty closed her eyes as those words of Thomas's once again came into her mind. *You are my destiny; I will love you forever.* But this time she felt less pain and guilt. Yes, she thought now, in a strange way she was Thomas's destiny, because although he wouldn't be the one to stand beside her at the manor, she would now do his work. And together with Justin, whom he'd also loved so dearly, they would make that work a memorial to his name.

"Yes, you are quite right," Kitty said.

They returned to the manor where they welcomed everyone, including the vitriolic Miss Wood and the dumbfounded Mrs. Bennett. Mr. Bennett hobbled over to Kitty and asked how her mother was. Kitty told him she was doing wonderfully, and he went away happy, pleased that his Mary had such a lovely daughter.

Later, Kitty escaped from the crowd. Justin accompanied her to the end of the driveway then stood watching her as she went along the lane. As she did, he was reminded of the strange dream he'd once had of a little girl laughing and picking flowers in the lanes.

Up the hill past Forde Kitty went, gathering a posy of flowers on the way to her grove. The beech and rowan trees had been cleared away, the area cleaned up. The grave had been remade, as it would stay for centuries afterwards. It was quiet and serene once again.

She smiled, thinking how fast the men had worked to do Justin's bidding, and her heart glowed at the prospects of what was to come. She knelt down and placed the posy on the grave. She didn't know what was beyond death but was very aware that there were things beyond common understanding. She closed her eyes and imagined Leah waiting with open arms to finally welcome Mary home across the river into that beautiful, peaceful garden.

"I'm so sorry that happened to you," she whispered. "So sorry for your suffering. But I shall bring flowers to you always. And after I die, someone else will. No one will ever forget you, Mary Jay."

And with that promise she got up and walked home to the manor.

Author's note:

This novel, begun in the 1980s, started out untitled, and was written about a young girl called Kitty, who lived at a farm called Forde. However, lacking focus, I put it aside.

On a visit to England in 1993, when someone gave me a newspaper article, I was reminded of Mary Jay and the legend of Jay's Grave. Being a native of Dartmoor, I had always been aware of the speculation surrounding the workhouse girl who purportedly took her own life after being *crossed in love.* Now I read that Mary was sometimes known as Kitty Jay, and it was thought that she had lived at a farm called Forde.

Inspired by the coincidences in my unfinished manuscript, I went to Jay's grave. Apart from a wild rabbit, no one was there. With the scent of heather and bracken in the air, surrounded by the wildness of the moors, I began to wonder whatever had possessed that young girl to take her life. What dreadful thing had come to pass that had made her give up her newfound freedom?

I suddenly felt compelled to write her story. I couldn't get her out of my mind. When I returned to Canada I dug out my old manuscript and, taking what I had already written, developed the story of *Mary's Child.*

Part of my research revealed that a well-respected author, Lois Deacon, also wrote a novel about Mary Jay. Although it was years out of print, I nonetheless managed to get hold of a copy, *An Angel From Your Door.* And it was that title that inspired me to include the lovely poem at the beginning of the book.

Although our stories differed, Lois saw Mary just as I did: a gentle, humble girl, who suffered through no fault of her own.

It is also Mary Jay and her fictional descendents who have inspired the sequels to *Mary's Child, - PastPresent I, Awareness, and PastPresent II, Resolution,* forthcoming from Twilight Times Books.

Author Bio

Celia was raised in Devon, England. After she emigrated to Canada in 1980 she had short stories published in magazines in the UK, Canada and the United States. One of these was translated into Braille; another sold to a South African magazine. She also wrote and co-directed a play, performed on Galiano Island, British Columbia.

Celia writes in several genres. Her novel, *Mary's Child,* the first in the Dartmoor Series, reflects her love and knowledge of the South Devon moors. Both it, and a short story, "Jay, the Farmer's Daughter" were inspired by the legend of Jay's grave, near where she used to live. There are two sequels to follow *Mary's Child* - *PastPresent I: Awareness,* and *PastPresent II: Resolution.*

Twilight Times Books has also published *Unraveled,* a mainstream, humorous novel spun around the Gulf Islands in British Columbia.

Over the years Celia's interest and focus on writing has grown. She is a tutor for Writer's Online Workshop (http://www.writersonlineworkshops.com) where she interacts with students wishing to focus on the short story.

Celia lives in British Columbia with her husband.

Don't miss any of these other
exciting mainstream novels

- Death to the Centurion
(1-931201-26-9, $16.95 US)

- Jerome and the Seraph
(1-931201-54-4, $15.50 US)

- Unraveled
(1-931201-11-0, $15.50 US)

- WolfPointe
(1-931201-08-0, $15.50 US)

Twilight Times Books
Kingsport, Tennessee

Order Form

If not available from your local bookstore or favorite online bookstore, send this coupon and a check or money order for the retail price plus $3.50 s&h to Twilight Times Books, Dept. IB706 POB 3340 Kingsport TN 37664. Delivery may take up to four weeks.

Name: ______________________________

Address: ___________________________

____

Email: ______________________________

I have enclosed a check or money order in the amount

of $__________

for ______________________________________ .

If you enjoyed this book, please post a review
at your favorite online bookstore.

Twilight Times Books
P O Box 3340
Kingsport, TN 37664
Phone/Fax: 423-323-0183
www.twilighttimesbooks.com/